Praise for

'A belter of a thriller with proper breathtaking, pulse-racing levels of tension. Tracking heart surgeon Anna as she grapples with an impossible moral dilemma, I almost felt I was going under the knife myself. Thriller fans will be in heaven'
LOUISE CANDLISH

'One of the smartest, twistiest thrillers I've read in years. A relentless, menacing story with an airtight plot and a deviously satisfying finale. Fans of *The Silent Patient* and *The Woman in the Window* will love it'
JOHN MARRS

'When you pick up a book to read the first page and then can't put it down . . . Amazing read'
SARAH PEARSE

'Brilliant. Relentlessly tense. This thriller gave me palpitations!'
LESLEY KARA

'Utterly gripping, addictive and brilliantly tense'
KAREN HAMILTON

'*Do No Harm* hooked me . . . What a terrifying ride!'
GILLY MACMILLAN

'With an agonising dilemma at its heart and a pace that never lets up . . . A corker of a thriller'
KATE RIORDAN

'A thrilling, nail-biting story that made me gasp out loud. This is not a run-of-the-mill, will she/won't she, thriller. I was constantly kept on my toes and double-guessing myself as the plot unravelled. Great plot, fantastic characters who I promise, you will either love with fierce abandon or hate with a passion. I thoroughly recommend it and enjoyed every delicious page'
NADINE MATHESON

'Seriously terrifying, chilling and unputdownable'
EMMA CURTIS

'An edge-of-your-seat, head-spinning thriller with emotion and depth woven through its heart'
LAUREN NORTH

'A brilliant example of psychological crime writing at its very best, always compelling, with fascinating characters . . . Something tells me Jack Jordan is going to be HUGE'
KATE RHODES

'The ultimate page-turning edge-of-your-seat thriller. Loved it'
NIKKI SMITH

'A real winner: gut-wrenching, nail-biting and thought-provoking'
ROBIN MORGAN-BENTLEY

Also by Jack Jordan

Anything for Her
My Girl
A Woman Scorned
Before Her Eyes
Night by Night

JACK JORDAN

SIMON &
SCHUSTER

London · New York · Sydney · Toronto · New Delhi

First published in Great Britain by Simon & Schuster UK Ltd, 2022

1 3 5 7 9 10 8 6 4 2

Simon & Schuster UK Ltd
1st Floor
222 Gray's Inn Road
London WC1X 8HB

Simon & Schuster Australia, Sydney
Simon & Schuster India, New Delhi

www.simonandschuster.co.uk
www.simonandschuster.com.au
www.simonandschuster.co.in

A CIP catalogue record for this book is
available from the British Library

Hardback ISBN: 978-1-3985-0567-4
Trade paperback ISBN: 978-1-3985-0568-1
eBook ISBN: 978-1-3985-0569-8
Audio ISBN: 978-1-3985-1269-6

Typeset in Sabon by M Rules
Printed and bound by CPI Group (UK) Ltd, Croydon, CR0 4YY

Sandra Jarrad

My constant inspiration for mothers who would do anything for their children, just as you have always done for me. This book would not have been possible without you.

'Primum non nocere.'

—HIPPOCRATES

'First, do no harm . . .'

—Hippocratic oath,
modern day

‘Doctors are subjected to a high level of psychiatric morbidity . . . It will therefore not be too surprising that some of the traits associated with a psychopathic personality . . . are perhaps selected out in those who rise to the top of our profession.’

—J. PEGRUM and O. PEARCE,
The Royal College of Surgeons, September 2015

PART I

1

Anna

Thursday, 4 April 2019, 16:32

There is blood on my neck.

A single drop, no bigger than a freckle. Minuscule in the grand scheme of things. A man lies before me with cut flesh and exposed bone; black, tar-stained lungs cranked apart to expose his heart. And yet for all the gore, all I can think about is that one small speck searing into me like a burn.

I switch the blade from my left hand to my right and roll my wrist until I feel the satisfying crunch beneath the skin. The room is so quiet that the sound carries a faint echo, ricocheting off the cold tiled walls.

Everyone in the room has their eyes on me, assessing the stillness of my hand, the glint of the scalpel beneath the bright strip lights, rosy at the tip from the man's blood. And yet despite the scrutiny, my palms remain dry, and my grip holds steady. But buried beneath my scrubs, my heart is pounding so fast that I can almost taste it.

Peter's heart, however, is stone cold.

Mr Downing's double coronary bypass was straightforward, until suddenly it wasn't. After cutting and sawing my way through the chest, I bypassed the blocked arteries using veins from his leg to return healthy blood flow back to the heart. By removing the clamp from the aorta to resume blood flow, and rinsing away the cold potassium fluid injected to keep it still, Peter's heart should wake from its medically induced slumber.

I stare down at his splayed chest, waiting for a twitch, a spasm, the first jolt to signify life.

Nothing.

'Lungs off, please.'

'Lungs off,' Dr Burke repeats.

'Return to bypass.'

'Returning to bypass,' Karin calls back from the perfusionist's station.

I pass the scalpel to my aide and wait in the deafening silence. When the heart is finally back on bypass, I feel the tension leave the room like a hot, stale sigh.

'Let's give it a minute,' I say, and clamp the aorta. 'Poor thing's probably knackered.'

'Aren't we all?' Dr Burke quips, giving me a supportive wink over the top of his glasses.

It is a thoughtful gesture, but we both know I am on my own. Each surgery is a collaborative effort up to this point: Dr Burke manages the medications, breathing tube and monitoring lines; Karin controls the heart–lung machine; the surgical care practitioner standing at the foot of the bed harvests the leg veins for transplantation; each specialist with their own aide. Beside me stands my own, Margot, assisting with every tool and swab. But when it comes to the heart, the responsibility is all mine.

A wave of heat scores my back, prickling across my shoulder blades.

Focus.

I assess the chest cavity. The bypass was done well: the grafts are good, with clean, airtight joins. We have given the heart time to recuperate, administered a cocktail of drugs to try and stimulate electrical activity, and run tests for metabolic abnormalities or any other complaints we might have missed. I have checked, rechecked and tidied my work, in the hope that it was due to a mistake I made and could ultimately fix. None of it worked.

I glance at the clock on the wall. We are fast approaching the end of the four-hour window we have before damaging the heart becomes inevitable. Once passed, each second ticked off the clock might as well be a nail hammering down the lid to the patient's coffin.

My top lip tingles with approaching sweat. I fight the urge to dab it dry, and recite the advice my mentor once gave me.

Never show your nerves. If you panic, they panic. You can't bring a ship into the dock if your crew has jumped overboard.

I squeeze the patient's heart in my fist, contracting and releasing in the rhythm it has followed so many times before, and gently lay it inside the chest cavity. The flesh has turned rosy-pink from my grip. In a strange way, it almost looks pretty, like a cheek flushed from the cold.

'Let's give it one last go,' I say, the implications pulsing behind my words.

I reach in slowly, prolonging the patient's life for as long as I can, and release the clamp's hold on the aorta. A river of blood flows into the heart.

Still, nothing happens.

I squeeze the heart repeatedly, but even with the potassium fluid flushed out it feels strangely cold; wet and slippery like a hog's snout.

Come on, Peter.

My shoulders tense where I hunch over the table and put all of my strength into manually manipulating the heart. Sweat gathers upon my face; Margot slips in silently and dabs each droplet away.

I'm not sure how much time has passed – a minute, ten – but when I look up from the chest cavity, glistening with perspiration and breathing heavily behind my mask, I realise that the whole team is staring at me, their eyes awash with pity. That is when it finally hits me.

This heart won't ever beat again.

Stress pains pulse behind my eyes, spasm in the knotted muscles of my shoulders. I look down at my hands, aching and trembling from seizing the heart so firmly, and release the smallest of sighs.

'Bypass off, please.'

Karin nods once and looks away. A man will die today, and we will orchestrate it. Me, with the command. Her, flicking the switch.

'Bypass off,' she confirms.

'Lungs off, please.'

'Lungs off,' Dr Burke replies.

And then we wait.

The heart–lung machine winds to a stop. The tubes clear of

blood as it returns to the patient's circulatory system. And then, the inevitable: the flatline of a motionless heart. The sound screams through all of us, piercing through the theatre in shrill echoes, ringing off every apparatus and stainless-steel tool.

I glance at the clock on the wall.

'Time of death: 16:53.'

2

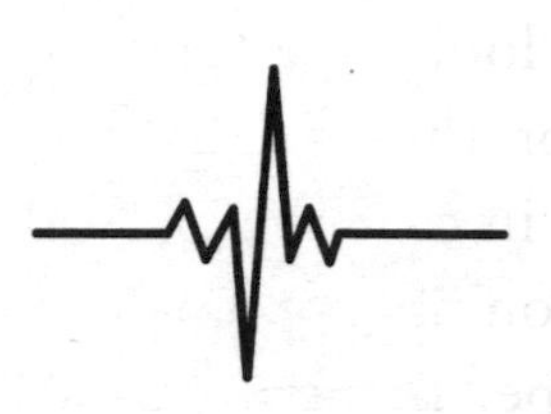

Anna

Thursday, 4 April 2019, 17:10

'I'm sorry for your loss.'

A weaker surgeon might look down at their feet at this moment. Too selfish to hold the gaze of the dead patient's loved one as their heart breaks. But I keep my eyes on Mrs Downing's and witness it all: the almost-silent gasp as the blow hits her, the tears sheening over her eyes. Nurse Val from the cardiology ward twitches nervously by my side.

I first met Mrs Downing during her husband's initial consultation, and watched as she left my office with a hopeful bounce in her step. It was a standard procedure, with a very low risk of Peter not coming home. My reputation and experience helped her sleep at night; they are what urged her husband to sign on the dotted line prior to surgery. She will come to hate me for this, once the shock has passed.

'Did he suffer?' she asks, her voice breaking.

'No. He wouldn't have felt a thing.'

She might think me cold, meeting her eyes without flinching, but I'm merely well practised. Over time I have learnt not to look at a patient's next of kin with too much sympathy, or they might find me patronising, nor too much sadness, in case they mistake it for guilt. If I had smiled too widely on my approach, I might have given Mrs Downing false hope. Being a cardiothoracic surgeon isn't just about fixing hearts, it is also knowing how best to break them.

'Mrs Downing,' I say calmly, stepping cautiously around her shock. 'My colleague Val is going to take you through the next stages now and answer any questions you may have. If you need anything, please don't hesitate to ask.'

Val takes Mrs Downing's hand and delicately guides her towards the chair; she manages to keep her sobs at bay until I shut the door behind me, that British stiff upper lip finally allowing itself to unfurl behind closed doors.

I close my eyes and take a deep breath to compose myself, before setting off down the corridor towards the changing room. I hadn't lost a patient in a while, not until today, and I have the sudden fear that I may be at the start of a losing streak, but swiftly bat the thought away.

This is one failure after a long line of successes. Keep it in perspective.

But whether out of conditioning or habit, I know I won't be able to get this procedure out of my head.

I step inside the changing room and yank off my scrub top

as I approach my locker, quickly losing myself in my thoughts as I strip and redress.

'You all right?'

Margot is stood at the locker next to mine, tying her hair into a ponytail. Her roots need doing.

'I'm fine.'

I had been going through the procedure again, obsessing over every detail in search of the moment Mr Downing's heart began to fail. Clearly, I'm not hiding my thoughts as well as I usually would. Failure often does that: it rattles the armour, revealing small glimpses of the tenderness within.

'There's nothing more you could have done.'

'I know,' I lie. 'Thanks.'

I feel her eyes linger on my face a beat too long. My tone had been flat and direct. Emotionless. She must think me callous. Perhaps she is right.

I am inhumanly cold before calling time of death. I rummage around a chest cavity with the same emotional attachment as an electrician rewiring a circuit. I don't think of the person hidden beneath the surgical drapes, or pay a thought to the family members sat outside the theatre, waiting to hear if their world is about to right itself or implode. I would go mad if I did. It is only when I leave the operating theatre that the weight of the repercussions presses down upon me, and I spend the rest of the evening redoing the procedure in my mind.

'Ready for Saturday?' she asks flippantly.

I had forgotten. Mr Downing's operation had distracted me. The stress seeps back into me in an instant.

In two days' time I will perform one of the biggest operations of my career: bypassing three blocked coronary arteries for Ahmed Shabir, MP for Redwood and, if the whispers are correct, the future leader of the Labour Party. He is referred to as Patient X by those in the know, sworn to secrecy to keep the procedure from going public so as not to affect his chances in the next election. There is nothing like having the fate of a potential prime minister dangling over one's head while brandishing a scalpel.

'Of course.'

Margot's phone rings. She checks the screen briefly and throws it into her handbag to ring out. I catch the name *Nick* before it vanishes into her locker, and take my own from my bag, reading over the messages that Zack and I sent one another earlier in the day.

Zack
Please don't make me go. U said u would come

He had sent it at lunchtime. While my son should have been playing, he had been texting me, worrying. I sent a reply between surgeries, feeling so nauseous with guilt that I had left my lunch untouched.

Me
I want to come on holiday with you more than anything, but I have very poorly patients who can't get better without my help. We will go somewhere in the summer holidays, just you and me. Start thinking about where you want to go, and I will sort it xxx

Zack
U always put them first

I hadn't known what to say to that.

'Up to much tonight?'

Margot is rolling a cigarette, running the tip of her tongue along the edge of the paper before folding it shut and sticking it behind her ear.

She has tried to force a friendship between us a few times now, almost as if it is a challenge that she has set for herself. But I don't muddy working relationships with personal affection. If colleagues become too familiar, errors inevitably follow. The operating theatre is no place to be relaxed. It is much safer if everyone remains on their toes.

I take my jacket from my locker and slip it on.

'Not particularly, no. My brother is taking my son to Cornwall with him and his daughter tomorrow for the Easter holidays, so I'll be spending the evening at home with him before he goes.'

She knows the life of an NHS employee well enough not to ask me why I'm not going with them. I am grateful to her for that, at least.

'How's he doing with everything?'

My hand freezes on the zip of my jacket.

'Pardon?'

Her eyes widen at the sudden sharpness of my tone. She drops her sights to my hand.

'Well, you're not wearing your rings.'

My cheeks burn with a quick flush of anger. I take my bag from my locker and slam it shut.

'That's private,' I snap, and turn for the door. 'See you in the morning.'

'Yeah,' she replies bluntly, and mutters quietly beneath her breath.

Bitch.

I pause at the door, a slew of words pooling on my tongue, and shut it behind me with a soft click.

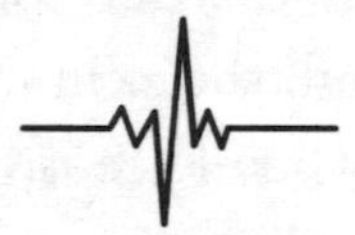

I reach my car and freeze.

In the distorted curve of the window, my face almost appears like a skull: dark, shadowy eye sockets; sharp cheekbones and a jutting chin.

Who on earth is going to want you now?

I clamber inside and chuck my bag on the passenger seat. The ignition turns over with a tired grumble, and lukewarm air blasts up from the vents to clear the fog from the windscreen. I lean back against the seat and close my eyes.

Zack will have eaten dinner by now and sprawled himself across the sofa in front of the TV, while Paula tidies my kitchen and completes any other chores she finds along the way. If one of my former neighbours in the city had offered to pick up my child from school and load my dishwasher, I would have slammed the door in their face and fixed the chain. It is amazing what a few miles and sheer desperation can do.

This is the first time I have sat down in six hours and I can feel my body seizing at the joints. The thought of taking the dog for an evening walk fills me with dread, but then I think of Bear's little face, and my heart sinks. In getting Zack the dog he always wanted, I had hoped it would make my absence less noticeable. But all it did was add another name to the list of people I seem to let down.

I think of my reflection in the car window, how exhausted

I looked, and pull down the sun visor to inspect myself closer. My skin appears pale and haggard beneath the thin veil of make-up, with dark shadows circling my eyes. The whites of them are a bloodshot pink, whereas my lips have almost no colour to them at all. I pull the skin taut with my fingertips to reverse time and freeze when I see it.

The fleck of blood is still on my neck.

I lurch forwards in a panic and scratch at my skin with my nails until it is red raw, my pulse drumming excitedly beneath my fingertips. It has dried to a crisp and peels away in flakes. When it has finally gone, there are long, jagged scratch marks in its place. I close my eyes and sink against the seat again.

The impulse is back.

It has been eating away at me since the heart refused to come off bypass. Like a worm in my brain, wriggling incessantly, eating away at my concentration. I crank open my eyes. The tired woman in the mirror glares back at me.

I peel off the strip of fake lashes on my right eye to reveal the near-bald lid. Only the odd strand has been left unpicked.

It has been weeks since I last gave into the urge. I have plucked at threads as I sat on the sofa of an evening, picked my cuticles until they bled, anything to distract myself from doing the only thing that calms me: the compulsion that has haunted me ever since I can remember.

My fingertips tingle as I imagine raising them towards my lids. I clench my hands into fists to squash the desire and inadvertently crush the fake lashes in my palm. I curse under my breath and try to straighten out the strip again, but it's no use: the lashes are crumpled like the legs of a dead spider, stiff in its web. I remove the remaining strip, roll them into a ball, and chuck it in the passenger footwell.

The impulse hasn't gone away. I push up the sleeve of my jacket and inspect the hairs on my forearm. Blonde, friable little things, some grown in at odd angles, others split in two after years of being plucked from the roots. If I am going to do it, I tell myself, I should use the arm. Easier to conceal. Less humiliating. But it just isn't the same.

I tentatively raise my hand to my eye, as if I can outsmart my own wits, and feel a lash between my fingers. The need grows until I can think of nothing else: that one, compulsive thought like a mass on the brain. I roll the lash between my fingertips to savour the moment, growing dizzy from the tug-of-war firing inside my skull, before I finally give in – and pluck. A tiny pop, followed by instant release. Relief washes over me. I finish the ritual by placing it on my tongue.

I jolt to the sound of my phone ringing, and catch a brief glimpse of my face in the mirror. My cheeks have flushed a riled pink, and I am so ashamed that I can't meet my own gaze.

I'm a freak. A sick, depraved freak.

I swallow the lash down and snatch my phone from my bag, Adam's name flashing on the screen. I answer the call through hands-free and set off.

Just get yourself home.

'Hi,' I say, flustered.

'Hi, you all right?'

'Fine. You?'

'I'm good. Just landed in Amsterdam for a meeting, thought I'd check in.'

There is a long, tense silence. We have only shared a few words and yet I can already feel my hackles rising. I reach the edge of the car park and pull out onto the main road. Only a few more turns and I'm home.

'Are you driving?' he asks.

'I just finished work. Is there a reason you called?'

I stop at the zebra crossing as Adam hesitates on the other end of the line. A woman hobbles across, hunched over her walking frame with her face braced against the chill of the wind.

That'll be you, the voice says inside my head. *Withered and alone.*

I clench my teeth until I hear the bones creak.

'My solicitor wants to renegotiate my sum,' Adam says finally.

The steering wheel rasps beneath my grip. I push my foot down on the accelerator. The engine growls so suddenly that the old woman jolts as she reaches the other side of the road.

'No, *you* want to renegotiate.'

'I'm sorry, Anna.'

'If you raise your sum, I will have to sell the house. You know that. Zack is already struggling with all of the changes.'

'I'm broke.'

I scoff. 'We're all broke.'

'No, I mean I'm *broke.*'

I turn off the main road and drive down The Avenue, a long, winding road of large detached houses. Mine is situated just around the bend off its own private lane tucked away from the rest of the street, with only Paula's house beside it and a small patch of woodland separating us from the back of the hospital grounds. To think Adam and I drove down here together for the first time just over a year ago, believing that the move out of London and into the outskirts would be the thing to save us. Bewitched by the long garden paths and our own little hide-away off the beaten track.

'The reason we're paying our solicitors a small fortune is so they can communicate for us,' I say as I pull down the private lane. 'You promised me that we'd leave the divorce to them and dedicate our communication to Zack.'

Gravel pings against the underside of the car. There are hedgerows to my left, the small mass of woodlands to my right. In the distance, the roof of my house slowly emerges through the trees.

'My solicitor *has* got in contact, Anna. You haven't got back to us.'

'I'm trying to balance a full-time job with being a single parent, for Christ's sake. You could cut me some slack.'

I reach the foot of the drive and slam down on the brake pedal.

Adam continues pleading his case, but it is nothing but noise. All of my attention is on the array of removal vans parked on the driveway. My front door is wide open and fluttering with the draught, and as I look closer, I spot shadows darting behind the windows.

There are people inside my house.

3

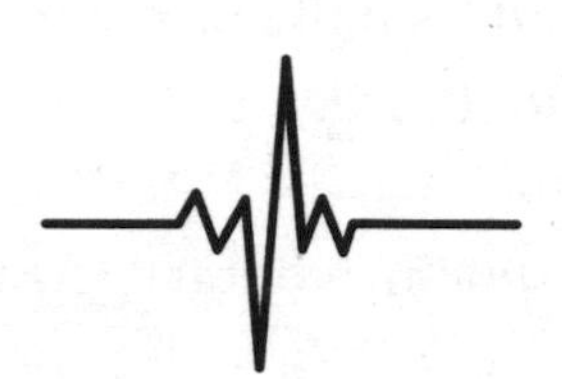

Anna

Thursday, 4 April 2019, 18:02

I take such a sharp intake of breath that I almost choke. The sound of it lodging in my throat stops Adam mid-sentence.

'What?'

'There are bailiffs at the house!'

'*What*?'

'*Bailiffs*! There are vans. There are people inside—'

'Are you sure? How would they get in?'

'Does it *matter*? Just how broke are you?'

'Look, don't panic, it's going to be all right. I'll make sure of it. I'll get everything ba—'

I hang up the phone and lift the handbrake, stumbling out of the car in a daze. Behind me, the engine is still running and the driver's door hangs open with a faint beeping from the dashboard. But all I can think of is Zack watching strangers ransack our home, his eyes brimming with tears as our belongings are filed out of the front door piece by piece.

Oh God. Paula will have let them straight in. She is too kind for her own good. That's what happens, isn't it? If they can get in it's fair game, and they take everything of value. They won't care which belongings are Adam's and which are mine.

Two men dressed in black overalls step out on the driveway and approach one of the vans.

'Stop!'

They continue their conversation in a language I don't understand, heading round to the back of the vehicle. I march towards them and prod the closest man in the shoulder.

'Excuse me!'

The stranger spins around. He is young and good-looking, with hazel eyes and dark stubble encroaching his cheeks. He mutters something venomously before turning his back on me again. A small droplet of saliva landed on my cheek as he spoke. I dash it away and wipe my hand on my trouser leg.

'Look, whatever this is about it has nothing to do with me. My husband and I are getting divorced. He doesn't live here anymore, and everything of his was taken when he . . . Are you *listening*?'

The men are still talking among themselves, laughing with their backs to me. Even if they don't understand English, surely they wouldn't just ignore me. I am about to start shouting when I jolt at the sound of a power drill and whip around.

It is coming from inside my house.

I storm towards the door with my heart lodged in my throat, and spot that groundsheets have been laid over the carpet. The plastic crinkles under strangers' boots as they snake in and out of my kitchen, my dining room, cross each other on the stairs. Everywhere I look, there are men with cropped hair, broad muscles, tattoos breaching their collars, black gloves covering their hands. The thought of them rifling through our things is so violating that I catch a sob at the back of my throat just in time.

I step inside and flinch at the sight of something hanging over me in my peripheral vision. A man stares down at me from a stepladder, towering over me with a power drill in his hand.

He is fixing what looks like a small camera into the wall.

I open my mouth to speak when plaster showers down from the wall in a thick, forceful mist. I stumble into the hall, coughing and spluttering into my hand as the drill blares behind me.

'Zack? *Zack?*'

There is grit in my eyes, cutting into them with each blink. Behind the tears I spot the large bulk of a man heading down the stairs, each step creaking beneath his weight.

How many of them are there?

'Paula?' I call out. The drill drowns out my voice. *'PAULA?'*

I rub my eyes and wince as the grit digs deeper. Tears stream down my cheeks and swing from my jaw as I turn blindly about the hall. Bear should be barking. Why isn't he barking?

'*Zack?*' I shout, just as the sound of the drill dies. My voice rings through the hallway and carries up the stairs to the landing. The terror is thick in my voice, even as it echoes.

Paula must have taken Zack next door. At least he doesn't have to see—

'Dr Jones.'

I spin towards the doorway to the living room with my chest panting.

'Join us,' a voice says from within.

The flippant invitation to step into my own living room is enough to vaporise any heartache I feel. Now my whole body is pulsing with rage, a venomous heat filling my chest until I feel sweat break out beneath my jacket. I wipe at my eyes with quick swipes and head into the living room.

Three men stare up at me in the doorway: two from the sofa, and one in the armchair, each with a mug of mine in their grips.

'Take a seat,' the man says from the chair, with the same calm voice as before. The other two men watch me intently from the sofa.

'Who on earth do you think you're talking to? Get out of my house!'

'Sit. Down.'

The man looks at me with such enraged conviction that I flinch when our eyes meet. I am so furious that I'm shaking, and yet I feel myself sinking compliantly into the free chair beside the fireplace.

The man in the chair is in his forties, his dark hair peppered with grey, dressed in a suit and shirt that look too tight for his muscular frame. The men on the sofa are slightly younger and covered in tattoos. One has a shaved head and a heavy jaw, the other with cropped blond hair and acne scars pitted in his cheeks. Above their heads, a tiny camera watches me from the corner of the room. Were it not for the setting sun on the other side of the window reflecting in the lens, I might not even have spotted it.

I turn in my chair in search for more, and spot another at the opposite end of the room. It is as small as my fingertip and white all over, blending into the walls and ceiling so seamlessly that it would be difficult to spot if I didn't already know this house like the back of my hand.

These people aren't bailiffs.

'You will find them in every room in the house,' the man says from the armchair.

His presence alone is commanding, from his deep, gravelly voice to the muscular girth of him practically breaching the chair. His eyes, however, are the most dominating. They are a cold, piercing blue, so clear and menacing that I feel myself shrink within my seat.

'What's going on?' I ask, feebler than before. 'Where is my son?'

The man leans forward and places the mug on the coffee table. The one I use every morning. Zack hand-painted it for me for my birthday two years ago. *To the best Mummy,* signed and dated on the bottom, covered in yellow stars and jagged little hearts. A lump forms in my throat.

'What I'm about to tell you is very important. I won't repeat myself, so make sure you listen to every word I am about to say.'

I open my mouth to protest.

'Your neighbour is dead.'

He says it with such ease that I almost don't register the gravity of his statement. But when it sinks in, the news hits me like a blow to my temple. A high-pitched whistle screams into my brain.

'. . . and we have your son.'

4

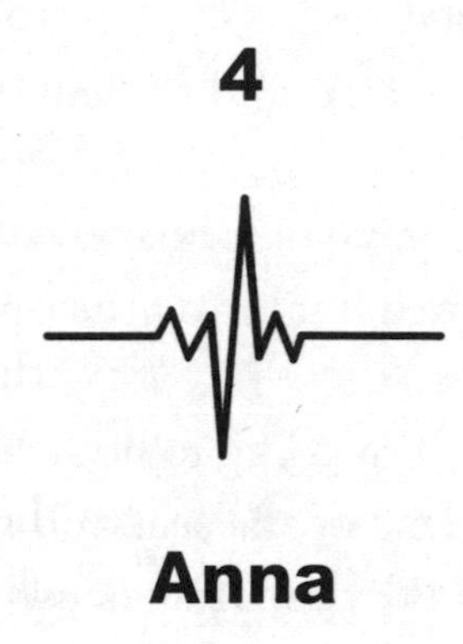

Anna

Thursday, 4 April 2019, 18:27

I sit in the armchair before the men, frozen in place.

For a brief second, everything stops. My mind is wiped clean. My heart stalls with a painful jolt. Air catches in my lungs. And then it all comes crashing back. I inhale a desperate, guttural breath as tears bite at my eyes.

This isn't real . . . It can't be . . .

'Dr Jones, I need you to focus. This is important.'

I nod obediently, a single tear falling silently towards my jaw.

'Your son is in a safe place, and no harm will come to him if you do as we say. There are rules you must follow, and if you break them, your son will pay the price.'

This man, this stranger, is using my own tricks against me. He is employing the same tone I use when I tell a patient's next of kin that they have died: sympathetic, yet firm. *I'm sorry for your loss*.

'All you have to do is complete one simple task, and you will get him back unharmed.'

My heart leaps, so fast and violently that a pain slices across my chest.

'A . . . a task?' I ask, my voice hoarse with fear.

'You must kill Ahmed Shabir on the operating table in two days' time.'

My stomach drops. I'm going to be sick. My vision is swirling. I grip on to the arms of the seat and push the heels of my feet into the carpet in the desperate need to root myself.

'If you repeat this to anyone, your son will die. If you are at any point discovered during your assignment, your son will die. If you fail to kill the patient, your son will die in his place.'

The two men on the sofa are watching me so intently that I can feel their glares burning into me, but I can't take my eyes off the man in the armchair. He is asking for the impossible. Not just ethically, but pragmatically. But just thinking of the consequences for not doing as he asks brings fresh tears to my eyes. I want to ask him why, but he speaks again before I can.

'Your locks have been changed so we can come in and out, and the cameras will survey your movements around the clock. This is the phone we will contact you on with the next steps.'

I stare down at the coffee table in a daze. There is a new set of keys, a cheap pay-as-you-go handset, and two phone batteries beside it.

'For your personal and work phones,' he says, following my line of sight. 'To trace your movements and monitor your communications.'

I hear the mutter of voices from the driveway and spin around. The men I first set eyes on are meddling with my car.

'They are fitting a tracker,' he says. 'If you try to remove it, we will know.'

This isn't real, I tell myself, and notice that I am rocking lightly in the chair. I bite down on the inside of my cheeks to feel something other than the horrendous pain behind my ribs.

'We will be watching every move you make,' he says, reaching inside his jacket. 'And if you slip up, I can assure you: you will regret it.'

He removes his hand and places a handgun on the glass coffee table with the quietest clink.

'Remember, Dr Jones: one simple task, and all of this goes away.'

On the outside I am deathly still, staring at the barrel of the gun on the table, but inside my mind is a chaotic scramble of emotions. My eyes fill with tears with the sudden rush of helplessness, before drying up as a bout of rage scorches through me. I feel faint, yet alert to the slightest sound. A tumultuous mess of misdirection is firing inside my brain.

And then, out of nowhere, I shock everyone in the room. I laugh.

I laugh until tears stream down my face and it hurts to breathe. I feel myself turning red. Through it all, the men watch in stony silence.

'You're joking,' I say, wiping my tears.

They stare back at me without a word.

My laughter dies in an instant.

'Where is he?' I ask, wild-eyed and frantic. 'Where's Zack?'

The man stares back at me in grim silence.

'Zack?' I call towards the hall, slowly tearing my eyes away from the man in the chair. '*Zack?*'

I jump up and head instinctively towards the stairs, bounding up them two at a time, and stumble just as I reach the top. A man laughs from my bedroom doorway, climbing down from a stepladder after fitting a camera in place. He has another in his hand, and I stare at the small white lens, the red and blue wires snaking out the back.

'*Zack?*'

I scramble to my feet and sprint along the hallway towards his bedroom, where another man stands testing a camera in the corner of the room.

'*Get out!*'

He jolts and whips around. When he sees the look on my face, he drops his eyes to the floor and mumbles something in his native tongue as he slips past me for the stairs.

Zack's familiar scent fills my chest. His bed is made, and the room is clear of mess but for the pyjama top poking out from the edge of the laundry basket. I have the sudden, urgent need to bury my face in it and inhale.

Zack isn't here.

His absence hits me instantly. It hadn't truly sunk in before, but now, as I take in the sight of his room, his toys, the pyjama top I peeled off him just this morning, it hits me. He is really gone. A desperate sound reverberates up my throat, caught between a sob and a yelp.

No. This can't be.

I slam the door shut and rip between the rooms, calling his name in furious panic and barging past the array of men filling my house, ignoring their laughter at my expense. Nausea comes to me in waves. I run and stop, run and stop, the urge to vomit clamping down on my stomach as acid stings up the back of my throat. I bound down the stairs and into the kitchen.

There should be pots and pans drying on the draining board, along with the plate and cutlery Zack would have used for dinner. But the surface is clear, and I spot drops of congealed jam on the countertop by the toaster where I had slapped our breakfast together in a rush.

'ZACK?'

My voice blares back at me. I stand in the middle of the room with my chest heaving.

Next door. They must be next door.

I turn for the hallway and bolt towards the front door, pushing past the man on the ladder. He yells something at my back. I hope he falls, cracks his skull on his own tools.

The cool air instantly dries the tears on my cheeks. A man is inside my car, manoeuvring it out of the way so that the vans can clear the driveway, while another rifles through my bag that I left on the passenger seat. It is all happening so fast, I just want to scream at them to slow down, give me a moment to make sense of it.

I sprint down the driveway, sweat breaking out beneath my jacket, and cross Paula's front lawn until I'm at the door, pounding on it with my fists.

'Zack? Paula?'

When I get no answer, I push over one of the potted bay trees flanking the entrance. Soil scatters across my feet, and I dig among the dirt for the spare door key. My head goes light and I brace myself on the doorstep, quivering on my hands and knees.

Don't fall apart.

When I open my eyes, I spot the glint of the key among the dirt.

I snatch it up and scramble to my feet. My hands are caked in mud, and my knees are soiled. I'm shaking so violently that I struggle to fit it into the lock, and turn it with such force that I fear it might snap.

The door swings open.

'Paula?'

I expect to hear her call back to me, to see Zack turn the corner as he runs to greet me with Bear bounding excitedly by his side.

Silence rings through the house.

I rip down the hall, checking first the kitchen, and then the living room, and stop before the fireplace to catch my breath. The silence continues to pierce through the room.

They aren't here, and yet, even with the evidence all around me, I can't comprehend it. If I keep looking, if I keep running, I will find them safe and well. This won't be real. My whole body is shaking, and it hurts to breathe, to think, with each new thought overcrowding my brain until I can't think straight and shake even harder. I stand in the middle of the room for at least a minute, staring at a framed photo upon the mantelpiece. It is of Paula and her daughter.

Maybe they took Bear on a walk to get away from it all. That seems like something Paula would do.

But wouldn't she have called me?

I instinctively paw at my pocket for my phone, my heart sinking when I remember leaving it in my bag. The very bag one of the strangers had been rifling through on the driveway.

I turn back on my heel and follow the soil I brought in with me from the doorstep, and bolt across the lawn once more. The evening is getting darker, and I have to strain to see the ground beneath my feet. Men are filing out of my front door one by one. Others are already packing up their equipment to the sound of van doors slamming shut.

They can't leave until I know where he is.

I rush back into the house and tumble as the groundsheet is tugged suddenly from beneath my feet. My hip hits the floor first, and pain ricochets down my thigh. I look around in a daze.

A man is standing at the other end of the entrance hall with the plastic sheeting in his hands where he had been rolling it up for transport. A smirk creeps across his lips. When he laughs, I have the instant desire to throttle the sound out of him. I stagger to my feet and stumble inside the living room. The three men are stood expectantly.

'Where is my son?'

I lunge at the man with the cold, blue eyes and snatch at his collar with such force that he stumbles back.

'*Where is he?*'

I pound against his chest with hard, desperate thumps, swinging and hitting blind until I clip the end of his nose. Blood bursts from his nostrils.

Hands grab me from behind and yank me backwards with such force that I am almost lifted from my feet; they slam me into the wall with a deafening thwack. Something clicks inside my neck. My vision spins. I can smell the blood from the man's nose, the sharp breath of the men pinning me to the wall.

'Cover her mouth.'

A large, gloved hand clamps down over my lips.

'*DON'T!*' I hear, as I bite at the stranger's palm. My head is knocked into the wall again, and a hot, stinging pain zings down my spine. The room spins violently. I heave for breath, moistening the leather of the glove.

I can't breathe.

The blue-eyed man is scrolling through his phone and sniffing back blood, his face lit a ghostly white from the screen. I squint against the light as he holds it before me.

It is a photo of Paula. Her skin has turned a noxious grey. Her eyes are open, and her lips are apart. In the centre of her forehead is a deep, dark hole penetrating into her skull. Her body has been abandoned in what looks like a well, lying in thick, black water that has soaked through her clothes.

I scream into the stranger's palm, and sob so hard that both men have to prop me up against the wall to keep me from buckling, and yet I can't tear my eyes away. The man returns his phone to the pocket of his suit.

'If you don't do what is asked of you, your son will join her. I will stick the bullet in his brain myself. Understand?'

The hand is lifted from my mouth. I gasp for breath.

'Why should I believe you? How do I know he isn't already dead?'

I'm shouting, sobbing, but I can't control myself. He stares at me with those cold blue eyes and sighs. A single drop of blood slips from his nostril and lands silently between his feet. He retrieves his phone and places it to his ear. We all wait, listening to the distant sound of the phone ringing.

'Put him on,' he says.

He approaches me and I flinch, expecting another slam against the wall, but instead he places the phone against my ear.

On the other end of the line, I can hear a shuffling sound, like trouser legs rustling together, and the echo of footsteps against a hard floor. A door creaks open and squeals on its hinges. I breathe heavily into the receiver with my eyes darting between the men.

'Mummy?'

The sound of his voice knocks the wind out of me. I freeze, open-mouthed, tears streaming down my face.

'Baby?'

Zack bursts into tears as if he has been trying to be brave all this time. I have never heard him so upset, and long to wrap my arms around him and stroke his hair, kiss every inch of his face. The distance between us only makes me cry harder. I bite down on my lip to compose myself, and force the words out as clear as I can make them.

'Baby, listen to me. Are you listening? You are going to be okay. I *promise* I will get you back. You hear me?'

'Mu-mu-mummy . . .'

Each sob is agonising. My chest is on fire. The men could beat me, strangle me, fire a round of bullets into my head; none of it would amount to this pain.

The man removes the phone from my ear.

'*No!* I didn't get to tell him I love him!'

The gloved hand is rising to my lips.

'*Please!*'

It clamps down over my mouth. When he ends the call, my legs buckle. The two men drag me to my feet.

'You know what's at stake now, don't you?'

I nod furiously behind the gloved hand, moist from my tears.

I can't breathe. I can't breathe. I can't breathe.

'Let her speak.'

The hand is lifted from my mouth. I gasp for air and exhale in a desperate sob.

'*Yes!*'

The men release me. I instantly drop to the floor and slam down on my coccyx.

Through the blur of tears, I watch as the two henchmen leave the room, and the man I hit takes something from his pocket. My phone. He removes the battery and replaces it with the other on the table, then again, with my work phone. On the driveway, headlights turn on in quick succession, lighting up the room until I can barely see through a squint. I lean against the wall, my head spinning, listening to the grumble of engines firing up outside and the distant patter of footsteps, the waggle of foreign tongues.

'One simple task, Dr Jones,' the blue-eyed man says. 'That's all it takes.'

The door shuts behind him with a slam, the sound shuddering through the rest of the house.

I sob for a while, holding myself as I rock against the wall, saliva strung between my lips. When the spinning stops, I open my eyes.

The room is dark. The house is silent.

And just like that, they are gone.

5

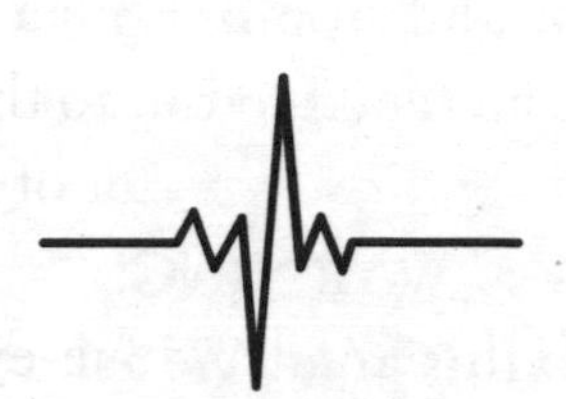

Margot

Thursday, 4 April 2019, 17:20

I'm not a bad person. That's what I keep telling myself.

I steal a look over my shoulder and cock my head to listen to the room. It has a devious layout, with the array of lockers forming tight little corridors and copious corners to hide in. But all I hear are gurgles from the pipes lining the walls, and the faint murmur of voices from the corridor on the other side of the door.

When I am sure that I am alone, I slip the money from Karin's purse and tuck it in the back of my jeans, closing her locker with a faint click of the lock.

If I were a bad person, I would have taken it all. I could have taken her phone, her debit card, the designer watch she always hides in the pit of her left shoe, but I only took ten measly pounds. But regardless of the excuses I conjure, I know that the reason I didn't clear her out entirely wasn't out of kindness, but a ploy to lessen the chances of her noticing anything was amiss.

The guilt flickers within my chest. I quickly snuff it out.

I'm not a bad person.

I head for the door and stop in my tracks when I spot that another notice has been taped to the back.

WARNING!

Thieves operate in this area. We ask that you keep your belongings safely secured, and only necessary valuables are kept inside the changing room unattended. All personal belongings are left at your own risk.

If you know of anything related to the recent thefts, please contact your line manager immediately.

My heart has picked up. Quick, nervous beats against my ribs.

It took months before anyone realised things were amiss. Months of hanging back until I was the only one left inside, rifling through my colleagues' belongings and debating what to take. What would they would miss the least? What could they spare? But the more I did it, the less I thought of their predicaments during my sprees. By the time people started to realise something was wrong, I had advanced to slipping inside people's lockers when they dared to turn their backs. I began to steal not only to get by and pay off my debts, but for fun, an itch that I never seem able to scratch.

I tell myself that I'm not a bad person. Perhaps one day I will believe it.

I open the door and flinch. My manager is standing on the other side of the threshold.

'There you are,' Kelvin says. 'I was looking for you. Can I have a word?'

Kelvin has never liked me. He is professional, and rarely lets it show, but occasionally I catch the way he looks at me when he thinks I'm not looking – he is trying to figure me out.

Maybe I am being paranoid.

'Can it wait until tomorrow? I have to dash off.'

My throat has restricted with nerves. We both hear it in my voice.

'It won't take long,' he replies with a tight grin.

He knows.

I mirror his smile. My heart is racing.

'Of course.'

He leads the way to his office in silence. Kelvin is short and stocky, with thinning wisps of mousey-brown hair and dark, round glasses that make his eyes appear far too small. When we find ourselves alone, Kelvin is usually the first person to force conversation to prevent any awkward silences, but now he isn't even attempting that.

He doesn't have to pretend to like me anymore. Not now he is going to fire me.

As we weave through the corridors towards his office, I think of all the ways my life will fall apart if I am let go. My debts will go unpaid, and I will fall further behind on my rent; I wouldn't be surprised if Sandy has changed the locks by the end of the month. Nick has already called me today and left a string of aggressive messages about the money I owe him, and I wonder how far I would have to push before he gets violent. The more I think of it, the more I panic, until I am shaking all over and my mind becomes fuzzy. As we reach the door to Kelvin's office, I am desperately trying to think of a convincing lie.

He opens the door with the sweep of his arm, ushering me inside.

Karin is sat before Kelvin's desk with Belinda, a fellow scrub nurse. They both turn to look at me as I enter and, by the expressions on their faces, they don't know the nature of the meeting either. Karin gives me a look of bewilderment. I shrug my shoulders.

'Take a seat,' Kelvin says.

I sit down beside Karin; her ten-pound note crinkles inside my back pocket. She gives me a quick smile and I force one back, the corner of my lips quivering from the strain.

Kelvin sits down and looks at each of us in turn.

'Thank you for coming on such short notice.'

'What's this about?' Karin asks, with a quick glance at her watch.

'Are we being made redundant?' Belinda asks, the panic evident in her voice, along with the smoker's husk of her twenty-a-day habit. I really should quit smoking if I don't want to look like her when I get older. Even the grim reaper would wince before he took her.

'No, no,' he replies, raising his palms in appeasement. 'I'm meeting with everyone in the unit to discuss the recent thefts in the women's locker room.'

Heat rises up my spine. When he glances at me, my eyelid twitches.

'Why just our unit?' I ask. 'We're not the only people who use the changing room.'

'No, but after tracking the dates and times of the thefts, we have worked out that each incident occurred when it was in our use.'

I hadn't thought of that.

'Now,' Kelvin says, clasping his hands together. 'I'd like to know: have any of you noticed any suspicious behaviour recently, or had anything go missing?'

I have stolen something from everyone in this room: money, cigarettes, food from the staff fridge. I can feel my cheeks burning, and grit my teeth together to force composure. The body is such a snitch. It gives away everything.

'I've had money go missing,' I blurt out quickly. 'Not much, just five or ten pounds, here and there. I thought I was miscounting at first, or forgetting what I'd spent, but then I tracked my spending. It didn't add up.'

'Right,' Kelvin says, nodding as he writes down my statement. 'Did you report this to anyone?'

'I've only just come to the conclusion myself. As I said, I thought it might have been forgetfulness.'

'I see.'

He doesn't look at me, so I can't gauge whether he believes my lie. I watch for the slightest tell: an arched eyebrow, the pursing of his lips. He gives nothing away.

'The same has happened to me,' Karin says. 'Never large amounts, as if it was done in the hope I wouldn't notice. But I have started counting my money after every shift and on a few occasions, I have been left five or ten pounds short.'

Five times, I think. *I have stolen from you five times.*

'I've had cigarettes go missing,' Belinda says.

Kelvin gives her a look. Belinda crosses her arms.

'I have, Kel. I smoke twenty a day, never a fag more or a fag less, and almost every shift I'm down one or two. That adds up.'

'Right. At least we know we're looking for a smoker.'

The rollie I tucked behind my ear burns against my temple.

It is pointed right at him. I run my hand through my hair to conceal it, careful not to knock it from its perch.

'Forgive me,' Karin says, leaning forward in her seat. 'But are you only interviewing women? Male staff can just as easily enter the changing rooms. We all know it's only a digit difference on the security code.'

I nod adamantly. '*One-two-three-four* and *two-three-four-five* aren't particularly hard to crack.'

'Exactly,' Karin adds.

You're one to talk, I think. *The code to your locker is one-one-one-one.*

Kelvin goes red in the cheeks.

'We will have the codes changed. And as for the culprit, we are confident it's a woman.'

'Why?' Karin asks.

He laces his fingers together upon the desk, his gold wedding ring glinting beneath the strip lights.

'Along with personal belongings, we have also had stock go missing. Stock that only a woman would need.'

Oh shit.

'Like?' Karin asks.

My heart starts to race, and the bag straps in my grip moisten with nervous sweat. I hate this room. It's so small and stuffy. I look to the window behind Kelvin's head, but it has been sealed shut.

'In the last few months there have been women's sanitary products going missing, but just recently . . . pregnancy tests.'

My cheeks scald. I look down at my lap.

'I see,' Karin replies. 'Well, you won't have long before the thief starts to show, will you?'

'That's if the person is pregnant, of course,' he replies. 'And it wasn't a negative—'

'Kelvin,' I interject. 'Isn't this a bit inappropriate? Members of staff shouldn't feel guilty for getting pregnant. If this gets out, you will be putting every pregnant staff member under unnecessary strain. This has turned into some brainstorming meeting, and I'm not sure I want to be part of that.'

'Me neither,' Belinda adds quickly, although I can see by her aggravated foot-tapping that her desire to leave isn't due to any moral dilemma, but her need to go outside and light up.

'You're right,' Kelvin replies, blushing again. 'I apologise. But if you do see or hear anything that might be connected to the recent thefts, I want you to know that you can tell me anything in the strictest confidence.'

The three of us stand in awkward silence, not a sound but for the scrape of chairs and the meaty thud of my heart.

'Have a nice evening,' he says towards Karin and Belinda. 'Margot, a word?'

I have given it away. He saw my cheeks flush, the nervous sweat shimmering above my lip and brow. I nod but remain standing, listening as the door clicks shut behind me.

'I just wanted to check in with you,' he says. 'See if everything is all right at home?'

I can feel the defensive venom seeping into my mouth. I do this every time someone attempts to pry; my tongue sharpens like a scalpel.

'Why would you feel the need to ask that?'

'Well . . .' He looks me up and down. 'You've lost quite a bit of weight recently.'

And you've gained some, I want to say.

'Is that an appropriate thing to ask? Discussing a female employee's body?'

His eyes widen a fraction; his spine straightens.

'I didn't mean anything untoward, I . . .' he stutters, and clears his throat. 'I was just concerned.'

'You needn't be. Can I go?'

He looks at me in bewilderment, as if he is trying to understand how his act of concern turned south so quickly, before releasing a small sigh.

'Yes, you can go.'

I nod curtly and leave without looking back, my heart racing rampantly in my chest.

If he has noticed I've lost weight, he might wonder if I'm the thief. I have stolen the man's lunch, for Christ's sake.

I head for the lobby and think back to what Karin said.

Well, you won't have long before the thief starts to show, will you?

My throat constricts with nerves. People start showing at what, twelve weeks? If that's the case, I have only three weeks left. Maybe I will be lucky, and be one of those women who hardly show, even in the later months. But Ma used to joke about how she waddled with the weight of me by six measly months.

You were my greedy little Maggot, forever wanting more.

I have always hated that nickname. *Maggot*. But by the time I realised what it meant, the name had already stuck: everyone knew me as Maggot Barnes.

I step outside the hospital and take a deep breath. The chill of the breeze pinches at my cheeks. I pull out my phone to check the time, and spot the latest message.

Nick
You're taking the piss now mate. Pay me by 5pm tomorrow or you'll be picking up your own fuckin teeth

Every drop of saliva leaches from my mouth. I try to read the text again but the words blur in my shaky grip. He gave me a large stash of weed when I was in his good books, and said I could pay him back when I had the money. Problem was, I never did have spare money to give him because my debts continued to grow. Clearly his patience has run out.

I take out Karin's ten-pound note and watch as it flicks in the wind. It is all I have to my name after my overdraft and debt repayments devoured this month's salary. Next payday won't help me either, because the same will happen again: my salary will be dragged into the red the second it lands in my account.

I jolt at the sound of my name and shove the note back in my pocket.

Karin passes me with a smile, her bag clamped firmly over her shoulder. I wonder if she has looked inside her purse yet.

'Night, love,' she says with a wave.

'Night!'

I head for the bus stop with my head down, my hair flattened to my scalp from the wind. The guilt is soon replaced with a churning hunger that makes me feel ill.

I am not as lucky as people like Karin, with a rich family to fall back on when times get tough, or a husband who pays half the bills. I am the type of working class that only has to stumble once for their whole world to fall apart, a single misstep that they will pay for for years. I think of Dr Jones driving to and from work in her Mercedes, the diamond rings she used to wear on her wedding finger, and swallow the resentment down.

They might need the money. But I need it more.

My stomach rumbles so loudly that it breaks my train of thought. I take the cigarette from behind my ear and light it within a cupped hand to quell my hunger. I will grab a box of chips from the kebab shop on my way home.

Cheers, Karin.

But inside the guilt swells. I remember the thoughtful smile she gave me as I sat down beside her, completely unaware that kindness was the last thing I deserved. I push on, dragging on the cigarette as I try to ignore Ma's voice whispering in my ears.

Greedy little Maggot.

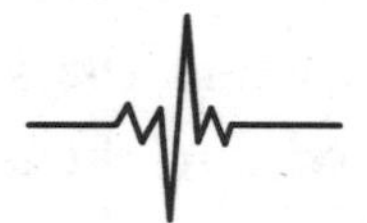

I open the front door and step into my empty flat.

Every sound echoes from the vacant space and naked, hardwood floors. The walls are bare without art or picture frames, the built-in shelves without a single book. All that is left is a single armchair facing the floor-to-ceiling windows and the cheapest TV I could find at the pawnshop when I was selling the flat-screen. It's a similar sight in the bedroom: all that's inside is a mattress on the floor and my clothes folded in piles along the back wall.

I flogged everything that wasn't nailed down: the sofa, the divan, every book from the cheap paperbacks to the signed editions my ex treasured. After the loan-repayment invoices started coming in, and I was pushed further into the red, I needed every available penny for rent. But all it bought me was an extra couple of months; that was a while ago now.

I shrug out of my wet coat and go to hang it up on the stand, only to remember that I sold it to someone online last week for fifteen pounds, which didn't last a day. I hang my coat on the bedroom door, trying to ignore my footsteps echoing around the empty room, and sit down in the armchair with a heavy sigh.

I can see the whole of Redwood from here: a large expanse of lights glittering beneath the clouds. I sit awhile, wondering what other people's lives are like behind the windows, if they are content, or if anyone is doing the same as I am: staring out from their rooms and wondering after the lives of others, daring to hope things might improve. Dan and I used to look out over the town together. We'd drink wine, smoke some green, and finish off the night with sex on the sofa that almost always ended up on the floor. We were happy.

I jolt at a loud bang against the door. My heart seizes like a clenched fist, sending a shiver of pain down my arm.

'Margot, I saw you come up. Open the door.'

Dan. He must have been staking outside the building waiting for me to come home. I sit, frozen, listening to him bang on the door, and wonder if he's figured out the truth about his stuff yet. I don't plan on being around when he finds out.

'Fine, ignore me. But you can't ignore the court when they summon you. This is the last letter from my solicitor. It's your final warning to let me get my things, Margot. You've had six bloody months.'

He slides an envelope under the door and I sit deathly still, as if he will sense my slightest movement. I stare at the envelope long after he has gone, wondering if he is still there, waiting for me to let my guard down. When I finally tear my eyes away and turn my sights back to the window, I place my hand above the little life growing inside me. The thing Nick put there.

He had simply knocked on my door to deliver some weed, the first time we did it. I would buy some from him whenever Dan went away for long work trips and the loneliness would set in. The weed numbed my sadness, and Nick's touch fed my need to be wanted. If only I hadn't asked him to stay and smoke a spliff with me that night, to keep my loneliness at bay. What followed was a lazy shag, slow and monotonous in tempo, ending with Nick's sour grunt as he finished before he rolled off me and fell straight to sleep. He woke up three hours later, stuffed his supply of weed in his jeans, and sidled out the door without a word, leaving me feeling more alone than I had before. But I didn't have long to wallow; Dan returned from his work trip early to find Nick making his way out the flat and drawing up his flies. Nick and I began to do it regularly after that until his generosity dried up and I missed my period.

I had decided to go through with an abortion, at the start. I'm not the mothering type: I'm selfish, reckless, and Ma didn't exactly set a good example. But the more the world took from me, the more I realised that this pregnancy might be all I have left that I can truly call mine.

What the hell I am going to do?

I head into the bedroom where I keep my stash, hidden away in a little wooden jewellery box, and place the necessary utensils on my bed: a lump of weed, tobacco and papers, and my grinder decorated with a bedazzled marijuana leaf with half the jewels missing. It has such a potent scent that when it wafts up towards me it makes my eyes water. I spot something else from inside the jewellery box, something I forgot I had hidden away.

I pull out the Polaroid photo of Dan and me, snapped by an old friend on a summer day in the park, sunlit and smiling. I thought I had finally made something of myself, back then. I had a decent man, a nice apartment, and a double income to rely on. All it took was the break-up and a couple of months of failed payments, and high-interest loans to send me back to where I belong. I should have left the flat rather than Dan, we both knew I couldn't afford that kind of rent alone, but I was desperate to hang onto the life I had, and terrified of where I might end up.

You'll end up right back where you belong, Ma whispers.

I shove the photo back in the box and roll a spliff to smoke the thoughts away. I shouldn't be smoking while pregnant, but I also shouldn't have to steal from my colleagues to feed us both. And a mother's stress is bad for babies, isn't it? At least this will mellow us both out a bit.

I flinch at the word. *Mother.*

When I was growing up, I vowed my life would be different to Ma's. I studied hard, went to university, learned to speak more posh than I am, and yet somehow, I ended up where I belong, walking in Ma's well-worn shoes and pregnant with a baby by a man I can't stand, stealing from good people just so I – so *we* – can eat.

I put the spliff to my lips and light it, inhaling hungrily. When the first few hits go to my head, I pick up the photo again and drive the end of the spliff into Dan's face. I watch in a trance as he shrivels and blackens, the luminous orange embers eating away at his smile.

I look around the empty room, dark with the evening's shadows, as my throat slowly constricts from the sudden desperation of it all.

I need to find a lasting solution, and quickly.

6

Anna

33 hours to go

Friday, 5 April 2019, 00:53

When I was fourteen I was hit by a car.

I had been late to meet a friend at the cinema on the corner of Edgware Street, back home in the city. Funny, I don't even remember what the film was now. As soon as my legs were knocked from under me, nothing else mattered. Everything I loved, every deep-seated belief and passion, were slammed out of me by that Ford pickup driving at forty-two miles per hour. All I could think about was the pain. The screams of pedestrians as they looked on in horror. The sound of my crown kissing the hot, metal bonnet. The windscreen cracking beneath my weight.

That is the only way I can describe it: the abductors came into my life and slammed into me with the force of a four-by-four.

I am still sitting in the dark.

My hip is throbbing where I fell after the groundsheet was tugged from beneath my feet. I have sat here for hours with my head against the wall, listening to the sound of my heart drumming against my ribs and the faint electrical hum of the cameras watching me from either end of the room. Maybe they don't make a sound. Maybe it's all in my head.

My eyes sting where the grit has burrowed beneath my lids, and my lips feel fat and swollen, tingling as if the stranger's hand is still clamped across my mouth. But nothing comes close to the agony that grips me when I think of Zack.

I keep hoping that I am going to wake up soon. That this is all some fever dream. When I think of where he might be, what he must be going through, how terrified and alone he must feel, the adrenaline surges again, and my breaths become shallower and shallower. Full-blown panic throttling the life out of me.

You won't help Zack by sitting in the dark.

I close my eyes and inhale deeply, ever so slowly clearing my mind of the paralysing fear. I feel the panic surge up, then simmer down again. In and out like a tide. I do this until I adopt the same razor-sharp focus I employ in the operating theatre and open my eyes.

I have to go to the police.

I can't do what they are asking of me. It goes against every promise I made to protect and preserve life. It is immoral, illegal. I would become just as corrupt as they are. Worse even. And even if I did, it would still mean leaving Zack God knows where, with violent strangers who mean him harm.

Fear envelops me quickly, and my fingers tingle with the relentless urge to pluck at my eyelashes. I curl my hands into fists and slow my breathing again.

Get up, Anna. Get up.

I put a shaking hand to the wall and stagger to my feet.

Maybe I won't have to go to the police at all – a neighbour might have seen or heard something. But if they had contacted the police, surely they would have made a house-check by now. Is there really something so unusual about removal vans driving along your road?

I think of the houses along our avenue. Everyone is wealthy and standoffish; there is no sense of community here. Our lives are so busy that we rarely even look up. I feel the hope slowly drain out of me, that sense of dread and loneliness encroaching further.

The moon is bright tonight, beaming through the window and reflecting in the glass coffee table. I stare at the shadowy silhouettes of the phones, the new set of keys, the mugs the men left behind. I feel like taking them outside and smashing each mug against the driveway until there is nothing left but small fangs of china. Everything they touched has been tarnished.

I step towards the coffee table to retrieve my phone and freeze at a sudden sound.

Scrape, scrape, scrape.

My heart flutters as I look towards the study door. A whine escapes from the other side.

I rush into the hall, tears of relief biting at my eyes. As soon as I open the door, Bear comes rushing out and runs about my legs in excited circles, small drips of urine escaping him after holding it for so long. I sink to my knees and snatch him up, inhaling his puppy-like scent. His fur soaks up my tears. I can feel his little heart pounding.

They didn't take everything. At least I still have you.

He wriggles out of my hold and hobbles towards the back door, small drops of wee trailing behind him. I get up and open the back door; he doesn't even sniff at the grass, the poor mite starts to go before he has even cleared the patio.

All this time, I have been thinking of no one but Zack, but finding Bear instantly reminds me of everyone else wrapped up in this.

Paula is dead.

The words hit me like I'm hearing them for the first time. Paula had quickly become an anchor for Zack and me when Adam left. The same Paula who could make Zack laugh in ways I never can. The same Paula who made it seem like I had everything together, even when I didn't, and that I was a good parent, which I'm not sure I have been. The same Paula we came to love as family.

And she's dead because of me.

I stand in the silence, lost at how to fix it all, thinking desperately of ways the men could be identified and held accountable. My mind drifts to the mugs on the coffee table in the living room.

There might be DNA left on the rim. I could seal them up in ziplock bags and preserve whatever traces they left behind. But each time I move, I have the inescapable sense that I am being watched. The sensation bristles the hairs on the nape of my neck. I turn to face the tiny camera above the door, so well disguised that I can barely see it in the low light, and stare straight down the lens.

Why me? Why Ahmed Shabir?

They aren't asking me to kill just any patient, but a Member of Parliament. Ahmed Shabir's death would bring a multitude of questions and instant interrogation. The hospital would go into PR overdrive; news outlets would cover the death day and night.

My career would never survive it.

How could it? My work – my duty – is to keep my patients safe from harm. It is what my entire profession depends on. Without our oath there would be no trust, and without that, the career I have dedicated my life to would cease to exist.

I glance at the clock on the wall – it is one in the morning. Is someone monitoring the footage every second? Perhaps I could pretend to go to sleep, and then wait a while – an hour, maybe two – and slip through the en-suite window and scale down the garage roof. If I leave the phones behind, and set off on foot, I could go to the police station and be back before sunrise.

My God, Anna. This is absurd. Plotting an escape from your own home.

Bear returns inside noticeably brighter and goes straight to his food cupboard. I shut the back door behind him before dropping a cup of dried food into his bowl, and limp into the entrance hall. I feel at a complete loss at what to do with myself, and wander aimlessly in the dark. Each time I go to flick a light switch, I stop myself; I refuse to give the men behind the cameras a better view.

I pause at the foot of the stairs and glance up the stairwell. To think that only a year ago I thought of this place as my dream home: five bedrooms, four baths, large expanses of glass and crisp white walls. I saw myself living here for ever. Now all of the love has been sucked out of it. Without Zack, without Adam even, this house is nothing but a hollow, lifeless shell.

Adam.

I return to the living room. My phone has been switched off since the battery was replaced. As soon as I turn it on, the screen is bombarded with notifications: missed calls, voicemails, text messages.

Adam:

Are you okay? What's happening?

Anna, call me as soon as you get this. Maybe I can talk to them.

Please talk to me.

I think back to the gun clinking against the coffee table.

If you mention this to anyone, your son will die.

My legs start to shake, and I sit down in the armchair, listening to the sound of Bear's food bowl dragging along the kitchen floor as he licks it clean.

Thank God Adam is away on business. Had he been in town, he would have come to the house to try and appease the situation, and who knows how the exchange would have gone then. I sense the sharp glare of the cameras on my skin as if they were eyes, and glance up towards the corner of the room.

Do they only transmit the sight of me? Or can they hear me too?

I look down at my phone, quivering in my white-knuckled grip.

Adam mustn't know until I've spoken to the police. Once Zack is safe, I will tell him everything.

I raise the phone to my ear, the cold screen jittering against my cheek. He picks up on the second ring.

'Why the *hell* didn't you call me sooner?' he barks down the phone.

After all the times he left me waiting at the end of the phone, crawling from bar to bar after business meetings in Amsterdam, eyes lit red from the lights of the district he swore he never visited, he has the audacity to be angry at me. Words of spite fill my mouth, but I quickly force them down. Now isn't the time; I must throw off any suspicions he may have. The abductors are listening.

'I got it wrong,' I say quietly.

'What do you mean you got it wrong?'

'They were removal vans, meant for another house on The Avenue. They thought they were at the right address.'

'But you said they were inside.'

'I told you, I got it wrong.'

'Well, why would you assume they were bailiffs?'

'Why do you *think*?'

He keeps on talking, but my attention drifts to the sight of blood on the carpet; dark maroon droplets hardened into the fibres where I smacked the intruder's nose. There are scuffs up the wall where they held me. I remember the feeling of the hand over my mouth, pushing the flesh of my lips against my teeth. I will never look at this room in the same way again.

'Anna, are you listening?'

'Sorry . . . I was looking at my schedule for tomorrow.'

He sighs heavily. While I had my reasons for ending the marriage, he did too: he said I worked too much, and didn't pay enough attention to him and Zack.

You always put them first.

Zack's last words to me before he was taken. Each one hits

me like a stone. He must have overheard Adam saying the exact same thing.

'Who moves house that late in the day?' he asks.

'They said something about having trouble obtaining the keys.'

'Oh, right.'

The awkward silence returns, and I fear that I have been found out, that he can sense me lying to him. The static of the call screams into my ear.

'Is Zack excited for tomorrow?' he asks.

A sharp pain digs into my chest at the sound of his name.

'Hello? Can you hear me?'

'Sorry, yes. He's excited.'

'Good. Will you let me know when he arrives? I'll give him a call.'

'*No!*' I shout. I regret it the moment the word leaves my lips.

'Why the hell not?'

Stay calm, Anna.

'I don't think that's a good idea.'

'*What?* Why?'

I should have thought about my lie sooner, I will need to remember every word I say. Not only must I convince Adam, I must appease the men who have my son. I imagine them listening in on the call, hanging on my every word. A headache pulses behind my eyes.

'Anna?'

'Zack doesn't want to speak to either of us at the moment. He heard us fighting earlier, and he . . .'

After all the times I berated him for lying, reminded him how much marriage relied on trust and honesty, here I am, lying through my teeth. Just as the guilt begins to rear up, I swallow it back down.

You're doing this for Zack.

'And he what?' Adam asks impatiently.

'He got really upset and stormed up to his room. He wouldn't even let me say goodnight. I think it would do him good to have some time away from us both. The break-up has really affected him, Adam.'

'He's eight, for Christ's sake. He doesn't need space, he needs love.'

'With all due respect, you don't know what he needs. I'm with him every day and I know what's best for him. Right now, that's space. It has been about us for so long; let's stop being selfish and do this for him.'

He sighs down the phone, and I know I have him.

'He can go to Cornwall with Jeff and Leila tomorrow and take his mind off everything,' I say. 'Jeff will keep me updated and Zack can call us when he's ready.'

'Fine, if that's what he wants. But update me as soon as you hear from Jeff.'

'Of course.'

My voice catches. I had almost believed my own lie: that Zack had gone away, but that he was safe, and would return happier than when he left.

'Are you sure you're all right?' he asks.

This is the first time I have missed Adam since the separation. Not the soft pucker of his lips, or the feel of the flesh beneath his clothes, but his strength; the sense of security that came with having him by my side.

'I'm happy if Zack's happy. Goodnight, Adam.'

I hang up and lean back in the chair, overwhelmed by the sudden sense of loneliness. I had been lonely all my life until I had Zack. Even when Adam and I married, I was trapped inside my own walls, refusing to let anyone in. But Zack broke them all down. Now my only anchor is gone. I sit, untethered and drifting, as the tears threaten to creep back into my eyes.

Bear pads into the living room sniffing at the floor, tracking the men's scent, and starts licking at the blood dried in the carpet. I lunge up to stop him when the burner phone vibrates against the glass table. I pick it up tentatively, my heart racing and the harsh white light stinging my eyes. A text message is waiting on the screen.

> Be careful how many stories you spin, Dr Jones. One mistake and it all unravels.

The phone vibrates in my grip. Another message.

> It will be Zack who pays the price.

Another message: a photo this time. I almost drop the phone. A sound rips from me, caught between a gasp and a howl.

The photo is of Zack.

He is curled up in the foetal position, fast asleep among old, dusty blankets on a concrete floor in the corner of a dark room, lit only by the flash of the camera. He is wearing the school uniform I had laid out for him this morning, and his golden-blond hair is ruffled from tossing and turning. But he isn't asleep by choice: embedded in the back of his small, pale hand is a cannula, with a clear tube running out of the frame.

They are sedating him.

Another text stings the palm of my hand. I can barely see the screen through the tears.

Don't let him down.

If I see them again, I will kill them. Tear the life from them with my bare hands. I move without thinking, grabbing my bag where it was discarded on the carpet and snatch up my keys: the old set from my bag, and the new, from the table. I find myself running for the car.

I stop on the driveway. The tracker will be ticking away, waiting to follow my every move. They will have watched me throw open the front door and bolt outside. Everything I do, everything I say, is done under their watchful eye. I wouldn't even know where to find them. I bury my face in my hands.

This is too much. I don't know what I'm doing.

Bear has followed me outside; I can hear the tap of his claws against the driveway, his nose sniffing at the grass. Something creaks in the night and my eyes whip towards the sound.

Paula's door is wide open. The key is in the lock where I left it, with soil sprawled across the doorstep; the bay tree is still lying on its side.

It won't be long before Paula's daughter calls me from Australia to ask me to check on her mother, wondering why she isn't answering the phone. When day breaks, the dog walkers who use the lane to reach the woodland will pass by the house and see the door swinging on its hinges, the mess at the foot of it. They will call the police, report a suspected robbery perhaps, and officers will arrive for a welfare check.

Then they will find my fingerprints all over the house.

I take a deep breath of the cold night air and swipe at my cheeks. If I want my son back, I must clean up the mess and make it seem as though nothing is wrong.

I must pretend the abduction never happened.

7

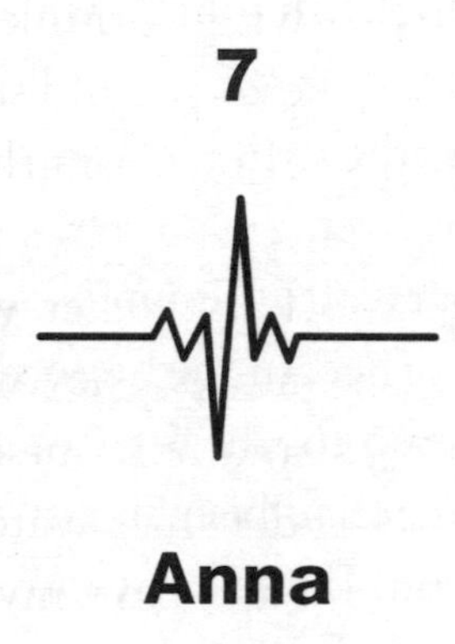

Anna

27 hours to go

Friday, 5 April 2019, 07:19

I haven't slept a wink.

I sit at my desk at the hospital and stare at my reflection glaring back at me from the picture frame. The stress of the last twelve hours seems to have aged me twelve years. My skin looks dull, and my cheeks appear gaunt from the shadows cast beneath my cheekbones. Before I began cleaning up the mess I made of Paula's home, I had scraped back my hair into a lopsided ponytail. I remove the hairband and shake it loose.

I cleaned until dawn. First Paula's house, then mine. I swept up the soil from her doorstep in the dead of night, vacuumed the carpet in the hall and through to the living room, before emptying the hoover bag into a bin liner and retracing my steps, disinfecting every handle and surface I remember touching. I scrubbed at the bloodstains on my living-room carpet until the sponge was frothing with pink foam and my nostrils stung from the bleach.

Ahmed Shabir's medical file is sprawled across my desk. I have been reading it over since I arrived, and have combed through today's papers after stopping at the petrol station before heading to my office, in the hope of finding out how the man I have been ordered to kill became tied up in something so dark. My first instinct had been to put his name into Google to see what came up, but I quickly stopped myself as I remembered that the police track those things.

I had thought about my situation as if I were going to go through with it.

But I won't. Of course I won't.

Shabir is featured on nearly every front page: the left-wing papers describe him as our only hope; the right-wingers have torn him to shreds. From what I can see, Ahmed is being featured heavily in the press for his work campaigning for higher defences against drug-trafficking into London. Redwood had once been used as a gateway for traffickers to bring their drugs to the heart of the city, but Shabir's crusade and the crackdown that followed saw a rise in drug-related convictions. Now he is promising to push for the measures to be implemented on a national scale should he become leader of the party, with the promise that the rates of violent crime will fall as a result.

Is this all because of drugs? Is that why this is happening to us?

The abductors must see me as the perfect catch. I am a newly single parent who has only been in Redwood for a year, having left London where all of our family and friends live, into a house down a quiet private track that is out of sight of potential onlookers and out of earshot from those living on The Avenue. They took Zack just before a planned two-week holiday, during the Easter break when children won't be missed from school, all while Adam was out of the country, and I was completely alone but for Paula next door, a widow whose only family lives on the other side of the world.

This was planned meticulously. These strangers learned everything about my life, my daily pattern, my loved ones. They must have been watching us for weeks.

I think back to the first time I met Mr Shabir: that warm, inviting smile, jet-black hair greying at the sideburns, his calm, soothing voice. He sat on the other side of this very desk, hands clasped at the knee, nodding his head as I went through the procedure, as if I weren't discussing sawing through his breastbone so I could slice at his heart. No foreboding of what was to come.

If he hadn't chosen our hospital, none of this would be happening to us. But Ahmed was firm on his choice: should the operation get leaked, he wanted it known that he trusted his local NHS hospital, rather than hiding away in a private facility and alienating working-class voters.

I sigh heavily and rest my chin on my fist. Reading about the patient has only made things worse. I had been secretly searching for signs that he is a bad person, so that killing him won't feel so bad.

Stop it. You're not going through with it.

There must be a way I can tell the police without being caught. If I leave my phone in my office, and head to the police station in a cab or on foot, the abductors won't be able to track me, surely?

Then I think of Zack's beautiful face, his blond hair that comes alive with threads of amber when the sun hits it, the way his eyes puff up when he first wakes and crawls into my bed for a cuddle.

But what if killing Shabir is the only way I will get him back?

I bury my face in my hands and toy with my predicament, mentally performing one heinous task, then the other. The consequences that derive from each decision seem impossible to fathom.

Either I abide by my oath, and kill my son.

Or I save Zack, and murder an innocent man.

I take a deep breath and sweep my hands through my unwashed hair, leaving a faint shimmer of grease on my palms. The photo of Zack that sits proudly on my desk is staring at me. I place the frame face down. I mustn't think of this as a mother. I must assess each case as a doctor, and triage.

In extraordinary and desperate times, we are made to choose between patients when only one can survive. The doctor who is given the ultimatum must assess the situation using statistics to consider who has a stronger likelihood of survival. What would normally dominate a person's decision-making is discounted: morality must be left at the door. I pick through the patient file and assess the facts.

Ahmed Shabir is a forty-year-old man with familial hypercholesterolemia in need of a triple heart bypass, with his chance of survival standing at around 90 per cent, should he not encounter any post-surgery complications. His life expectancy after the surgery will stand close to that of the general population, but after ten years post-surgery, his mortality rate will drop to 60–80 per cent. His familial hyper-cholesterolemia will continue to cause him problems in the future. This might be his first operation, but it is unlikely to be his last.

As for social aspects: he has a wife, but no children he will be leaving behind. Mr Shabir and his wife will be considering death as a possible outcome. They will have been preparing for this risk.

I bite down on my bottom lip.

Focus on the facts.

Zack Jones is eight years old and in perfect health, bar lactose intolerance and a penicillin allergy. His favourite colour is green. He has many years ahead of him. He hasn't had even a quarter of the life experiences that Mr Shabir has been lucky enough to have. Zack has barely started living.

And he's mine.

My phone rings, breaking through the silence of my office. I jolt so suddenly that something clicks at the back of my neck, and the memory of being thrust against the wall hits me in an instant. I can smell the blood from the man's nose, the hot, sharp breath of the men pressing against me. I pick up the phone in my quivering grip and look at the screen. My brother's name flashes up at me.

I stand from behind the desk and pace on shaking legs. Through all of the mayhem, I forgot that Jeff would be collecting Zack this morning.

If you tell anyone, your son will die.

The phone keeps ringing, and ringing.

I mustn't answer it; the abductors will be listening. I sit back down at my desk and wait for the call to end. As soon as it stops, I pick up my work phone from its dock and listen to the dialling tone shrieking in my ear.

Could they have tapped my office phone too?

I place the phone back on its cradle and stare at it, as if I will find signs that it has been tampered with if I look at it long enough.

My office phone might be tapped, but Dr de Silva's won't be.

I brace myself against the desk with a sudden dizzy spell. Spots dance in my eyes. I am exhausted, and the day has barely begun; there are two surgeries on today's schedule.

One step at a time.

I take a deep breath and open the door to my office. Sounds from further within the hospital echo through the vast network of corridors, but thankfully there is no one in sight. I step out of my office and make my way to Dr de Silva's office next door, pressing down on the handle as quietly as I can. I slip inside and close the door behind me.

'Anna, good morning.'

I spin around.

Dr de Silva is sat at his desk.

'I'm so sorry . . . I didn't think you'd be in this early.'

'So you thought you'd come and raid my chocolate drawer?' he says with a wink.

I force a laugh. The false smile makes my cheeks ache.

'What can I do for you?'

'I was hoping to use your phone. Mine is playing up and my mobile didn't charge properly last night.'

'Of course, go ahead.'

'No, it's fine. It's a somewhat private call. I'll ask at the nurses' station if they wouldn't mind if I use their—'

'No, no,' he insists. 'If you take your call at the nurse's station the whole hospital will know your business by lunchtime. I was about to go and grab a coffee anyway.'

He gets up from behind the desk and heads for the door, but as he gets closer, his smile fades.

'How are you doing?'

I must look awful: pale complexion; flat, unwashed hair; dark circles around my eyes.

My eyes.

I had planned to glue fake lashes on when I arrived at the office, but quickly forgot when I opened Ahmed Shabir's file. I look down, cheeks burning.

'I'll be fine.'

'All right. But remember, if you need someone to talk to . . .'

If I talk to you my son will die.

'Thanks.'

He pats me on the arm.

'And if I don't see you beforehand, good luck for Saturday. Not that you'll need it.' He opens the door and turns back with a smile. 'You have the rest of us green with envy, you know.'

Take it, I think. *I don't want it.*

He gives me another wink and finally leaves the room.

I perch on the end of his desk with a sigh. I have barely begun and already there are so many layers of deception, so many lies to keep track of, and yet the truth seems to be written all over my face.

I reach for the phone and type in Jeff's number, dreading the next jumble of lies that are about to fall out of my mouth.

'Hello?'

Hearing his voice makes my heart leap. I instantly want to burst into tears and tell him everything. I grip the side of the desk as hard as I can.

'Jeff, it's Anna.'

'Oh hey!' he says spritely, the sound of a man who is about to head off on holiday without a care in the world. I am so jealous I could weep.

'Where are you calling from?' he asks.

'Oh, my phone is playing up. I'm using a colleague's.'

First lie.

'You're at work already? I was hoping to see you when I popped over to collect Zack. Is Paula minding him?'

'Look, Jeff, I'm afraid I have some bad news . . .'

The anticipation burns up my throat. I feel so awful, crushing his happiness, but there is also a wicked part of me that longs to bring him misery, just so I don't feel so alone in mine.

'I was up half the night with Zack,' I say.

Second lie.

'He has been really looking forward to going away with you, but after all of the changes recently, the thought of being parted from me made him really anxious. I think it's best he stays at home with me.'

Third lie.

'Oh gosh,' he says. 'I'm so disappointed.'

'I feel awful, but it is such a raw time for us; our emotions are all over the place. I think he needs as much stability as possible until we settle into our new normal. I'm so sorry.'

'Don't be, I would do the same for Leila. Oh God, Leila . . . she is going to be heartbroken.'

At least she is safe.

I swallow the resentment down.

'Jeff, I'm so sorry to drop this on you and run, but I've got an operation this morning and I need to see the patient. Just know that Zack and I will make it up to you both. Perhaps we could all go away together later in the year.'

If I get him back.

'That sounds great. Look, Anna, before you go . . .'

He pauses briefly. I hold my breath.

'Are you all right?'

I'm giving it away. Dr de Silva saw it written all over my face; Jeff can hear it in my voice.

'Yes . . . why?'

'Well, you're going through a lot at the moment what with the divorce, and work, and being a single parent. Just know I'm here if you ever need help. Even if it's just to take Zack off your hands one morning so you can catch up on sleep. You sound exhausted.'

Tears spring to my eyes. I clear my throat.

'Thanks, Jeff. Look, I really must dash, but have a great holiday and make sure to send us a postcard.'

'Will do. Love you, Annie.'

I end the call quickly and close my eyes, holding my breath through gritted teeth.

I can't fall apart. I must be strong for Zack.

When I am sure it is safe, I open my eyes again and spot fine, golden hairs littered across my lap.

I had been picking at my arm.

I brush them off urgently and focus on my breathing again, slowly tying up each of the lies I have told.

There is no fear of Adam calling Jeff directly. Jeff loathes him since the infidelity during his work trips came to light. Zack won't be expected at school for another two weeks, and everyone believes he is in Cornwall, whereas Jeff thinks Zack has stayed home with me. I will go to the police station the first chance I get, and they can try and find Zack while I play the abductors' game. As long as I keep up the façade, and keep each story thread from breaking, I can sort all of this out. No one has to know.

It will be my little secret.

8

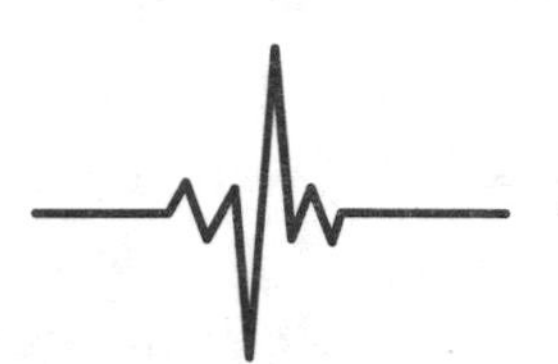

Rachel

Friday, 5 April 2019, 08:36

The body is at the bottom of the well.

At least it isn't in view of the sun, where the heat can get to it. Even the flies haven't found her yet.

The motor of the retrieval winch is purring like a cat in the sun and, deep within the well, the chain bringing up the body is creaking with the weight. The sound makes my teeth ache.

Crime-scene personnel were suspended down at daybreak. They took photographs, collected water samples, searched the body for evidence that might have been damaged with the move. Now they lie in wait with the rest of us, ready to flock around the body as soon as it is transferred to the pop-up tent shivering in the morning breeze.

The body was found by a dog walker as the cliché goes,

whose yappy terrier caught its scent and tracked it to the well, and set off barking with its front paws upon the wall. It was as the owner went to retrieve it that he caught sight of the body down below: her head cocked as if she was looking up at them, mouth open in a silent scream for help. It is fair to say he won't be walking his dog on Littlebrook Farm ever again.

The body appears. Dark water falls from her in heavy streams, exuding a foul stench that instantly hits the back of my throat.

The victim's skin has a sickly green hue to it. Her clothes are hanging off her from the weight of the water. She has a shoe missing, and in the centre of her forehead is the unmistakable sight of a gunshot wound. The woman must be in her sixties; not exactly someone one would associate with this sort of crime.

'A mugging?' Detective Sergeant Mark Ryan asks beside me.

'That's a lot of effort for one woman's handbag.'

'There's been a rise in muggings this year.'

'I'll bet you fifty quid right now that none of the victims were shot clean through the head.'

Just as I say this, the winch reaches the end of the line, and the body turns slowly where it is suspended above the well, giving us a flash of the exit wound at the back of her head. The white hair beneath her crown is now dark burgundy.

'This isn't the work of a petty criminal,' I say. 'This was an execution.'

I watch the retrieval team begin lowering the body from the winch. DS Ryan can't take his eyes off it either.

'Still signs of rigor mortis,' he says, eyeing the victim's ramrod legs. 'At least we know it happened in the last forty-eight hours.'

DS Ryan's skin is so fair that he practically glows in the path of the sun, with a thick cluster of freckles across the bridge of his nose. His auburn hair is even brighter than my son's. There must only be a couple of years between them. My son would have been about twenty-five now.

'Do you think her killer was someone from around here?' he asks.

'No. Not in Littlebrook. There are only six or so houses in the hamlet. The culprit would be sniffed out by noon. The killer will have known that the farm was abandoned and travelled here to dump the body.'

'The well has been out of use since the 1980s, when the farm went bust,' he says. 'They must have thought she wouldn't be found down there.'

'Inspector Conaty,' a voice calls. It is the pathologist, Diane Reed, ushering us over to the body with a gloved hand.

I give her a nod and make my way over, lifting my feet to clear the long reeds of grass. By the time we reach her, my trouser legs are soaked through with dew.

The smell is even worse up close.

'She wasn't down there long,' Reed says, lifting her mask. 'No maggots, and still showing signs of rigor mortis. At a glance, this happened in the last twenty-four hours.'

I stare at the stumps where the end of the victim's fingers should be.

'So her fingertips were cut off then? They didn't rot?'

'Definitely cut. You can see signs of a serrated blade in the skin.'

The victim is wearing a pale-blue cardigan with buttons that imitate pearls, and smart navy trousers with an ironed crease down the front of each leg. A small shard of skull is tangled in her hair.

'Any idea what sort of firearm was used?'

'Looks like a handgun at close range.'

'How can you tell?' DS Ryan asks.

'There are burns around the entry wound,' Reed answers. 'And if the perpetrator used a larger weapon, there'd be a bigger mess to clean up.'

'How'd she get into the well?' I ask.

'I suspect she was dropped or pushed. There were signs of broken bones when we transferred the body; she is exhibiting damage that we would expect to see if she had jumped from a third-floor window.'

I stare at the victim's face. She would have been pretty when she was alive. Nice bone structure, warm hazel eyes, lips that would have formed a kind smile before her teeth were removed. When I was called to attend the discovery of a body in a well, I had suspected the sad but usual sight of a rough sleeper, who perhaps climbed inside and couldn't get back out; or maybe a junkie who paid the price of a bad drug deal. Not someone's grandmother with a gunshot wound to the head.

'Were the teeth knocked out or pulled?'

'Pulled,' Diane replies, curling back the victim's top lip to reveal bloody craters in her gums. 'Takes longer, but ensures there won't be anything viable left behind.'

'So it's safe to assume our killer removed her teeth to prevent us from identifying her through dental records.'

'That would be my guess.'

'Thanks.' I turn to DS Ryan. 'Let's go look at the well.'

I lead the way, squinting against the morning sun. The dew has soaked through my shoes, and makes a jarring squelch with each step. I reach the wall and peer over the lip.

'What's next, boss?' DS Ryan asks behind me.

'We need to find out who she is, and where she was killed – this is just the dumping site. We won't have much to go on until we do.'

I glance down the shaft and a wave of vertigo shakes my brain.

'Our first port of call is sifting through any missing person's reports raised in the last few days. If we don't find anything, we'll get an artist's rendering mocked up and share it on social media. Hopefully someone will recognise her and get in touch. I want to know her name by tomorrow morning.'

I hear the click of a camera behind my back and turn around. The white tent illuminates with each bold flash, as the team snapshot every scratch, every hair. The entrance to the tent flaps briefly with the wind, giving me a glimpse of the victim's face. Her eyes are wide open: searching, pleading.

'This isn't the sort of person who gets mixed up in the wrong crowd. Let's find out who she is, and how the hell she ended up here.'

9

Margot

Friday, 5 April 2019, 09:09

I have less than eight hours to give Nick his money.

My eyes are bone dry after spending most of the night awake trying to find a way out of my predicament, but it was a night wasted: there is no way I can pay him back by tonight. I can't even afford milk after spending Karin's money on phone credit and a box of chips, let alone over two hundred pounds in arrears. And then there is the rent I need to pay, bills, food. Sandy called twice this morning chasing after my rent, but I didn't have the guts to answer.

I lay out Dr Jones' tools for the morning operation in silence, lined up in the order she will need them: scalpel, oscillating saw, rib retractor, forceps, scissors, needle driver, sutures, ticking them off the checklist as I go. At the foot of the bed the surgical care practitioner's aide, Beth, is lining up the tools for harvesting veins for the coronary bypass. Karin has checked the heart–lung machine twice.

Just two days ago, I had been cursing so many routine procedures. I wanted something meaty – a transplant, a valve repair from exterior trauma – something I haven't seen every week for the last five years. But today I am relieved. With everything else so uncertain, it is a comfort to be assisting with a procedure I know well.

'Switch the forceps and the scissors,' Dr Jones says over my shoulder.

The theatre is so quiet that I jump at the sound of her voice.

She isn't usually here at this point; she waits until the patient has been put under and wheeled in before gracing us with her presence. And that isn't the only thing off about her this morning: she looks like shit.

Even behind her mask and eye shield, I can tell that she has been up half the night. Her eyes are bloodshot and puffy, and if anyone dares to talk to her, she snaps back at them. Something has really got under her skin, and her foul mood has infected the entire room. In the corner of my eye, I can see Beth laying out each tool with the utmost care, terrified that she might make too loud a sound and get one of Dr Jones' sharp glares.

I stifle a yawn behind my mask. When I finally did fall asleep last night, I almost wished I had kept my eyes open, for I had the same recurring nightmare rolling around my mind in a loop: I had been running through the corridors of the hospital with my teeth falling from between my lips and tinkling on the lino floor behind me. Every time I tried to call out for help, I choked on them. I kept on running until the final tooth fell, and turned back to see Nick following the trail I'd left behind me. It always ended with him grabbing me, but I'd wake just as he spun me round.

No doubt where that came from.

I can't take out another payday loan. It was their high interest rates and late-repayment penalties that got me into this mess in the first place, that first month when I couldn't meet my rent. My overdraft is at its limit, and my credit score is so bad that if I were to call up my bank and ask for a loan or a larger allowance on my credit card, they would howl with laughter as they disconnected the call. I am too proud to ask my family for money, and friends are pretty thin on the ground these days, which tends to happen when you take their money and fail to pay them back. I'd go to the local food bank, but I'm terrified of being recognised by a patient. Kelvin would definitely start to suspect me.

I could tell Nick I'm pregnant. Maybe he won't hurt me then.

But deep down, I'm not sure he would care.

The prep-room doors open and the sedated patient is wheeled in. She is forty-four according to her chart, with bright auburn hair and a frozen face from expensive anti-ageing procedures: her cheekbones look unnaturally large, and her lips appear swollen, throwing the symmetry of her face off kilter. But what catches my attention most is the gigantic diamond ring on her finger, sparkling under the strip lights. All of the saliva evaporates from my mouth.

'Wait,' I say. 'She's wearing a ring.'

'What?' Dr Jones snaps.

I point at the patient's left hand.

'Christ. She can't wear that in here. The nurses know that.'

I can't take my eyes off it.

The diamond is huge.

It must cost a fortune.

It could pay my debts to Nick, every rent payment I have missed in full, enough food to last me months.

'Is there a next of kin in the hospital who can keep it safe for her? A partner?'

No. It's too risky. I can't.

'She came alone,' Beth says, flicking through her file.

'I don't want delays today, team. Someone needs to take care of it.'

'I'll do it,' I hear myself say.

Everyone in the room looks at me.

'Kelvin has a safe in his office. It will be secure there.'

'All right,' Dr Jones says. 'Be quick.'

I nod and seize the ring on the patient's finger, twisting it against the skin. It has been there for so long that it has created a groove in the flesh. It feels like I am prising jewellery from a dead woman.

'Christ, Margot,' Karin says. 'You don't have to take her finger with you.'

'Sorry.'

I tuck the ring into the pocket of my scrubs, noticing how the white gold band is still warm.

'I'll be ten minutes.'

'Make it five,' Dr Jones replies.

I nod quickly and head out through the prep room to the hall as quickly as I can, terrified that Dr Jones might change her mind and have someone else run the errand instead. My heart is racing so fast that I feel dizzy.

I slip inside the changing rooms and check for anyone inside. The clock is ticking on the wall, counting off the seconds until I have to be back in the operating theatre. I open my locker, slip the ring from my pocket, and admire how the diamond glistens with every turn. I slide it on, but it doesn't look as good on me: my nails are bitten to the quick, and my skin is cracking between my fingers. The woman on the operating table has probably never done a hard day's work in her life.

This could be the answer to all of my problems, I think, as I hide it away inside the small compartment of my bag and zip it shut.

Or it could destroy everything, a voice whispers back.

I slam my locker shut and head for the door.

10

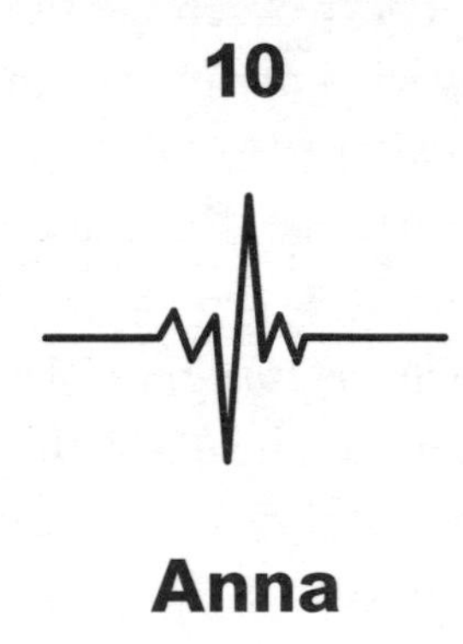

Anna

22 hours to go

Friday, 5 April 2019, 12:14

I walk into the women's locker room and stare longingly at the bench flanking the middle of the changing bay as if it were a bed with freshly washed sheets. I would love to lie down, even for a moment. My legs are trembling and there is a persistent ache in the small of my back. But I can't waste my break on sleep, no matter how much I need it. If I don't go to the police now I will miss my window.

I peel off my scrubs, feeling where the fabric stuck to my sweat during the morning's surgery, and shove them down the laundry chute in the wall.

I can't kill a man. I won't.

Mummy . . .

Mu-mu-mummy . . .

I clamp my eyes shut and sink down onto the bench.

Every time I think of defying the abductors' rules, I think of Zack on the other end of the phone. Remembering the desperation in his voice sucks the life out of me. I hide my face in my hands, careful not to press down on the fake lashes, and feel myself drifting off when the door to the changing room opens with a long, high-pitched screech.

Margot.

I must look awful: spine curled, tummy protruding over the waistband of my underwear, dark circles around my eyes.

'Going out?' she asks.

'I just need to pick something up. I won't be long.'

She shrugs as if she couldn't care less, but if I hadn't told her, the nosey little cow would only have pried until she found out.

As I take my clothes from their hangers and slip into them, I watch Margot from the corner of my eye. She opens her locker beside mine, checks on something, then takes out her phone and scrolls through the messages. She sits down on the bench with a sigh.

'I hate men. Don't you?'

I flick my hair out of the back of my blouse and slip into my shoes.

'You have no idea,' I reply, as I take my bag from my locker and lock it behind me. 'I'll see you in an hour or so.'

Margot shrugs, her eyes never leaving her phone.

I leave the changing room and head for the lift, only stopping when I hear a man call my name.

'Anna, glad I caught you.'

It is Dominic Keller, chair of the cardiothoracic department.

He is tall and broad-shouldered, and always has an air of impatience about him. I swallow down my panic and force a smile.

'Dominic, what can I do for you?'

'Just checking you'll be dropping by my office before the end of the day. I'd like to go over protocol for Patient X tomorrow.'

My eye twitches at the mention of him. I force my smile wider.

'Of course. I should be out of surgery around five. Mind if I drop by then?'

'Great,' he says, and pats my arm before heading the way I came. 'Look forward to it.'

As he heads off down the corridor, I step into the lift, my heart racing in my chest. I'm panicking at just the thought of the surgery, but how will I feel when the time comes, when people are watching my every move? When all of the heightened security measures are put in place?

I couldn't kill the patient even if I wanted to.

I glance at my watch: I have one hour and forty-five minutes until I need to get back.

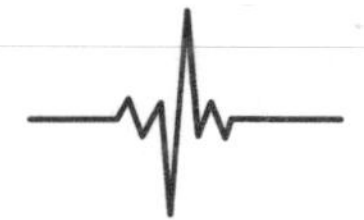

I jump into the first cab in the taxi queue outside the hospital.

'Police station, please.'

I expect to see a flicker of worry on the driver's face, but he doesn't even flinch. He merely turns up the radio and pulls out onto the road.

I strap myself in and tap my foot against the footwell to the music to keep myself awake, glancing over the man's shoulder and into the side mirror.

No one is following you. You're being paranoid.

I close my eyes and rest my head against the seat.

What will I tell the police when I get there? I realise how it will sound when I say it aloud: strange men have set up CCTV throughout my home to monitor my every move. They murdered my neighbour, kidnapped my son, and the only way I will get him back is if I kill a politician on the operating table.

They will think I'm mad.

The driver slams on the brakes and my eyes shoot open. He is shouting profanities out the window, gesticulating wildly with his hand. A cyclist flips him the bird and pedals out of sight.

I must have fallen asleep for a moment; nausea is coiling in my gut and there is a vile taste in my mouth. I pinch the skin on my wrist to keep myself awake.

Almost there. Just a few more turns.

I still don't know what to tell the police. If I mention the CCTV cameras, they will want to search my house to see for themselves. But how can they, with the men watching on the other end? I couldn't even bring the phone with me to show them, to stop the abductors tracking me there.

I turn and glance through the rear windscreen, but I don't notice anyone blatantly tailing the car, just a red Focus behind us, and an Audi behind that.

See? I tell myself. *You're being paranoid.*

I take my handbag from the seat beside me and take a couple of gulps from my water bottle, fighting the urge to splash it all over my face.

The cab comes to be an abrupt stop.

'Seven-eighty.'

I fish around in my purse and pull out a ten-pound note.

'Keep the change,' I reply, and get out of the car.

April has finally shaken off the chill, and the sun beams down on my face, far too bright for my tired eyes. I take my sunglasses from my bag and walk hesitantly towards the station, stopping in the shade beneath the trees opposite the entrance.

If you tell anyone, your son will die.

I dig my heels into the ground and remind myself that there is no other way. If I don't tell the police now, I will be expected to kill a man in the morning. That isn't an option.

If you fail to kill the patient, your son will die in his place.

I think of Zack curled up in the dusty blankets in the cold, dark room, a drip snaking into the back of his hand with God knows what being pumped into his veins.

I check my watch: I have to be back in the operating theatre in an hour. This is my only chance. I stare at the police station doors, willing my legs to move.

I stay rooted to the spot.

If I walk inside and tell them everything, there is no guarantee Zack will be saved. I would be gambling with his life, trusting that the police could somehow infiltrate the abductors' plans of harming him if I fail. But there is a high chance that the police will have no idea who they are, or where they are keeping him. It could take them weeks to track the abductors down. It only takes a second to pull the trigger on a gun.

Mu-mu-mummy . . .

I shake the sound of his cries from my mind and pace beneath the trees.

I can't believe I'm considering this.

Each time I think of another solution other than murder, I imagine how it might play out. Zack dies every time. I watch him die so many times that I can't bear it, flinching as the imaginary sound of a gunshot rings in my ears. The best possible chance I have to get him back is by following their rules. Everything else relies on hope, and trust.

I turn back for the road, just as undecided and terrified as I was before. Both outcomes end in disaster. I can't lose my son, but I can't knowingly harm a patient either.

I look up from the path and freeze.

The black Audi I spied from the back of the cab is parked up on the other side of the road, with a familiar face behind the wheel. It is the man who I met on my driveway yesterday afternoon. I remember his hazel eyes, the spittle landing on my cheek as he spoke.

They followed me here.

Zack.

I walk on with my head down, picking up the pace with each step, my heart pounding. The sun burns into my back. In the corner of my eye, I spot the Audi pull out of its parking spot beside the path and follow behind me.

I turn at the corner and run. Run so hard that my vision blurs as my eyes jar in their sockets. Run until the hot air leeches every drop of moisture from my mouth.

I'm running towards the phone.

Running to hear if they have killed my son.

The doors to the lift open on the third floor. I step out, struggling for breath and soaked through with sweat. My feet are cut up with blisters. But it's all meaningless. All I can think about is Zack.

'Christ. Did you swim here?' Val asks from the nurse's station.

I am too breathless and terrified to respond, so stride towards my office and shut myself inside, leaning against the door as I pant for breath. The burner phone is vibrating inside the drawer of my desk.

I hobble across the room and open the drawer, answering the call with a held breath. A drop of sweat lands silently on the desk. I wait, listening to the stranger breathing on the other end of the line and the desperate racing of my pulse.

'Pull a stunt like that again and I will send you his hand.'

The call ends.

I stand deathly still with the phone pressed to my ear.

Then I fall to my knees and hurl my guts into the wastebasket beside the desk.

11

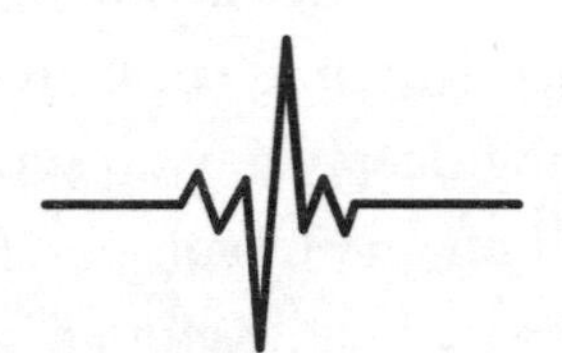

Margot

Friday, 5 April 2019, 19:28

I stand in the lift, glistening with sweat. I haven't done a large food shop in so long that I forgot how much of a chore it was lugging all of the bags from the shop to my building, but the thought of eating properly kept me going, and has my mouth sopping with saliva. But with the joy of having food comes the guilt from how I got my hands on it.

The patient's ring sold for a measly grand at the pawnshop on Hammerton Road; practically daylight robbery for the size of the diamond. But I didn't have time to wait for a higher offer elsewhere: I'm running late in paying Nick back, and I've already visited every other pawnshop in town. Turning up with a ring like this would raise even the most immoral soul's brows.

Each time my mind drifts to the woman I stole it from, I try to imagine her doing terrible things to ease my guilt, like kicking a dog or shouting at a baby. She has kicked the imaginary mutt so many times that if it were real it would be dead in the ground by now. My phone starts ringing from inside my bag, but I ignore it. It will only be Sandy chasing after the rent again.

Kelvin lost it when he found out about the ring. I was dragged into his office and made to watch him pace back and forth, his face growing deep crimson until I genuinely feared he might give himself an aneurysm.

You weren't in your office, Kelvin ... Dr Jones asked me to rush straight back, so I put the ring in my locker and fixed the padlock. It's not my fault that a thief broke in and stole it – a thief you have known about for months and have failed to stop ...

He didn't say much more after that.

The lift arrives at the fourth floor with a high-pitched ding. As I step out and make the turn to the left of the corridor, a hand snatches a fistful of my hair. I let out a sharp yelp, arms flailing, and feel the bags slip from my grasp. Produce spews down the stairwell to my right in a succession of thumps and clatters against the railing. I am just about to scream when the stranger slams me into the wall, the bobbly plaster cutting into my cheek. A strong hand snatches my wrist and yanks my arm behind my back.

'Where's Nick's money?' a woman spits, millimetres from my ear. Her breath is foul.

I spot Nick standing just a few feet away, leaning against the wall of the corridor with his arms crossed and a smirk creeping across his face. He has shaved his head since I last saw him. He looks like a fucking bowling pin.

'I have it, all right?'

The woman twists my arm further and I yelp again, sure that my arm is about to pop out of its socket.

'I'm *pregnant!*'

Still, she keeps twisting. Sparks flash in my eyes.

'Let up,' Nick says begrudgingly.

The woman hesitates, as if deciding whether to follow his orders, and reluctantly lets go of my arm. I stumble to face her and press myself against the wall, cradling my throbbing elbow in my palm.

At first glance I take the woman for forty or so, but as I look closer I realise she is far younger, and a hard life has ruined her complexion. Her teeth are stained from years of chain-smoking, eyes yellow from too much drink and God knows what else.

'Aren't you going to invite us in?' Nick asks. He nods towards my door and gives me a wink. He either hasn't connected the dots that I'm pregnant two months after we had sex, or he doesn't care.

I snatch up my bag from the floor where I dropped it in the scuffle. The strap has snapped on one side. The whole corridor smells of milk where it leaks through one of the bags, pooling on the carpet. I unzip my bag for my keys and approach the door, with the woman stalking behind me like my shadow. She shoves me inside the moment I turn the key in the lock.

Nick's laugh echoes round the empty room.

'Shiiiiiiiiit, you weren't joking about being broke, were you?'

His smug smile makes me feel ill. To think I have let this man touch me.

'Money,' the woman says, clapping her fingers against her palm. 'Now.'

I pull my bag up towards me with the broken strap and sift

through the envelope of cash with shaking hands, making sure to keep it hidden from their greedy eyes. I just count off the right amount in my head when the woman snatches my wrist and yanks the envelope free.

'Christ, you've been hiding it away, haven't you?'

She puts the lot in the back of her jeans.

'No way! I only owe two hundr—'

All I see is a quick flash of gold from the rings on her fingers before her knuckles slam into my stomach. I buckle over with a retch and slump to my knees on the hardwood floors.

'Think of the rest as interest.'

I can't breathe; she completely winded me. It feels like every organ has been jolted out of place. I slink further to the floor as my lungs croak for breath, listening to them laugh and the faint crinkle of the envelope as she hands it over to him and heads for the door. My eyes water from the pain.

She's killed it. It was such a heavy blow, and it's still so early. Oh God, she's killed it.

'Here,' Nick says. He puts his hand out to me, and for a second I think he is offering to help me up. Then he flashes a fifty-pound note between his fingers and flicks it at my face. 'Buy yourself a lamp or something, yeah?'

He heads for the door, laughing through that same, vile smirk. I listen as they make their way down the stairs until I am alone, breathing in the sour scent of milk drifting in from the hall, a single tear of frustration slipping down my cheek.

I am back to square one.

12

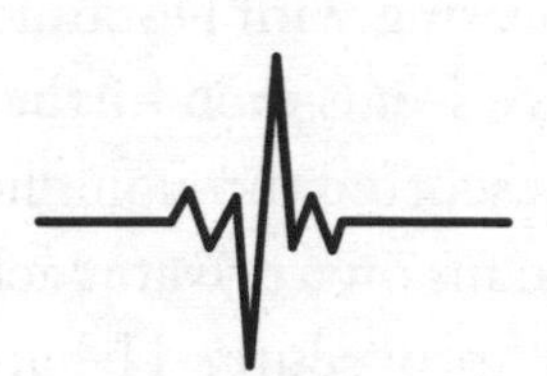

Anna

11 hours to go

Friday, 5 April 2019, 22:59

I wake on the sofa with a harsh, guttural gasp.

My head is pounding, and I feel unbearably hot. The clothes I slept in have twisted around me, and the microwave meal I fixed for myself and struggled to eat is on the floor, the plastic container and the metal fork licked clean by Bear, who is looking up at me from the beneath the coffee table, his tail wagging with guilt. Ahmed Shabir's file is strewn across the top of it.

I had been planning the murder.

I know what my options are, and that only one will save Zack, but the idea of taking a life is too awful to compute. I tell myself that I am only planning it hypothetically, to see if what they are asking of me is even possible, but I struggle to believe my own lie. I know that with every second that passes, I am that bit closer to having to make a decision, and the longer I delay, the worse it will be. I glance at the clock on the wall: it is 11 p.m. In less than twelve hours I will be expected to kill a man. But after my meeting with Dominic to discuss the security protocols, the task seems even further out of my control.

Mr Shabir will be escorted through the back of the hospital at dawn and guided to his own private room on the ward where he will wait until the procedure. The cardiothoracic theatre wing will be completely shut down, with other procedures moved to different floors. The corridors will be cordoned off and guarded around the clock.

Don't think of that now. Anything else but that.

I place my hands on either side of me to push myself up and feel a familiar sensation in my right hand. My eyes slowly drift towards it, my heart filled with dread.

There are five strands of my hair laced between my fingers. I must have been hair-pulling in my sleep. The stress of all this is making my trichotillomania worse.

I couldn't say when or why the compulsion started, only that I can't remember my life without it. My first memory of my mother is her slapping my hand away to stop me from plucking. The same woman who would take my chin in her hand each night before bed and count aloud the amount of lashes I had. If I woke up with less, I was grounded and had my pocket money taken away. As if I could control what I did in my sleep.

I take the hairband from my wrist and sweep my hair back to remove temptation, tying it into such a tight bun that I feel my face pull taut.

Stay in control.

I reach for my phone nestled among the paperwork on the coffee table and find a text on the screen.

Adam
How was Zack's day today? Has he spoken to you yet?

Adam has never been this attentive. He often goes a week without getting in touch. But if he thinks Zack is angry with him, Adam will be quick to prove him wrong and show him why he is the best father there is. I didn't realise I had married a narcissist until our honeymoon.

Me
Jeff says he's having fun. Hasn't spoken to me yet. Give him time, Adam. This is good for him.

I take a series of deep breaths and pick up the case file from the coffee table.

Focus on the task at hand.

The patient isn't an extreme case. The procedure itself shouldn't be difficult, and the success rate is high, which means causing an error would be an even riskier task. If the patient died unexpectedly, the coroner would wonder why. Not only that, everyone will be watching me while I work: the anaesthetist, the perfusionist stood by the heart–lung machine, the practitioner at the foot of the bed, the aides by their sides. Margot will be the closest of them all, stood right beside me watching my every move. I will be literally surrounded, and every move I make will be scrutinised.

Every time I think of a way to kill him, I find a way to solve the problem. Heart surgery is so tried and tested that it is nowhere near as fatal as it used to be, and if there is a way to save him, everyone in the room will work together to find it. The only way I could kill Ahmed Shabir and get away with it is by causing a catastrophe.

The burner phone vibrates against the coffee table with an incoming call, and the memory of our last conversation comes to mind.

Pull a stunt like that again and I will send you his hand.

I snap up the phone and place it to my ear.

'H-hello?'

'These are your next steps,' a deep voice says. 'Write down everything I tell you. Memorise it, then burn it.'

I snatch up my notepad from the coffee table and flick through until I reach a clean page.

'Tonight, you will leave two pairs of hospital scrubs on your doorstep. In the morning you will send a text with the exact location of the operating theatre and an in-depth description of any security measures around the patient, with the locations where they will be in place. Two of my associates will be waiting for you to confirm his death – you must make contact with them as soon as your task is complete. They will accompany you as you take the body to the morgue and confirm the death of the patient en route. Once this is complete, and no suspicions have been raised, we will begin putting into motion the return of your son.'

My heart leaps.

We will begin putting into motion the return of your son.

I look down at my notes and what he has asked of me. The sense of dread quickly returns.

'What you are asking me to do isn't that easy . . . I will have eyes on me the whole time. Even if I were able to kill the patient without getting caught, a junior doctor would be the one to close up the chest cavity, and it would be nurses who would clean and prepare the body for a porter to take the patient down to the morgue. Usually I leave the operating theatre long before these tasks are completed. It would be very, very odd for a surgeon to do all this.'

'Make an exception.'

'You're not listening – it will set alarm bells ringing. If you want me to do this without raising suspicions, I have to follow the correct protocol.'

I expect him to pause, to reflect on what I have told him. But he doesn't hesitate for a second.

'You will do as we ask. You know what will happen if you don't.'

The call disconnects with a faint beep.

13

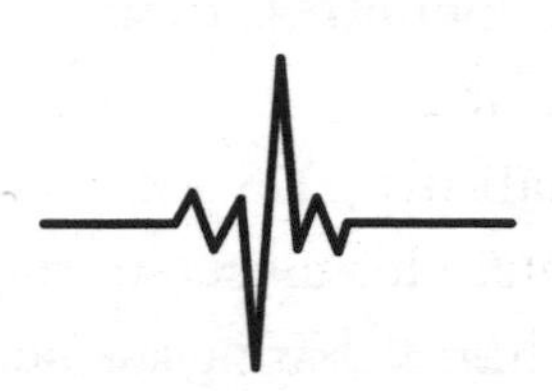

Rachel

Saturday, 6 April 2019, 08:02

'The victim's name is Paula Williams.'

Everyone in the conference room looks towards the artistic rendering of the victim's face, pinned to the board behind my back. There are photographs of the well, of the body on the pathologist's carving table, the stubs of her fingers where the tips were sawn off. Strangely, the photo that haunts me the most is a snapshot of her feet taken at the scene: the left is swollen inside her shoe, but the other is bare, veiny and mottled. The pads of her toes wrinkled in the water.

'The well is located on an abandoned farm in Littlebrook, a small hamlet roughly thirty miles out of town. As of yet we have no reason to believe the victim had ties to the area. The more likely scenario is that the body was dumped there to avoid attracting attention and leaving a trail back to the culprit.'

I drag my finger along the map pinned to the board, from Littlebrook and into town.

'Paula lived down a private track off The Avenue, an affluent road at the back of Redwood Hospital – none of the houses are worth less than a million.'

'How the other half live,' DS Amy Slater mutters from the other end of the table. Her over-plucked eyebrows make her features appear too harsh, but I have come to think she does it for this very reason; it is hard to gain control of a situation when you stand at just over five feet.

'Not the sort of person you'd expect to find in a well with a bullet through her brain, is it?'

'Exactly,' I reply. 'The victim was a sixty-five-year-old widow who hadn't had so much as a parking ticket.'

'Maybe her husband was dodgy?'

'We checked,' DS Ryan replies. 'He worked in oil in the 1980s and sold up at just the right time. Both of them were squeaky clean.'

'Who confirmed her identity?' Sergeant Anthony Chesnick asks. He is a quiet, straight-talking man. I don't think I have ever seen him smile, but I have a kinship with him that I can't quite explain. Perhaps it is because we are the oldest people in the room.

'A member of the local W.I. got in touch after seeing the artist's rendering. Supposedly the victim attended too and, according to the source, would regularly collect a neighbour's child from school. We managed to get hold of a range of CCTV footage following the route from the school to the supposed home address. The tech team spliced this together for us.'

I raise the remote to the TV and the CCTV footage starts to roll.

Paula Williams walks as if she hasn't a care in the world, wearing the same light-blue cardigan she would be found dead in. Even in the footage I can see the precise line down the front of each trouser leg.

The footage jumps from street to street, until she is no longer alone and has a small boy in tow. A cute, blond thing, caught on the cusp of being young enough to skip, but old enough to stop himself when they pass children around his age. Although the footage is silent, it is clear the pair are close. Their heads turn towards each other as they walk in conversation, and Paula rests her hand on his shoulders when he veers too close to the road.

Then the footage cuts to an empty street, and the time stamp in the bottom right corner shows it has been just over six minutes after the last shot of them.

'Where'd they go?' DS Slater asks.

'Exactly,' I reply, and step aside to show the map on the board. It features a harsh red line, drawn in dashes like Morse code. 'This is the journey they would have taken. The last time we see them is here, the street to the left of the park. They would have crossed the green, and should have come out here, two streets away from The Avenue. They didn't.'

'Is there no CCTV footage around the park?' Slater asks.

I shake my head.

'Here's what perplexes me: we have received no reports of a missing child matching the boy's description either. We have a woman who has been dead for forty-eight hours and a potentially missing child, and no one has come forward to claim them.'

The team's attention drifts behind me to the still of the boy from the CCTV footage, printed and stuck to the board with a garish red circle around him, leading to a note written in capital letters by a sharp, urgent hand.

WHO IS HE?

'Mark, I want you to track down the victim's next-of-kin, and see if they can come in and identify the body. Failing that, get her GP on the phone and ask for them to step in. I want her identity confirmed by noon.'

'Yes, boss,' DS Ryan replies.

'Amy, I want you to scope out the park. Stop by around school pick-up and ask passers-by if they recognise the pair and if they saw anything untoward on the afternoon they went missing.'

'It's Saturday, ma'am,' she says. 'And it's the Easter break. The kids won't be back for another two weeks.'

I often do this when I sink my teeth into a case. I work so often that I forget that other people stop to take a breath, and I slept so little last night that the days have blended into one. I still have the crook in my back where I fell asleep at my desk, determined to find out as much as I could once I learned about the boy.

'Of course. Still, take a couple of uniforms with you and ask around. Knock at the houses overlooking the park, and if you see anyone with a child around the boy's age, ask if they know the pair. If they live close by, it's likely they will use the same route to walk to the school.'

'Yes ma'am.'

'Anthony,' I say. 'Make sure you have at least four officers free for me. I suspect we'll need them later.'

'Yes, ma'am.'

'As for me, I'll be submitting a search warrant this morning, in the hope of us gaining access to the victim's property later today. We've got a body and the well she was dumped in, but we won't get anywhere until we know where she was shot, and by who. But priority number one . . .'

I point to the photo at the centre of the board.

'Find out who that bloody kid is.'

14

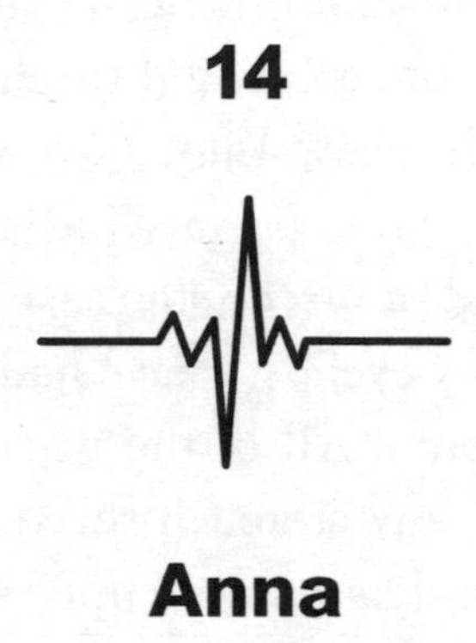

Anna

3 hours to go

Saturday, 6 April 2019, 07:03

The surgical scrubs I left on the doorstep have gone. Taken silently in the night.

I stand in the doorway with my eyes on the mat. To think that the strangers were just here on the other side of the door and I didn't suspect a thing. They are my closest connection to Zack, and it almost feels like he was here too. So close that I could have snatched open the door and held him. To have the opportunity ripped away from me, even though it was entirely imagined, has left a deep, ceaseless ache in my chest.

I finished planning the murder at three this morning. Not a single method I found was foolproof: as I went through the potential ways to kill him, I imagined the specialised tool that would be passed to me that would rectify it, all of the procedures and protocols that would be followed to try and bring him back to life. But after hours of plotting, I found a way. It is definitely not without risk, and it takes an element of sheer luck, but it is possible. Now I just have to decide if I can go through with it.

I close the door and sit on the staircase with the butts of my palms pressing into my eyelids. I have had a headache burning at my temples for hours. All of the usual cures have evaded me. If I eat or drink, my stomach threatens to bring it back up, and taking painkillers on an empty stomach only makes it worse. Sleep is pointless, for the second I close my eyes, I dream of Zack. Dream, after dream, after dream, even if I only close my eyes for a moment. I see him die countless times, but sometimes I save him, only to wake up and have him snatched away from me again.

I force myself to my feet and walk to the mirror in the hall. My skin is lily-white, and my eyes are pink and swollen. I seem to be nothing but bone now: my cheeks could cut steel.

I take the false lashes from my bag and unscrew the lid on the glue. I have grown to like the smell, the harsh chemical burn in my nostrils. The process is so drilled into me that I run the nozzle along the strip without having to think, and raise it towards my right eye. I stare at my lid and my hand starts to shake.

There is only one eyelash left to pluck.

I stand before the mirror, admiring the way it arches from the lid, growing fairer towards the tip. The glue on the strip will harden if I wait too long. I will have to pick it off, start again. But I can't stop staring at that one, lone lash.

I place the strip on the sideboard and raise my hand to my eye. When the lash bristles against my fingertip, a euphoric shiver runs down the ridges of my spine. It is sickening to think that one, fine hair has so much power over me. I pinch it – hard – and pluck it out with hate. It rests on the tip of my finger, curling at one end, a tiny white follicle at the other. I place it on my tongue and swallow it down.

My left eye has more: four lashes at different stages of growth. I pluck them out with the same force, watching as the soft skin puckers with the vigour of each yank. I pluck and swallow, pluck and swallow, until my eyelids are completely bare. I wait for the relief to wash over me, but I don't feel a thing.

I press the strip against my eye and hold it there with one hand, as I trail the glue along the other, and hold them both in place for over a minute. Once they are glued down I open my eyes and stare blankly at the woman in the mirror. I didn't realise how much I hated her until now. When Zack went, he took all of the parts I'd learned to like about myself with him. Maybe there were never traits I liked at all, and they were all him reflecting in me.

The burner phone vibrates inside my bag. I have become so accustomed to the silent house that I brace at the sound, and pain shoots from the crook in my neck. Immediately I am transported back in time, pressed against the living-room wall with a gloved hand clamped over my mouth, and strangers' bodies crushing against my chest until I can barely breathe.

I ground myself and fish through my bag. I have three phones now: my personal phone, my work phone, and now the burner phone too. I have come to distinguish which alert belongs to which. The phone the abductors gave me is harsher, deeper – violent.

I press it to my ear, expecting to hear the gravelly voice of the blue-eyed man, telling me what I already know: that in a matter of hours, someone will be dead.

'Mummy?'

The sensation I feel when I hear Zack's voice is how I imagine it feels to be punched: a violent jarring of the senses, followed by a bout of pain. I clasp the phone to my ear like it is the most precious thing in the world.

'Zack?'

I listen as he starts to cry, each breath escaping in a small whimper. Just the sound of his voice submerges me in physical pain: my throat burns, my chest aches. The headache intensifies so suddenly that I feel dizzy.

I hear the murmur of a deep voice on the other end of the line. Zack tries to stifle his tears.

'The man . . . he says we don't have long.'

God, how I hate them. Giving him to me in small bursts, only to snatch him away again, all while using Zack as a pawn. Exploiting his tears and his terror to make me do what they want.

'Are you okay? Are they hurting you? Where are you?'

'I don't know, I . . .' He stops talking as the deep voice murmurs in the background. 'He said I have to ask you something.'

Tell the man I'm going to kill him.

'What is it, baby?'

I listen to him breathing. I never knew I could love someone so much that I would adore the sound of each breath. They sound so small, so delicate.

'The man said . . .'

'What did he say, sweetheart?'

'He said to ask . . . are you going to save that man, or me?'

I cover my mouth and smother a sob, shaking silently behind my hand.

'Mum?'

I swallow it down and inhale sharply.

'You, baby. Always you. I promise I won't let anything happen to you.'

The man murmurs again, and I hear a quick fumbling on the other end of the phone.

'Zack? *Zack?*'

The call ends.

I scream so loud that my ears ring, and throw the phone towards the door. The back flies off with the impact. I hear the screen crack.

I brace myself against the wall, my hands pressed against the plaster with my head towards the floor, locks of hair moving with each frantic breath. I never used to think of myself as an angry person, but these men have clawed a rabid animal out of me. I want to kill them, slowly, painstakingly, until they are begging for their mothers. We are all so blind, thinking that we know who we truly are. It is only pain like this that reveals what we are really capable of.

I stay against the wall until my heart slows and my lungs calm. Suppressing the emotions until I am numb again, and the only thing on my mind is the task at hand.

My only chance of getting away with it unscathed is by doing everything right until the last step. The coroner must see that I did everything correctly. Then I will rupture the aorta and stall until the patient's life bleeds out of him. I just have to make sure nobody sees me make the cut.

If I fail, I will inject a bubble of air from a syringe into the heart. A pocket of air so small that it would almost be naked to the human eye, but once stuck in a vein, becomes a bomb. But regardless of the method I use, one thing is clear.

Ahmed Shabir must never wake up.

15

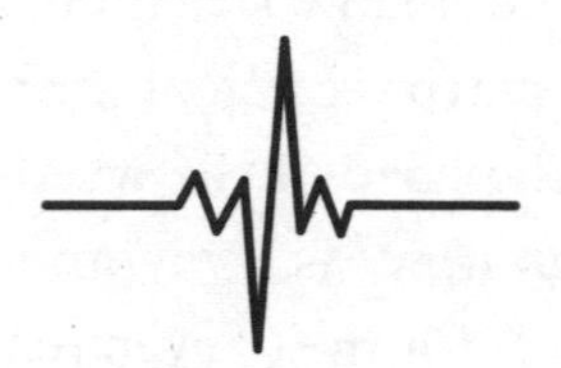

Margot

Saturday, 6 April 2019, 07:40

I keep checking for blood, but so far there isn't any.

The first thing I did when I woke up was search for spotting on the sheets. Then when I used the bathroom, I inspected my underwear expecting to find old, dried blood flaking from the cotton. Nothing yet. It is tough, like me. It will need to be.

I sit on the end of my mattress on the floor and stare into the hand mirror I stole from the nurse's station a week or two back. There had been a beautiful floor-length mirror in the flat before Dan left. It sold for forty-five pounds online.

I stare at my reflection and see where the stress has been wreaking havoc on my complexion. There is a small cluster of stress spots by the corner of my mouth, and the skin around my eyes looks translucently thin and friable.

My stomach is throbbing from the woman's fist. I unwrap my dressing gown and look down at myself, but the only sign that anything occurred is a small strip of bruised skin where one of her rings left its mark.

I pick up my hairbrush and pull it through my wet hair until my scalp feels hot, and a slow stream of water works its way down my spine. The sharp scratch of the bristles makes me feel something through the haze of the weed I smoked last night, clinging onto me even now, as if my mind is a beat behind. It takes me a few seconds for me to even realise that my phone is ringing. I pick it up off the bed and answer without thinking.

'Oh,' Sandy says. 'You're not dead then?'

Shit.

I close my eyes, scolding myself silently.

'Margot? I can hear you breathing . . .'

'Hi, Sandy. What's up?'

She emits a dry laugh. 'Oh, I think you know, Margot.'

I stall for a second to try and change tack, plucking at the hairs wound around the bristles of the brush. Her posh accent and her uptight tone scream of a privileged upbringing. She's never going to be able to sympathise with me, whatever I tell her.

'I'm sorry I've missed your calls, work has been so busy—'

'Frankly, Margot, I'm not in the mood to hear one of your excuses, so let's not waste any more of each other's time.'

No more delays. No more chances. I thought she had a bit of a way to go yet before she did anything drastic, but I can hear by her tone that I've misjudged her. My heart rate climbs.

'I'll pay you back the couple of months' rent next week, I promise.'

'*Three* months' rent, and your promises don't mean much,

do they? I understand you're in a difficult position, what with your partner having left, but I can no longer shoulder your domestic issues. I'm making too much of a loss.'

She sighs on the other end of the phone, as if her next words pain her to muster. I don't believe that for a second.

'You've got until Sunday night to transfer that money to me. If I don't see it in my account by then, I'm changing the locks.'

I feel sick. She has never put her foot down like this before. It isn't like she won't get the money; whenever I fell behind in the past, I always made up for it. But that was when my credit score had a shred of respectability, and I could take out a loan to cover another, or I could sell more of Dan's things. Now all of my wage is devoured by my overdraft and my debts, and the flat is empty. I have nothing to fall back on; not even Sandy's patience.

'I'll get it,' I say.

'Make sure you do.'

The call ends and I let my hand fall, the phone landing face down on the bed.

I get up from the floor and wander out of my bedroom and into the living area, empty and void but for my memories of better times. I only have to look around to see a physical manifestation of how bad my life has become. Every time I step in through the door, my heart breaks.

I hate it here. But I have nowhere else to go.

I slip into the changing room and listen out for signs of life: footsteps, sighs, the rustle of scrubs being pulled on by tired hands. But all I hear are my own frantic breaths. The fear of being turfed out of my flat has me by the throat.

'Morning!' I call.

No one answers.

I make a quick dash around the room, checking each changing bay. When I find myself alone, I take out my phone and get to work. I open the notes app where I typed out everyone's locker combinations. For such intelligent people, they can be very stupid. Not one of them has changed their lock combinations in recent weeks. I only know a handful, from those who I could get close enough to watch as they opened and closed their lockers, but even if I knew my way into every locker, it wouldn't be enough to pay Sandy back. But maybe if I give her just enough, she will allow me some more time to collect the rest.

I have to do something.

I start with Karin's, pocketing every bit of cash from her purse, the designer watch from her shoe, her phone. Desperation has made me lose all reason, swiping things I would never have risked taking before this. Every time I try to think rationally, I shake my head roughly, pummelling the thoughts to dust.

I take Beth's gold bracelet and cash, down to the short change in her purse, shoving each finding into the pit of my bag until the straps are digging into my wrist. I just finish cleaning out Belinda's purse and stash of cigarettes when I hear the door handle turn behind me. I slam the door to her locker and open mine, shoving my bag inside, clinking like a money pot.

'Morning, love,' Val says, shrugging out of her coat.

'Morning.'

I don't dare turn around, for my cheeks are red-hot. I take out my scrubs and chuck them on the changing bench.

'Did you hear? A patient is suing the hospital.'

I slip my top over my head, amplifying my nervous breaths. The warmth of each exhale flushes my cheeks.

'We lost her engagement ring, apparently. Worth a whopping fifty K.'

I freeze, my top still half over my head, the chill in the air nipping at the bare flesh on my stomach. I yank it off and stare at her. My face is scalding hot and my hair has frayed out of its bun.

'*Fifty?*'

'That's what I heard,' Val says over her shoulder, rubbing cream into her hands. Whatever it is, I can smell it from here. The floral scent hits the back of my throat. I come over all dizzy and grip onto the edge of my locker to anchor myself.

I sold a fifty K ring for a measly grand.

'The board is going mad,' Val says, kicking off her shoes. 'I feel sorry for the fool who lost it.'

'Me too,' I mutter.

Val keeps talking, but I tune out the words. I usually find a way out of these situations. Gift of the gab, Ma called it. But I'm in too deep this time. It feels like everything I have done is finally closing in around me.

I slip into my scrubs, *uhming* and *ahhing* along to everything Val says, as my nerves continue to tighten around my neck like a noose.

Something bad is going to happen. I can feel it in my bones.

16

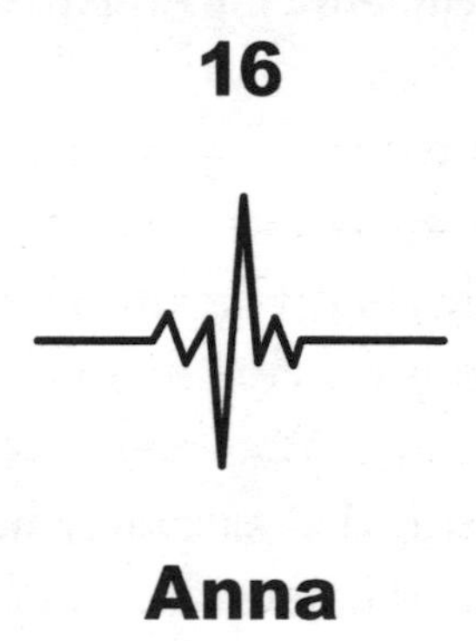

Anna

1 hour to go

Saturday, 6 April 2019, 08:59

I pause in front of the double doors leading to the ward.

It is time to see the patient.

I have stepped foot on this ward countless times, and never once have I hesitated before these doors. I never had time to notice the scuffs and swipes in the paintwork from passing trolleys, or the small, spindly crack working its way through the glass panel on the left.

I spent my first hour at the hospital going over my plan, lapping the halls around the operating theatre in the cordoned-off ward with my eyes on my stopwatch to try and gauge how long it would take the security guard to make each lap. I walked at my own pace, then tried to walk like a man might, with wider strides, different tempos. The overall average was one minute and thirty-two seconds. That's how long I will have to wheel out the body, meet the abductors, and head towards the lift for the morgue.

After I've killed a man.

'Excuse me, Doc,' a voice says behind me.

It's Val and a colleague wheeling in a patient. I step aside and watch as the bed is ushered in, one of its wheels spinning out of sync. The sound of the ward creeps through the open doors: a patient pressing the buzzer from their bed, the nurses' shoes scuffing against the lino floor.

I take a deep breath and walk inside, forcing a smile when nurses glance my way, inclining my head with polite nods as I pass patients' beds, and slip down the narrow corridor towards Mr Shabir's private room. I stop at the door and peer through the glass panel.

The patient is sat up in bed talking with his wife. Despite the stress of what is to come, they are smiling at each other. Their hands are clasped so tightly that I can see the whites of his wife's knuckles.

I can't do this.

'Come in, Doctor,' Mr Shabir says behind the glass.

I snap out of my trance and step inside with a forced smile.

What with my focus being purely on the couple, I hadn't noticed the woman sat in the opposite corner of the room nearest to the door, typing incessantly on her laptop. When she notices me, she shuts it down with a polite smile, only to give a sly glance to her phone as an alert pings through. I bid her good morning and head for his bedside.

Mr Shabir is a handsome man, but he is clearly unwell.

The strain on his heart is evident: he has lost the usual vibrancy to his complexion, with colourless, cracked lips and puffy bags beneath his eyes from being kept awake; each breath he takes sounds laboured. His PR team must be experts at keeping his health out of the papers. I wonder how they hide his physical symptoms when he is in front of the cameras.

'Good morning, how are we all doing?'

Mrs Shabir's perfume fills my nostrils. I can practically feel the anxiety radiating off her.

'Nervous,' he says.

'But *positive,*' Mrs Shabir adds. I notice she gives his hand a quick squeeze.

'That's the best way to be,' I reply. 'Nerves are inevitable, but positivity is very important.'

I hear the woman clear her throat behind my back; Ahmed gives her a gracious smile.

'This is Tammy, my PR manager,' he says. 'She is here to execute damage control if I keel over.'

'*Ahmed,*' Mrs Shabir says, grief etching her face.

He pats his wife's hand and looks to me with a sympathetic smile.

'Sorry, Doctor. I joke to get through these sorts of things. I mean no harm.'

First, do no harm . . .

My oath whispers in my ears. I listen to my young, innocent voice reciting it with pride, believing every word.

'None taken,' I force, and reach for his chart at the bottom of the bed. 'Now, I'll run through what's going to happen today, and then if you have any questions for me, please don't hesitate to ask.'

'Is he more at risk because of his health condition?' Mrs Shabir asks. 'The familial hypercholesterolemia?'

I flinch when I meet her eyes. So full of hope. Of trust.

You can't trust me.

Ahmed laughs and pats his wife's hand.

'She said *after* she has run through things, darling.'

Mrs Shabir laughs nervously. 'Yes, of course. Sorry.'

'Your husband is at slightly more risk of complications due to the fact that we have three coronary arteries to bypass, which will mean more time under general anaesthetic and more time on the heart–lung machine. As for Mr Shabir's hereditary high cholesterol, there is a high chance your husband will need to have further bypasses in the future.'

'So if I die, that means you can blame my father,' he grins towards his wife – but she doesn't laugh.

'Don't, Ahmed. It doesn't bear thinking about.'

The clipboard starts to shake in my grip. I hold it so tightly that pain shivers up the tendons of my wrists. I clear my throat.

'So, my plan today, once you're under, is to—'

'What sort of drugs will he be on?' she asks. 'To put him under, I mean?'

'Mindy, please.'

'It's fine,' I say.

She gives me a grateful smile. I look down towards the chart.

'Ahmed will be put under general anaesthesia, and some medication to thin his blood and avoid clotting.'

'Thank you,' Ahmed says to me, before turning to his wife. 'Now let her speak.'

She nods with a closed smile, as if forcing herself to keep quiet.

'So the procedure shouldn't take more than three hours. Once you're sedated and set up on oxygen, I will open the chest to access the heart, set you on the heart–lung machine, and administer medication to cool down the heart so that it is nice and still.' I watch Mindy's face pale. 'He will still be alive, Mrs Shabir. It's like switching a plug from one socket to another – the electricity is still powering the device, but from a different source.'

I look away, uncomfortable beneath her trusting eyes, and yet I can still feel them burning into me. The clipboard quivers in my grip.

'Once the machine has taken over, I will get to work on each of the three bypasses, using veins from your leg. When this is complete, I will flush out the medication and transfer circulation from the machine to the body. Once the heart is beating happily I will close the chest and send you to the recovery ward. The TV signal is poor but the nurses are lovely and will take great care of you.'

I force a smile, trying to put them at ease, but I hate myself for it. While I might be soothing the patient's nerves, his wife will hang on my every word. It is her I will have to deal with once he is dead.

'See, it doesn't sound so bad,' Ahmed says.

Mindy nods, but her eyes fill with tears. She stands quickly and faces the window. I can see her shoulders shaking.

'Will we be kept updated frequently?' Tammy asks from behind me. 'We have several people eager for news.'

I don't like her, but it isn't her fault. She is doing her job, like I should be doing mine, but the additional pressure and the impending guilt sharpen my tone.

'Usually we practise the no-news-is-good-news strategy, so we can work without being disturbed, but we can make an exception.'

Her eyes cool. 'I'd appreciate that, thanks.'

I turn back to the patient. Mrs Shabir is still looking out of the window, sniffling to compose herself. Mr Shabir sits quietly, turning his wedding ring around his finger. On his other hand, he is wearing what looks like a sovereign of some kind; not the sort of style I would imagine a politician wearing.

'You will need to remove those before surgery, I'm afraid.'

He looks up at me, breaking away from his thoughts. 'Oh yes, of course.'

He slips them off one by one and places them on the bedside table with a quiet clink.

'Do you have any more questions for me?'

'We're good,' he says. 'Thank you.'

'I will see you soon.'

I give him my hand. I feel the warmth of his flesh, the life radiating from him. I have to fight myself not to squirm out of his touch.

'Thank you, Doctor. I know I'm in great hands.'

I nod quickly, a forced smile pinching at my cheeks, and turn for the door.

I can't do this.

I am halfway down the corridor with tears stinging at my eyes when Mrs Shabir catches up to me. I blink furiously and turn with a smile.

'I just wanted to say thank you,' she says.

'Oh, there's no need to—'

'And to ask something else.'

The pain in her eyes is killing me. She clearly worships the ground her husband walks on.

'Yes, Mrs Shabir?'

'What was the survival rate again? I know we went through

all this at the pre-assessment appointment, but my brain is so scrambled today, I don't trust my own memory.'

'I understand, but you're doing extremely well. So with your husband's pre-existing condition and other factors like age, weight, smoking status . . . he has a ninety-per-cent chance of surviving the surgery.'

She stares at me, unsure whether it is good news or bad.

'That is a very good percentage, Mrs Shabir. If you have any more questions, the nurses will be happy to answer any—'

'There's one more thing.'

I bite down on the inside of my lip.

'You will do your best, won't you, Dr Jones?'

She stares into my eyes so intensely that I feel sick with guilt, bile burning the back of my tongue. I nod furiously.

'Of course,' I lie. 'Your husband is in safe hands.'

She smiles and reaches for my hand. I flinch at her touch.

'Thank you,' she says, fear croaking in her voice.

I watch as she walks away, her long, black hair swishing behind her, seeming lighter than she had before, elevated by my lies.

I am about to destroy her life.

I walk towards the doors as the fear wraps around my throat, and head down the main corridor until I reach the cordoned-off operating ward.

In a matter of hours, it will be over, and Zack and I will be free.

17

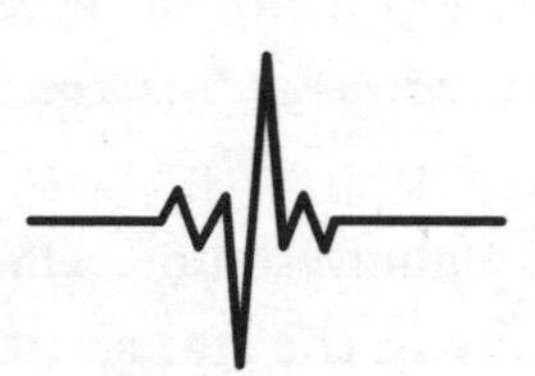

Rachel

Saturday, 6 April 2019, 09:50

A dead person's home is a mind-boggling thing to behold. Not the house, with its bricks and mortar, or the run-of-the-mill drainpipes and double-glazed windows, but the home – the very heartbeat of the building that pulses from the walls.

Paula Williams' home was clearly her pride and joy. It isn't just the cleanliness, with dust-free skirting boards or the starched white valance on her bed, but the small, intricate touches that make the space hers, from the bone-china ornaments on the mantelpiece, to the floral print on the curtains, the family photos framed on the walls. I wonder what will happen to it all when she is buried six feet under.

After the victim's daughter was found to be living in Australia, the GP confirmed the body was that of Paula

Williams, and the magistrates' court approved the search warrant first thing. The doctor's reaction to her death keeps replaying in my mind.

I just don't understand how she could have gotten herself into this mess. This was a woman who lived for gardening and made pottery in her outhouse. When I say she is the last person I would expect to meet this kind of demise, I mean it. It's nonsensical.

'This house puts my flat to shame,' DS Ryan says behind me, as he makes his way down the stairs, each step crinkling from the baggies over his shoes. 'It's so clean.'

'It certainly is.'

'You thinking it's a clean-up of a murder scene?' DS Ryan asks, and stands at my side before the mantelpiece. He applied too much aftershave this morning; the musk of it stings my nostrils.

'No, she didn't die here.'

'How do you know?'

'The residents of The Avenue would have heard the gunshot, and the bullet was fired at close range. The victim's blood would have splattered all over the ceiling.'

We both look up. The ceiling is spotless.

'But can you smell that?'

DS Ryan sniffs at the air.

'Vanilla?'

'And?'

He sniffs again. His brow creases when he catches it.

'Bleach?'

'Disinfectant,' I reply. 'All of the windows were closed when we arrived, which meant the smell was trapped inside, but it wouldn't have lasted for long.'

'You think the place was cleaned after she died?'

'We'll see what the white-suits say.'

I turn for the door and stroll out of the house to breathe in the fresh morning air, and watch as the crime-scene personnel comb over each inch of the house and grounds, their suits rustling every time they move.

Pathologist Diane Reed is stood at the foot of the drive staring up at the house with the hood of her suit pulled down, revealing her unkempt silver hair fraying from its bun.

'It's days like this I wish I hadn't quit smoking,' she says as I reach her. 'It's like Malcolm can sense when something bad is coming, and books the week off so I can pick up the slack.'

'You make a great interim crime-scene lead. A superior one, in fact. Although if you tell him I said that I'll have to kill you.'

'Please don't. Malcolm would find a way to bring me back from the dead to clean up the mess.'

We share a brief smirk before the solemnness of the scene takes hold again, and watch the crime-scene investigators comb through the front lawn. Their white body-suits are so bright that the sun's rays bounce off their backs.

'What've your guys found so far?'

Diane points towards the porch.

'Soil deposits on the front step, which match that found in the plant pots. The one to our left is looser than that on the right. Looks like it was disturbed recently.'

'A struggle happened there?'

'Or something was hidden inside.'

'What have the fellas found on the lawn?'

'Shoe prints.' She nods her head towards the house next door. 'Leading there.'

I look at the house next door: an ultra-modern home, almost

double the size of our victim's, with large expanses of glass and stark white walls. A quick bit of research this morning showed that while the houses lining The Avenue were styled after the Victorian era and built around forty years ago, the two houses down this private lane were new developments, built within the last five. The house next door sold for almost two million.

'Know who lives there?' Diane asks.

'Someone with a ton of money,' I reply wryly. 'Not yet. The officers knocking up and down the street should come up with something within the next hour or two.'

'Well, whoever left the footsteps did so in a hurry. The depth and placements in the earth suggest the person was running.' Diane looks up the private lane towards the cordoned entrance. 'Walk with me?'

I nod and follow in step beside her. She pulls out a packet of cigarettes and a pink lighter.

'I didn't really quit smoking.'

'I know, Di. I could smell it on you.'

She gives me a wry smile. 'My eldest begged me to stop. I pretend I've quit, in the hope that one day I'll believe it myself. I sneak a few in when I can.'

'No judgement here.' I kick a stone up the gravel path, listening to the flick of Diane's lighter behind her cupped hand as we leave the crime scene. 'Thank you for doing the postmortem so quickly.'

'No problem,' she replies, white smoke escaping from her lips. She picks something off the tip of her tongue. 'Shame about the bullet.'

Diane's prediction had been correct: the flesh track in the victim's head had matched a semi-automatic Glock shot from close range. Selfishly, I wish it had been a registered firearm. It would have been far easier to track the person down. A Glock would have been a black-market purchase. As for the bullet: it went straight through her skull.

'I'm hoping we'll recover it from the scene of the murder.'

'You'll have to find the murder scene first, doll.'

She holds out the cigarette to me and I take it, drawing on the end until thick smoke fills my lungs. I haven't smoked in so long that the one measly hit goes straight to my head. Diane slips it from my fingers and takes another hungry drag.

A plane is flying overhead, leaving a thick contrail in its wake. I think of the victim's daughter flying over from Australia, processing her mother's murder in the tight squeeze of economy class.

'Rachel,' Diane says, and comes to a stop, gravel crunching beneath her feet. 'Are you going to be all right working this case?'

I pause and kick a stone a few feet ahead, watch as it rolls down the small verge towards the patch of woodland.

'Why wouldn't I be?'

The smell of her cigarette creeps over my shoulders. I wish I hadn't taken that drag; the toxins almost make me feel drunk.

'You know why,' she replies with a loud exhale. 'The boy.'

I kick another stone, saying nothing for a while. Someone had to ask, and I had been preparing myself for it, but Diane has caught me off-guard. I clench my jaw; harden myself against the pain.

'I'll be fine.'

I keep walking, determined not to speak another word about it. Diane sighs and follows behind.

As we reach the top of the lane, cordoned off with blue and white caution tape fluttering in the breeze, Sergeant Chesnick is returning from conducting the door-to-door enquiries with his officers. He is headed straight for us.

'Get anything good?' I ask.

Diane ducks beneath the tape to stamp out her fag.

'A good start,' he replies. 'The house next door belongs to Dr Anna Jones, a heart surgeon at the hospital.'

I give a stray look over my shoulder, where the roof of the hospital is just peeking over the top of the small woodland, spotting brief flashes of white as investigators search between the trees.

'Is she the neighbour with the kid?'

'Yes, ma'am.'

I look to Diane.

'How big were the footprints on the front lawn?'

'Size six or seven,' she says, bowing under the tape again.

Too big for a child, but a potential match for an adult female.

'Did any of the neighbours recall seeing the victim recently?'

'A couple saw her walking to collect the boy on Thursday afternoon.'

'But no one saw them walking back?'

'No, ma'am.'

Fits the theory that the pair were intercepted on their walk home.

'The resident on the corner there, Mrs Jenny Howard, seemed to know the victim well. She might be one to talk to.'

'That's great, Anthony. Thanks.'

I turn back for the lane, walking faster than I had before, eager to peek through the windows of the house next door.

'Someone smells a rat,' Diane quips.

18

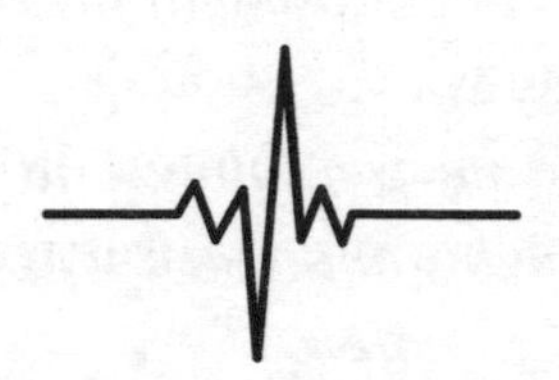

Anna

10 minutes to go

Saturday, 6 April 2019, 09:50

I stand at the scrubbing sink, staring through the glass partition and into the theatre.

Ahmed Shabir is lying unconscious on the operating table waiting for the tip of my scalpel. I stare at his bare feet teetering towards the end, watch as his chest rises and falls, the window of flesh in the surgical drapes. Dr Burke has fitted the breathing tube, and Karin is testing the heart–lung machine ready for bypass. Today's practitioner is prepping the patient's leg for harvesting the veins for transplantation.

There's no point to any of it. In a matter of hours, he will be dead.

I look down at my hands, lathered in suds from my elbows to my fingertips, rosy pink around my thumbnail where I worked too hard with the scrubbing brush and stabbed at the bed of my nail. My hands are shaking violently. I clench them into fists and bubbles form between the grooves of my fingers. This never happens to me. I'm known for my steady hand. I run the tap and rinse the suds away.

They will all see me trembling and know something is wrong. I will get caught, and Zack will die, and I will go to prison for the rest of my life.

The cordons at each of the corridors leading onto the ward have been made to look as inconspicuous as possible, using cleaning notices so as not to attract suspicion. David will be the security guard lapping the halls, away from his usual post at the main entrance of the hospital where we greet each other every morning, and I dare to hope that should he stumble across us in the act, I will be able to charm my way out of it.

Once the deed is done, I will have to act quickly in wheeling the body towards the lift. It is a mere six metres of corridor I have to travel, but I will only have one and a half minutes to convene with the abductors, reach the lift, and slip inside before David crosses our path.

Don't think of that yet. You have a much bigger task to execute first.

Execute. The word makes the hairs on my neck stand up.

I take a moment to let the water drip off me into the basin and close my eyes, steeling myself against the onslaught of fear. That's when I hear him, calling to me.

Mummy . . .

I shake my head.

No. Not now.

... are you going to save that man, or me?

I can't breathe.

... you will do your best, won't you, Dr Jones?

My head spins so fast that I feel sick.

If you fail to kill the patient, your son will die in his place.

I snap open my eyes. My hands are quivering beneath me in tightly furled fists. The pressure has caused a dark bead of blood to escape from beneath my thumbnail. I hold it beneath the tap and watch it burst and trail away, swirling insidiously around the drain.

Remember your triage. Zack has a higher chance of survival, more years to live.

I dry my hands, slip on my mask, and force myself to step into the theatre before I lose my nerve, as every fibre of my being tells me to turn back and run.

'Gloves,' I say aloud, with my arms aloft and bent at the elbow. Margot holds each glove open for me to slip my hands inside, places the visor over my eyes. We have done this so many times that we could do it in our sleep. But this surgery isn't like the others. She will discover that soon enough.

I turn to face the operating table, my legs quivering beneath my scrubs.

'How're we doing?' I ask the room. My question sounds throttled, and I feel a ligament pull in my neck from the strain of my smile.

'Ready to go when you are,' Dr Burke says.

His tone isn't as chirpy as usual, and I fear that he can see right through me, the cruel intention flashing in my eyes. Then I remember what day it is and grin behind my mask.

'Someone's not happy to be working on the weekend.'

'Got to do them occasionally, I suppose,' he replies, giving me one of his winks.

'How's the patient?'

'Stats are good, responding well.'

'Everything up and running?' I ask Karin.

'Good to go.'

'Great. So, we have a triple coronary bypass consisting of the circumflex artery and anterior descending artery on the left, and the coronary artery on the right. Nothing we haven't faced before.'

I look down at the patient, his face slack with sleep, and admire his long, thick eyelashes that would be so satisfying to pluck if they were mine. He looks so peaceful.

He will never open his eyes again.

My mouth is dry with nerves. When I lick my lips behind my mask, it feels like sandpaper running across the flesh. My pulse throbs beneath my jaw.

Margot slips in and places tape over the patient's eyes, and delicately picks up the surgical drape to cover his face.

I take a deep breath, moistening the inside of my mask, and stare at the mass of blue drapes on the operating table. The only sign of a human being before me is the small window of flesh at the chest, and his bare legs towards the other end of the table.

Just like that, with his eyes taped shut and his faced covered, Ahmed Shabir is gone. All that lies before me is a sea of blue and a puzzle to solve. My emotions are gone, smothered beneath indiscriminate logic, and what had once been a coping mechanism to save lives has now equipped me to take one away.

I think back to the look Margot gave me in the changing rooms the other day, as if I were a cold, hard machine, void of humanity.

Maybe I am heartless, after all.

I look down at the patient's chest, freshly shaved and blank like a canvas. I rub dark antiseptic over the skin where the incision will be made and feel the faint tremble of his heart beneath, the warmth of his flesh thrumming through the tips of my gloves. But it doesn't register.

Ahmed Shabir is nothing but a circuit of arteries and flesh.

'Let's begin,' I say, and put out my hand. 'Scalpel.'

19

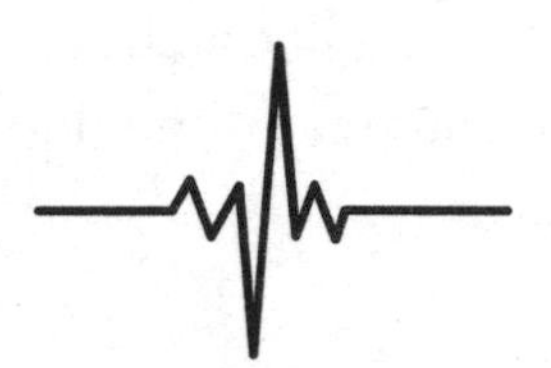

Margot

Saturday, 6 April 2019, 10:02

I watch Dr Jones run the scalpel silently over the patient's chest, the flesh blooming open like a blood-drenched flower.

'Swab, please,' she says.

I reach in to dab the bleeders and watch as she cauterises the persistent vessels with the faint singeing of flesh emitting the smell of burnt fat, a scent I've oddly grown to like.

The human anatomy never ceases to amaze me. As soon as a procedure begins, all of my personal problems evaporate and I become transfixed by the body: its skin, bone, design and flaws. A lot of people would faint at the sight of a man's ribcage peering out through parted skin, but I look at it in amazement; I get to see parts of the human body that the majority of people never see. Sometimes I wish I could stay inside here for ever witnessing cut after cut, watch the dance of a naked heart beating right in front of me. It makes me forget everything that is happening on the other side of the walls.

'Saw,' Dr Jones says.

I pass her the oscillating saw. The sound of the metal hitting the bone rips through the room, the pitch of it going up and down as she cuts the ribcage in two.

'Rib retractors.'

We exchange tools, and I watch her fit the metal teeth within the break and slowly part the sternum, revealing the other world that exists beneath the skin. The heart is beating inside its protective sac, a sight both beautiful and revolting.

'Scissors.'

I pass the scissors and watch as she cuts open the sac, two layers of cloudy, fibrous tissue oozing with clear fluid, which is quickly suctioned away.

A healthy heart would be a lively shade of pink, but Mr Shabir's looks dark and angry, with layers of yellow fat clinging to it like barnacles on a hull. I stare at the squirming muscle, no bigger than a clenched fist, jolting inside the chest cavity. All of life's problems seem so inferior when I watch a human heart at work. It is so simple, yet enchanting.

'Ready for bypass, Karin?' Dr Jones calls.

'All set.'

Karin's aide hands over the two pipes for the bypass. Dr Jones fits one into the right atrium, working against the heart's wriggling as if it is trying to escape her touch. The other is inserted into the aorta through a small incision.

'Turn on bypass,' Dr Jones asks.

The machine whirls, and blood slowly leaves the patient, trailing up the tube and away from the body. The heart continues to beat even when it is empty.

'Clamp,' Dr Jones asks.

I pass her the clamp, a pair of scissors with soft blue padding in place of blades. She reaches in to clamp the aorta to stop blood from the bypass machine from fuelling the heart and seize its beating.

'Full flow,' Karin announces.

The attachment of the clamp changes things, instantly shifting the atmosphere of the room. As soon as it is fixed on the aorta, the heart starts to die. I have always loved the Shakespearian tragedy of that: to fix a heart, you have to thrust it towards death's door.

'Potassium solution, please.'

Dr Jones takes the syringe and injects the solution straight into the heart, and I watch in awe as it begins to slow as the solution gets to work, paralysing the muscle and cooling down the flesh to prevent decay before, finally, it stops, and the lungs are switched off. The patient exists purely by machine.

'Thank you,' Dr Jones says, and passes the syringe to me.

Our gloved hands touch briefly, and I flinch.

I felt her hand trembling.

I watch as she picks up the heart, moving it around in the chest cavity and twisting to see the back, eyeing up the arteries she needs to reroute with dissected veins. The heart vibrates silently in her shaky grip. She lays it back down inside the chest and flexes her hand.

Perhaps she had another late night. Her skin is just as pale as it was yesterday, with the same dark rings around her eyes. It couldn't be the reason that any normal person would assume.

Dr Jones has done countless surgeries – there is no way her hands would be shaking from fear.

20

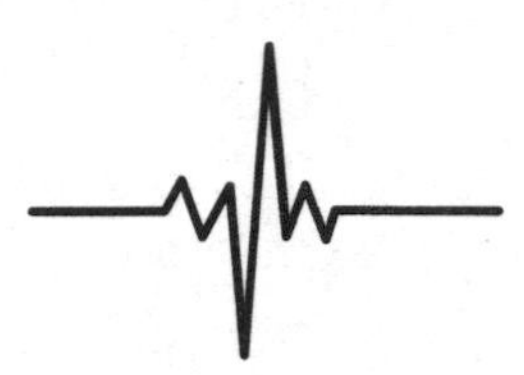

Anna

Saturday, 6 April 2019, 11:20

I can't stop my hands from shaking.

Every time I grip onto a tool, the bright lights shimmer against the vibrating steel, practically screaming for everyone to look my way. When I pick up the heart, the flesh trembles. They must have noticed the state I am in by now. Sweat is beading all over my face, running down my temples in hot, salty trails.

Dr Burke's radio is playing. On any normal day I would tune it out, but today it seems as though the song is playing on full blast, and from the other side of the room the clock is ticking on the wall, taunting me from its perch.

'Be my, be my baby . . .'

Tick. Tick. Tick. Tick.

'Be my little baby . . .'

Tick. Tick. Tick. Tick.

I grit my teeth to tune out the noise and stare into the chest cavity.

The right coronary artery has been bypassed successfully. It is a good graft, and despite the sweat running into my eyes and the lack of sleep curdling my brain, the sutures are neat and even. But the second bypass for the circumflex artery is proving trickier. Whichever way I grasp it, the needle driver slips in my shaky grip and my hold on the surgical thread loosens, or it tangles before I can tie the knot. I try for a third time as the song blares in my ears, one particular word chipping away at me. The tension on the thread jitters in my grip.

'Baby . . .'

Stop.

'Baby . . .'

Please.

'Baby . . .'

No, no, no, no–

'Be my little baby . . .'

'Turn that bloody thing off!'

The music dies in an instant. Silence rings through the room.

Everyone is staring at me.

'I'm sorry,' I mutter. 'I need to focus.'

It is quite possibly the worst thing I could have done. Now the room is deathly quiet. I can feel the animosity strumming in the air, the heat of their glares on my hunched shoulders, eyeing the stammer in my grip.

'Margot,' I say. 'Sweat.'

She reaches in and dabs at my face with gauze.

'Burke, stats.'

'Responding well,' he says curtly, clearly bruised by my admonishment.

'Good.' I nod at him. 'I'll be administering more potassium after this graft, make sure it's to hand.'

The room falls silent again, and the tension is stifling. A trail of sweat slips down my ribs. I can almost feel them exchanging looks at my expense.

You're being paranoid. Focus.

The clock is louder now, almost as persistent as my pulse drumming at my temples. I want to rip it from the wall and stamp on it until the glass cracks and the motor is broken into a thousand pieces.

The vein graft slips in my grip. I bite down on my bottom lip to stifle the building frustration, only stopping when I taste the faint trace of blood on my teeth.

'Margot, hold this a second, please.'

She takes the needle driver from me. I can't help but notice how still it is in her grip compared to mine.

My hand is burning. I can feel the muscles twitching every time I hold a tool. Even the bones ache, stiffening at the joints in my fingers. I flex my hand repeatedly, gripping it into a fist, before stretching my fingers as taut as I can. But as soon as I take the driver back, the steel shakes and the aching returns.

'Thanks.'

I reach inside the chest cavity, hooking the needle through the vein.

Mummy . . .

No. Not now. Please, not now.

I clamp my eyes shut. Press my feet into the lino floor.

I hear his cries as if he were next to me: the abrupt catches in his breaths as the sobs take hold, exhales shuddering out of him in whimpers. What's worse, I can only imagine what he must have looked like as he spoke, and my mind paints the worst possible picture. I see tears glistening on his cheeks and the phone pressed to his ear, his eyes fixed on the barrel of a gun pointed towards his head.

Mu-mu-mummy . . .

'Are you okay, Dr Jones?'

Margot is staring right at me, eyes wide with concern. I must have spaced out.

'I'm fine,' I reply, and turn back to the chest cavity. 'I just have a headache.'

She has been breathing down my neck, figuratively and literally, for the last hour and a half, but no matter how many times I snap at her, she becomes even more attentive. As if she knows exactly what I'm doing.

No. She has watched me work dozens of times. She might think I'm nervous because of the patient's status, but she would never suspect I was intending to cause him harm.

But the way she looked at me raised the hairs on the nape of my neck. She is close enough to see everything, watch every tremor in my hand, smell the sweat pouring off me.

Just keeping going, I think, forcing myself to focus on the job at hand. *You haven't even got to the finale yet.*

21

Anna

Saturday, 6 April 2019, 12:30

I have completed each of the bypasses to save the patient's life. Now all I have to do is kill him.

I am exhausted. My eyes are bone dry, and the tension in my shoulders is so great that it hurts to move my head. I need to use the bathroom, and I long for a tall drink of water; my mouth is so parched that my tongue keeps tacking to my teeth. But I don't have much longer to wait.

I have joined the graft veins to each of the coronary arteries and flushed them with solution to check the joins are airtight, but the other ends are hanging free, ready to be sutured to the aorta. By a cruel twist of fate, the heart no longer needs to be isolated from circulation for this final hurdle: I have to make his heart beat again before stopping it for good.

'Coming off clamp.'

I release its hold on the aorta, and blood streams towards the heart. The colour of the flesh brightens from the circulation and flushes out the potassium fluid. Slowly but surely, it starts to beat again. I could let him live now, if I wanted to. I could do the right thing. Suture the vessels to the aorta and sew him up again.

'Partial clamp,' I ask.

I pass Margot the first clamp in exchange for the second, and reach in to fix it in place. It is designed to allow us to work on attaching the bypasses to the aorta without stopping the blood flow completely. Except for me to kill him, I need it on full flow to cause as much loss of blood as possible.

I must wreak havoc.

My heart races. I feel the echo of it in my throat, my temples, pulsing at the tips of my fingers. I place the clamp on the aorta incorrectly, with too little pressure on the artery.

'Almost done, team. All there is left to do is fix the grafts to the aorta, and we're sailing. How are his stats?'

'Nice and steady,' Dr Burke replies.

'Blood volume?'

'Full flow,' Karin calls back.

'Great.' I turn to Margot. 'Sweat.'

She reaches in with some gauze and dabs the droplets from my face, eyeing me inquisitively. I never usually sweat much, but today I must have perspired a litre of it during the last hour alone. My scrubs are sticking to me and my hairline is sopping wet. I wonder if she can feel the pounding of my heart as she pats the gauze against the droplet trailing down my neck.

'Scalpel, please.'

She passes me the scalpel. It feels heavier somehow, weighty with the repercussions of my next cut. The sharp tip glints beneath the lights.

To fix the grafts to the aorta, I need to make small cuts in the artery so that the blood can pass through the new passageways. In theory, if the partial clamp were in place correctly, excessive blood flow would be kept at bay.

Everyone is watching. I can feel their eyes on me, flicking back and forth from my face to the scalpel in my hand. At no point have their eyes diverted collectively. If one of them looks away, another remains. Margot is so close to me that I can feel the heat from her body radiating through her scrubs.

'You're in my light,' I say.

'Who?' Dr Burke asks.

'You,' I say, and glance over my shoulder. I just see Margot's eyes widen before I return my gaze to the chest cavity. 'Move back.'

She shuffles slightly.

'*Further.*'

She takes a dramatic step back. I can't see her face, but I can feel her rage practically burning the flesh off my back.

'Thank you.'

I sense everyone in the room sharing a look. I have never been so abrupt, and have snapped at all of them at some point during the surgery. I had hoped that it might have been taken for nerves due to the high-profile patient on the operating table. Now I fear that they might suspect something darker.

I need everyone to look away.

I can feel Karin's eyes on me; Burke's too. The blade quivers in my grip, light flashing in the steel as it jitters, and the inside of my gloves are moist with sweat. I reach in slowly, the tip of the scalpel just meeting the wall of the aorta.

'What's the time?' I ask, as flippantly as I can muster.

I sense everyone glance towards the clock.

And cut.

It is a long, deep incision that instantly begins to fill the cavity with bright red blood, sloshing around the heart and coating the lungs. Machines start wailing. Everyone looks back in shock, their questions almost completely silenced by the cacophony of alarms.

'What the hell happened?' Dr Burke asks.

I pretend to frantically search the cavity for a bleeder, my once-blue gloves now slathered in red. Small splashes of blood coat the sleeves of my scrubs.

'It's the aorta,' I say, finally. 'My God, it's torn almost in two.'

The vast volume pouring through the cut is causing it to tear wider and wider, until layers of the artery are peeling away before my eyes.

'It's too damaged,' I say loudly over the noise. 'I'll need to replace it.'

'He's losing too much blood,' Karin says.

'Oxygen levels depleting,' Dr Burke says.

'Start a transfusion,' I say. 'Quickly.'

I turn to Margot. 'Put pressure on the tear.'

She grabs a handful of gauze, but before she can place her hands upon the tear, it shreds to the incision where I inserted the pipe for the heart–lung machine. The pipe comes free and rains down on her like a hose: blood splashes up her chest, her neck, her face. She gasps with shock as it hits her.

'Apply pressure now!'

She jumps in with the gauze and presses down on the aorta as hard as she can, dripping with the patient's blood and panting. The visor over her eyes fogs up with her anxious breaths.

I take the pipe and force it beneath her grip, feeding it as far down the aorta as I can to clear the break.

'Hold it in place while you apply pressure. *Don't* let up, not even for a second.'

I move down the bed and snatch scissors from the tool table, cutting a circle through the drapes above the patient's groin to access the femoral artery. My heart is beating so fast that I can feel the thrum of my pulse in my grip.

'Where's that transfusion?'

'*It's coming*,' Karin snaps back.

'Oxygen levels are dangerously low,' Burke says.

'Turn on the lungs!'

I squirt the antiseptic solution over the site and rub it in with my hand, before snatching up the scalpel.

'The blood loss is too great,' Dr Burke says.

'Apply more pressure!' I shout towards the other end of the table. Margot looks back at me in terror.

'There's barely anything to apply pressure to! It's completely shredded.'

Karin and her aide are panicking on the other side of the table, feeding the transfused blood into the patient.

'We aren't making a dent,' she says breathlessly, her eyes meeting mine over the table. 'He's losing more blood than we can put in.'

'Keep going.'

I cut the flesh of his groin to reach the femoral artery, causing more blood to empty onto the table, and cauterise the heavy bleeders before making an incision in the artery for the machine.

'Pass me the tube. Quickly!'

Margot pulls the pipe from beneath the gauze, but just as our hands meet around it, we both freeze.

There is no blood coming from the tube.

I can't see the patient's heart, due to the vat of blood lapping in the chest cavity, but I know it isn't beating; there are no air bubbles rising to the surface, no jolting waves from the struggle of the muscle beneath.

Margot slowly raises her hand from the gauze, which is now completely red. Nothing more than a slow trickle escapes from what is left of the aorta.

I look to Karin holding the last bag of blood, too late to feed it into him. Beside her, Dr Burke is staring at the chest cavity looking paler than I have ever seen him.

I peer down at myself. Blood is dripping from my scrubs and tinkling quietly onto the lino floor. Margot looks as though she has been attacked with a butcher's knife. There are red droplets hanging from her jaw, and her scrubs are soaked in it.

The room is deathly quiet but for the high-pitched ringing in my ears. I place down the scalpel, clattering briefly against the other steel tools, and clear my throat as I look to the clock on the wall.

'Time of death . . . 12:43.'

22

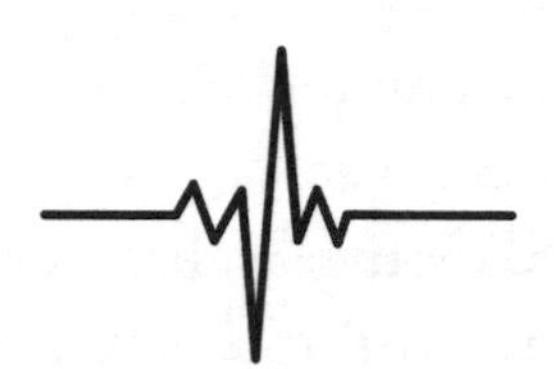

Rachel

Saturday, 6 April 2019, 12:45

'What can you tell me about Dr Anna Jones?'

Jenny Howard is sat in the armchair on the other side of the coffee table, while DS Ryan and I are crammed on the small sofa in the bay window with our shoulders touching and the sun warming our necks. A tray of tea and scones rests on the table, wisps of steam rising from the teapot.

Jenny rubs the scrunched-up tissue beneath her nose. She has been crying since we arrived, but I have yet to see an actual tear.

'Anna and her family moved from London to The Avenue about a year ago. I could tell they were from the city. They had no sense of community. We like to socialise here in The Avenue. Paula and I were particularly close.' She pauses for dramatic effect, glancing towards the window as if to compose herself. 'But Anna has always been very stand-offish.'

DS Ryan bites down on a scone, and crumbs drop onto the saucer in his lap. I give him a look. He slowly places the plate on the coffee table.

This isn't a social visit.

'Anna and her family, you say?'

'Yes. She has a husband called Adam and an eight-year-old son, Zack. Although, perhaps I should say ex-husband. They separated about a month ago. I can't say I'm surprised, you could see they were dysfunctional.'

'What makes you think that?'

She sighs and looks to the window, rolling the scrunched-up tissue in her hands. Fine white fibres coat her lap like dust.

'Well, we aren't that close, what with Anna being rather cold, but they both have very busy work schedules. I often feel sorry for the boy. I see him riding his bike up and down the lane for something to do. I don't think he has made many friends since the move.'

'Who looks after Zack when his parents are at work?'

'Paula did. I don't know why she pandered to that woman. I always thought she was very ungrateful for everything Paula did for her. I think Paula missed caring for her grandchildren – her daughter lives in Australia now, did I tell you that? She must have wanted to bestow her affections on someone.'

'What sort of things would Paula do for Dr Jones?'

'What the boy's mother should be doing,' she replies sharply. She notices the tissue dust on her lap and begins to pick flecks from the fabric. 'Paula would cook and clean, fetch the boy from school each day—'

'Was that a usual occurrence? The school pick-up?'

'Oh yes, every day. Anna would drop him off at school early in the morning and leave him at breakfast club. Then Paula would collect him at the end of the day.'

I write her answers down on my notepad. DS Ryan clears his throat.

'When was the last time you saw them?' he asks. 'Anna and her son?'

'I saw Anna and Zack on Tuesday morning when I popped by to visit Paula next door. They were just pulling out of the driveway. Paula had mentioned that Zack was set to go on holiday with his uncle for the Easter break – I think it's odd, a mother handing over her young child for two weeks like that.'

'Did she say when Zack was to leave for the holiday?'

'He went on Thursday, or yesterday, I can't quite remember. Typical working mother – as soon as the holidays come around, she shifts the boy over to someone else.'

I bite down on the tip of my tongue. I notice she hasn't shared any judgements on the boy's father, who worked just as many hours as the mother, by her own description.

She realises her mistake.

'Oh, I didn't mean *you*, dear ... If you have children, of course?'

I feel DS Ryan tense beside me. A brief silence fills the room. I clear my throat and force a smile.

'I did.'

Her face falls slack. That's when I see the recognition spark in her eyes.

'Oh my ... I'm so sorry. I thought I recognised you—'

'Please, there's no need,' I say, raising my hand to stop her. I change the subject as quickly as I can. 'Did you see Paula at all on Thursday?'

'Thursday?' she repeats, collecting herself. 'No. Usually, I might have seen her walking to the shop to collect her morning papers, but I had gone into town early for an optician's appointment.'

'And what time did you return?'

'Oh, about ten, I should think.'

'And did you notice anything unusual down The Avenue that day? Anyone you didn't recognise? Any unfamiliar cars on the road, perhaps?'

'Well, there were the removal vans after dinner. Around half-six . . .'

Who moves house that late in the day?

'Who was moving?'

'No one that I know of,' she replies. 'That's why I found it odd to see them down The Avenue.'

'Could they have been delivery trucks?' DS Ryan asks.

'It must have been a big delivery, there were at least five vehicles.'

Thank God for nosey neighbours, I think to myself, and try not to let on to her that she might have mentioned something important. Some people tend to embellish the truth when the spotlight is on them; Mrs Howard seems just the type.

'Can you remember any number plates? Or the name for the moving company? Sometimes it's printed on the sides of vehicles.'

'Oh, I couldn't see any of that, I'm afraid. After all the tests I'd had at the optician's, my eyes were exhausted. I'm near-sighted, you see, and it was getting dark.'

'Could you see which direction they were going in?' DS Ryan asks.

Mrs Howard looks towards the window, deep in thought.

'They were leaving; I could see their taillights.'

'But you couldn't see which house they were driving away from?'

'I'm afraid not. It was just a second's glance.'

She could be mistaken; perhaps the trucks weren't out of place at all, and Mrs Howard simply isn't acquainted with the family who moved. But I know her type: tenaciously inquisitive, seeing privacy as a challenge rather than a virtue, and wanting to know every scrap of gossip they can get their hands on. My guess is Mrs Howard could tell me the secrets of every family living on The Avenue.

'Thank you for answering our questions, Mrs Howard. If you remember anything else, don't hesitate to get in touch.'

I slip my card across the coffee table, and watch as she picks it up, nodding silently. When she meets my gaze again, she gives me *the look*. The same, pitying glance I get every time someone is about to mention my son.

'Again, I do so wish to apologise in case I caused any upset. I didn't recognise you before. The story of your boy is just heartbre—'

'Like I said,' I interject, harsher this time. 'There's no need. Don't get up, my colleague and I can see ourselves out.'

By the look on her face, something tells me Mrs Howard isn't rendered speechless very often. But mourning mothers often cause that; no one ever knows the right thing to say.

'I don't think she meant anything by it,' DS Ryan says as the front door shuts behind us.

First Diane, now Mark. I can practically hear the eggshells cracking around me.

'Go ask DS Chesnick to have his team enquire about the removal trucks,' I ask as I head up the garden path. 'Confirm if anyone actually did move out of The Avenue on Thursday, and check if any other neighbours saw the trucks.'

'Yes, ma'am.'

I push open the gate and step out onto the road.

'What happened to him, ma'am? Your son?'

His question stops me in my tracks.

'I'm sorry to ask, but everyone at the station knows but me and—'

I can hear the struggle in his voice: he seems anxious about prying, but sounds equally as eager to know the answer.

To answer his question, I have to think back. Think of him. I see Jamie's sweet, smiling face and tears instantly sprout in my eyes. It hits me like a punch to my gut every time.

'I took him to the beach,' I say hoarsely. 'And while he was playing, I dozed off. I'd worked the nightshift, and my ex-husband had to work. When I woke up he was gone. Someone had managed to coax him away while I slept and . . .' I clench my teeth to keep back a sob, and hold my breath until it passes. 'I never saw him again.'

I exhale sharply and dash the tears away. I hate to open up, especially on the job. When I turn to face him, I see the same sympathetic smile that Mrs Howard had given me.

'Once we get back to the office,' I say, 'I want you to do as much snooping into Dr Jones' background as you can. Mrs Howard mentioned Zack was on holiday with an uncle – start by confirming whether Anna or her husband do in fact have a brother. Look into her husband's life too.'

'You think she might have made it up about the boy going on holiday?'

I stare down the private track, the roof of the surgeon's grand home just clearing the trees. No one's life is this perfect.

It doesn't matter how rich or successful a person is. We all have something to hide.

'I don't know what it is we're dealing with. I'm sure Dr Jones is telling the truth. But it's important we look at this from every angle.'

Because something tells me she's lying.

I turn back for the road and stop in my tracks.

'And DS Ryan?'

'Yes, ma'am?'

'Never ask me about my son again.'

23

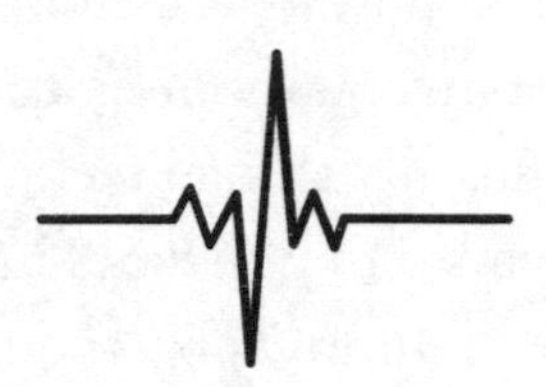

Anna

Saturday, 6 April 2019, 12:53

The patient's blood has turned the water red. I watch it stalk the drain in the scrubbing sink, round and round and round, pinkish soapsuds floating on the surface.

I really did it. I killed a man.

I should feel something. Anything. But there is no anguish, no pain, no relief, just the same persistent ringing in my ears, high-pitched like a scream.

None of my colleagues have been able to look me in the eye since I called time of death. I had been short-tempered and refused to work as part of a team, one of the most important aspects of surgery. Margot scrubbed out as quickly as she could, too furious to meet my eyes. None of the others said a word to me as they filed out of the theatre. Not even Dr Burke.

They might not suspect me of wrongdoing yet, but should anyone suggest foul play, might my irritability be a red flag they remember?

Stop, I tell myself. *This isn't over yet – I have to tell the patient's wife.*

I wait for the guilt to hit me, crush down upon my chest or knock the wind out of me, but nothing comes. I am completely numb with shock. The only thing I feel is the urge plucking at me from within. The need to pull hairs has never been greater. I want to snatch at my hair and rip, and rip.

It is almost over.

I dry my hands and check myself over in the mirror on the wall for any blood I might have missed, and fail to recognise the woman reflected back at me. I have aged years in just a few days. My cheeks look hollow, and my skin is the colour of ash. It seems like the old me died with the patient. I am no longer a surgeon, a mother.

I am a killer.

I step out of the operating theatre and stop in my tracks.

They must have heard the hinges squeal, for the door to the operating theatre on the other side of the corridor opens and two men step out, dressed in the scrubs I laid out on my doorstep the night before. They look shiftily up and down the corridor for the security guard as they approach.

'Where is the body?' the man on the left asks. His accent is thick, his tone abrupt. It sounds Eastern European, something I hadn't been able to pin down before. I recognise him from the day this all started: he was the first man I encountered on the driveway. The man with hazel eyes.

So he does speak English.

I recognise the other man too. He was the one who pulled

the groundsheets from beneath my feet, laughed as my face creased with pain. They are standing so close that I can feel the warmth of their breath.

'It's not ready yet,' I tell him in a harsh whisper. 'I have done what you asked. Now I have to tell the patient's wife that her husband has died.'

I go to pass him and a hand snatches my arm. I swing back around.

'You have five minutes,' he says.

I yank my arm away and head down the corridor, my skin stinging from where his nails dug into me.

I pass the cordon and turn off for the ward. The closer I get, the more I start to panic, remembering how Mrs Shabir had looked at me before the procedure: her eyes washed with pain; palpable, gut-churning fear.

You will do your best, won't you, Dr Jones?

I pause before the door, my hand resting on my stomach.

It was her husband, or my son. Her pain or mine.

I take a deep breath and step into the room.

Mrs Shabir is sat in the hard chair beside the bed, her spine slouched and her face slack with grief. Ahmed's PR manager perks up at the sight of me and places her laptop to one side. The sound rouses Mrs Shabir from her trance.

When she spots me in the door, her eyes spring to life and she jumps up from her seat. Then she notices the look on my face. Her eyes immediately brim with tears.

'No . . .'

'Mrs Shabir, I'm—'

'*No!* He can't be. You said he had a ninety-per-cent chance of survival. *Ninety per cent!*'

She bawls into her hands; her legs look ready to buckle at

the knees. The noises that are coming out of her sound like a dying animal: pure, unrestrained agony.

I did this.

'Mrs Shabir . . .' My voice comes out strangled. I cough to clear it, but it only seems to get tighter. 'We performed the triple bypass surgery to each of the blocked arteries, but upon finishing the procedure, your husband's aortic artery ruptured. We did all we could, but he lost too much blood. There was nothing more we could do to save him. I'm sorry.'

I'm not even sure she heard me. She is sobbing so hard, teetering on hyperventilating. I edge towards her to coax her down towards the seat.

'Maybe you should sit—'

'Don't touch me!'

She sinks down onto the seat, her face hidden by her hands and locks of dark hair.

In the corner of the room, Tammy's jaw has fallen slack, and her complexion has lost all colour.

'He . . . He can't have,' she says. Something clicks behind her eyes. 'I need to make a call.'

I look towards the door and lock eyes with Val, where she is peering through the glass partition. Everyone on the ward must have heard the commotion. I give her a nod and meet her at the door.

'I just informed her of her husband's death. She's in shock. Would you sit with her?'

'Course,' she replies.

'I don't need to remind you that whatever you hear in this room is not public knowledge?'

She nods knowingly and perches down beside Mrs Shabir.

When Val rests her hand on the woman's back, Mindy's hard resolve crumbles in an instant. Val rocks her back and forth.

I did this. I'm a murderer.

I head back up the corridor, so overcome with shock and exhaustion that I am almost swaying, and cross the ward in a blur, curious glances burning into me as I pass. When I cross the cordon and close in on the operating room, I hear a door creak open behind my back from the theatre adjacent to mine: the door is ajar, and piercing eyes stare out at me.

The men are waiting.

'What's taking so long?'

'I'm following procedure,' I hiss. 'If you want me to get away with this you need to back off and let me do my job.'

'Hurry up,' he spits, and closes the door with a quiet click.

David appears at the bend in the corridor.

'You all right, Doc?' he asks.

If the others have told him of Shabir's death, he hasn't let on. But even once he knows, he will be expected to continue keeping the area secure until Shabir is taken away. David's protocol is to station himself beside the body in the morgue until communication with the government has been made. My blackmailers must be in and out by then.

'Yes,' I lie. It comes out sharp, and his smile vanishes.

I must look rattled, for he gives me a curious look, before giving me a swift nod and carrying on down the corridor. I wait until he has cleared the bend before I step back into the theatre.

It is deathly quiet now. A junior doctor stands at the operating table, finishing up the closure of the patient's chest. Two nurses wait to wrap up the body for its trip to the morgue. There is blood all over the floor.

'I'll do the rest.'

The junior doctor jumps at the sound of my voice.

'Oh,' he says. 'I was told that I should—'

'And now I'm telling you that I will do it.' I look at the nurses, who have stood up straight after slouching against the wall. 'That goes for you, too. I will do the rest and take the body down. If you want to make yourselves useful, you can clean the floor when I'm gone.'

They leave in silence but for the scuff of their shoes, sharing looks at my expense as they go.

I have never been so abrupt, but it seems to be the only way to keep people from asking questions. If I'm cruel, they recoil, but they do as I say.

I pull on a clean pair of gloves and approach the body.

The drapes have been peeled away. The skin on his chest is still open, revealing its fleshy underside and the white bone of his sternum. The junior doctor had been sewing it shut with wire thread.

As I pick up the needle driver, my eyes drift towards his face.

The tape is still over his eyes, and his jaw is slack where the breathing tube had been forced between his teeth. I reach up and close it, and peel the tape from each eye. A long, black lash is stuck to part of the tape. The urge burns through me again.

Not now.

I scrunch the tape in my hand and place the ball on the tool table.

Ahmed really was handsome: defined cheekbones, strong jaw, full lips. Lips that his wife will never kiss again.

I lean in until my lips are millimetres from his ear. He smells of disinfectant and blood.

'I'm sorry,' I whisper.

I stand straight, forcing myself to harden. I can't risk myself unravelling until everything is complete. I refuse to look at him again, and get to work sewing up the last of the sternum, before pulling his skin taut and firing staples along the incision line. There is no point sewing him up, the coroner will only cut him open again, and the junior doctor has sutured the wound at his groin.

The clock is still ticking on the wall, only it isn't a taunting sound now, but a soothing backdrop to the empty room. I clean down the body with the supplies the nurses left, wiping away each speck of blood and disinfectant that resembles tar.

I wrap the body up in sheets, tipping and tilting him with the greatest care. It usually takes two nurses, and I struggle at points, huffing and cursing beneath my breath, but soon it is done, and my horrendous deed is wrapped head to toe. I pull the concealment trolley towards the operating table. I can't lift him alone and have to roll him onto it, apologising to the dead in whispers. I place the blue tarp over the trolley to conceal him and kick off the brakes by the rear wheels.

I bend down and retrieve my stopwatch from beneath the scrubbing sink and listen for life on the other side of the door. I hear David's familiar whistle as he turns the bend, the relaxed shuffle of his boots hitting the lino floor.

I listen until he tails off around the corner and hit the button on the stopwatch: we have one minute and thirty-two seconds to get to the lift.

I open the doors and wheel out the body, and spot the two men emerging from within the adjacent theatre. We meet each other's eyes and set off silently down the corridor.

The trolley is old and rickety, and each squeak of its hinges echoes up the vast corridor. The men follow close behind with their shoes practically clipping at my heels.

I reach the doors and tap the button on the wall. My heart is racing, and my palms grow moist where they grip the trolley. I glance at my watch: sixty-five seconds until David reappears. I tap my foot against the lino, listening as the lift slowly rattles up the shaft.

Come on, come on, come on.

I check my watch again: fifty seconds to go. Sweat breaks out under my arms at the sound of David's footsteps approaching from around the bend, his high-pitched whistling echoing up the corridor.

When the doors open, I rush inside and fix the brakes, reaching over to press the button for the basement. The two men slip in beside me just before the doors close. We had only twenty-five seconds to spare.

The lift starts to move.

'Open it,' the hazel-eyed man says.

I pull back the cover on the trolley and unwrap the sheets from Ahmed's face and chest. His mouth has fallen slack again.

The man takes Ahmed's jaw in his hand, turns him roughly from side to side.

'It's him,' he says.

The other man is holding his fingers to Ahmed's wrist, checking for a pulse. His technique is wrong; he should be checking for his pulse at his neck, but I am certainly not going to correct him. He uses the stethoscope hidden beneath his scrubs to listen for a heartbeat, as if it weren't obvious by the sight of the large metal staples running down the centre of his chest. The lift is tight and hot, and I can smell the sweat and breath from the men, the lingering scent of disinfectant creeping from the body.

He straightens with a satisfied nod.

'You can close it,' the hazel-eyed man says.

I wrap the body again, getting hit by a brief whiff of blood, just as the lift arrives at the basement. The doors open with a creak.

I kick the brakes and wheel the trolley out of the lift, struggling with Ahmed's weight and the rickety wheels twisting in different directions. The men remain inside.

'We will be in touch with next steps,' the hazel-eyed man says.

I stare back at them until the doors shut.

24

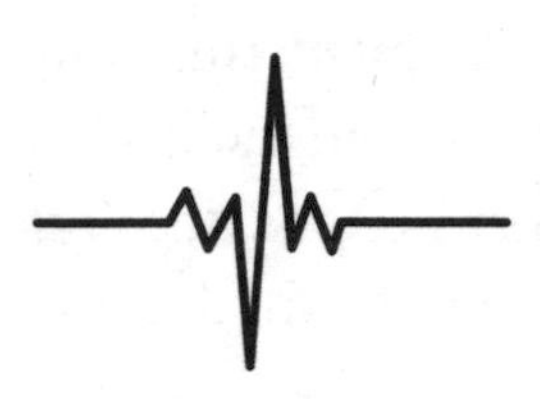

Margot

Saturday, 6 April 2019, 13:25

I think I just watched Dr Jones kill a man.

I step out of the toilet cubicle in a daze and catch my reflection in the mirror above the sink. My complexion is pale with shock, and my lips are red raw from running my tongue anxiously across the flesh. Three quarters of an hour have passed and I am still trembling.

Dr Jones had been foul to me throughout the operation, snapping at me at every opportunity she got. Now I realise why. I was the closest person to her, and could see everything she was doing. She asked me to step back to stop me from seeing her make the fatal cut. What she didn't realise is that I stepped forward to assist her just as she performed the deed.

I remember the blade slice along the aorta. The gush of blood that followed.

I have to tell someone. But who on earth would believe me?

Dr Jones is a highly respected surgeon. When it was announced that she would be transferring to Redwood, there was a buzz of excitement around the hospital that can only be likened to the time one of the royals made a visit, as if she is some sort of celebrity within medical circles. To make such a horrifying claim, I would need absolute proof – but I am the only witness. Everyone else had glanced at the clock, only looking back when the machines started wailing.

Who are they likely to believe? A renowned surgeon with decades of experience under her belt, or a scrub nurse who steals to make ends meet?

I walk to the sink and wash my hands, which are shaking almost as violently as Dr Jones' had been during the procedure, and check myself over in the mirror for any last remnants of the patient's blood.

Something in my gut told me that I shouldn't take my eyes off her. Dr Jones had been acting strangely since the beginning of the surgery, and for the first time I didn't trust her with the blade. I can't forget the sight of how vigorously her hands were shaking. She was nervous, erratic, and when she asked for the time, everyone looked at the clock. Everyone but me. That's when I saw her take the scalpel and drag it along the aorta.

There was no fumbling of the blade.

She didn't gasp as if it had occurred by mistake.

She purposely manipulated everyone into looking towards the clock, penetrated the wall of the aorta as deeply as she could, and sliced along the artery.

She killed him deliberately.

I rub my damp hands against the nape of my neck, listening to the anxious rush of my heart.

I have to tell someone.

I give myself a once-over in the mirror and dry my hands before heading for the door. Kelvin might not like me, but I am sure he will believe me, considering how serious the allegation is. He has to.

The corridor is awash with staff and visitors following the colour-coded lines on the floor leading to different wards. I walk down the corridor in a daze, and when I pass the changing rooms on the way to Kelvin's office, I stop and double-take: he is standing in the doorway, talking to someone inside.

'Kelvin,' I say as I approach, 'I need to talk to you. Something's happened.'

When he turns to look at me, he doesn't smile or soften. He stares at me as if I'm vermin.

'Yes, something has.' He looks into the changing room. 'She's here.'

A security guard steps out. It's Sonny. He always smiles or gives me a wave when we cross paths. He isn't smiling now.

'What's going on?' I stammer.

'Come with me,' Kelvin replies.

I glance into the changing room and see the door to my locker hanging open. My heart drops.

'Kelvin, I—'

'Save it for the office, Margot.'

I follow him in panicked silence, my heart rate climbing with each step. I pick up the pace each time I feel the clip of Sonny's shoes at my heels.

I try to conjure a lie, a way to explain away my fate, but it's useless. I knew something bad was going to happen. I had felt it all morning, a sinking feeling in my gut. When I saw what Dr Jones did in the operating theatre, I selfishly hoped that her actions were the reason for my dread; that it was some sort of freak premonition. Little did I know the dread was meant for me.

Kelvin opens the door to his office and ushers me inside. I have never seen him so angry, it is almost shivering off him; his cheeks are scalding red. I step inside and take a seat, clamping my shaking hands between my thighs. Sonny waits by the door, his thick arms crossed at his chest, and Kelvin sits behind the desk. Everything I stole is laid out across the surface.

Kelvin clears his throat.

'After our chat yesterday, I thought long and hard about what you said. Although your delivery left a lot to be desired, I believed that you were right: I needed to take a stronger stance on catching the person responsible for the recent thefts. This morning I received authorisation to search the women's locker room. Imagine my surprise when I opened yours and found these stolen items inside.'

I sit in silence, shaking in my seat. I feel like a little girl again, dragged into the headmaster's office and scolded for stealing. Ma's motto creeps into my mind.

If you get caught, you deny the lot, even if you're lying through your teeth.

'Don't you have anything to say?'

The look he gives me is so sharp that I flinch when I meet his eyes. He must think I'm scum. I will lose my job, my flat. Ma would be proud.

'Not even "sorry"?'

My throat starts to burn, but I hold the tears at bay. I will never let him see me cry. I clamp down on my hands as hard as

I can, until the skin on my wrists turns pale and my fingertips throb with blood.

He sighs.

'You're fired, effective immediately,' he says. 'The police are on their way.'

His words hit me like a blow to the gut. In the back of my mind, I hear Ma laughing.

'That thing you wanted to tell me,' Kelvin says. 'I suppose it wasn't a confession. What was it?'

I grit my teeth together to steel myself against the tears, keeping my eyes firmly on my lap.

'It doesn't matter,' I reply croakily.

No one will believe me now.

25

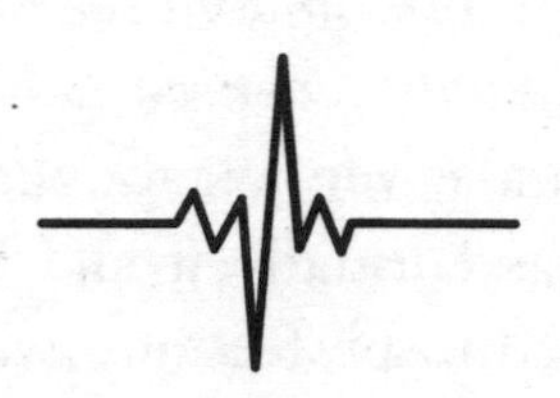

Anna

Saturday, 6 April 2019, 16:04

Once the patient is dead, and no suspicions have been raised, we will begin putting into motion the return of your son.

I can't stop repeating the same line in my head. I pace the house with the burner phone clamped to my chest, the cameras searing into me as I pass beneath them. My free hand twitches at my side, itching to reach up towards my head and pluck. Every so often I do it without thinking, and only come to when I feel the faint stinging from my scalp. I have done it a few times now; I keep passing long, blonde hairs on the carpet.

I'm a murderer.

Shabir's lifeless face flashes constantly in my mind: the slackness of his jaw; the smell of him as I leaned in towards his ear; that one lone lash stuck to the tape. I can't stop thinking about the shocked expression on Dominic's face when I told him. I watched every drop of life drain from his complexion.

They are going to find out what I did. What if someone saw me make the cut? Is that why they couldn't look me in the eye? The coroner will open him up and see the tell-tale signs of a scalpel incision, and I will never see Zack again.

I stop in the hall and cover my face with my hands.

I did everything as I usually would before the fatal cut. Each graft was joined to perfection. Every correct step was taken, both before and after I killed him. There is little chance the aorta will show signs of foul play; it was so shredded that Margot struggled to apply pressure to it. But the doubt continues to chip away at me.

I should have opened him up when I was alone with him. I should have covered my tracks better.

The doorbell rings.

I freeze, listening to Bear's excited barks as he runs into the hall. The phone didn't ring. Wouldn't they call, if they were going to bring Zack home? But the thought of him standing on the other side of the door obliterates all sense. I run towards it and throw it wide.

Two strangers stand at the threshold.

The woman must be in her fifties, with mousey-brown hair and pale-blue eyes, wearing a boxy black suit and flat, masculine boots. The man beside her is considerably younger, and almost a foot taller than she is.

They both hold badges within their grasps.

'Dr Anna Jones?'

I can't take my eyes off their credentials. My heart is clambering in my chest.

'Yes?'

'I am Detective Inspector Rachel Conaty. This is my colleague, Detective Sergeant Mark Ryan. May we come in?'

I am too shocked to speak. They couldn't have learned about the operation this quickly. The hospital would want to conduct their own investigation into any allegations before calling the police. They couldn't risk news like that getting out; it would be a PR disaster. They would need proof.

'Dr Jones?'

I can feel the camera staring down at me in the doorway, its line of sight burning into my crown. Bear is wriggling beside me, trying to squeeze past my legs to get to the visitors. I shove the burner phone in my pocket.

'I'm afraid now really isn't a good time.'

She frowns.

'We are currently investigating a serious crime within the area, and have spoken to your neighbours throughout the day. It won't take long.'

They've found her.

The abductor's words ring inside my head.

Once the patient is dead, and no suspicions have been raised, we will begin putting into motion the return of your son.

... no suspicions have been raised.

If they come inside, the abductors will know. I pull the door to.

'I'm sorry, but I'm afraid it will have to wait until tomorrow.'

The detective gives nothing away. Her mouth is set in a firm line. The man beside her, however, takes a curious glance behind me to see inside the house.

'We're investigating a very serious crime, Dr Jones,' she says, flatly. 'I'm afraid it can't wait.'

The panic swells in my chest, and tears of desperation sting at the whites of my eyes. I clear my throat and step aside.

'All right, but I'm expecting an important call so I can't be long.'

They step inside, passing beneath the camera. I lead the way into the living room on shaking legs and offer them both a seat. They sit on the sofa, seeming to take it in turns to glance around. One of them always has their eyes on me.

'You have a lovely home,' DI Conaty says.

'Thank you,' I reply, as I take to the armchair.

I can feel the camera glaring at me from above their heads. It takes all my strength not to glance up and stare pleadingly down the lens.

It's not my fault.

'You said you were investigating a serious crime?'

'I'm afraid we have some bad news,' DI Conaty says. 'Your neighbour, Paula Williams, was found dead yesterday morning.'

I clap my hand over my mouth. The tears that had been building at the door seize their chance and begin to work their way out.

'Oh my God . . .'

'I understand this must come as a shock.'

'How?' I stutter. 'When?'

'That's what we are trying to find out. It appears to have been a homicide.'

'A *homicide*? No, that doesn't make sense. Was it during a burglary or something?'

'We don't think so, no. Have you noticed any new faces popping by? Any changes in Paula's routine?'

I pretend to think back, but all I can focus on are the cameras watching us. One on my face, and one on theirs. I imagine the abductors watching the footage while a gun is pointed at my baby's head.

'No,' I answer. 'Nothing. Paula is – *was* – a lovely, normal lady. She was exceptionally kind. She became like family to us.'

'Your neighbour Mrs Howard said that Paula used to help you with childcare?'

My heart sinks at the thought of them speaking to Jenny. She is the local gossip, and has had it in for me ever since I declined to join her local book club and the Neighbourhood Watch committee.

'Yes. Paula would help for an hour or two after school, after I found myself struggling to balance full-time work and child-care. Being relatively new in town I didn't have anyone around to help. Paula's daughter had not long moved to Australia, and I think she was lonely in the house by herself. I needed help, and Paula needed the company. It benefited us all, and my son and I will miss her immensely.'

'And she collected your son from school, too?'

'That's right.'

'Who collected Zack on Thursday?' she asks.

'Paula did.'

I notice the male detective perk up at that. He sits straighter in his seat.

'That's what we're struggling with,' DI Conaty replies. 'Because according to CCTV footage we have of the two of them, they didn't come home.'

'No, they didn't.'

DI Conaty frowns. Her partner looks to her, then back to me.

'You don't sound too concerned?'

'Well, no, because Paula wasn't meant to bring Zack home

on Thursday. They went to meet my brother. Jeff has taken Zack on holiday to Cornwall for the Easter holidays.'

'Wouldn't he have a suitcase? He didn't look to be carrying anything in the footage.'

My thoughts and fears stumble over one another in my tired brain, and a wave of nervous heat flushes through me. I force out the first lie that comes to me.

'My brother and I had arranged that beforehand so Zack and Paula wouldn't have the stress of carrying it,' I blurt out.

'Okay. Where did they meet?'

They are asking so many questions in such quick succession that the lies are toppling out of my mouth without me having time to remember everything I have said. DI Conaty has a way of speaking that makes it seem like she doubts everything I have to say.

Maybe that isn't her tone at all ... maybe she realises I am lying.

'I'm sorry,' I say, running my hands through my hair. 'This is all rather overwhelming. I'm struggling to think straight.'

DI Conaty smiles, but it seems forced. I wonder if she has noticed that I'm forcing it too.

'I understand. Perhaps we can arrange a date to chat next week, when the news has sunk in. We can meet at the station.'

Yes. Any day but today.

'Thank you, yes. I think that would be better.'

'I'll just need your brother's contact details to confirm everything you've told me.'

I feel my expression drop, which DI Conaty clocks immediately. She seems to catch every stray thought that enters my mind, every flicker of fear on my face. I run with the first lie that comes to me.

'I'm afraid that won't be of much help to you. Jeff has to make calls in the next village over, you see, as the call reception is so poor. But I will happily take your details and pass them on to him so he can get in touch.'

'In this day and age?' she asks. 'Where is it they're staying?'

'Maybridge – a very small town, more of a village really. It's unlikely you've heard of it.'

She hesitates for a few seconds, staring at me from the other side of the room. I don't care what she suspects. All I want is for them to leave my house. My eyes briefly flick towards the camera.

Please don't kill my baby.

'I see,' DI Conaty says, reaching into her blazer. She places her card on the coffee table. 'I will need your contact details too, to get in touch about meeting at the station.'

I give her my number, waiting as she types it into her phone.

My personal phone vibrates on the top of the coffee table with an incoming call. Next to it is my work phone. We all stare at it until it stops.

They saw me with the burner phone at the door.

I look up at them, a shock of nerves shooting down my spine. Both of the detectives are looking at me intently.

'Now you have mine.' She looks at the two phones on the table, and then back to my hand where I had held the burner phone to my chest when I answered the door. I can feel it burning against my thigh from inside my pocket, and wonder if she can see it. 'Three phones?' she asks. 'You must be a very busy woman.'

They rise from the sofa. There is a tension between us as I lead them towards the door. I can feel Conaty's eyes on me, taking in my body language, searching my person for the burner phone. I wonder if she has noticed that my legs are shaking. I open the door and a breeze slips into the hall.

'I will call soon and schedule a date for you to come in,' she says. 'If you think of anything in the meantime, don't hesitate to get in touch.'

'Thank you.'

They give me a nod and step out onto the drive. I close the door behind them and immediately start pacing back and forth.

She didn't trust me one bit. She knew everything that came out of my mouth was a lie.

I continue to pace, going over the conversation in my head to the sound of the car pulling off the driveway, the faint crunch of gravel as they depart.

The burner phone rings inside my pocket. I answer it on the first ring.

'It wasn't about Ahmed Shabir,' I stammer into the receiver. 'I have done everything you asked. Now give him back to me.'

I breathe heavily into the receiver, the sound crackling down the line.

'You said as soon as I killed the patient you would—'

'It's not over yet,' the man says at the other end of the line.

My legs falter. I rest a shaking hand on the banister.

'Remember, you not only need to kill the patient, but get away with it.'

A sob bursts out of me.

'No! I have done everything you have asked of me. *Give me back my son!*'

'As soon as the police investigation blows over. Make sure they don't suspect you, Dr Jones. Your son's life depends on it.'

The call ends.

'No!'

My legs buckle as if I have been kicked. I sink down to the floor, wails of despair clawing out of me, and thrash my fists against the carpet until the fibres burn my knuckles, and spit flies from my mouth. When I have no energy left, I lie down defeated with my knees pressed to my chest. My tears soak silently into the carpet.

PART II

26

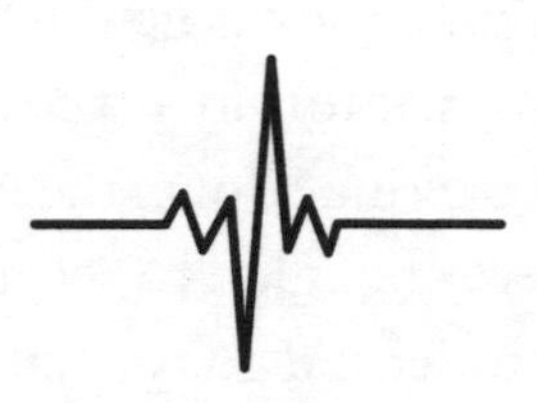

Margot

Monday, 8 April 2019, 08:32

I wait at the top of the steps at the rear of the police station, my hip leaning against the railing with the charge sheet tucked in my back pocket. They sent me out of the exit situated along a backstreet, presumably to keep the riffraff out of sight.

My clothes reek. The officers took them from me after handing over an old grey tracksuit to wear during my time in the cell, but this morning I had to pull them on again, creased and stained with old sweat. I remember changing into them at the hospital, and pacing back and forth as I wrestled with what I had witnessed.

Dr Jones killed Mr Shabir. It is all I have been able to think about since she called time of death. I circled my eight-by-ten cell going over the memory repeatedly: the shimmer of steel sinking into the aorta, blood surging out. It wasn't an accident, that much I do know. She thrust the blade with conviction. Dr Jones must have entered the theatre fully intending to kill Ahmed Shabir.

But why?

The sound of an engine growls up the back lane and I freeze on the spot, bracing myself for my lift to arrive. When I spot a police car appear and continue down the lane, I sigh with relief; the only time I have ever felt glad to see a copper.

When it was time to let me go, the custody officer asked if there was anyone I could call to collect me, and I stared at her in silence as I tried to force out a name. I hadn't realised how alone I was until that moment – I couldn't think of a single person who had my back. When the officer began to suggest I take the bus fare instead, a name flew from between my lips in an attempt to claw back some of my pride. A name I have regretted uttering ever since. It is sheer luck that his number has stayed the same.

I haven't seen my brother in years.

Damien grew up to be just like Ma: treating every word she said as gospel, and went about his life with the belief that the world owes him something, taking whatever he wants regardless of the cost. But unlike Ma, there is a heart in there somewhere. Or at least there used to be.

You could be describing yourself there, Maggot.

I rub my face, blood tingling beneath the tired skin.

No, this is different. I did what I had to do to get myself out of a hole, whereas Ma thrived on digging the family deeper. I'm nothing like either of them.

I hear Damien before I see him: the brutal rag of the engine, zooming down the back lane. A black Mercedes pulls into view and brakes sharply at the foot of the steps.

We stare at each other, listening to the engine purr beneath the bonnet. He is wearing sunglasses with lenses that reflect my image back at me: my shoulders have sagged with exhaustion, and my face is deathly pale. He gives me a curt nod. I nod back and stub out my fag, my heart pounding in my chest.

'Fuck. You reek, Maggot,' Damien says as I slip in beside him. The car pulls away before I have time to fix my belt.

'Nice to see you too.'

He lowers the windows to let out the smell and leans over me to reach for the glove compartment. The door knocks against my knees. He takes out a packet of cigarettes before clicking it shut again, giving me just enough time to see the handgun concealed inside, the barrel pointed right at my gut.

'Where am I dropping you?'

'My friend's place,' I lie, clicking my belt into place. 'End of London Road. Nice car, by the way. Who'd you nick it from?'

He turns the corner sharply. I grip on to the door handle until every drop of blood is squeezed from my fingers.

'How do you know I haven't made a living for myself since you've been gone?'

I scoff at the thought.

'Whoever did the respray for you missed a spot. The paint around the door join is bright blue.'

He laughs with the cigarette between his teeth, taking his eyes off the road to light it. He takes a drag and fills the car with smoke.

'You never did miss a trick. What'd they keep you in for?'

'Theft. My hearing's in a month.'

He emits a high-pitched whistle.

'That can get you up to seven years, you know that?'

'Less time than you'd get for stealing a car.'

'I'm not stupid enough to get caught.'

I roll my eyes and stare out the window.

'You say that like you haven't been locked up before.'

As my temper simmers, I notice we are bickering just like we used to as kids. We haven't seen each other in fifteen years, but it might as well have been fifteen minutes, and it pains me to admit that I have missed him. But I daren't tell him that; it would give him leverage to rein me back in.

'Sure you don't fancy dropping home for a bit?'

'Home? You're still at Ma's place?'

'My place now,' he says.

No, I tell myself. *We are not going down this road. There is a reason why we're not in each other's lives.*

'My friend is expecting me.'

'*My friend is expecting me*,' he mocks in an overly posh tone. 'Not meeting that rich boyfriend you ran out on us for?'

'You haven't seen me in years. You could ask me how my career is going, what I've been up to with my life. But all you can do is rib me.' I exhale sharply and turn towards the window. 'And you wonder why I've never come home to visit.'

'All right, how's your career going?'

I drum my fingers against the sill of the window.

'Come on, you wanted me to ask.'

'I got fired.'

A brief silence hangs between us, with only the growl of the engine filling the car. Then I hear him laugh behind closed lips. He tries to stifle it, but all it does is make him laugh harder. It isn't long before he is bellowing, slapping the wheel with his palm. When I meet his eyes, a smirk creeps across my lips. He pushes me playfully and suddenly I'm laughing too, until tears wet my eyes and my stomach aches. He pulls the car down London Road and parks a stone's throw away from my apartment building.

'I've missed this,' he says, the smirk still flickering on his lips.

I wipe my eyes and force the laughter down. For a flicker in time, I had forgotten to keep my guard up and longed to wrap my arms around him. My big brother, here in the flesh. I clear my throat and straighten my spine.

'Come home with me,' he says. 'Have dinner with us.'

'*Us*? You actually met someone who will put up with your bull?'

He avoids the bait. 'Come on. You wouldn't have called me if you didn't want to, you would have called this mate you're going to see. It's just dinner. And for the record: yeah, I've met someone. His name's Rick, and you'd really like him if you gave him a chance.'

Damien has found love and settled down, and I missed out on all of it. I shock myself by considering the invitation.

No. Don't let him reel you in. He's just like Ma.

I look down at my lap and unclip the belt.

'Thanks, but I've got plans.'

He goes to say more, before clenching his jaw shut. He nods sharply.

'Fine.'

'Thanks for the lift.'

'Yeah,' he says dismissively. 'Good luck in court.'

I get out of the car and head for my building with Damien's eyes burning into my back. I step inside and immediately take to the stairs to avoid waiting for the lift, holding back tears as if I'm a little girl again.

Grow up, I scold, as I reach the fourth floor and fish around my bag for my keys. *You can't let him back in, because you can't trust him. You know that.*

I cross the landing and freeze, my line of sight focused on the note taped to my door.

Your stuff is in storage. Text me for the address
Sandy

I snatch it off and read it repeatedly, until finally the words sink in. I hide my face in my hands, listening as the paper crinkles in my grip and tears sting at my eyes.

She really did it. I'm homeless. No job. No home. What am I going to do?

'Your friend not in?'

I jolt at the sound and drop my hands. Damien is standing at the top of the stairs, leaning against the banister, his sunglasses pushed to the top of his blond buzzcut. He must have followed me up. His playful smirk softens when he sees the tears, and I spot a shimmer of pity in his eyes.

'Come on. We'll have a chippy tea later, my treat.'

I stand frozen before the door, as if I have any other choice. It feels so good to finally be taken care of, but the consequences of going back to the past that I have been running from for so long scream at me to stay where I am; I would be better off at some women's refuge or on the streets. I look down at the note. My tears have made the ink run.

I don't have any other choice.

He beckons me with his hand and I step towards him, as every fibre of my body tells me not to. He slings his arm over my shoulder and pulls me close.

'But first you're having a bath, you stinky cow.'

I laugh, sniffling against the tears.

Having my big brother look after me has made me feel safer than I have felt in a long time. But as we make our way down the stairs, panic slowly coils around my neck.

Once I go back, he will make it almost impossible for me to leave.

27

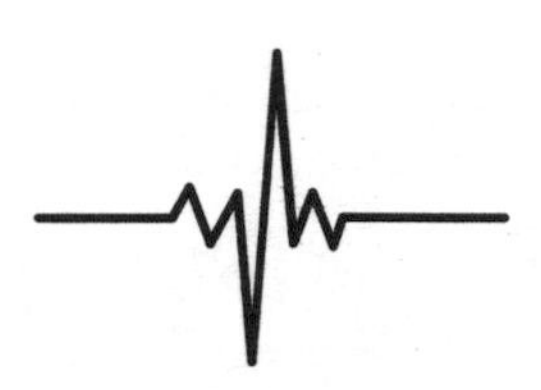

Anna

Monday, 8 April 2019, 08:40

All I seem to do now is shake. From fear, from rage, from lack of sleep and the benzodiazepines keeping me calm. I tear my eyes away from the hospital on the other side of the windscreen and drop two yellow tablets into my palm, swallowing them down with a gulp from my water bottle.

I did everything they asked. I lied, I cheated, I killed a man in cold blood, and they still won't give him back to me.

I drifted in and out of a fitful, self-induced coma for the whole of Sunday. Dreaming of Zack, calling out for him in my sleep so loudly that I woke myself, only to be crushed by the pain that awaited me. Then I would swallow some pills and drift back to sleep. I still feel half-asleep even now.

The burner phone the abductors gave me has been silent, but

I know they have been watching me. Whenever I broke through the medically induced sleep, I felt the cameras' glares on me, twitching all over my skin.

I check my reflection in the sun visor. I am dressed in a white blouse and smart black trousers as if it is just another Monday, but when I look closer, I can see that my hair hangs lifelessly about my shoulders, noticeably thinner from relentless plucking. Even behind my make-up, my skin looks tired and haggard, and the whites of my eyes have turned pink from crying.

Pull yourself together. Zack needs you.

No one can suspect that anything is wrong. I must be strong, indifferent. Impenetrable. I take one last look at the woman in the mirror, watching as I slowly harden behind the eyes, and slam the visor shut.

If I don't act convincingly, they will kill him.

I take a deep breath and get out of the car.

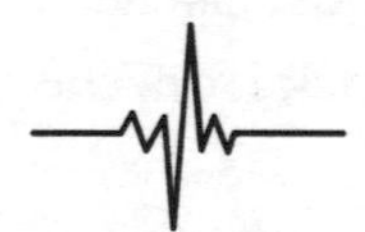

I step onto the ward, listening to the familiar rustle of my scrubs and the soft patter of my clogs. On any other day, I would go about my business without a second thought, but now it takes every ounce of my being to force the faux smiles and morning greetings. Holding the lies together with the last shred of control I have.

I reach the nurse's station and meet Val's eyes. She gives a swift nod towards the beds lining the ward where Dr de Silva is standing by my patient's bed.

My heart jolts.

'What's this about?'

'I'm not sure,' she replies. 'You hear about Margot?'

'What about her?'

'She was the thief. Got fired on Saturday and was taken away by the police.'

'Christ. I wouldn't have expected that.'

That's a lie. I totally expect it of her. I think back to all of those times that she tried to befriend me in the changing rooms; she was probably trying to shift my attention away from my open locker, or get me to trust her so I wouldn't suspect her if fingers started pointing her way. Clever girl. Just not clever enough.

At least she is one less person to worry about.

'Did Dr de Silva say anything about taking on my patient?'

'No, he just asked for your chart. He had the right hump.'

Which means someone higher up lumbered him with the work.

'Thanks.'

I reach Dr de Silva just as he is turning away from the patient's bed, ticking a task from the clipboard. My clipboard.

'Good morning.'

He looks up and instantly blushes.

'Anna, good morning.'

'Are we trading patients? I know it can be a bit monotonous day-to-day, but this is a new one.'

He doesn't even force a laugh. His pity makes me flush hot.

'I think you should speak to Dominic.'

'Anything I should be concerned about?'

He stutters briefly, his eyes never wavering from his clipboard. 'Just swing by his office when you have a moment.'

I force a smile and turn on my heel, heading for the doors out of the ward. Val watches me as I pass.

Dominic had been shocked by the news of Ahmed's death. I replay the moment in my mind, remembering how his expression fell, and a ream of concerns seemed to cross his mind: what effect an MP's death will have on the hospital's reputation, the effect on *his* reputation, the PR fiasco that will be coming his way. He no doubt thought back to all of the times he boasted to those in his close circle, and realised he would have to eat his words. But I didn't think it would lead to this; there is only one explanation for a surgeon's patients being taken over by another.

I reach the door of his office and knock hesitantly.

'Come in.'

I step inside the office, and when Dominic looks up at me his frown vanishes.

'Anna. Good morning.'

'Morning, Dominic.'

I cross the room and take a seat. The circles around his eyes tell me he hasn't been sleeping well. I wonder what my appearance says about me.

'Dr de Silva is handling my patients?' I ask, my tone shifting between a statement and a question. I sit, straight-backed and tense, but every so often I feel a flicker of vulnerability pluck at my resolve: the occasional twitch in my eye, a nervous tug at the corner of my lips.

'Yes,' he replies. 'I thought it would be best, until we know what to expect when the news breaks.'

'So you're suspending me?'

'No,' he says, too quickly. 'Or at least, not for any wrongdoing. I'm not punishing you for what happened. It was clearly out of your hands. But . . .'

'But?'

'The board feels that the right thing to do in this situation is to allow you to take a step back while we deal with any potential repercussions from the press.'

He seems so afraid to say the wrong thing, rock the boat any more than Shabir's death already has. I want to shake the words out of him.

'Dominic, you needn't tiptoe around me. I'd much rather you be direct.'

Put me out of my misery.

He nods slowly, and finally meets my eyes.

'This is out of my hands, Anna. The board has requested a thorough investigation into Mr Shabir's death and a temporary suspension of duty to avoid any hounding from the press.'

Investigation.

'Ahmed Shabir is one of the most prominent MPs of the moment, with tremendous public backing. We are expecting a lot of press interest in the coming days.'

'And it would be easier if I weren't here.'

'Yes,' he replies frankly.

I nod calmly, but inside I'm screaming. This wasn't part of the plan.

If the investigation finds any wrongdoing on my part, Zack is dead.

I clamp my hands between my thighs to stop them from shaking.

'An investigation ... Do they suspect me of negligence or something?'

'No one is suggesting that, but I'm sure you see why it's necessary. We will have questions from the press, the government ... We need to show that we understand exactly what happened.'

He doesn't need to say any more. I look down at my lap to compose myself and force the panic down before meeting his eyes again.

'So, what happens now?'

'There will be an investigation and a series of interviews with yourself and those who were in the theatre, except for Margot, who unfortunately had to be let go for another matter. The coroner has examined the body, and a second opinion is being sought from outside the hospital.'

He stalls, reluctant to voice what comes next. We both know it's coming, collectively holding our breath.

'You're suspended from your duties pending the outcome of the investigation. Here is the date and time of your interview to address the board.' He slips an envelope across the desk. 'If it goes beyond that . . . It won't, of course, but if it does . . . I'd contact a solicitor.'

My throat burns furiously. I sit in my seat, every muscle in my body taut.

'How long until it goes public?' I ask, my tone flat.

'I'd say you have until the end of the day.'

I nod quickly, teeth clenched to force composure. I expect him to say something encouraging. *You will get through this* or *Call me if you need anything,* but all he can do is avert his eyes.

I stand in silence and turn for the door.

'Anna . . . I'm sorry.'

I cannot respond, not with words, not even a nod. I simply stare back at him before opening the door to leave his office, and walk as fast as I can towards my own, shaking as if I am about to implode. I slip inside and lean against the door.

An investigation means they will be scrutinising every move

I made. Every cut. Every tool. I should have opened him back up to reassure myself before I took him to the morgue.

My personal phone rings from the top of the desk, and I jolt at the sound. My nerves are fried. I pull myself away from the door and practically sway towards the desk.

DI Conaty is calling.

I pick it up with a shaking hand, and debate letting it go to voicemail, or turning off my phone altogether. But I know she won't stop; she is as determined as I am. I take a deep breath and answer.

'Hello?'

'Dr Jones, it's Detective Inspector Rachel Conaty. I was hoping you would be able to come to the station today to continue our chat. Is there a good time for you?'

My legs shake wildly, panic and fear building into a scream behind my teeth.

'Must it be today?'

There is a brief beat of silence. I stand listening to the pounding of my heart.

'Your neighbour has been murdered, Dr Jones. The sooner we speak to everyone on our list, the sooner we can find out who killed her. It's a very important matter.'

'Of course. I am not suggesting it isn't, it's just . . . I am struggling for time at the moment.'

'Is midday okay?' she asks.

'Fine. If that suits.'

'You know where we are?'

'Yes.'

'See you at twelve.'

The dialling tone screeches in my ear.

I place the phone face down on the desk, notice the trembling of my fingers, skin white with shock. I listen to the silence ring about the room.

I was a fool for believing I could ever get away with this. A guileless, desperate fool.

28

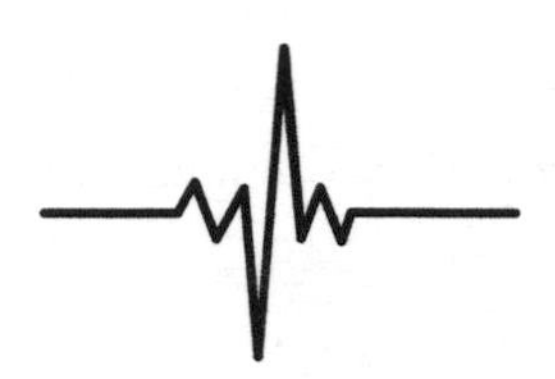

Rachel

Monday, 8 April 2019, 09:32

Last night I dreamt about the boy.

The CCTV footage of Zack Jones is grainy: no features, no details, just a form of white skin and blond hair reflecting the sun's rays. But in my dreams he was in focus, my mind morphing him with memories of my son, borrowing his freckles and the bright blue of his eyes. We were at the beach, and my eyes flickered shut with sleep; when they opened again he was gone, and I woke from the dream to the sound of myself screaming his name.

I couldn't get back to sleep after that.

I sit at my desk and rub the nape of my neck, looking at the printouts strewn across my desk.

Most of what Anna Jones told me has checked out. Her

brother Jeff Dunn, a therapist based in London, has a second home in Cornwall, and Zack's schoolteacher confirmed the boy spoke of spending the Easter break with him. But none of this explains why I have yet to hear from Mr Dunn, nor does it explain Dr Jones' recent behaviour.

I remember the panic that flashed across her face as I called her phone during our first interview in her home. The fear in her eyes told me everything I needed to know: she has something to hide.

No one needs three phones.

What's more, when I told her that we were there to discuss a serious incident, she had glanced unconsciously towards the victim's house.

Dr Jones knew of Paula's death before we told her.

I look down at the documents Diane faxed over: the traces of soil found outside the front door were also discovered inside. Someone appears to have run across the lawn, knocked over the plant pot, and entered the house, attempting to clean up after themselves before they left. If there was a key beneath the pot, it wasn't there when we arrived.

Why would Dr Jones not mention entering her neighbour's house on the day of her death? What does she have to hide?

The door to my office opens, and I break away from my thoughts, sitting up straight as Detective Chief Inspector George Whitman steps inside.

'Conaty, good morning.'

George is a burly man in his fifties: peppery hair, deep black eyes. His voice is low and gravelly, and his face is hard-set, but get a few drinks in him and his femininity slips out. I once asked him why he felt he had to hide himself away, and he laughed so hard he coughed up half of his pint. The force definitely has its issues with equality, no matter what the diversity posters plastering the halls claim.

'Morning, sir.'

'How's it going?'

'Good. I have the victim's neighbour coming in for an interview at noon, and I'm following up some inconsistences in her story as we speak.'

'Good start,' he replies, as he sits on the other side of the desk. 'Do you have any other lines of enquiry?'

'None that are as fruitful as this one. Footprints were found leading from the surgeon's house and across the lawn to that of the victim, whom she was close to. Her child might have been the last person to see Paula alive.'

'Her child,' he repeats.

My hackles rise at the word.

'Yes, sir. Is there a problem?'

He raises his palm in mock surrender.

'No, there's no problem. But I'd like you to keep other avenues in mind.'

'As in, other avenues that don't involve a child?'

He exhales sharply and sits forward.

'I'm just saying that we need to look at this from all angles.'

'What other angles would you suggest? I have been following the line of enquiry with the most unanswered questions: why is Dr Jones averse to talking to me about her neighbour's death, the very woman who she entrusted with her child's care every day after school? Why are there footprints across the victim's lawn, which suggest an adult was running between the two properties? And who would know the victim better than the woman who lived beside her, saw her every day, and trusted her with son's welfare?'

'But that isn't what's bugging you the most, is it?' George asks calmly. 'It's that you can't confirm her son's whereabouts.'

'Why is that so strange?'

'Because neither of the boy's parents have reported the boy missing, and while you pool all of your focus on the Joneses, you're neglecting the signs of highly organised criminal activity: pulled teeth, severed fingertips, the ligature marks around her wrists which suggest she was tied.'

'My team are working on all of this.'

'Then why aren't you?'

We stare at each other across the desk.

'I read your case notes,' he says. 'I'm not saying what you've found shouldn't be followed up, but I would like to see a more well-rounded take on the motive: previous crimes matching the same MO, potential ties to known criminal rings. So far this is lacking.'

He gets up from the chair and straightens his blazer as he turns for the door.

'Have your interview with Dr Jones today and see what comes of it. Get in touch with the local police down in Cornwall and ask for them to do a welfare check on the boy if you have to, but then pass these duties to another member of the team. I want you tackling the bigger fish here.'

I sit silently behind my desk, picking at my cuticles until strips of nail litter my lap.

'Dr Jones wouldn't have been the one to pull out the victim's teeth or saw off her fingertips, would she?'

I swallow my pride and meet his eyes.

'No, sir.'

The words come out strangled, forced from behind clenched teeth. He nods, seemingly satisfied, and gets up for the door.

His hand freezes on the handle. I know what's coming, and feel the frustration rising through me.

'Rachel, if you need to talk to anyone—'

'I don't,' I reply quickly. 'I'll do what you've asked.'

Whitman lingers a moment, watching me as I pick at my files on the desk. When the door clicks behind him, I clear my throat and pick up my phone, typing in the phone number from the open file on my desk.

'Hello, is this Adam Jones? This is Detective Inspector Rachel Conaty from Redwood Police. I'm calling to ask a few questions about your wife.'

29

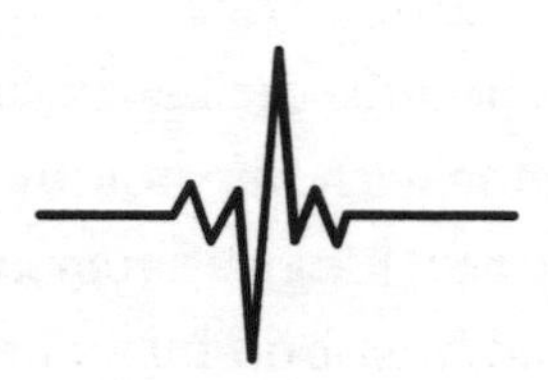

Margot

Monday, 8 April 2019, 11:03

I look up at the house I grew up in and feel my whole body fill with dread.

It is an ugly sight. There are weatherworn brown bricks on the bottom half of the house and cracked rendering on the top, with slips of green mould trailing beneath the windowsills. My bedroom window is still cracked. When the sun hits it at just the right spot, it sheds a slice of rainbow on the wall. I used to stare at it for hours.

Damien climbs out and slams the door behind him.

I get out of the car, twitching with reluctance. The air has the same old smell it always had: the tang of putrid water from the slip of river stagnating behind the estate that we used to frolic in as kids, the occasional kick of gasoline from the petrol station on the main road where Damien first taught me to steal. But perhaps the most overwhelming is the unavoidable stench of old cigarette smoke radiating from Ma's house, as if she is still in there puffing away, waiting for me. If the council were to ever knock the place down, orange tar would bleed from the walls.

I follow Damien as he slips the key in the lock, turns it to the left, and barges the door with his shoulder to release the catch. It has been like this for as long as I remember.

As he steps over the post and kicks off his shoes, I remain at the threshold, reeling from the familiar scents drifting out to greet me: a concoction of smoke from cigarettes and weed, lard radiating from the kitchen where the smell has fried into the walls. If I listen closely, I can still hear it crackling in the pan, the smell of bacon drifting into the hall. It was the only thing Ma knew how to cook.

'Come on, then,' he says, holding the door open, a flash of underarm hair creeping from his short sleeve.

I step inside and jump silently as the door closes behind me.

It is exactly the same as when I left. Bobbled plaster on the walls, with dizzying swirls of Artex above my head. There are countless memories stained into the shag carpet beneath my feet, worn and frayed from dirty soles.

I slip out of my shoes and trail behind Damien into the living room, my heart rattling against my ribcage and the smell of Marlboro Reds filling my lungs. I stop dead in the doorway when I see it.

Ma's armchair. I remember her so vividly, as if she were right before me, with her legs curled beneath her and smoke trailing from the end of her cigarette, dressed in the pink dressing gown that was littered with fag ash, and cropped dark hair, wild and knotted with silver emerging at the roots. I wonder what she'd say if she saw me now.

You got fat.

Damien sits down on the settee and kicks his feet up; the same suite I remember from my childhood years. He takes a long spliff from a tobacco tin and lights it.

'How've you been, then?' he asks, his voice strained from holding back smoke. 'You still got that boyfriend?'

The rich one you left us for, Ma whispers in my ear.

'We broke up,' I reply, frozen in the doorway.

So you thought you'd come crawling back.

The air has been slowly leaving my lungs since I stepped inside, but standing before Ma's chair – seeing her, hearing her, smelling the cigarette smoke and bacon fat – my airways close shut. I look to Damien, teetering on the verge of laughing or crying, and turn for the front door as quickly as I can, just getting a brief taste of the fresh open air before he slaps his hand against it and slams it shut.

'Don't do this,' he says, his breath reeking of ganja. 'Don't leave again. Not yet. Just give yourself a minute.'

'I can't . . . breathe,' I hiss.

'You fucked off for fifteen years, don't you think you owe me a minute?' He turns me towards him and cups my face in his hands, hard. 'Come on, I've missed you. Please.'

I stare at the latch, willing it to turn.

'Go have a bath and wind down, you're just in shock, that's all.' He lets go of my face and rubs my back softly. 'It's not like you have anywhere else to go.'

I glance up the stairs to the shadows on the landing, taking short, sharp sips of air into my lungs.

I used to be so afraid of the dark that I would often stand

at the doorway of my bedroom, too scared to walk across the landing to use the bathroom. I wet myself so many times, and would crawl back into bed, damp and shaking, knowing Ma's rage would erupt when she saw another puddle soaked into the carpet.

It's not like you have anywhere else to go.

'Go on.' He nudges me towards the stairs.

I nod, too exhausted to fight him, and climb the stairs, the floorboards creaking familiarly beneath my weight. When I reach the last step, I see the family photo is still hanging on the wall at the top of the stairs: Ma, Damien, the Alsatians Penny and Spike, back when they were alive. But I'm not there.

Ma had cut me out.

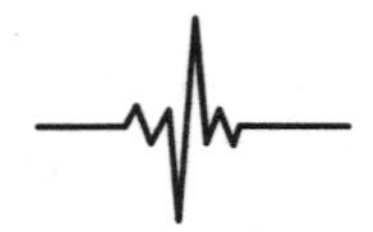

The small box room I used to call my own has been stripped bare of my existence. There are tape marks on the wall where my Nirvana posters once hung, and the single bed pressed up against the wall is being used as a dumping site for mounds of tat: a dusty clock that stopped ticking long ago, cardboard boxes that never made their way back through the loft hatch above my head. The desk beneath the window is the same. On the back of the door hang some clothes and a sticky note with my name on, written in Damien's scrawny handwriting.

I slip into the clothes in the middle of the room, shivering all over as I hop into the jogging bottoms and knot them at the waist. I stayed in the bath until the water turned cold and my skin pruned. My hair is still damp, plastered down my back.

I slip the white vest over my head, then the hoodie that

drowns my small frame, until there is nothing more I can do but stand in the centre of the room and take it all in. I look at the desk beneath the window where I used to study into the early hours, desperate to learn all I could and escape. To think that it was all for nothing, that years later I would be back. I push the junk up the bed and perch on the corner with a sigh.

I am about to be a single mother, with no support, no job, no home. I will never work in nursing again with theft on my record. Hell, I could be facing prison. The qualifications I strived so hard for are now worthless pieces of paper. I'm back exactly where I started.

My hand drifts to my belly. If I'm convicted, I will have to give birth in prison. They will take the baby away and give it to some middle-class couple, and I will forever be known as the wayward mother who couldn't care for her child. I imagine the baby as a girl, small and innocent as I was when Ma had me, growing up and realising that her mum was just as rotten as mine; a lineage of bad mothers corrupting their young.

The chain stops with me. I'll do whatever it takes.

The only thing holding me back is money. People say it doesn't make you happy, but I have never been as miserable as I've been when I'm poor. If I had the funds, I could run. Skip bail and start over with a new name.

I hear Ma's voice whispering in my ears, repeating the last words she said to me before I walked out the front door.

However far you run, however many lies you tell yourself that you're better than the ditch you were born in, it'll always be in your blood. You can't outrun your DNA, Maggot. But I'm sure you'll die trying.

I would love to say she was wrong. Wrong about everything

she ever said to me. But I'm back here, exactly where I started. Just like she said.

How would I get the money? It's not just thousands I'd need, but tens of thousands.

There is no way I could steal enough to raise the sum I'll need, and if I were caught and charged for running, I wouldn't be granted bail again. I've only got one chance, and I have to do it right.

The only way I'll get it is if I know someone with a lot of money to spare.

I sit in silence, thinking of names and faces and batting them away, one after the other, until one appears, and finally sticks.

Dr Jones.

She has a Mercedes, the large diamond rings, the big house behind the hospital. Christ, she has money to burn. And I just witnessed her commit murder.

A plan starts to form in my head, and my heart thumps wildly, as one word comes to me and makes everything fall into place.

Blackmail.

I glance down at my stomach. A shiver of panic runs down my spine at the thought of it swelling with life. This kid will have a better start in life than I did, even if it kills me. I feel my will to fight return, like a fire in my gut.

I've got someone else to think of now. If I don't do this, I'll go to prison and they'll take the baby away. Give it to a pair of snobs like Dr Jones. I'm not the bad person here – she's the one who killed a man. I'm merely making her pay for what she's done.

As the guilt starts flickering within me, I think of the scalpel slicing down Mr Shabir's aorta. The gush of blood filling the cavity behind his ribcage.

She made her bed the moment she stuck the blade in him.

I catch sight of the slice of rainbow shining on the wall where the sun is hitting the crack in the windowpane, and reach out to touch it. All I feel is cold plaster beneath my fingertips, but it reminds me of how I felt when I was young, staring up at its beauty in innocent wonder: hope.

I'm getting out of here – I just have to stay on Damien's good side until I get enough money to run.

I pad barefoot to the door and stand on the landing with my dirty clothes bundled in my arms, listening to the silence of the house. Damien had called up the stairs while I was in the tub to say he was off to collect Rick, which gave me time to calm down, to see this place as nothing more than a house. Ma's memory, Ma's voice, they are all in my head. But as I stand on the landing, the memories still call to me in whispers.

I walk down the stairs and put my clothes in the wash, using muscle memory to work the machine, then head into the lounge and sit on the sofa opposite Ma's armchair, curling my bare feet beneath me to warm my toes.

The armchair morphed to her shape over the years. The cushions have dipped from the weight of her, and the arms look worn from her grip. On the side table, she would keep a packet of Marlboro Reds and the crystal ashtray she nicked from the pub, surrounded by half-empty pill trays.

Everyone knew that Ma was a drug addict. Everyone, that is, except Ma. She said she took pain meds for her *bad tooth*, the molar that turned completely black with decay. Sometimes, as a child, I'd catch a whiff of it rotting at the back of her mouth.

They killed her, of course, not six months after I left. She took so many pills that she actually stopped her own heart while she slept. I heard down the grapevine that Damien was trying to find me to tell me the news and bring me home for the funeral, but I never did come back. With no father in the picture I became an orphan overnight, for Ma took his identity to her grave; one last thing to hold over us for eternity. Maybe that's why I still see and hear her so clearly: I didn't get the closure I needed. I didn't get to see her dead.

I hear a key enter the lock on the door, followed by the shoulder barge to lift the latch. It isn't long before the smell of fish and vinegar seeps into the living room.

'Thought we'd have it for lunch instead,' Damien calls from the kitchen.

He makes his way into the living room with another man close behind, a pretty mixed-race lad with long eyelashes and cropped black hair.

'Rick, this is my sister, Maggot.'

'Hi,' he says with a smile. 'I'll go and dish up.'

Damien hangs behind, waiting for my verdict.

'He's lovely.'

Too lovely for the likes of us.

Damien smiles proudly and passes me a plastic bag.

'I got you some things, thought you might need them.'

I peer inside and find cigarettes, deodorant, a toothbrush and paste. The grateful smile falls from my face when I see the box of tampons.

'Thanks,' I say. 'Look, I need you to drop me somewhere later.'

He doffs an invisible cap and drops a bow. 'Anything else, princess?'

'Maybe. Got any advice for extorting someone for a shit-ton of money?'

I watch as the words hit him: his eyes come alive, and a

smirk pulls at the corners of his lips. I imagine Ma smiling too, nodding approvingly from her chair.

Good girl.

'And I need you to get me a car.'

'Christ, you don't want much, do you?' he says, with a laugh. 'What do you want a car for?'

'I'll need a way to get out of town if shit hits the fan. How fast can you get one?'

'I gather you've got no money to pay for it?'

'You want me to pay for a stolen car? Can't you just ... take one?'

'I don't do the legwork anymore,' he says, looking slightly bruised that I thought so low of him. But he seems to consider my request, and nods with a sigh. 'My guy owes me a favour. I'll see what I can do.'

'Thanks.'

'Hey, I'm doing it for me too. Just earning my cut, right?' he replies with a wink.

Everything comes at a price. Ma taught us that. Damien isn't doing this for me: he wants the money he thinks he will get from me if he plays along. It's a shame he isn't wise enough to realise that I'm playing him at his own game.

'Of course,' I say, forcing a smile.

30

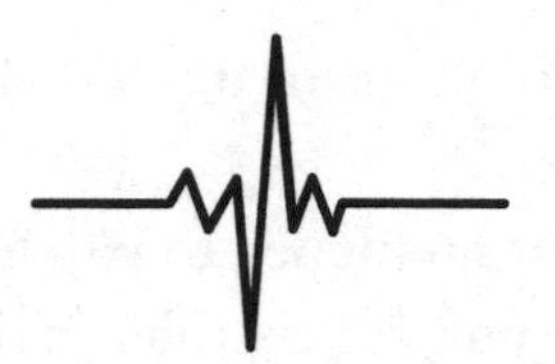

Anna

Monday, 8 April 2019, 11:05

After leaving the hospital, I drove around Redwood for hours planning what I was going to say to the police. I couldn't go home. I had to feel like I was fleeing, even if I was only going in circles. I wonder what the abductors must have thought, watching me drive around and around.

I pull down the private track towards home, taking deep, calming breaths.

Zack needs you. Your wits have got you this far.

But nearing the house only makes my anxiety worse – the place I felt safest has now become one of my biggest fears. The men didn't just break into my home. They took it from me. Even when the cameras are gone, and the locks are changed, and I finally get Zack home, there will be no going back. I will always feel their glares on my skin as I walk from room to room, remember the feel of the intruder's hand clamped across my mouth to stop me from screaming.

I reach the end of my driveway and slam on the brakes.

Adam's car is blocking the way. I spy him sat on the doorstep, glaring furiously at me behind the wheel.

'Oh God,' I say aloud. 'Not now.'

He rises to his feet and strides towards the car. I can tell he is angry just by the way he walks.

'What the hell is going on?' he asks as I step out.

Detective Conaty must have told him. I open my mouth to utter my first lie when I stop abruptly with a sudden thought.

If the house is bugged, maybe the car is too. Listening to me as they track my every move.

I slam the door shut and take him by the hand, leading him towards the end of the driveway.

'Not here.'

He yanks his hand from my grip. 'Our neighbour has been murdered and you didn't think to drop that into the conversation?'

'Adam.' I stare at him pleadingly. 'Not here.'

I turn away from the house and cross the lane towards the woodland. Adam follows behind me, the angry thump of his feet reverberating against the ground, his breaths quick and harsh behind my back. I walk between the trees and stop roughly fifty feet away from the treeline.

'I can explain everything, but first you need to calm down.'

'*Calm down*? I had a call from a detective this morning asking questions about you, about Paula's murder, and you expect me to act calmly?'

'Adam, please—'

'You changed the locks. I had to sit outside my own front door like a dog.'

'It's not like that—'

'First I'm not allowed to talk to my son, then you avoid my calls. I turn up to find out what's going on and discover you've locked me out. How the hell am I supposed to see it?'

'I'm being watched, all right?'

He stares at me in silence, mouth agape. We stand looking at one another, listening to the sound of an ambulance pull into the hospital beyond the trees.

'Have you lost the plot?'

'I got caught up in something, but it's all a misunderstanding.'

'You think you're being *watched*?' Whether consciously or not, he takes a step back. 'You're paranoid, you know that, right?'

He stares at me as if I'm mad.

'You know Ahmed Shabir? Our MP?'

'Of course I bloody do,' he spits. 'I'm not an idiot.'

'Well, he's dead.'

A mess of emotions crosses his face.

'Well, what does that have to do with you?'

'I killed him.'

'*What?*'

'I performed his open-heart surgery on Saturday, and he didn't make it.'

I watch as his shoulders unfurl, and his breathing begins to slow.

'That doesn't mean you *killed* him, Anna.'

I did. I killed him.

'I've been suspended and there is an internal investigation happening in the hospital. What if they find a way to blame me?'

'Now that *is* paranoid,' he says, and takes a step closer. 'You did nothing wrong.'

If only I had the privilege of being able to believe my lie too. It would be so much easier to bear.

'But Detective Conaty has it in for me. I was so stressed about what was going on that I must have seemed suspicious when she came to ask about Paula.'

'What, she thinks you killed her?'

'No, but—'

'Then what?'

'I don't know! She just has it in for me. Perhaps because Paula and I were close and I have been reluctant to talk to her. She must think I have something to hide.'

'Well you don't, so you have nothing to worry about.'

He gives my arm a comforting squeeze.

My tough upper lip starts to quiver from the comfort of his touch, and suddenly I long to be able to tell him what is happening to Zack and me. For him to take care of things for a moment so I can come up for air. But I know what will happen to Zack if I do.

He isn't going to back off unless I hurt him.

When I don't visibly calm from his words, he slowly lowers his hand.

'*Do* you have something to hide?'

'Don't be absurd.'

I pull away and walk absently back and forth.

'I'm stressed, all right? I have to go to the police station soon to talk about Paula, and then I have the internal interview with the hospital coming up, and the press is going to be reporting on Mr Shabir's death any minute and make my life a misery. I just need you to cut me some slack.'

'*Me?*' he protests. 'What have I done?'

'You're constantly pressuring me about Zack not having called, asking when I've spoken to him, when you think he will call you. I can't deal with all this and reassure you at the same time.'

I watch his expression fall, the guilt seep into his eyes.

'Well, I didn't think of it like that.'

'Zack needs space, and so do I. Let Zack enjoy his holiday without thinking of the divorce, and let me deal with the shit I'm in. When Zack gets in contact I'll call you. Until then, back off. We're divorcing, Adam. Start acting like it.'

He exhales sharply, and looks towards the trees.

'Is that why you changed the locks? To make sure I got the message?'

'Yes,' I lie. It comes out so abruptly that I almost wince.

'Wow,' he says, shaking his head. 'Well, message received.'

He turns back for the road, calling back to me as he cuts through the trees. 'You're blocking my car.'

I follow behind him, my hands shaking with adrenaline. The tension is palpable, and I can see by his tense shoulders and wide strides that he is upset.

'Adam,' I say, as we walk up the drive to our cars.

He turns back and I flinch. His eyes have sheened over. It's very rare that he will let me see him cry.

'If the detective calls again, please tell her to hash out her issues with me directly and leave you out of it. I don't want her causing more issues between us. If she doesn't let up, just ignore her calls until she stops.'

'You want me to ignore a police detective?' he asks. 'Won't that make her suspicious?'

'Give yourself some credit. You can be very deceptive when you want to be.'

He flinches at that. I had said it with venom, anger that had been festering in me since the separation. I used to keep my voice low and my words precise so as not to upset Zack in case he overheard; now the fury is finally working its way out.

He bites his bottom lip, as if keeping words at bay, and nods sharply. I watch as he unlocks his car and opens the door. He stops just before he climbs inside.

'Why do I have the feeling that you're lying to me?'

My heart rate spikes. I cross my arms.

'Not everyone lies to their spouses, Adam.'

I get in my car and slam the door behind me, swinging out of the drive and onto Paula's so he has room to reverse out. My hands are shaking at the wheel, my knuckles bloodless and white. I wait until he pulls away and speeds down the lane, road dust billowing around the car until he is out of sight.

I exhale slowly, the tension seeping out of me, and check the clock on the dashboard. It's time I left for the police station.

31

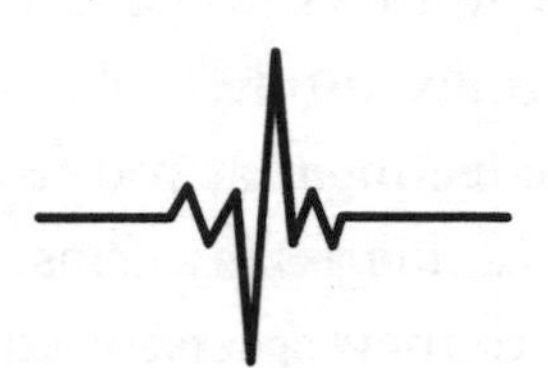

Rachel

Monday, 8 April 2019, 11:49

'Could you please say your name for the tape?'

'Anna Jones,' she says in a crisp, calm tone from the other side of the desk.

Her posture is straight, body language tight and composed. She is dressed in a smart blouse and trousers, with not a single hair out of place, and yet there is still something off about her. I notice her eyes are an aggravated pink. Either she hasn't been sleeping well or she has been crying.

'Thank you for coming in today. I appreciate that it was quite a shock when we first spoke. I trust you feel able to talk more with us today?'

'Yes,' she replies flatly.

'Great.'

I clasp my hands on the desk and lean forward. DS Ryan sits poised beside me.

'I'd like it if you would describe the relationship you had with Paula Williams, and share the ins and outs of your day on Thursday, fourth of April. Hopefully this might shed some light on what happened to her.'

'Of course,' she replies calmly. 'I'm happy to help. Although I'm afraid I didn't see Paula at all on Thursday.'

'When was the last time you saw her?'

'When I arrived home from work the previous evening around six o'clock.'

She didn't even have to think about it. No brief pause to sift through her memories, no sight of her eyes darting with recollection.

Almost as if she has rehearsed what she plans to say.

'Paula had collected Zack from school and made dinner for him and me, as she usually does. Zack had eaten and was in the living room doing his homework with the television on, while Paula was reading a book. It was a very normal scenario.'

Dr Jones appears to be a very cold person. She speaks with a cool, monotone voice, with no bubbling inflictions or accompanying facial expressions. She speaks straight and her face is motionless, despite the conversation being about her murdered friend. I can't imagine her having friends at all.

'Did you pay Paula for these services?'

'I asked if I could pay her multiple times, but she refused. Her daughter had moved to Australia and her husband had passed away not long before we moved in next door. She wanted to feel useful. Her words, not mine.'

'You're a lucky woman. Many people would kill to have an arrangement like that.'

I wait to see if she reacts at the word, and spot the corner of her mouth twitch.

'How did you become friends with Paula?'

'Detective, haven't we've gone through this—'

'It's for the benefit of the tape, Dr Jones.'

Her eyes linger on mine, and I watch as frustration bubbles up behind them.

'Through my son. When we moved in next door, Paula and I would greet each other when we crossed paths; usual neighbourly etiquette. Zack often rides his bike up and down the track, and it was then that they started talking to one another while she gardened. It grew from there.'

'Your other neighbour . . .' I pretend to remind myself of her name and glance down at my notepad. 'Jenny Howard, she described your son as a lonely boy, with few friends.'

I see a crack appear in her façade. Her lip twitches again, and her eyes narrow.

Her weak spot is being criticised as a mother.

'Perhaps. We had just moved from London. Although I'm not sure what that has to do with Paula's death.'

Another deflection. Any mention of her son and she quickly bats it away.

Why is she so reluctant to talk about her child?

'Of course,' I reply. 'What I meant was, perhaps that's what Paula saw and instigated her desire to befriend him, and vice versa.'

'Perhaps.' She smiles politely, but it doesn't reach her eyes.

'So I assume that helped bring you and Paula closer?'

'Yes, we would stop and chat for longer, and Zack and I would wave at her in the mornings where she sat at the window drinking her morning coffee. She noticed I was struggling to balance full-time work and Zack and offered to help out. Our friendship blossomed from there. We became particularly close after my husband and I separated.'

'It sounds like she became a big part of your life. You trusted her with your child, and she cooked and cleaned for you every day. That sounds like quite the set-up.'

'One that benefited us all,' she replies matter-of-factly.

'You said you would wave at her every morning,' DS Ryan says from beside me. 'Did that continue after Paula started assisting you in the afternoons?'

'It did.'

'Only you just told us you last saw her on Wednesday,' he replies. 'You didn't wave at her on Thursday, fourth of April?'

She thinks back, glancing upwards.

'You're right. That's when I last saw her.'

'The morning of her death?' I ask.

'Yes. Zack and I waved at her as we made our way to the car. She waved back. Then I spent the day at the hospital. I'm sorry, I forgot about that. It was such a brief exchange.'

'Did you ever step onto the lawn to say hello?' DS Ryan asks. 'Approach the window to chat?'

She frowns. 'Not that I can recall. Why?'

'Our forensic team found footprints leading from your house, crossing the victim's lawn towards her front door. Do you remember anything about that?'

I watch her throat bob with a nervous swallow.

'I . . . well, no, I don't.'

'What size shoe are you?'

'A seven,' she replies, reluctantly.

'Our prints match a woman's size-seven shoe.'

'How odd,' she says, clearly flustered.

'They appear to have been left at a fast pace, as if the person was running.'

I can see her scrambling for an excuse, her eyes busy with thoughts.

'Oh! Of course, that was me.'

'It was?' DS Ryan asks curiously.

'My dog,' she says. 'I was rushing out of the house that morning and he slipped by me. I had to chase after him and bring him back inside.'

'Another thing you forgot about that morning?' I ask.

'I was in a rush. I'm a single parent who works full-time, Detective. Mornings never run smoothly.'

'I see.' I glance down at my notes, trying to hide my frustration. The woman can excuse anything.

'When speaking to Mrs Howard, she also mentioned seeing several removal vans leaving your end of The Avenue, on the day of Paula's death.' I watch her eyes widen a fraction. 'Do you know anything about that?'

She composes herself quickly, and smirks, seemingly amused.

'Mrs Howard is . . . a character. She likes to stick her nose in other people's business. I would take everything she says with a pinch of salt.'

'Noted. But that still doesn't answer my question.'

The smile falls from her face. 'My husband and I are divorcing. He was having some of his things taken to his new address.'

'And he can corroborate that?'

'If it's really that important to your case . . . yes, I'm sure he would.'

She is brilliant at condescension. So effective that it almost makes me doubt myself.

'You had arranged for Paula to escort Zack to meet with your brother for the trip to Cornwall, is that right?'

'That's correct.'

'Where was the handover expected to happen?'

'They met by Kathleen's Diner. It's halfway between the school and the M1 junction Jeff uses to reach Redwood.'

'Why didn't Jeff pick him up from school?'

Her eyes reveal a flash of fear. Almost as if she had failed to rehearse an answer to the question.

'What do you mean?'

'Well, if Jeff was driving from London to Redwood, why not drive to the school directly, and cut out the middleman?'

'Cornwall is a long drive,' she says. 'Shaving off a detour like that seemed logical. That way he could avoid the traffic from school pick-up and simply collect Zack and pull back onto the M1.'

'That's a long way for a woman in her sixties to walk, isn't it?'

She frowns.

'I'm not sure I agree with that. Forgive me, but you're what, in your fifties? Do you think you'd be incapable of walking a few miles in a decade's time?'

'Not for a necessary purpose, but the reason is a bit trivial, isn't it?'

She is starting to crack. Her cheeks have flushed, and I can see a vein elevating in her neck.

'You also said during our first interview that you and your brother Jeff organised an exchange of your son's luggage prior to the trip. Are you saying your brother drove all the way from London, packed your son's luggage in the car, and drove all the way back home again, only to drive to Redwood and meet

Paula and Zack at the diner to shave off the ten minutes it would have taken him to drive to the school?'

She crosses her legs, a protective gesture. Her arms move as she rings her hands in her lap beneath the table.

'I'm sorry, I am a bit lost here. What does any of this have to do with Paula's death?'

Another deflection. I lean forward until I am close enough to smell her perfume: floral, yet sharp.

'As far as we can tell, Paula was last seen by your son and your brother at the diner. She didn't make it home, which suggests she was intercepted on her route home. Validating the details of where she might have been and why she was going there is of tremendous importance. So, how did you organise the exchange of luggage, Dr Jones?'

I watch her eyes twitch nervously as she thinks. Whatever she is about to say isn't coming from her memory – she is spinning a lie.

'My brother had some business close to Redwood last week, so he and I arranged to hand over the luggage then.'

'But surely there would be items Zack would need during that week? His toothbrush, for example?'

Her eyes narrow.

'I like to plan ahead. It's in my nature, due to my profession. I bought him travel-sized toiletries and a disposable toothbrush. If he loses anything it won't be such a big deal, because the items are only temporary. My brother can tell you all this when he calls.'

'Which reminds me. Why hasn't he?'

Her cheeks flush further, deepening until blotches form on her neck like hives.

'Forgive me, I didn't think it would be the highest priority on your list. You're investigating a murder – I wasn't aware knowing what my son was doing on his holidays would be of such interest to you. I will give him your contact details tonight.'

'You haven't spoken to your son or his protective guardian since Saturday?'

Her eyes fill with fury, and her glare burns. A few more prods and she'll break.

'I am a heart surgeon, Detective Conaty. I don't exactly have much time to spare. I had a very difficult procedure on Saturday, and then I got home and found two detectives on my doorstep, telling me one of my closest friends had died. This was after a long week of negotiating the details of my pending divorce. I needed a day to process everything. But now I know it's of such grave importance, when my brother calls tonight I'll ask that he get in touch. Now, do you have any questions for me about Paula? Or are you going to continue asking me questions about my private life? I thought I was here to help you gain insight into my neighbour's life, not to satiate your interest in mine.'

We stare at each other over the table, the tension pulsing in the air.

'As soon as we know Jamie is where you say he is, we can move on.'

She frowns and looks to DS Ryan at my side. I spot him turn towards me in the corner of my eye.

'Zack,' he says. 'The boy's name is Zack.'

I realise my error and look down at the surface of the desk, too embarrassed to meet anyone's eyes. My cheeks burn.

'I'm sorry. My mistake.'

I wish the floor would open up and envelop me whole. The tension we built has been shattered by my mistake, and all of the scrutiny that had been funnelling towards Dr Jones is now directed at me. Mark has tensed up beside me. The confidence he usually has in me is gone; he doubts me. Dr Jones is staring at me intently with the smallest of smirks on her face.

'Thank you, Dr Jones. If we have any more questions, we will give you a call. Until then, please do contact your brother. I would like to speak to him as soon as possible so that we can move on.'

'Yes,' she replies, standing up. 'I would like that too.'

'My colleague will show you out.'

DS Ryan escorts her from the interview room, and I sit alone, listening as the door clicks shut and the tape continues to roll.

His name is Zack, I remind myself, saying it over and over again to drill it into my brain.

Jamie is gone.

32

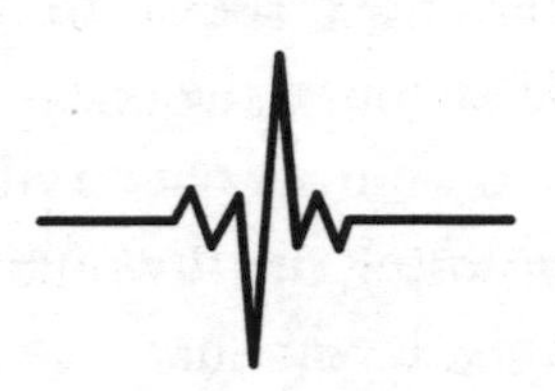

Anna

Monday, 8 April 2019, 12:57

The engine stalls for the third time.

'Shit!'

I slam my palms against the steering wheel and look anxiously in the rear-view mirror as the car behind honks its horn. I fumble with the keys, cursing under my breath. The light has turned green. The car sounds its horn again. When the engine finally turns over, I slam my foot on the accelerator and zip down the road.

The lies are catching up with me. There are so many of them that I am struggling to remember which lie belongs to whom. To convince one person, I must lie to another, and then another, and another. A never-ending spiral of deceit. Can a spider get caught in its own web?

Detective Conaty knows something isn't right. She doubted every word I said, pulled at threads in my story that I hadn't even known were there. Every time I open my mouth, I am merely borrowing time to think of my next step, but I cannot escape the feeling that everything I say and do will ultimately be my undoing. That the very lies I use to evade punishment will be used to persecute me in the end.

I jolt at the sound of the burner phone vibrating inside my bag.

They will have traced the car to the police station.

I pull into the nearest lay-by, hand searching frantically to retrieve it.

'Hello?' I say breathlessly.

'You will meet us tonight,' a deep, gravelly voice says. 'Ten p.m. in Littlebrook, at the old abandoned farm. It is signposted on the main road leading into the village – pass the gates and don't stop until you reach a barn. Don't be late.'

I open my mouth to speak just as the call ends. I sit in stunned silence, the dialling tone screeching in my ear. I drop the phone in my lap and rest my head against the wheel.

Do they think I co-operated with the police? He didn't give me a chance to explain that I was complying to try and shift the attention off me. If the abductors think I am betraying them, they will hurt Zack. Maybe they have already. I haven't heard his voice since I killed Shabir.

What if keeping Ahmed alive was my only collateral? The only thing keeping Zack safe? What if they killed him as soon as I did what they wanted?

My breaths grow shallower and shallower, until I can barely draw air.

Calm down. Zack needs you.

I close my eyes and lean back into my seat until the

hyperventilation slows, and my heart calms. When I open my eyes again, sparks of light dance each way I look. My gaze settles on the phone box situated on the corner of the street.

Jeff.

I unbuckle the seatbelt and snatch my purse from my bag. The noise outside hits me all at once: cars whizz past me on the road, brakes squeal sharply as the traffic lights turn red. I break into a run and shut myself inside.

The phone box smells of urine, and the phone itself is filthy, the keys smudged black with dirt. I take it from the cradle, force loose change into the slot and dial the number.

'Hello?'

'Jeff, it's Anna.'

'Anna? Where are you calling from?'

It sounds like he is outside. I can hear the crash of waves in the distance, and the occasional whistle of the wind crackling into the receiver.

'A phone box. Look, Jeff, I don't have much time.'

'Are you all right? You sound—'

'Something's happened and I need your help.'

'Okay.' He says it in his calm, therapist tone. I hate when he treats me like one of his clients.

'I'm going to give you a phone number for a police detective. She has asked for you to call her.'

'A *detective*?'

'I got caught up in something bad, Jeff. Really bad. I can't talk to anyone about it, but please trust me. I can't do this alone.'

'Do what alone?' he asks. The wind crackles into the receiver. 'Anna, you're scaring me.'

Could I tell him? I left the phones behind in the car. There are no cameras watching me in here, no microphones listening in. But the risk of hurting Zack with my words makes me freeze to the spot, tears of frustration burning in my eyes.

'The detective wants to speak with you because she thinks you're looking after Zack.'

He pauses on the other end of the line. I hear a gull squawk, and then Leila's voice. Jeff must have covered the receiver, for he replies in muffled words before the sound clears again, and Leila is gone.

'Why would the detective think that?'

'Because that's what I told her. Zack is in danger, and it is imperative that I keep the truth from the police to make sure he's safe.'

'You're not making sense—'

'*It doesn't have to make sense!*'

I sigh heavily, the anger seeping out of me.

'To keep Zack safe, I have to say that he is with you in Cornwall.'

'Well, where is he?'

'I can't tell you.'

'You can't expect me to lie to the police and not know why. Anna, I'm really concerned—'

'Do you trust me?'

He stalls. I hear a door click shut, and the noise of the coast vanishes.

'Of course.'

'Then please, just do this for me.'

'But Anna—'

'If you love Zack, if you love me, you will do this. I can't tell you why. I will, but only when I know Zack is safe.'

'You're asking me to commit a crime. If I lie to the police, and I'm later found out, I could go to prison. Leila would lose her father.'

'And if you don't do this, I will lose Zack for ever.' My voice breaks as the tears rise. 'Please, Jeff. I'm begging you. I know I'm asking a lot of you, but I wouldn't do this if I had any other choice. Please.'

'Dad!' Leila says on the other end of the line. 'I want to go back outside.'

I wait with bated breath.

Please, Jeff. Please.

'I'm just talking to Auntie Annie, poppet. I'll meet you out there.'

I hear a door open and shut. Jeff sighs deeply. Looking at his daughter must have plucked at his heartstrings, for when he speaks again, his tone has changed. The judgement is gone, and it is softer and passive.

'Okay.'

I sigh with relief, finally able to draw breath.

'Thank you.'

The call starts to beep. I open my purse, but I only have enough change for two more minutes.

'Do you have a pen and paper?' I ask. 'I don't have much time, and I need to give you the detective's number and tell you everything you need to say.'

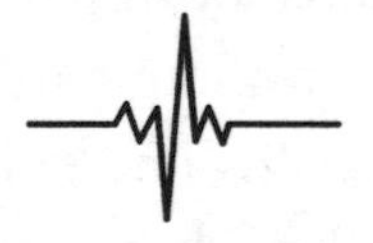

I wake with a jolt and a quick gasp for breath.

The dreams are getting worse.

When I am home alone, all I do is sleep. I drive myself

mad, pacing up and down the hall waiting for word from the abductors. When I sleep I can shut the world out, but each time I wake, the memory of my predicament hits me as if for the first time.

I lift myself up on my elbows and peer about the room through a tired squint. My vision is foggy, and there is fuzz on my tongue.

I am in the living room. The lights are off, but the blinds are down. The only light in the room is from the TV in the corner. The pills must have knocked me straight out.

I lift my feet from the sofa to the floor and sit up, my elbows on my knees, and rub my eyes until they sting. The tablets block out the noise inside my head, numb the pain in my chest, but the more I take them, the harder it seems to come round from their hold. I was prescribed them just before the move when my marriage was at its worst, but I decided not to start them in fear they would interfere with my work. I take a soothing breath and run my hands through my hair. Three long hairs drift towards the carpet.

I swipe my hands through my hair again, feeling the nervous tremble of my fingers working their way across my scalp. When I pull away, there are long, blonde hairs woven between my fingers. Shame washes over me, and I long to close my eyes again, fall back into the dark, painless abyss where the guilt can't reach me. I must have been plucking in my sleep again; pluck too much and surrounding hairs shed from the stress.

My eyes drift to the TV. The volume is so low that the broadcaster's voice is nothing but a mumble. But the breaking news headlines crawling along the bottom of the screen are clear as day.

BREAKING NEWS: REDWOOD MP AHMED SHABIR DEAD AT 40 • SECRET HEART OPERATION GONE WRONG • PM'S STATEMENT EXPECTED IMMINENTLY

I stare at the breaking-news banner, reading the words over every time they loop back around. *AHMED SHABIR DEAD* screams back at me. I snatch up the remote from the coffee table and turn up the volume.

'With this breaking news comes the speculation that Ahmed Shabir's heart disease was kept secret so as not to affect his re-election as Redwood MP, or hinder his widely assumed ascent to leader of the Labour Party—'

Bear barks at the sound of the door, breaking me from my trance.

My immediate thought is of the press. Could they be staked outside the house? That's what happens when a big story breaks, isn't it? But I didn't see or hear any mention of my name on the news.

Calm down. Don't think so far ahead.

But the cogs keep turning, and turning.

I get up from the sofa, envisioning hordes of journalists waiting for a statement. What if it is the detectives? They will have seen the news, adding another layer to their suspicions.

My lies are catching up with me.

I glance at my reflection in the mirror in the hall, teasing the knots and wild flicks out of my hair, and open the door.

The person stands alone, in the shadows of the night. A sly smile pulling at the corners of her lips.

It's Margot.

33

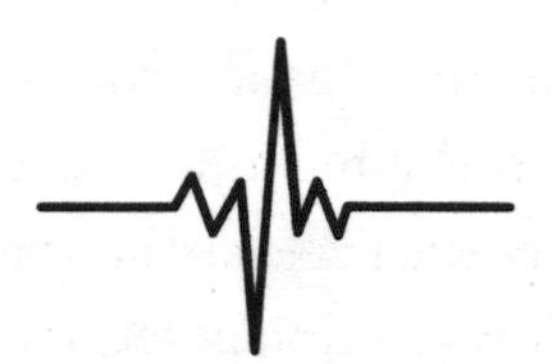

Margot

Monday, 8 April 2019, 20:25

The door opens slowly, until I see a slither of a face: Dr Jones peering through the gap. She frowns as she recognises me and opens the door wide.

She looks awful. Her hair and clothes look slept in, and her eyes have a drunken sheen about them, but something about her demeanour tells me it isn't drink. Growing up with a mother addicted to prescription pills makes it very easy to spot the side effects in others.

'What're you doing here?'

Everything I rehearsed has gone. I might be a thief, but extortion is a whole new game, which takes nerves of steel and a lack of conscience. It is stealing, yes, but now I must look her in the eye as I do it.

She releases an exacerbated sigh, as if my mere existence is a waste of her time. My guilt vanishes instantly.

'I know what you did,' I blurt out.

The frown vanishes from her brow, and her eyes widen; little hints of the vulnerability she usually hides so well.

'What?'

'In the operating theatre. I saw you do it.'

She looks at me as if she has no idea what I'm referring to, but she can't hide the panic in her eyes, the nervous bobbing of her throat as she swallows. A dog pokes its head around her legs and stares out at me, its pink tongue jumping with its breaths.

'Do what, Margot?' she asks, stepping down from the doorstep and pulling the door to.

'You killed Ahmed Shabir.'

She stares at me for a long time. Frozen like a deer.

'I watched you do it. You took the scalpel and ran it along his—'

'All right,' she snaps. 'Wait here a minute.'

She steps back inside, and I stand shifting anxiously from side to side. When the door opens again, she has the dog on a lead.

I take a nervous step back as they approach.

'What're you doing?'

'Come with me,' she says, and heads towards the woods.

This wasn't how I imagined it. I thought I would tell her what I know, and what she would need to do to keep me quiet, and it would be done. She would promise to abide by everything I asked. But somehow she has snatched the reins.

'Come on,' she hisses from the shadows.

I follow her into the dark, the gravel on the lane crunching beneath my shoes.

'Watch the verge.'

I stumble down a small ditch beside the track, scuffing my knees. My cheeks burn with embarrassment.

'Where are we going?' I ask, dusting myself off.

'Somewhere private.'

She walks on towards the woods, with only the light from the moon to guide us, until she slips beneath the dark canopy of the trees. I look in from the woodland edge.

'This is far enough.'

I listen to the snap of twigs beneath her feet as she makes her way back to the edge. We stand a metre apart: me in the clearing, her in the shadows. She unleashes the dog and it sets off beneath the trees, sniffing at the earth.

'I assume you've come to try and blackmail me.'

'Something like that, yeah.'

'And you think people will believe you?'

The wind rustles the trees, shedding brief seconds of moonlight on her face. Her lips are set in an obnoxious snarl.

'If you were to tell anyone at the hospital what you *think* you saw, can you honestly say that people would take your word over mine? I mean, who are they more likely to believe? A renowned surgeon with an impeccable record? Or a disgruntled ex-employee who was fired for stealing?'

I cross my arms tightly over my chest.

'The hospital might think that, but the police will want to look into it once I've filed a report with them. Your record won't be so clean then. And with the police breathing down their necks, the hospital will look a little closer and see the tell-tale signs of that cut you made. That's if they aren't already feeling the heat from seeing Ahmed Shabir all over the news. It won't be so easy for them to dismiss me when the evidence is right under their noses.'

The wind picks up again, blowing my hair around my face. I pinch the locks away and tuck them messily behind my ears.

'The difference between us, Anna, is that I have nothing to gain from lying, and you have everything to lose – your son, your career, wealth. The police will see that too.'

She falls silent. I search for her face in the dark in an attempt to read it.

'What do you want?' she asks finally.

'Fifty grand.'

She bursts out laughing. I jolt at the suddenness of it.

'That's absurd.'

'You earn more than double that in a year. There's a gigantic sum of money in bricks and mortar over there, and a brand-new Mercedes on the drive. You've got more than enough to spare.'

'I really don't.'

'That's your concern. I want ten thousand by midday tomorrow as a down payment.'

'And if I don't?'

'I'll go straight to the police, then the press – I'm sure they'll pay handsomely. I'll get my money, Anna. I don't care how. It's up to you whether you want this to go in your favour.'

I stare into the darkness, catching only the faint movement or flash of skin when the trees move with the wind, casting slips of moonlight onto her face.

'You have a choice to make,' I say. 'You can walk away fifty grand lighter, or in handcuffs. Think about how much your freedom is worth. How much your pride will cost you when your son is left without his mother.'

I turn back for the lane, bidding my final words over my shoulder.

'I'll call your work phone at ten a.m. tomorrow and tell you where to meet me.'

'*No*,' she says abruptly, stopping me in my tracks. 'Don't call me. Meet me round the back of the hospital at eleven. By the bins.'

'Fine,' I reply. 'Don't be late.'

I walk on, heart thumping, a smile creeping across my face.

Tomorrow morning I will be ten thousand pounds richer.

I can't help but laugh to myself in the dark.

34

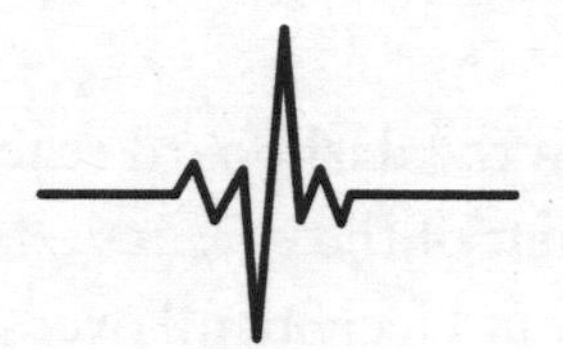

Anna

Monday, 8 April 2019, 21:50

I pull up outside the barn on Littlebrook Farm where an array of cars are parked out front, and eye its towering doors, the edges aglow from the light within. I recognise the Audi that tracked me to the police station all those days ago.

I grip tightly onto the steering wheel as stress pulses at my crown. Thin blonde hairs litter my lap where I have been picking at my arm on the drive. I am being pulled in so many different directions, what with the abductors, the hospital, the police, and now Margot, and I long to scream until everything stops.

I knew there was something off about Margot, but I never thought she would be capable of blackmailing me. Just remembering that smug look on her face as she stood on my doorstep is enough to make me feel sick.

One thing at a time.

I am early. They told me not to be late, but I'm not sure if they will appreciate me arriving too soon, either. I sit listening to the sound of crickets dancing and muntjacs barking in the distance as I try to calm myself down, stop myself from shaking. But I can't stop imagining all the things they might have planned when I walk inside.

When the clock on the dashboard reaches 21:58, I turn off the ignition and get out of the car.

The night is cool, but I feel hot all over. My heart is rampant and sweat coats my palms. Even the gravel crunching beneath my feet sounds sinister. When I reach the door, I hear the murmur of voices fall at the sound of my presence, and rap my knuckles against the wood.

'Come in,' a man says.

Ten men greet me with silence, stood shoulder to shoulder, dressed in black suits and crisp white shirts. The blue-eyed man stands in the centre with a sly smile on his face.

'Close the door.'

My hands jitter at my sides, both with nerves and the urge to lunge at him.

This monster has my son.

I turn and shut the door behind me.

'I did what you asked,' I say.

'You did. Now you must get away with it.'

Ten pairs of eyes stare back at me. The shaking gets worse, rattling down my spine to my legs. I clench my knees together and grip my hands so tightly behind my back that I hear a knuckle click.

'You're losing control of the situation. The police are closing in, and the hospital is investigating you. How do you think that looks to us?'

'I'm not losing control,' I stammer. 'I'm doing everything I can.'

'They haven't backed down. You are still a person of interest to them.'

He comes closer, his steel-capped boots crushing the dead hay littering the ground. I feel every muscle in my body tighten. When he brings his arm from behind his back, I flinch, expecting a strike across my cheek. He watches me squirm and smirks.

In his hand is a black folder.

'Use this to deter the police investigation into your neighbour's death,' he says. 'As for the death of Ahmed Shabir, well . . . the police will be led by the hospital investigation, yes?'

'I . . . believe that is the case.'

'Then convince them.'

He says this with such a searing stare that I flush and look away. I feel the heat of his breath against my lips.

'Look at me,' he says sternly, until I meet his eyes. 'Tell me you'll convince them.'

I nod quickly.

'I will.'

'Then you and your son will live. Do I need to remind you what will happen if you don't?'

I shake my head.

'You may go,' he says, waving his hand dismissively in my direction as he turns away. The rest of the men join him and turn to leave down the long corridor of stalls, where another door stands ajar, creaking in the night.

'How do I know you're telling the truth?' I ask, my voice quivering. 'That he isn't already dead, and I'm doing this for nothing?'

He turns and charges towards me, his face a furious shade of red. I back away nervously and bump into the set of doors, and yelp as he raises his foot and kicks them open. I land on my back in the dirt, breathing in the cloud of dust, and lose my grip on the folder he gave me. Papers scatter with the wind.

He snatches me by my jacket and pulls me roughly to my feet.

'*What are you doing?*' I cry out as he tightens his grip on my collar and drags me into the darkness.

My hair is caught in his grip on my collar, snagging at my scalp until my eyes water. I try to pull away. He grips harder. In the distance, a moonlit clearing slowly appears. I spot the mouth of a well and my legs buckle.

I think of Paula staring up from the murky water. The dark hole in the centre of her forehead.

This is where they dumped her body.

'*No! No, please! I'm sorry!*'

My feet scuffle along the ground, and the night air gets caught in my throat. My flailing hand knocks against the gun at his waistband. I imagine Paula dead at the bottom of the well, the bullet hole in her brain.

'*I am doing everything you asked!*'

We get closer, and closer, until I can see the moss covering the bricks, smell the stagnant water below. He thrusts me over the edge and I scream.

I sob desperately, dangling above the mouth of the well. The only thing keeping me from plummeting is his fist clutching my collar and hair. The stone lip of the well is digging into the bones of my hips, and I watch helplessly as debris breaks away from the wall and take seconds to finally reach the water. If he were to let go, it would be the end of me.

'Do you recognise it?' he whispers in my ear. His breath

smells of cigarettes and something sharp and sweet, like bourbon. He drops me an inch and I scream.

'Yes!'

He keeps me there, his hot breaths rasping in my ear, as I quiver in his grip and my tears fall to the water below.

'You do not ask me questions,' he hisses. 'You do as you're told, or you and your boy will be found down there with metal in your skulls, understand?'

I nod quickly, my voice escaping in a blubber of tears.

'Yes.'

He drags me back and chucks me to the ground. I scramble upright and thrust my back against the well, my chest heaving and tears streaming down my face as he walks off into the night.

'Please don't hurt him!' I shout at his back, my words echoing through the trees.

I close my eyes and stay there huddled against the well, shaking and struggling for breath, until the sounds of their engines dies off down the lane, and I am alone but for the shadows and the dancing crickets.

This is why he brought me here: to show me where they'd find our bodies if I fail.

I can't bear to think of Zack with these men, being a victim of their sudden bursts of violence.

I'm failing him.

A sound breaks me away from my thoughts, and I stare about me for the cause. A crisp white page from the file the man gave me has become caught among the long reeds, flapping with the breeze. I scuffle to my feet and rush to snag it before it flies away.

I hold it in the path of the moon, squinting to see the

words in the darkness. It is a photocopy of the front page of a newspaper. I read the headline repeatedly, and look to the photos beneath. One of a child. Another, of someone I have met before.

A smile creeps across my face, nervous laughter working up my throat.

This changes everything.

35

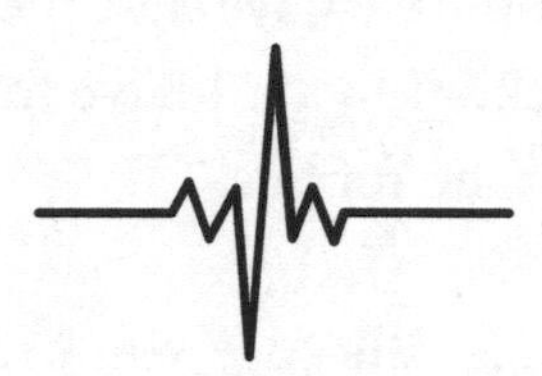

Margot

Tuesday, 9 April 2019, 09:45

'They're really just going to give me a car?' I ask from the passenger seat.

Damien is sat behind the wheel, the faint smell of ganja drifting off him whenever the breeze slips in the open window.

'No,' he replies. 'They're giving *me* a car that I'm passing on to you.'

He places two cigarettes between his lips and lights them, his eyes briefly leaving the road, before handing one to me. I feel the urge to take the wheel every time his attention drifts.

'That surgeon,' he says. 'She really killed that bloke?'

'I saw it with my own eyes.'

I grip the door handle as he speeds round the bend.

'She dangerous?'

'Only to people who trust her, and I don't.'

'Well, if she can kill that MP, I bet she wouldn't think twice about doing the same to you.'

I scoff and take a drag on the cigarette.

'She isn't a threat – she's a coward. He was unconscious, for Christ's sake. She wouldn't have had the balls to do it if he'd been able to fight back. Why do I have to stay in the car?'

'It's safer that way,' he replies.

'Safer for whom?'

'*Whom,*' he mocks. 'Who are you kidding with that shit? You sound like a proper twat.'

I roll my eyes and set my sights on the long country road tailing out of Redwood.

'Well, how long until we're there?'

'It's down the next left,' he replies, and glances over at me in the passenger seat. 'I mean it about staying in the car.'

'Yeah, I heard you.'

It's a rare sight, seeing Damien nervous. I haven't seen him scared since he was twelve years old and the owner of the corner shop caught him with a rucksack filled with stolen cider cans and threw him out the door by the scruff. Maybe he just got better at hiding it than I did. But he certainly seems nervous now.

'Look, if this is too big an ask, or will leave you with some kind of debt, I can find a car another way.'

'It's fine. I want to.'

He's not doing this for you. He's doing it for the money.

I didn't realise how alike he and Ma were, before I left. He talks like her, laughs like her, even his teeth are starting to turn like hers, a hardy yellow with a smoker's stains between each ridge. He must have a heart in there, beneath all of the hardness and the bravado. But then, this is the Barnes way: we take from everyone around us to protect ourselves, even our own. Isn't that what I'm doing, using him with the promise of a false reward?

I spot a mound of scrap metal above the shrubs lining the road, gleaming in the sun as it shines briefly through a break in the clouds. Damien slows the car and turns down the next left, marked with a large sign reading 'Redwood Quality Metals', which, ironically, is rusting. Beneath the name is a round symbol. It looks like two snakes coiled together, their heads meeting in the middle. They might be good with metals, but they're shit at branding.

Damien follows the long, bumpy track, scarred with pot-holes and craters in the earth. At the other end is a large warehouse surrounded by a wall of crushed cars piled on top of one another, and a small security hut where the lane meets the yard. Damien pulls up and winds down his window.

'Here to see Jax,' he says.

The man inside nods and waves him through.

'Who's Jax?'

'The less you know, the better.'

He pulls up beside a mound of metal and lifts the hand-brake, as the warehouse door opens and three men wearing black suits step out onto the forecourt.

'Wait here until I say,' he says sternly, and slams the door behind him.

I watch him cross the yard towards the men, shaking hands in that humorous masculine fashion, hurting each other to prove their strength, and glance at the dash for the time: it is almost ten o'clock. In an hour, I will meet Dr Jones and be ten grand richer.

I must stop calling her that. It makes it seem like she is my superior. Anna Jones is nothing more than a murderer.

I take a drag on the cigarette and catch sight of something in the corner of my eye. It's Damien, waving me over. A black Audi has been brought around and parked on the forecourt: it's the latest A3 model, and stunningly clean. It will be the nicest thing I have ever called my own. The men are nowhere to be seen.

I tried to live right for so long: I cut myself off from my family, went back to school, worked myself to the bone, only to end up right back where I started. And yet all I had to do to get a car like this was ask.

I step out onto the forecourt, shaking away the dark thought as soon as it forms.

Maybe Damien has it right.

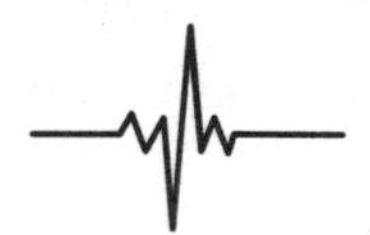

I park up the car a street away from the hospital and head towards the meeting place on foot. I was on a high for most of the journey, but as I got closer my nerves began to overtake me. One of my bail conditions was to stay away from the hospital unless it was a health emergency. This could see me locked up until my court hearing.

Maybe that's exactly what Anna wants. She could be leading me into a trap.

No. I'm being paranoid. She doesn't have a leg to stand on.

I follow the path towards the rear of the hospital, passing the outbuildings where they test the blood samples and biopsies, the scent of the bins following the breeze, and turn the corner.

Anna is waiting for me.

She looks better than she did yesterday. Her hair has been washed and blow-dried, and her clothes look expensive. Even her complexion looks better, rosy-cheeked beneath her sunglasses. But her expression is cold and uninviting, with straight-set lips and her head held high.

'You're late,' she says.

My fingers fidget at my sides. What I wouldn't give to shake the arrogance out of her.

'Got the money?'

She reaches into her bag and pulls out an envelope. Even from here I can see it is filled with cash, bulging against the confines of the paper. Saliva fills my mouth. I snatch it from her grasp and peer inside, counting off the fifty-pound notes.

'Erm, is this a joke? There's only five thousand in here.'

'You have to earn the rest,' she says calmly.

The anger fizzes up instantly. I have held it down for so long, biting my tongue, taking every blow life has given me. But her indifference tips me over the edge. I stride towards her and pin her up against the nearest bin, my forearm pressing into her neck.

'I don't think you understand,' I hiss. 'You don't get to negotiate. Either you give me the money, or I talk. That was the deal.'

She has the nerve to smile. I press down harder. A vein swells in her forehead.

'No, you won't,' she replies, her voice hoarse from my arm pressing into her gullet.

'You want to test that?'

She reaches up over my hold on her neck and slips off her sunglasses, and we stare one another dead in the eyes.

'I know you won't because you can't afford to. You don't care about doing the right thing, or you would have done it already. All you care about is money. But you're not a bad person deep down, however much you try to hide the fact. So whatever shit you're in to make you act this way must be pretty bad. You obviously need this money desperately. Play by my rules and you'll get it.'

I look her in the eye, considering my options, until I let go with a frustrated growl.

'You're the most infuriating person I've ever met,' I spit.

'Likewise.'

I light a cigarette behind a cupped hand and take a long, heavy drag. When I look over at her, she is fixing her hair, and runs a delicate hand over her neck; the skin has flushed a riled pink from my arm.

'If you want my money,' she says, 'you'll need to know everything I'm up against. But once I tell you, it's done. There will be no going back.'

If my predicament is bad enough to make me blackmail a person, hers must be even worse to justify killing someone. I look down at the envelope of cash in my hand, shaking in my grip. Five thousand won't be enough to start a new life.

'Go on then,' I say with a nod. 'Tell me.'

'I mean it, Margot. If I tell you, you're in this too. I can't take it back.'

She looks at me for a long while, her gaze intense and unflinching. I swipe my tongue nervously across my lips. She seems to take my silence as consent.

'Lift up your top.'

'*What?*'

'I said lift up your top. I need to check if you're wearing a wire.'

I laugh, both from nerves and dismay, but she merely waits in silence. I roll my eyes and whip up my top, flashing her my bra.

'Turn around,' she says, twirling her finger.

I want to punch her. Knock the self-assured expression from her face. Instead I bite my lip and turn, lifting my top to flash her my back.

'Okay,' she says, as I face her. 'Now give me your phone.'

Now I *really* want to punch her. She is commanding me like she would a dog. *Sit. Lie down. Roll over.* I stare at her vehemently, my hands shaking by my sides.

'You could be recording on your phone,' she says impatiently. 'You'll get it back once I've said everything I need to say.'

I shove my hand into my pocket and thrust the phone into her palm, watching as she presses the home button to check if I'm recording, then turns it off and slips it in her bag.

Seemingly satisfied, she sighs, as if searching her mind as to where to begin.

'The day of Peter Downing's surgery, I returned home to find strangers inside my house. They had killed my neighbour and abducted my son. I was told the only way I would get him back alive was by killing Ahmed Shabir on the operating table. I tried to fight it, but there was no other way. That's why I did what I did. To save my son.'

I stand open-mouthed. I don't know what I had been expecting, but it wasn't this. She has been particularly vile recently – was it the stress of having her child ripped from her?

'*Bullshit,*' I scoff.

She stares back at me in silence.

'What, and I'm just supposed to take you at your word? This could be a lie to make me pity you and get me on side.'

She takes her phone from her bag and holds it up to me.

It is a photo of a child. At first, I think he is sleeping among a mess of blankets, but the closer I look, I see dirty, cold concrete on the walls and floor, the harsh lighting of a camera flash in the dark, and an IV needle poking from the back of his hand and snaking out of frame.

My mouth drops.

She's serious.

She pockets her phone again, maintaining that cold sense of control that makes her seem so inhuman.

'I did what they asked, but they still haven't given him back to me. Not only did I have to kill the patient, I must get away with it without detection – but the police and press interest have made them nervous. I won't get him back until everything dies down.'

There is not a flicker of emotion on her face, no waver in the pitch of her voice. Either she is reluctant to be vulnerable around me because I'm a threat, or she really is the coldest person I have ever come across.

'Cameras have been fitted inside my house – there is a tracker on my car; my phones have been tapped. If they find out I've told you, not only will they kill my son and me . . . they will kill you too. I meant it when I said there was no going back.'

My stomach drops as if I've been kicked.

'Wait, *what?* You said nothing about putting me in danger.' I chuck my fag to the ground and head for the path. 'Fuck you for pulling me into this.'

I feel her hand on my wrist. She yanks me back. When I turn, our noses are practically touching. She tightens her grip.

'You're in this now,' she hisses. 'If you speak a word of it, we'll both be dead. My son will die. He is eight years old, Margot. *Eight.*' She stares deeply into my eyes, hers watering at the mention of her son. 'I told you there was no going back.'

I yank my arm away and pace, running my hands through my hair.

'If you can see I'm already going through hell, why put me through more? What is *wrong* with you?'

'Don't be such a hypocrite. You came here to exploit me. You can't claim the moral high ground now that I've done the same.'

I light another cigarette, but this time it shakes in my grip, and the lighter refuses to flame. I push down so hard on the button that I'm sure it'll break. Anna wraps her hand around mine. It is cold, yet still. She slips the lighter from my grip and ignites it first time.

'We have to work together now,' she says quietly. 'This way, we both win.'

I stare deeply into her eyes, the cigarette growing soggy between my lips.

Don't trust her, I tell myself.

I hold my cigarette to the flame and step back, inhaling the toxins.

'Okay, well . . . Who's *them*? Who took your kid?'

'I don't know,' she replies, and chucks me the lighter. 'That's what I need you to find out.'

'*Me?*'

'I told you, they're following every move I make. And now I have the police after me, and the hospital starting an investigation into Shabir's death. I can't go anywhere without being traced – but you can.'

She glances down at her watch. When she meets my eyes again, her face has grown a shade paler, and her eyes look wider with worry.

'I don't have long. Do you have a good memory?'

She speaks with such conviction that every sentence is punchy and scolding, as if she is clicking her fingers at me to hurry my reply. I am not her comrade in this; she doesn't respect me enough for that. It is evident every time she speaks or looks at me; the self-righteousness in her tone.

'Good enough. Why?'

'Good,' she says, and takes a step closer. 'I need you to find out what Shabir was tied up in to get into this mess. I'm sure it has something to do with the anti-drug-trafficking measures he campaigned for in town, and all of the officials he was able to influence. If we find out what he was up against, we find out who these men are who have my son. I will get you a copy of Shabir's health records, there might be something there, but the rest is up to you. I'll give you the other five grand when you find out what he was up to, and then once I have my son back, you'll get the remaining forty grand.'

I thought I was getting money for simply staying quiet, but somehow I have been drawn into her mess. It has all happened so fast that I don't even know if I ever agreed to all of this.

I should have just taken the five K and run.

'There's no backing out of this now,' she says. The panic must be evident in my eyes. 'I've told you something that could risk my son's life.'

Every part of me is screaming to turn back. I couldn't possibly trust her enough to help her. I'd be watching my back more than my front.

'How would they know that you told me? I could walk away, and pretend you didn't say anything.'

'Because if it comes to them taking my life and that of my son's, I will tell them who you are, what you know, and how to find you. You'll be on the run for the rest of your life. You put my son and me in danger by trying to extort me; I won't forget that.'

This was a trap from the very beginning. She was never going to fear me, I was stupid to believe that. She is too intelligent, too calculating. I wouldn't put it past her to have concocted this plan while we spoke in the woods. She always seems to be one step ahead.

'So, you can turn around now and run until they find you, or you can work with me and leave town with a clean slate and fifty thousand pounds richer. I will need your answer in an hour's time. If you do decide to help, I need you to go and buy two untraceable phones while I'm gone. Meet me back here at half-twelve with the phones and we'll go from there.'

I watch in stunned silence as she takes my phone from her bag and hands it to me. She slips on her sunglasses and heads for the path.

'Where are you going?' I ask.

'To my interview with the board. When I come back I will bring the files with me. If you're here, we're on.'

'And if I'm not?'

She stares at me, her gaze searing through her sunglasses. I hate her, always have, but I realise now that she must hate me too.

'Then I wish you the best of luck. You'll need it.'

She walks away and vanishes behind the corner, leaving me alone behind the bins, the cigarette burnt to a nub between my fingers.

36

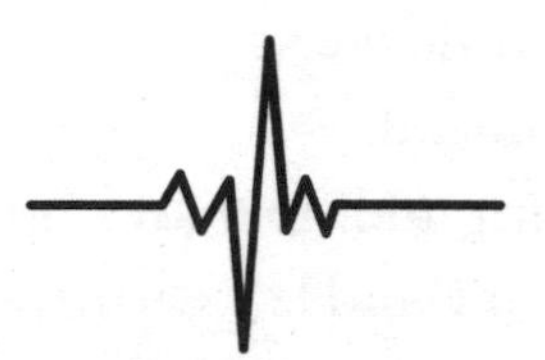

Rachel

Tuesday, 9 April 2019, 11:30

'Conaty,' DCI Whitman says from the doorway of his office. 'A word.'

Everyone in the room looks in my direction where I stand beside DS Ryan's desk. We all know that that tone of voice means something bad. I walk towards the office with my head high and my eyes straight ahead.

George is sat behind his desk.

'Take a seat,' he says.

I shut the door and sit down, watching as he rubs his hand over his buzzcut and emits a slow, full-bodied sigh.

'There's no way to beat around the bush with this, so I'm just going to come right out and say it: I got a complaint about you while you were out this morning. Someone called and claimed you're harassing them.'

My jaw drops.

'*What?* From who?'

'Dr Anna Jones.'

A burst of laughter leaves my lips.

'You must be joking.'

He stares at me, his eyes stern and unrelenting.

'She is concerned for your welfare.'

'My *welfare*?'

'Concerned that you might be projecting your own grief onto her child.'

I can imagine her using her dominating presence to lead the conversation. She has that ability to pull the focus of a room simply by stepping into it, I wouldn't put it past her to assert the same over the phone.

She has been looking into my past, and for what, to find ways to discredit me?

'That's absurd, sir. Of course I'm not. I'm just doing my job.'

'No, Conaty, you're not.'

He picks up Paula Williams' file.

'This isn't a child-abduction case, Rachel. It's a murder case with clear ties to organised crime. But instead of tracking down the victim's killer, you're obsessing about a child who, according to both of his parents and his current guardian, isn't missing. And yet you're still chasing it, even when I told you to back off. Why?'

He throws the file back down on the desk.

'Are you kidding? If Dr Jones' and her brother's accounts are true, this Jeff and the child were potentially the last people to see the murder victim alive. According to CCTV footage she didn't make it home, which must suggest she was intercepted en route. So validating the details of where she might have been leading up to her disappearance is of tremendous importance. And quite frankly, I couldn't give a damn about what the kid's family says – no one from law enforcement has confirmed his whereabouts.'

'Which brings me to the second complaint.'

'You have *got* to be kidding me.'

'Cornwall Police has been in touch. Apparently you're calling and berating officers?'

'Berating? I'm asking them to do their damn jobs, sir. They said they went to the address I provided for the suspect's brother and no one was there, and when I told them to stake out until they returned, they refused.'

'They can't just hand over two of their officers for them to sit on their arses all day for a kid that hasn't been reported bloody missing. They've been even more affected by budget cuts than we have and, believe it or not, Conaty, they have their own cases to work on.'

'This is about checking the welfare of a child.'

'*Who no one has reported missing*,' he snaps.

I jolt at the boom of his voice, and watch as the anger slowly seeps from his face. He sighs and looks to his lap as if to collect himself and his thoughts.

'I listened to the recording of your interview with Dr Jones.'

My heart sinks. I knew my mistake would come back to bite me.

'You mistook the boy's name for that of your son.'

Sweat trails down my ribs. I can feel it beading above my lip, moistening my palms.

'It was an honest mistake.'

'You're getting too caught up in this. The boundaries are blurring. I won't warn you about this again – if I hear of any more behaviour like this, I'll reassign the case.'

He stares at me across the desk, his frustration slowly giving way to concern. He picks up a handful of files from his desk and hands them to me.

'These are previous cases with the same MO that matches the murder. Work on these, nothing more. This is what you should have been doing all along.'

I know I should keep my mouth shut, but I can't help myself. The words tumble out before I can stop them.

'But sir, if I've heard through the grapevine that Dr Jones was Ahmed Shabir's surgeon, then you will have too. It can't be a coincidence that the surgeon's neighbour is murdered just before the death of such a high-profile—'

He raises his hand, his index finger pointed right at me.

'If you start spouting conspiracy theories about Shabir's death I'll reassign the case right now and refer you to psych.' He picks up the Paula Williams file and waves it back and forth, his eyes never leaving mine. 'If I find out you've been doing anything other than this, I'll hand your arse to you, understand?'

I hold his gaze until I can't bear it any longer. I give in and nod.

'Good. Now get to work.'

I stand and head for the door, my legs trembling with rage.

When I step out into the main office, everyone looks up at me expectantly. They must think I'm chasing a dead-end too. I glare back, watching as each pair of eyes falls to the surface of their desks, head to my office and shut the door firmly behind me.

Dr Jones used my own missing son against me. For a split

second, my impartiality seeps away and I hate her. A hot, simmering loathing burning in my chest. I know something is going on with her child, I can feel it, in the way that only the parent of a missing child can. Something is wrong with her son – Dr Jones knows it, and I know it. But why go to such great lengths to keep it hidden? What kind of mother doesn't report her child missing?

Her brother Jeff is just as shifty as she is. When I finally spoke to him on the phone this morning, he managed to find an excuse for everything I asked of him. Just like Dr Jones.

The police can come to the cottage, but I can't promise we'll be here. We have lots planned and I'm not going to spoil their holiday by waiting around. I can't take Zack to the station either, I'm afraid. It's two towns over, and the car is in the shop. I hit a rock in the road and it screwed the suspension.

You can't speak to him right now. They're both taking a nap after their swim.

I'd much rather you let us enjoy our holiday in peace.

Deceit must run in their blood. They seem to thrive on it. But if Dr Jones thinks that using my child's disappearance will make me back off, she's wrong. Now I want to find her son more than anything – and I won't stop until I do.

I sit behind my desk and pick up the phone, watching through the glass partition as DS Ryan answers the call at his desk.

'Come chat with me for a sec.'

I hang up before he can reply, and watch as he rises from his desk and heads for my office.

'Close the door,' I say, as he enters.

He sits on the other side of the desk, noticeably nervous.

'Yes, ma'am?'

'I need you to keep working on the Dr Jones lead.'

I watch his expression fall. His body tightens.

'Ma'am, I—'

'If you don't find anything, I'll drop it. But taking his parents at their word isn't enough for me. If you're found out, it'll be me who gets a bollocking, not you. Will you do it?'

He glances over his shoulder towards the door, as if looking for someone to back him up, or maybe even to do a runner. Leg it before I can drag him down with me.

'What do you want me to do, exactly?'

'Look into the journey the boy and his uncle would have taken to Cornwall. There will be hundreds of cameras between there and here. Trace his number plate for footage at laybys, speed cameras, the lot. No one could make that journey with two kids in the car without stopping. If you don't find anything, I'll drop it.'

I stare deeply into his eyes. He finally breaks contact and looks down at his feet.

'Yes, ma'am.'

'Look at me,' I say, and wait until he does. 'Thank you, truly.'

'I'm just following your orders, ma'am.'

My smile falls. I am sure that is exactly what he will say if we're found out.

37

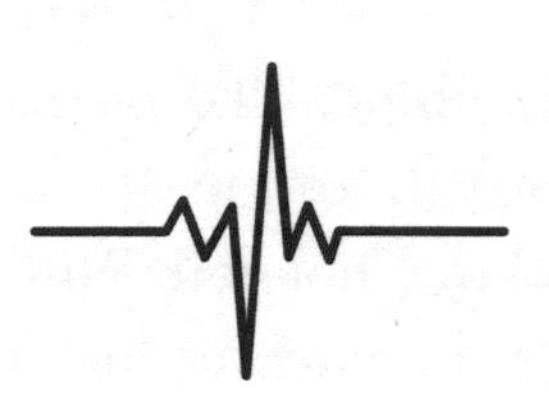

Anna

Tuesday, 9 April 2019, 11:50

I sit outside the interview room, my hands wrapped tightly around the handles of my bag.

I have gone over my story so many times that I could tell it in my sleep, but I have to stop myself from rehearsing it now, for fear of getting too complacent. I must say the words with conviction, use my nerves, allow myself time to recollect my next thread of lies as if thinking back to real memories, rather than having each stage of my story immediately to hand. It must come across as naturally as possible. I wonder when I became such a good liar.

My morning went to plan. When I woke, I did so without the burden of fear crushing down on my chest. Margot's plan to extort me should have made me feel worse, but I soon realised it was a gift. She has given me something – or someone – to control. I might not be able to move undetected, but she can, and she will; the stakes are almost as dire for her as they are for me. And then there is Detective Inspector Conaty and the file the abductors gave me, detailing the account of her son's disappearance.

I'm sorry about her son, I really am, I said to DCI Whitman. *She has been through an awful time. But that doesn't mean it is acceptable to harass my family and me. I'm sure you understand my frustration.*

I explained that if DI Conaty believed me uncooperative or on edge, it was due to the stress of my job, alluding to Shabir's surgery, and reminding him of my vow of discretion when it comes to my patients. He apologised profusely over the phone and promised he would handle the matter. All I had to do then was withdraw the cash from the bank and wait for Margot to walk into my trap.

I feel sorry for what Detective Conaty went through, but not at the expense of losing my son. She wants Zack to be safe, but what she doesn't realise is that by digging into our lives, she is putting him in the very danger she is trying to prevent. I will do all that I can to stop her. Even if it means destroying her career.

After putting in the call to the police station, I walked straight to the bathroom, flushed my pills down the toilet, and tied my hair into a tight bun to prevent any tempting stray hairs slipping from the fold. I can't fall apart anymore; I need to control myself. Self-pity and destructive coping mechanisms will get me nowhere. Zack needs me.

The door to the interview room opens, and the managing director of surgery, Keith Montague, appears.

'We are ready for you now, Dr Jones.'

He steps aside, giving me a view of the panel of desks accommodating the board of directors. They are all watching, waiting. I rise from my seat and step towards the interview room. Montague gives me a flicker of a smile; whether in alliance or pity, I'm not quite sure.

I slip out of the women's bathroom with folded tissue paper tucked beneath my underarms, and my face is still red and blotchy from the stress; my make-up practically wore off from perspiration.

I might have answered each of their questions calmly and rationally, using every word and phrase I had rehearsed, but the body doesn't lie.

Anyone would be a nervous wreck in that situation, whether they're guilty or not.

I tell myself this repeatedly, hoping that if I say it enough it finally will stick. But that doesn't stop the last question they asked me from ringing in my ears.

Is there anything you believe you could have done differently, or wish you had?

No, I tell myself as I reach the lobby. *I would do it all again, if I had to.*

Outside, the sun is beaming as if last week's chill hadn't occurred at all, and the stagnant air hits me like a hot slap. I follow the path leading behind the hospital, quickening my pace as I check my watch: I am twenty minutes late to meet Margot. That's if she is even there.

By the time I near the bins, the tissues beneath my arms are damp, and my face is speckled with perspiration from the stress and the heat. I turn the corner sharply with an intake of breath.

She isn't here.

Shit!

I pace back and forth, the rage in me building. I fight the urge to strike at the bins with my feet.

I had been so sure she would play along. Of course she would run, the little coward.

Despite the blackmail and the money, Margot had been my ray of hope; she was the one thing I could control. The thought of getting Zack home without her help seems impossible now.

I feel something land between my feet and look down to find a cigarette end burning on the ground.

Margot is stood with her arms crossed and a telling smirk on her face.

'Panic?' she asks.

I would sigh with relief if it wouldn't please her so much.

'Don't flatter yourself,' I reply, fixing my composure. 'I was worrying about the board meeting.'

'Sure you were,' she says. 'I've had time to think.'

My heart leaps. *Oh God, what now?*

'You've put me in danger by pulling me into your mess.'

'You wouldn't have been in this position had you not tried to blackmail me, Margot.'

She scoffs, running the tip of her tongue back and forth along her lip, as if holding back what she really wants to say. She steps forward until we are a metre apart.

'If you want me to run around town after you, I'll need more than fifty grand.'

'I don't have any more money to give you.'

'It's not money I want.'

She stares at me in silence, teasing out the tension until I feel sick.

'Oh, for Christ's sake, just spit it out.'

'Your rings.'

'My . . .'

My jaw drops, and I silently scold myself for showing weakness in front of her. I shouldn't care what becomes of them, they were given to me by a liar and a cheat. But it's the principle. They represent the entirety of Zack's life.

'It's not like you need them anymore,' she says. 'You'll give me the engagement ring when I get some dirt on Shabir, and the wedding ring when this is all over.'

A vile smirk creeps across her face. I hate her for it.

'Fine, but you're going to earn every penny.' I open my bag and thrust the files toward her. 'A copy of Shabir's health records.'

She takes the file from my grasp and slips it inside her bag.

'I want to know how Shabir was linked to this by tonight.'

'What? That's ridiculous. How am I supposed to—'

'I don't care. If you want my rings and my money, you'll earn them. My son has waited long enough. Did you get the phones?'

She pulls out a black box and hands it to me.

'I charged it some in the car on my way over. The number for mine is in there.'

I take the phone box from her with a little too much force and shove it in my bag.

'Good.'

We stand in awkward silence for a while, unsure of what to say next. We have both laid out our terms, both know what the other wants.

And clearly, neither one of us trusts the other.

'Well, get going,' I say. 'You've got money to earn.'

Her glare sharpens. I watch as she turns without another word and disappears behind the corner of the building.

I have no intention of giving her any more money – I couldn't even if I wanted to. I can't sell anything of value because all of our assets are tied into the divorce, and although I have money saved away, it isn't enough to meet the amount she is demanding. I was only allowed to withdraw ten thousand from the bank. She has half now, and I have kept the other so I have means to keep her quiet should she push me for more money later. But that's as much as she will get out of me; all I have to do is make sure she is too busy to realise what is going on until it is too late. I would have promised her anything if it meant getting Zack home and safe, and I wonder if she has plans to shaft me too.

If I want to get out of this unscathed, I need to figure out every move she plans to make. I must be one step ahead at all times.

38

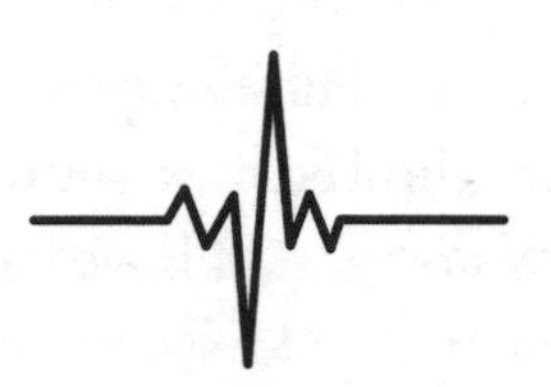

Margot

Tuesday, 9 April 2019, 13:16

I pull up at the kerb outside Damien's house wondering what prison food tastes like. Whether it is as bad as they say it is.

I should just cut my losses, head to the police station now, and admit to what I did. I'll probably be safer locked up than out here in whatever Anna is dragging me into.

I imagine myself pacing back and forth in my cell, my hand on my lower back to ease the weight of my pregnant belly. Some women have a partner to rub their swollen feet, and only eat organic food to make sure their baby has the most nutritious diet. All I would have is some lowlife cellmate and prison slop.

No. I'll get this money and I'll run. I won't let this baby hate me.

Anna is much more calculating and vindictive than I gave

her credit for. I always knew that she was cold, but I had no idea how deceptive she could be, how quickly she could shift the power balance and take control. How does she expect me to find out why someone wanted Shabir killed by the end of the day? It's preposterous. Perhaps this is part of her plan, setting me up to fail to justify not handing over the money.

I will just have to prove her wrong.

I get out of the car and knock on the door to be let in. The front door opens and Damien is stood on the other side, flashing his stained teeth in a smile. He is high as a kite, with glazed, heavy eyes and dopey smile. It was Ma who gave us our first ever spliff.

'Come in, come in,' he says gaily, ushering me in with his hand. 'I'm just making lunch.'

'Munchies?' I ask, as I step inside. The house reeks of weed and bacon fat, just like it used to smell when Ma would stand at the stove.

He chuckles, almost like a child. 'Big time.'

'Rick here?'

'Yeah, go sit down,' he says, and wipes his sweaty hands on the front of his T-shirt. 'I'll bring you in a sandwich.'

I find Rick lying across the sofa with his shirt off, dragging on a spliff. Don't they ever go to work?

'Here she is,' he says, his face as dopey as Damien's. 'We were just talking about you.'

'Good things, I hope,' I say as I cross the room. I go to sit on the floor by the TV; I would never sit in Ma's chair.

'Nah, come here,' Rick says, struggling up from the lying position.

'I'm fine.'

'Don't be daft.'

He pats the sofa beside him, and offers me a drag as soon as I sit down. He smells of old sweat; the sharp scent stings my nostrils.

'No thanks.'

He shrugs his shoulders and takes another hit. 'I hear you've got a good money-making scheme going on . . .'

'She sure does,' Damien says as he enters the room, and places a tray on my lap: a plate of bacon sandwiches and a pint of Coke; the colour of it reminds me of Ma's rotten tooth. 'Eat up.'

'What's the plan then?' Rick asks.

He raises the spliff to his lips again, and I catch a glimpse of the ring on his finger. It looks familiar, but I can't think where I've seen it before.

'You can tell him,' Damien says as he heads back to the kitchen, calling back to me. 'He's one of us.'

One of us.

Being lumped in with these people makes me feel a thick wave of shame. I tuck my hand beneath my top and stroke my belly, whispering to it inside my head.

We're nothing like them.

'You seen the story about the politician on the news?' I ask.

'Oh, yeah. Dodgy heart, right?'

'More like dodgy doctor,' Damien says as he returns with two plates. 'Maggot watched the surgeon kill the bloke on the operating table.'

Rick's jaw falls open and takes a plate from Damien.

'No way.'

'Yep, and she's rich, ain't she, Maggot?'

I nod. 'I thought I'd make it worth my while.'

Damien nods his head approvingly as he sits down in Ma's

chair, a smug smile on his face. He doesn't half look like her, sat there.

'How'd the meeting with her go?' he asks, reaching out to Rick for the spliff. I watch as their hands meet. Damien and Rick are wearing the same ring.

I've seen someone else with one just like it, and remember the design from somewhere, but whether it's the weed in the air or the morning I've had, I can't pin the memory down.

'It all went according to plan.'

I refuse to tell him about Anna's wedding rings or he will want his fair share, and if I tell him how wrong it went, how conniving and controlling Anna has turned out to be, he will lose faith. I know all of his attentiveness is down to me lining his pockets, but I still want it.

'She give you the deposit?'

So that's why he's asking all these questions. He wants to know if I have his share of the money.

'Yeah, but I'm keeping it in a safe place for now.'

Rick frowns. 'It would be safe here, wouldn't it?'

No.

'She's a clever girl,' Damien says, taking a bite out of his sandwich. A glob of ketchup glistens on his chin. 'We'll get our cut when it's the right time. Maggot knows what she's doing. Don't you?'

He gives me a smile, but it doesn't reach his eyes. In a roundabout way, he is putting me in my place, reminding me what will happen if I betray them.

'Right,' I reply timidly.

He smiles wider. 'See? She's a good egg. I helped raise her, after all.'

I pick up the sandwich and bite into one of the corners. The bacon has been fried to a crisp and scratches all the way down my throat. As Rick tucks into his, my eyes flick towards his ring again.

I know where I've seen it before.

On the ring are two snakes, coiled around one another with their heads meeting in the middle like a kiss. It's the same logo I saw on the signage at the scrapyard, but the memory that throws me the most is from a time before this all began: Ahmed Shabir had a ring just like it. I remember spotting his rings on the table beside his hospital bed before the surgery: a wedding band and the sovereign. I remember, because I had wondered how much I would get for them.

Why would someone like Ahmed Shabir be wearing the same kind of ring as these two lowlifes?

'Do you two work together at the scrapyard?' I ask.

'Yeah,' Rick says, mouth full, and nods towards Damien. 'That's how we met.'

'How'd you get into it then, Rick?'

'A friend of a friend,' he says. 'His Uncle Faheem runs it. When he heard how many years I'd been selling gear—'

'Rick,' Damien warns.

So it isn't about stealing cars at all. It's drugs they deal in. The cars must be a sideline.

'What's his last name?' I ask, as flippantly as I can muster. 'Maybe I know him.'

'Doubt it. Name's Shabbar.'

'Not Shabir?'

'Nah, definitely Shabbar. You're thinking of that guy.'

'Oh yeah,' I reply, picking up my sandwich. 'Silly me.'

Shabir. Shabbar. It can't be a coincidence that their names are so similar. But why would a high-profile MP be tied up with people like this?

The glint of Rick's ring catches my eye as he bites into the sandwich.

I raise my leg impulsively, tilting my tray until the pint of Coke pours all over Rick's lap and plate.

'I'm so sorry!'

It has soaked into his tracksuit bottoms, and his sandwich is swimming in it, bread breaking away and floating in the dark pool. He stares down at himself, eyes wide with shock, and then looks across to Damien. They burst into laughter until they're both red in the face, and my brother is practically rolling around on the carpet. Rick dabs at the tears filling his eyes. He probably wouldn't find it so funny if he weren't stoned out of his mind.

I get up and take the plate from his lap, Coke dripping over the sides, and place it on the tray where it fell on the floor. I glance at Rick's hand out of the corner of my eye, glistening and wet. The ring should slip right off.

'Go get changed,' I say. 'We'll clean up.'

I get up and offer him my hand, leaning back with the weight of him as he gets to his feet. The ring slips off his finger effortlessly.

'You're not mad?' I ask.

'Course not, it was funny. Come here.' He grabs me and clamps his arms around me in a hug, pressing my cheek into his wet chest. I squirm against him and I can feel myself turning red in the face, but I'm locked in his grip, which only makes him and Damien laugh harder. I hate them both in that moment. When he finally lets me go, he ruffles my hair and heads off down the hall, stumbling and laughing as he goes.

I slip the ring in my pocket and snatch up my bag.

'It's like a hit and run,' Damien says with a laugh.

'Sorry,' I say as I turn for the hall. 'I've got to head out again. See you later.'

'Maggot,' he says, coaxing me back, the smirk slipping from his face. 'You are going to share that money with us, aren't you?'

His expression grows hard, and his eyes piercing. Damien has a way of threatening a person without even having to open his mouth. Goosebumps break out on my arms.

'Course.'

'Good,' he says, with a wink. 'Good.'

He gives me another one of those smiles that doesn't reach his eyes, and a shiver runs down my back. I force a smile and head straight for the door.

When he realises I've taken off with the money, he will make it his personal mission to make me regret it.

After this is done, there is no going back.

39

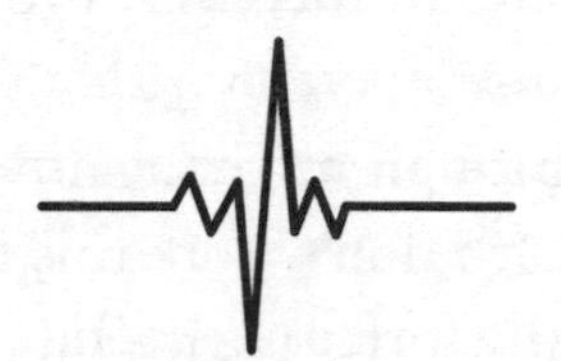

Margot

Tuesday, 9 April 2019, 17:10

I sit before the computer in the library, my head pounding. I have spent hours scouring through news articles, public police reports, newspaper archives, and reading over Ahmed Shabir's medical history file until I feel I know it as well as my own. But still, I can't make anything stick.

I press my earphones deep into my ears and play the video clip on the screen. Shabir is on a televised panel describing addiction as a pandemic that has run rife through our country, and how it is the responsibility of the government to implement change and reform.

How can a man who holds such a strong stance on ending drug-trafficking be tied up with the Shabbars?

After looking into Ahmed's career, I followed Anna's hunch

and searched online for drug-related statistics. Shabir has been widely praised in the press for the increase in arrests and convictions relating to drugs charges, but looking at the statistics on drug-related deaths in Redwood and in the city, the numbers have remained the same. The drugs are still entering town as they did before, despite the increase in convictions.

It doesn't make sense.

I run my hands through my hair, my elbows on the desk, and my neck bowed. If I don't work this out by the end of the day, I will be practically forfeiting the money, and without that I can't run. I think of myself pacing the cell heavily pregnant again, my shoulders aching from the responsibility weighing down on them. My eyes settle on the medical file.

Shabir's health records show no red flags. He has had the name Shabir since his records began. All of the things he said about his past during interviews were true: his name was on each of the online school records, from primary all the way to the University of Oxford. If journalists went looking into his past for dirt they wouldn't find it; on paper, he appears squeaky clean.

A headache is burning at my crown, and my arms are mottled with goosebumps from the air-conditioning unit rattling above my head. I pick up Rick's ring from the desk and slip it on, admiring each of the snake's gold bodies as they wrap around the other. According to the web, they symbolise the good and evil that live in all of us, a kind of moral yin and yang, writhing in harmony. The idea of 'good' drug dealers is a stretch, but I'm sure it helps them sleep at night.

Shabbar and Shabir are too similar. It can't be a coincidence, not after the MP was murdered on the operating table. This link has to be the reason he was killed.

I press my fingertips firmly into my temples, trying to make each of the threads bind together in my mind.

I pick up his health file and begin reading it front to back again, going over the same words I have read a dozen times. Diagnosed at twenty-five; first medical intervention at thirty. I read over the diagnosis of familial hypercholesterolemia, until I stop suddenly, my finger frozen on the page beneath mention of his father.

Ahmed didn't change his name. But maybe his father did.

I wake the computer mouse and bring up the page for the *Gazette* archives storing the official public record, where I had searched for any changes to Ahmed's name. I learned about changing names via deed poll when I was younger and fantasised about shedding any connection to Ma and my past. But by the time I could afford the fees, I had built a career by which everyone already knew my name, and had a boyfriend who refused to call me by another. I type in the father's details and search through the files. There isn't a match.

Shit.

I felt sure the father was the right call. I pick up the file again, and flick to the notes attached to Ahmed's medical history, breaking down the familial nature of the disease, and how the condition manifested in his father, whom he inherited from. My finger freezes on the date of his diagnosis: just a month after entering the country in November 1977, when his records began. His case was already severe, which means he had to have had treatment before then. I glance at Ahmed's date of birth – he was born six months after his parents arrived. The close timing of three such big events seems far too perfect to put down as luck.

If only I could read the father's file. But no one is going to look on the system for him and just give me the information after I've been fired.

I try to think of someone at the hospital I can call to help, but everyone I think of, I have stolen from.

Then I think of Val. She was heartbroken when her brooch when missing before Christmas. It had been her mother's, and Val cherished it. I wouldn't have stolen it if I'd known it meant so much to her, but maybe the offer of giving it back might motivate her to help me.

I check the time; she will still be at work. She won't have her mobile on her while on the ward floor. I pick up my phone and call the nurse's desk, my foot tapping nervously against the floor.

A voice I don't recognise answers the phone.

'Is Val there?' I ask.

'Who's calling?' the woman asks.

'Her daughter,' I blurt out.

'Hang on, love, I'll check.'

I listen to the hold music, trying to ignore the guilt chipping away at me. There's no way I'll be able to get her that brooch back. I flogged it as soon as I got my hands on it. But this will mean the baby and I can get out of here, and it could help save Anna's kid too.

It's all for the greater good.

'Hello, lovey,' Val says as she picks up the phone. 'Is everything all—'

'It's not your daughter, Val. It's Margot. Don't hang up – I've got something you want.'

'My money back for a start,' she quips. 'You've got a nerve, calling here when you—'

'I've got your mum's brooch, Val.'

Val falls silent.

'Do you want it back?' I ask.

'Of course I do you little . . .' She bites her tongue. I wonder what she planned to call me.

'Then I need you to look up a file for me.'

'You know I can't do that,' she snaps.

'Of course you can. It just depends how much you want the brooch, I guess . . .'

She falls quiet again, torn over what to do, and I sit listening to the background noise of the ward. My heart aches for it.

'What's the name?' she says at last.

'Sadiq Shabbar. I want to know if and when he was last treated by us, and if he went by any other name.'

'If I do this, and you don't give me my—'

'I'll tell you everything you need to know, Val,' I answer.

'Fine. Hang on.'

She types into the computer, and I wait on the other end, my heart thumping in my chest.

'No other name,' she says. 'And he hasn't been treated here since 1976. No record of him after that.'

No way.

Ahmed's parents must have left the country, changed their names, and then returned as Shabirs to prevent a paper trail; and just six months later, Ahmed was born. It's kind of genius.

'Now I want my brooch,' Val says, whispering into the receiver.

'Your best bet is the corner of Simmons Way.'

'What– what do you mean?'

'The pawn shop on the corner. I cashed it in there right after I nicked it.'

'Oh, you little thieving cu—'

I hang up the phone and grin from ear to ear.

It can't be a coincidence that a family tied to a potential drug-trafficking syndicate would change the family name mere months before Ahmed was born.

Why would they change his name, only for him to go on to lead a career path designed to destroy the family business?

But then he didn't, did he? There might have been more arrests, but the statistics have remained the same.

The answer is there in my mouth, burning on the tip of my tongue. So tauntingly close that I feel I could raise my hand and pluck it out.

Almost as if competitors are being rounded up so that one drug-trafficking syndicate can dominate the market.

When the idea clicks into place, it takes all my power not to jump up and scream. This isn't a case of irony – it must be how the whole scheme was designed. Who would ever suspect that the MP fighting for stronger penalties for drug-trafficking and distribution would be tied up in it himself? Christ, the Shabbars must have raised him with the sole intention of infiltrating government. To what, push anti-drug-distribution measures to oust their competitors and rule their domain?

Who better to find a loophole in the crackdown legislation than the man who helped bring it into fruition?

I glance back up at the computer screen and tap on the tab for Ahmed's panel discussion. In the tagline of the article, Ahmed is called the future of the Labour Party; Redwood is just the start of what the Shabbars have planned. Ahmed used his power to influence a crackdown on drugs entering London, but if he did become the leader of the party, and then went on to become prime minister, his influence would have been endless.

He would have been able to oust every one of their

competitors trafficking drugs into the country. The Shabbars would have been the gatekeepers of drug-trafficking on an international level.

I stare down at the medical file and back to the screen, reading the words over until my discovery finally sinks in.

Everything Ahmed Shabir said during his political career was a lie.

The abductors must have wanted Ahmed dead to protect their business, meaning Zack and Anna are merely collateral in all of this: the abduction of Zack is their way of pushing Anna into doing their bidding. It would have happened to anyone who was assigned to do the procedure. Of course, they had to make it look like a surgical death; had there been anything even remotely suspicious, the police would have to employ the most robust investigation they could, what with the whole country watching. But by having him die at the hands of a trusted surgeon during an extensive surgery, the element of suspicion goes away.

The burner phone rings from inside my bag, but I daren't answer it here. I gather up my things, exhausted and starving, but the adrenaline has me bounding down the steps towards the main entrance. The phone starts to ring again just as I near the doors.

'I've figured it out,' I say, practically panting as I step out onto the street and search my bag for my cigarettes.

Anna is silent on the other end of the line. I like to think I've stunned her. She obviously didn't expect that I might be as clever as her.

'We shouldn't talk about this over the phone,' she says finally.

'I bought untraceable phones,' I reply, slipping a cigarette from the pack. 'It's secure.'

'I'm not taking any chances. Meet me in the woodland by my house. Don't drive down The Avenue; park up somewhere and make your way on foot. Text me when you're there.'

She hangs up before I can say another word.

I sit down on the bench outside the library and light my cigarette, exhaling away the rage in a cloud of smoke.

Why, after all the hassle of buying the untraceable phones, is she so reluctant to use them? Maybe she was afraid the abductors might be listening in somehow. Or maybe she suspected I might have been recording her like she had assumed before.

Anna doesn't trust me one bit.

Good, I think, as I take a long, fat drag. *I don't trust her either.*

I take out my phone and write out a text, the cigarette burning between my lips.

> **Me**
> Bring the next cash instalment or I'm not telling you anything.

I wait for a response for a few minutes, but nothing comes.

I reach the woodland edge and text Anna to tell her I've arrived.

The night is warm. Warmer than the last. I reach into my bag to feel the envelope of cash Anna gave me earlier in the day. I told Damien that I had the money in a safe spot, and it is. I'll keep every penny Anna gives me on my person at all times. There is no way I'm leaving it somewhere for someone else to find, especially not where Damien or Rick can get their hands on it. I run the tip of my thumb across the wad of cash.

Light casts down Anna's driveway, with the elongated silhouette of a woman stretched across the paving. I spot her in the doorway, and hear the faint jangling of her keys carrying on the breeze. The door shuts and I watch for her in the dark, only spotting her when she is a hundred feet from me, cutting across the green with urgent strides. I hear the panting sounds of a dog and spot the blond mutt by her side.

'Did you bring the money?' I ask as she nears.

She waves a white envelope in the dark.

'Tell me what you know first,' she says.

'No. Last time we did this you gave me five grand when we agreed on ten. That didn't exactly instil trust.'

She sighs and hands it over.

'Five grand. It's all there.'

I take my phone out of my pocket and turn on the flash, shining the light on the envelope to count through the cash.

'We haven't got time for this,' she snaps.

'I've got all the time in the world. You're the one in a rush.'

She crosses her arms and taps her foot against the earth as I run my thumb along the wad of notes, counting off the fifties under my breath.

'Christ, would you get on with it?'

I shove the envelope in my bag and turn off the light. It has left a blot in my vision, following me wherever I look.

'What did you find out?'

'Sure you don't want to frisk me first? Check I'm not wearing a wire?'

'You just took a bribe. If you're recording, you'll have incriminated yourself too. Now start talking.'

I dig my hand in my pocket for Rick's ring and tell her to put out her hand. It is cold and soft; I imagine she lathers them in expensive creams before bed.

'What is it?'

'The same ring I saw Ahmed Shabir wearing before his surgery.'

She hesitates, and I dare to wonder if she is impressed.

'Put on the light.'

I take out my phone and shine the torch on the ring. The gold shimmers as she turns it back and forth.

'I remember seeing it too. Do the snakes mean anything?'

'Symbolises the good and evil in us all. Obviously theirs is out of whack.' I take the ring from her grip and turn off the light. 'I know where else I've seen it too. There's a scrapyard on the outskirts of town with a logo on the front exactly like this.'

'So what, Shabir was dealing in metal? That information hardly helps me get my son back.'

'No, it's a cover. Shabir was dealing in drugs.'

Even in the dark, I see her face change. It feels good to have knocked her usual superior expression off her face.

I tell her everything I have learned, from Ahmed's father changing his name, to my brother's connection to the business, and the name Faheem Shabbar.

'That's how I got the ring. My brother works for them.'

'So you've been to this place?'

'I was there this morning.'

She falls silent for a while, thinking in the dark. I don't like it when she is quiet. She has a way of twisting everything to her advantage.

'This still doesn't tell me who the abductors are or where my son is.'

'No, but it's our connection to finding out.'

'What do you mean?'

'Well, if we go there and explain what happened, they might help you.'

She laughs at me in the dark.

'You think it's a good idea for me to go to Ahmed Shabir's family and tell them that I killed him? But oh, I'd like their help to get my son back, if it isn't too much trouble?'

'They'll know you had no choice, and that you were just their means to do it without raising suspicion. If we tell them why it happened and who is really responsible, we'll be *helping* them. We should go tonight.'

She scoffs, but quickly falls silent again, thinking it over.

'Why don't you ask your brother to do it?'

'So you can keep your hands clean? Not a chance. Besides, my brother wouldn't do anything without payment. You got another fifty grand lying around?'

Her silence tells me she doesn't.

'There is still no guarantee that they would help me get my son back. It's way too much of a risk.'

'What other choice do you have?'

We both jolt at the sound of her phone. The sound carries an echo through the trees.

'That's them,' she says. Her tone has changed completely. She usually seems so self-assured, confident in every word she says. But now she sounds truly scared. 'Don't say a word.'

She puts the phone to her ear.

'Hello?'

I hear the distant muffle of a man's voice on the other end of the line. Deep and abrupt.

'I'm walking my dog.'

Christ. They really are tracking her every move.

The man speaks again. Even from here, his tone sounds threatening.

'I have everything in hand,' she says. 'I used the information you gave me. The detective won't be bothering me any—'

She stops mid-sentence with a sharp intake of breath. My eyes have adjusted to the dark now, and I can see brief details of her face: the glimmer of her eyes reflecting the moon, the parting of her lips. I hear the sniffle of tears.

'Oh sweetheart,' she says. 'I'm here. It's okay.'

The dog starts whining at her feet. I instinctively take the lead from her grip and crouch down to pet the dog and keep it quiet. Anna turns her back and wanders a few steps, dashing the tears from her face.

'I know you're scared, darling, I know. But I'm doing everything I can to get you back. I love you, okay? Don't ever forget it. I love you with all my—'

She stops abruptly, until all I can hear is the sound of the wind howling through the trees. The dog whines at me with a huff of breath against my face. I had stopped stroking him, too entranced by the scene.

'Yes,' she says into the phone. Her tone is back to how it was when she spoke to the man. 'I know. I'm going to the hospital tonight to see what I can find out about their investigation. I'll stay there all night if I have to.'

The man must be talking, for she doesn't say anything for almost a minute.

'Yes,' she says finally. 'I know what's at stake.'

She lowers the phone and slips it into her pocket, saying nothing as she wipes the tears from her cheeks and sniffs. The dog seems bored of me now and is staring towards her, its tail knocking against my knee.

When Anna turns around, the tears have stopped, and her face is hard and cold again.

'We'll go tonight,' she says matter-of-factly, and takes the lead from my grip as I stand.

'Was that your son on the phone?'

'Yes,' she replies flatly. 'They track my every move, so you'll have to tail me to the hospital. We can go from there.'

'All right,' I say softly, and watch her tense up at the slightest sound of sympathy. I harden my tone. 'I parked on Straight Road. Give me ten minutes to get there and then I'll follow behind you.'

She nods once, her jaw tensed shut, and turns to leave.

'Aren't you forgetting something?' I ask.

She stops in her tracks. When the realisation comes to her, she snatches off her engagement ring and chucks it at my feet. She leaves without another word, the dog bouncing gaily beside her.

That was the first time I have seen something truly human about her. But she locked it all down in a matter of seconds. Smothered it in her usual chill.

I kneel down and pick up the ring, the diamond glinting beneath the moon. I slide it on. The band is still warm.

If she can conceal all of that pain, I wonder what else she is capable of hiding.

40

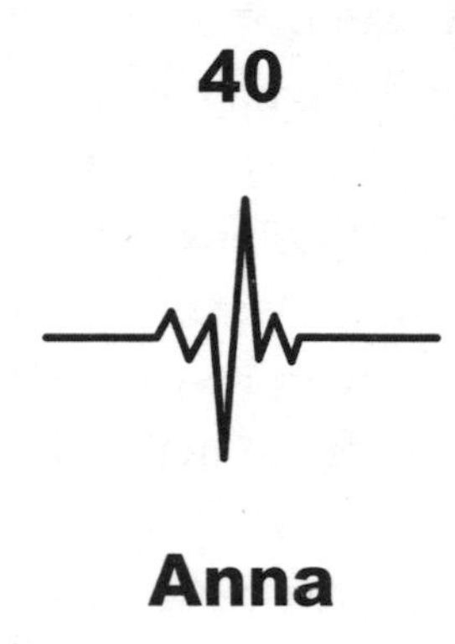

Anna

Tuesday, 9 April 2019, 20:09

I park up at the hospital, place the tapped phones in the glove compartment, and set off towards the building on foot.

This is the first time I am truly going against the abductors' orders, and I feel so anxious that I am wild with it, jumping at the slightest sound. Every crack of a twig or swish of the trees has me snap my neck towards the disturbance, expecting to find the abductors approaching me in the shadows. It's not like they haven't followed me before. I take out the burner phone and text Margot.

Me:
Meet me behind the hospital, where we met before.

I couldn't even look at her when we parted ways. She had looked at me with such pity after hearing me on the phone with Zack. But she can't pretend to have a soul, not when she is continuing with her plan to extort me and take my rings without a shred of guilt. In my eyes, she is just as bad as the abductors. Just as corrupt. Just as callous.

I turn the corner of the hospital, taking a sly glance over my shoulder to check I am not being followed, and try to exhale all of the rage out of me. I can feel it pressing on my chest, reverberating through me like heat. I wonder what my brother would say with his expertise.

You're angry with her for witnessing your flaws; your vulnerability. For being anything but perfect, like mother raised you to be.

I guess I am angry with Margot for a lot of things.

I reach the bins and stand in the dark, listening to the quiet whistle of the wind. My thoughts return to Zack.

He had sounded terrified on the phone. His speech was slurred from the sedative they are pumping into his veins; he must be so frightened and confused, slipping in and out of consciousness and waking up to the sight of strange men, holding a phone to his ear with my voice at the other end, seemingly a world away. A lump burns in my throat at the thought of him curled up in the dusty blankets, in the corner of some strange, cold room, an IV pinching at his hand.

I come to with the sound of a car. Headlights shine up the narrow road leading to the rear of the hospital, and I imagine the abductors turning the corner in the black Audi that had followed me before. I hold my breath, waiting to see the model of the car behind the lights, listening to the beat of my heart throbbing in my ears.

An Audi comes into view.

My heart jolts with the sight of the four-ringed emblem on the grill, feel bile kiss the back of my throat as it pulls up at the kerb. I stare through the window with the beat of my heart pounding in my ears.

Margot is behind the wheel.

I sigh with relief and feel the panic slowly shiver out of me.

'Were you followed?' I ask as I climb in the passenger seat. The car smells of cigarette smoke and cheap perfume.

'No,' she replies, pulling away before I have a chance to fix my belt. 'We're good.'

The car is far too nice for someone who has to steal to make ends meet and wears the same set of clothes day after day. I want to talk to her as little as possible, but my curiosity gets the better of me.

'How can you afford a car like this?'

She reaches the exit of the hospital and pulls out onto the road, pressing the accelerator with such force that I am thrust into the back of my seat.

'I can't. I got it from the Shabbars.'

'They gave you a car? Why would they do that?'

'They steal cars too,' she replies. 'My brother works for them. I asked for a car and he got it for me.'

I hadn't thought about the threat of her connection to the Shabbars. If her brother is working with them, and Margot is getting a car without paying a penny, perhaps she has a better relationship with them than she is letting on.

Maybe it's a trap.

'I didn't realise your brother was so well connected.'

'He doesn't know about Ahmed Shabir's connection to the Shabbars, if that's what you're thinking,' she replies. 'I don't think many of them do. When I mentioned Ahmed's name, he didn't even flinch. My brother likes to brag; he would have let on.'

'So you told him,' I say. 'About what I did . . .'

She says nothing for a while, no doubt angry at implicating herself. She glances at the sat nav and turns left, off the main road.

'I told him days ago,' she says finally. 'If he knew about Ahmed's connection to the Shabbars and told his boss what you did, you'd have had the repercussions by now.'

I wonder how it feels to be so confident in one's own beliefs. To blindly trust one's own judgement. I can't do a single thing without second-guessing myself.

'You said he had a big mouth.'

'Unless there's something in it for him.'

'You're giving him some of the money?'

'He thinks that, yes. But as soon as you deliver, I'm gone, and I'm taking the money with me.'

If she can turn on her own family, she wouldn't think twice about betraying me.

The brakes squeal as we stop at a set of traffic lights. I look at her face, her eyes the colour of blood from the stoplight. If I didn't dislike her so much, and she wasn't so scruffy, I would probably describe her as pretty. But however hard she tries to appear, her eyes give her away. She is just a scared little girl.

'They let you talk to Zack, then?' she asks.

I don't like hearing his name come out of her mouth. She makes it sound dirty. I avert my eyes to the road.

'Only when they want to remind me what's at stake.'

The mention of him has my guard wavering. I can feel the sadness bubbling up, the fear clawing its way out. Then I see my engagement ring on her finger. Any sadness I feel evaporates from the heat of my rage.

Stay focused, I tell myself, and stare ahead as the lights change.

'How do we know they won't just kill me for doing the abductors' dirty work?'

'We don't,' she replies.

Neither of us says a word after that.

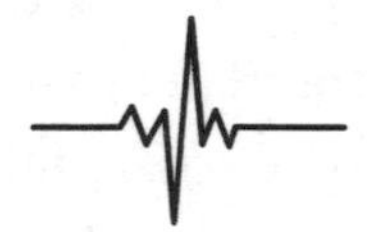

'We're here,' she says, slowing the car.

My blood is pumping so fast that I can hear the rush of it in my ears. I wipe my palms against my thighs and feel the plucked hairs on my lap where I had been picking at my arm in the dark.

She pulls the car down a lane that is scoured with potholes, sending the car back and forth, side to side. The jolting about makes the acid in my stomach slosh up into my throat. I grip onto the door handle until my fingers turn bone-white.

Margot still has that hard, absent look on her face, but her eyes are wider than they had been, and her hand quivers when she reaches for the gear stick. I watch in silence as she thrusts her hand in her pocket, takes out the gold ring, and slips it on.

There is a security hut up ahead, big enough to fit one guard inside, where one lone bulb hangs above his head. Margot pulls up to the window and puts her foot on the brake. Moths and other insects are fluttering against the glass of the hut. The man slides the viewing panel and smears their little bodies into green trails.

'I'm here to see Jax,' she says, after lowering her window. Her tone is calm and direct, but when I look closely, I can see the loose hairs hanging from her ponytail are shaking with her body. The sight of them makes my scalp itch.

Pluck, the voice says. *Pluck.*

The guard looks down at her right hand and eyes the ring, glinting from the light inside the hut, and nods. As we pull away, I see him raise a phone to his ear.

'Who's Jax?' I ask.

'I don't know. My brother asked for him when we came here.'

'Did you know the ring would work like that?'

'No, but it was worth a shot.'

No wonder her life has ended up this way. She seems to make every decision on a whim, without any thought of the consequences. The realisation makes our driving here seem even more reckless. I am just about to tell her to turn the car around when she pulls up outside a large outbuilding. Heaps of crushed cars have been placed on top of one another and left to rust, forming a wall around the grounds. The door to the outbuilding opens and sheds a long rectangle of light along the potholed ground.

'This is too dangerous,' I say, and find myself grabbing at her wrist. 'There has to be another way.'

She looks me dead in the eyes, and slowly peels my fingers from around her wrist.

'Your son is with people like this, Anna.'

My stomach plummets at the thought.

How dare I be scared, when he is going through so much more? I certainly won't allow her to be braver than me.

I nod silently and reach for the door handle.

The night air is cool and still. The crushed cars are glittering from the downpour we drove through en route, and rain drips and drops from one car to another in a chorus of high-pitched pings. Three men are stood outside the building with the light from the doorway beaming behind them, making them appear as dark, faceless silhouettes. Margot slams her door shut and heads towards them. I follow a step behind her.

'Jax?' she asks.

The man in the middle nods his head. I can see their faces now that we're closer; the man named Jax has hair darker than the night and deep, impenetrable eyes.

'We need to speak to Faheem.'

'If there's a problem with the car, you deal with me.'

'It's not about the car,' she replies. 'It's about Ahmed.'

His eyes widen a fraction, but only for a second.

'Who?'

'Do you really want me to say in front of these guys?' she nods at the man on his right. 'My brother works for you and has no idea about who he is ... as in, who he *really* is. I'm guessing it isn't common knowledge around here?'

I look back and forth between them and watch the confusion etch between the other men's brows. Margot sounds so confident, but when I look behind her back where she is hiding her hands, I see she is twisting the gold ring nervously around her finger.

'Go inside and shut the door,' Jax says to the men at his side.

Despite the confusion still thick on their faces, they nod silently and turn for the door. The door shuts behind them and the three of us are thrown into darkness.

'Speak,' he says.

He looks taller without the men on either side of him. Now I can see the sheer size of his arms, the bulk of his shoulders.

'Ahmed's death was deliberate,' Margot says.

He looks her up and down, then me. We must look like such an odd pair.

'Prove it,' he says.

She raises her hand and points over her shoulder.

At *me*.

'She's the surgeon who killed him.'

Fear zings through me. He looks me dead in the eyes, and my legs tremble.

'It's not her you want,' Margot says. 'One of your rivals abducted her son. If she didn't go through with it, they were going to kill him. Ahmed's blood is on their hands, not hers. She was just their means to do it without being caught.'

He hasn't stopped looking at me, hate pulsing in his glare.

'Wait here,' he says.

He bangs on the door with his fist and steps through the doorway as soon as it opens.

'Watch them,' he says, and walks out of sight.

The two men step outside again and tower over us.

I can't think. I can't breathe. I stand frozen before the men, willing my legs to stop shaking and run. Margot stands in silence too. I will her to turn and look at me, to reassure me of her reckless plan, but she continues to stare straight ahead, twirling the ring around her finger behind her back.

Sounds of footsteps come from inside the building. Lots of them. Heavy boots against what sounds like a metal staircase. They get louder, and louder, until it drowns out the thud of my heart.

The door opens and the two men step aside.

Four men appear at the doorway, their faces hidden behind black balaclavas over their heads.

They are heading straight towards me.

'What're you doing?' Margot asks.

But I can't see her anymore. The men are surrounding me, hands grabbing my wrists, my shoulders and neck. I am turned around so fast that my hair whips against my face. A black four-by-four pulls on the forecourt. When a black pillowcase is yanked over my head, I can't help but scream.

'It's not her you want!' I hear Margot say. *'Oi! I said, it's not her you—'*

She is cut short suddenly. All I can hear now are my loud breaths inside the pillowcase, my feet scuffling against the ground. I reach the car and stumble, hitting my shin against the step.

I can't breathe.

'Get up,' a man snaps close to my ear.

I put out my hands blind, feeling their palms all over me as they manhandle me into the car. Two men climb in beside me and crush me between their bulk.

Car doors shut. An engine turns on.

I am driven away in silence.

41

Rachel

Tuesday, 9 April 2019, 20:34

There are whispers around the office. Whispers about me.

I thought I was being paranoid at first. That I was mistaking people's perfectly simple glances for prying eyes, taking it personally whenever I stepped into a room and the conversation stopped dead. But then I heard my name spoken between the bathroom stalls. Then Jamie's.

> *Conaty is obsessed with the kid angle, isn't she? Almost as if she didn't see that dead woman in the well with her own eyes. It's a murder investigation, for Christ's sake.*

> *Totally. It's like she sees this random kid as Jamie. It's kind of sad. Did you read that article I sent you?*

Yeah. So fucked up about what happened to him. But if she can't let it go, she shouldn't be doing this job, should she?

One of the voices belonged to DS Slater, from my own team. Both of the women bid me farewell as they left for the day, false smiles plastered on their faces.

The office is deserted now, which is a blessing in some ways, and a hindrance in others. I can work without being watched from the main office, and I can go to the bathroom or make a coffee without feeling ostracised by my own team. But the silence of the office allows my mind to work on overdrive and, slowly but surely, the doubts begin to appear.

What if they're right?

I never used to distrust my own judgement. When my gut told me something, I followed it. But once Jamie went missing, I immediately began to doubt my abilities as a mother. Good mothers don't lose their children. Good mothers don't stop looking for them, even when the world grows tired of the story and moves on. The doubts spread to every aspect of my life. But there is one thing I know for definite: if I don't find a strong lead soon, this case will grow cold.

We have no murder scene. No murder weapon. No suspects. Paula Williams was just an ordinary, middle-class woman enjoying retirement, until she was plucked from the street and found dead in the well. There is no obvious reason for a person to want to kill her: there is no sign of strange activity on her phone records or bank statements to suggest extortion or money troubles, no new friends with ulterior motives, no known quarrels or tension between neighbours. There are no romantic relationships to pick apart, or work colleagues to question. Her body showed no signs of sexual assault. The only reasons for her death that I can possibly fathom are all linked to the boy.

I sigh heavily, my breath ruffling the pages strewn over the surface of the desk. I'm not sleeping, and when I do, I dream I am back on the beach, running around and screaming at strangers, asking if they have seen my son. Work keeps me occupied, and gives me a reason to stay awake, but it makes my dreams worse when I inevitably fall asleep. A toxic cycle I can't break.

There is a photograph of Paula's body poking out of the corner of the murder file. I pinch it free and scan her once-pretty face spoiled by toothless gums, the gunshot wound in the centre of her head, the odd fang of skull tangled in her hair.

The only people who leave this kind of destruction behind them are criminal organisations with in-depth knowledge of how we operate, and the areas they work in usually fall into two categories: drug distribution or sex-trafficking.

It has been long suspected that my Jamie fell victim to the latter.

Tears prick my eyes. I hold my fingers to my eyelids, pressing down with a firm hold.

Ever since I saw that little boy on the tape, I have been haunted by the gleeful bounce in his step, the way he held Paula's hand as they made their way home from the school gates. Just the thought of someone wanting to harm a child so innocent, so untarnished, makes bile sting up the back of my throat. It doesn't matter how hard I push against my eyelids; I feel the tears oozing out, trickling down the grooves of my smile lines. Everything I felt when Jamie was taken is slowly rising to the surface again.

'Ma'am?'

I jump in my seat and snap my neck towards the door. DS Ryan is standing in the doorway.

'What're you doing here?' I ask, swiping at my face furiously. 'I thought you went home.'

'Thought I'd hang on for a bit,' he says. 'Help with that favour you asked of me.'

If he has come with bad news, I don't know how I will take it. I fix myself in the chair, my spine straight, bracing myself for a blow.

'And?'

He brings his hand from behind his back and holds it out to me.

I flip open the file, my heart pounding my chest.

'I think it's safe to say you were right about the boy.'

42

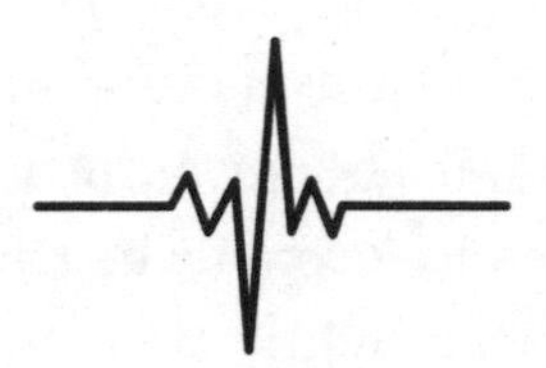

Anna

Tuesday, 9 April 2019, 20:45

We must have been travelling for twenty minutes, but still no one has said a word.

I can't breathe. It feels as if my lungs have inflated and can't release, suffocating me on my own breath. Someone fitted a zip tie around my wrists as the car pulled away from the scrapyard, and they are bound so tight that I can feel my pulse drumming at the tips of my fingers. But these are the last things on my mind.

Zack must have been taken just like this. A hood thrust over his head, wrists bound. I imagine the zip tie cutting into his beautiful, soft skin. Hear his terrified whimpers inside the pillowcase. He must have been so terrified.

If I die, no one will know what happened to Zack. The only person who knows is Margot. What if they kill her too?

In the privacy of the pillowcase, I let the tears fall silently, until I can feel them trembling at the edge of my jaw. I can't stop thinking of Zack experiencing this exact same fear.

They will never find him. No one will know where to look. If I am killed, and Margot runs, no one will know what happened to us.

The car starts to slow, gravel crunching beneath the tyres. My breaths get shallower and the air inside the bag grows hot.

The brakes squeal and we come to a halt. Doors open and slam, and the car rocks lightly with the lumber of bodies. A hand clamps down on my arm and a frisson of fear jolts through me.

'Get out,' a man says.

I shuffle along the seats, knocking my head against the lip of the doorway, and step down blindly onto the gravel. The night air blows the hood against my face. My tears turn cold.

'Walk.'

I am guided across gravel, listening to the crunch and pop of it beneath my soles, as the men talk in a language I don't understand. The gravel turns to grass, wet with dew. My heart races faster and harder. I can almost taste it, a metallic tang in my mouth.

What if Margot made a mistake, and these men are connected to Zack's abductors? What if I walked straight into a trap?

My right foot skids on the wet lawn, and the stranger's hand digs into me as I'm dragged up to my feet again. Perhaps they are leading me into the middle of a clearing, and any moment now they will order me to my knees and raise a gun towards the back of my head.

'Ple-ease . . .' Fear has a hold on my neck. I take a deep breath and choke on it. 'Don't kill me. My son—'

'Be quiet.'

'Please—'

I am silenced by a loud banging sound, and am pulled to a stop. His grip is burning now, like the twisting motion Jeff used to do to my wrist as a child. My legs are shaking and useless.

A metal bolt slides and snaps, followed by the sound of a door whining on its hinges.

'Walk.'

I stumble forwards, my fingers splayed pointlessly beneath my bound wrists. The door slams behind me. The sound echoes around the room and jars my senses.

My mouth is so dry with nerves that the insides of my cheeks are sticking to my teeth. Heavy footsteps stalk either side of me. I stand, shaking and silent but for my short, panicked breaths rasping inside the hood.

I am shoved, suddenly and violently, and fall back with a loud cry. A chair breaks my fall.

'I'm sorry,' I stammer. 'They didn't give me any choice. My son—'

The hood is yanked off my head and I am blinded by bright, white light. I blink furiously and see the four masked men stood in pairs on either side of a metal door fitted with heavy bolts.

I peer anxiously around the room. Dark-grey concrete covers the floor, the walls, the ceiling above my head where a single bulb dangles, swinging where one of them pulled the cord. It's the sort of room I imagine Zack is in, cold and alone.

Oh God, what if they really are working with the abductors, and this is the same place that Zack is being kept? I broke one of their rules by telling Margot, and now they are going to make me pay for it.

The door opens.

A man steps into the room. He too is wearing a balaclava over his head, and a jet-black suit, but he towers above the rest. He walks toward me, stopping just before my knees. I feel his breath on my face. It is hot and sharp. All I can see of him behind the mask is tanned skin at the opening of his shirt and deep brown eyes. I feel like I have seen those eyes before, and slowly realise who they remind me of.

This is Faheem Shabbar.

I killed this man's nephew.

I part my lips, stammering as I find the courage to speak.

'I didn't want to do it,' I say desperately. 'But they said they were going to kill my son if I didn't. They still have him. His name is Zack. He is only eight years old.'

I look down to my lap as the tears flow and yelp as he snatches my chin, forcing me to look in his eyes.

'Who are "*they*"?'

'I don't know,' I stutter. 'They didn't tell me anything.'

His hold on my jaw tightens. The hatred in his eyes makes me squirm beneath his glare.

'Describe them.'

I try to think back to the day I returned home and found them in my house, but it is as if I have been given a blow to the back of the head. Everything is jumbled. I close my eyes and try to imagine the scene.

'The man who did the talking . . . He was white, about forty or so, with dark hair and bits of grey at the sides. He had blue eyes, and spoke with an accent. All of the men did. It sounded Eastern European, but I couldn't say which country. They had tattoos.'

Faheem speaks over his shoulder to the men in his mother tongue.

'Do you know who I'm talking about?'

'Yes.'

My heart leaps.

'They have my son! I would do anything to get him ba—'

'How do you know who I am?' he asks. I can feel his pulse fluttering against the base of my jaw. Calm, methodical beats.

'I have been trying to find out who the abductors are so I can find my son, but to do that we needed to find out why they wanted Ahmed dead. I won't tell anyone who you are, or what you do. All I care about is getting my son back.'

'*We*. As in you and the Barnes girl?'

I nod furiously.

'She saw what I did and is extorting me for money. My wedding rings, too. I told her that I would only give them to her if she helped me and my son.'

He glances down at my wedding ring, nodding calmly, and slowly lets go of my face. A silent beat fills the room.

'Kill her.'

He turns for the door as a masked man steps toward me, slipping a gun from his hip.

'*No, no, no, no!* Please! My son will never be found!'

Faheem opens the door to leave as the masked man reaches me and pulls back the slide on the gun. I hear a bullet slot into the chamber.

'I will do anything! Please!'

The cold metal nozzle presses against my forehead. The fear is physical, zinging through me like a current. Tears stream down my face and I sob without restraint, my face scrunched with anguish and saliva stringing between my lips. I blurt out the first excuse that I can muster, words tumbling from between my lips in a scream.

'You might need me! Ahmed's condition was hereditary!'

I spot the man's finger tense on the trigger and clamp my eyes shut.

'Wait.'

I sit, panting for breath, my eyes clamped shut and my pulse hammering in my ears. I feel the gun pull away, listen as footsteps cross the room. A hand snatches my jaw and my eyes snap open.

'What did you say?' Faheem asks.

He is looking at me with an almost violent curiosity. His eyes search my face, his lips pressed into a snarl. I look up at him desperately, my tears wetting his hand.

This is my only chance.

'Ahmed's condition was hereditary. If you or members of your family ever showed symptoms, but couldn't get help through official routes because you're crimin—' I stop myself, blink back the tears. 'Because of what you do ... I could treat you.'

'Treat me how?' he asks impatiently.

He is looking at me intently, his eyes searing and unblinking.

'Medicine. Surgery. Whatever you needed, I'd find a way to do it.'

I look up at him pleadingly, eyeing what I can see of his face. His eyelashes are long and thick, like Ahmed's had been.

'I would do anything to get my son back. I won't tell anyone who you are. I wouldn't be able to tell, even if I wanted to. I'd be incriminating myself. All I want is to save my son.'

He stares down at me for a while, searching my eyes, scanning my face, the trembling of my lips.

'Please ...'

He slowly releases my jaw. I feel my blood resume its flow, where it had been trapped from his grip.

'Follow me,' he says, and walks towards the door behind my back.

I sit quivering in the chair, realising how narrowly I had just escaped death, before forcing myself to rise. My legs quiver beneath my weight and sparks of light drift in my eyes.

'Where are we going?' I stammer, as I turn slowly for the door.

He clicks his fingers at one of the men.

'To meet the patient.'

The hood is thrust over my head from behind.

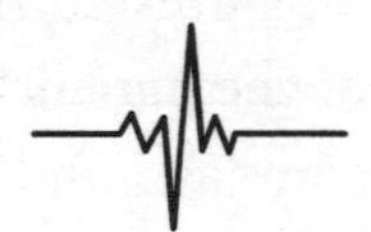

I must have been led into an outhouse, for we cross the grass again, through light rain and cold winds, towards another doorway. I am ushered inside, shoes squeaking against hardwood floors, the men who brought me here following close behind.

Faheem takes my bound wrists and places my hands on a banister, and I climb the stairs with caution, shaking from head to foot.

Just do as they say. Do whatever you have to do to get out of here. Zack's life depends on it.

I reach the end of the banister and follow behind Faheem as he snatches my bound wrists and guides me down a long hallway. After fifteen steps, he stops and knocks on a door. The masked men are standing so close that I can feel a man's breath against the back of my hood. I hear the click of Faheem's fingers again. Someone takes hold of my wrist, and I feel the graze of cold metal, hear the snap of the ties. Circulation flows into my hands again.

The door opens with a creak.

'Step inside, but don't remove the hood until I say.'

I walk blindly into the room, my hands braced by my sides. The air has the same medical tang as the hospital. I can hear a crackling fire, and a hissing sound.

'Remove the hood.'

I slowly raise my hands and peel it away.

I am in a bedroom. The ceiling is three times the height of me, with wood-panelled walls, and two armchairs before a grand fireplace. The tall windows are shielded with long, heavy drapes.

I am stood at the end of the patient's bed.

The man looks about my age and deathly ill. His skin is sickly grey, and his chest rises and falls with rasping breaths behind an oxygen mask, the source of the hissing I heard. He stares back at me silently.

'My other nephew,' Faheem says, arriving at my side. 'Ahmed's cousin. There is a warrant out for his arrest. If he were to walk into a hospital for treatment, he would wake up in handcuffs.'

Beside the patient stands a woman, looking at me with caution. She too is wearing a balaclava to protect her identity, but I can see long, dark hair trailing out the back, and beautiful hazel eyes peering out of the holes in the mask.

'This is his nurse,' Faheem says.

She gives me a silent nod and hands me a file.

'These are the notes I've kept. I hope they're adequate.'

She seems cold towards me, and I notice that she is holding the patient's hand, with a large diamond ring shining on her finger. This must be his wife.

'Sit,' Faheem says. 'And read.'

I take the seat nearest the fire, shivering from my damp clothes where we got caught in the rain, and open the file with shaking hands.

The notes are handwritten in small scribbles, but after years of working in medicine, I have become used to it, and read through the notes as quickly as I can, aware that I am being watched. Doing what I know best gives me a welcome sense of calm, and I focus on the task at hand. They have the patient on at least a dozen medications. None of them will be enough to keep him alive for much longer.

'How long has he been bedbound?' I ask the nurse.

'Nine months,' she replies. 'He would get so breathless that he would lose his balance.'

'Would he faint?'

She nods from his bedside.

'It says here you were able to get him an angiogram?'

The nurse nods and opens the small cupboard at the patient's bedside. She crosses the room and hands me the x-ray.

I hold it up to the light of the fire as the nurse returns to the patient, and see that all four of his main coronary arteries show signs of blockage, but not enough to debilitate him as he is now.

'This was taken a while ago?'

'Last spring,' she replies.

Which means the arteries have become significantly worse in only a year. I cross the room towards the bed and hand her back the files. She has a stethoscope around her neck.

'May I?'

She follows my line of sight and nods, unhooking it from her neck. The patient is looking me up and down.

'Can I have a listen?' I ask.

He blinks twice in quick succession.

'That means yes,' she says.

'He's too breathless to speak?'

'He's having a bad night. Some are better than others.'

I hook the stethoscope into my ears and listen to the patient's chest. His heart is beating dangerously fast for a man lying in bed. I would expect this sort of heart rate from someone who has just completed a four-mile run. I place my fingers to his neck.

'Sorry if my hand's a bit cold,' I say with a small smile, my usual line to try and put the patient at ease, but he says nothing. I listen to his heart for a full minute, tuning out the tick of the clock in the corner of the room, the rain pattering against the windows, the heat of Faheem's stare. I count one hundred and thirty beats, and erratic beats at that. This man should be in hospital. When I glance at his face, I notice his eyes have closed with sleep. I suspect he often dozes from lack of oxygen.

'It's severe. He needs surgery as soon as possible.'

Faheem ushers me over towards the fireplace. I cross the room with his hand in the small of my back and my heart pounding, and sit down before him. The flames reflect in his eyes.

'You think you can save him?'

'Yes, with the right equipment and support.'

He stares at me for a long time. I spot flashes of anger, flickers of doubt.

'I wouldn't . . . repeat what happened.'

He continues to stare, and I can't help but squirm beneath its intensity.

'How can I trust you?' he asks finally.

'No more than I can trust you. For all I know, I will do the procedure and you'll kill me anyway.'

He nods silently, as if the thought had crossed his mind;

my stomach drops at the thought. It is terrifying how little my life means to him. He could kill me without a second thought.

'I can save your nephew, Mr Shabbar. But only if you save my son.'

'Oh, so we are negotiating now?' he replies, a smirk twisting his lips. 'And here I was thinking you would do the surgery so I didn't lodge a bullet in your skull.'

I remember the cold metal of the gun against my forehead and swallow hard.

'I only care about my son.'

He watches me for a long time. I listen to the clock ticking from the other side of the room, the slow hiss from the oxygen tank filling the patient's lungs.

'Okay,' he says finally. 'Do the surgery, and in return we will retrieve your son.'

My heart leaps. I part my lips to thank him when he speaks again.

'You realise what will happen to you and your child if my nephew doesn't survive?'

He will kill us.

I nod silently, as it dawns on me that I am merely exchanging one threat for another.

But at least this way Zack and I have a chance.

'Who has Zack?' I ask. 'Who is doing this to us?'

'One of our competitors, the Volkovs. Ahmed's influence helped us with our business, but hindered theirs. This is them fighting back. Clearly they thought they could use you to get away with it.'

That's all Zack and I are to them. A way to even the score.

'When can you get him? He's in danger, and he is so young . . . He will be so scared—'

'It all depends on the surgery,' he interjects. 'The sooner it is performed, the sooner you get your son. So when we retrieve him is down to you.'

I stare at him blankly, trying to think my way out of the corner I have painted myself in. I can't just perform an impromptu, unscheduled surgery, especially without leaving a paper trail. I'd need an operating theatre, a team, drugs. I'm not even supposed to be on hospital grounds; my being there would be a red flag in itself.

Faheem is watching me, waiting. I look nervously towards the patient and try to talk myself out of what I know I am about to say. I repeat the thought I had just before I entered the room.

Just do as they say. Do whatever you have to do to get out of here. Zack's life depends on it.

'Tonight,' I blurt out. 'We will do it tonight.'

The nurse stands urgently, and whispers something in the language I don't understand. Faheem raises his hand to silence her, never once taking his eyes off mine.

'Your nephew is already at tremendous risk,' I say, with as much authority as I can muster. 'He won't last another week in the condition he is in. He should have had the surgery a long time ago. The quicker we do this, the likelier he is to survive.'

And the quicker I get my son back.

He watches me for the longest time, and I stare back, refusing to give into the tension.

The nurse speaks again, glaring at Faheem's back.

'We must trust her,' he replies in English. 'She is our only hope.'

Tears of relief bite at my eyes.

To think, after all this is done, I will have Zack home. I don't know how I will make this happen, but once I have performed the surgery, and the Shabbars have dealt with the abductors, they will all be out of our lives, and Detective Conaty will retreat once she sees Zack is safe. All I have to hope for is that the hospital investigation concludes in my favour. That is, until another worry begins to niggle at me. One thread I have yet to tie up.

'There's one more thing,' I say, and glance at the nurse beside the patient's bed. 'Something we must discuss alone.'

Faheem turns to the woman and speaks in his native tongue. She glares at me and leaves the room without another word.

Only then, when the door is shut and we are left alone with the sleeping patient, do I speak.

43

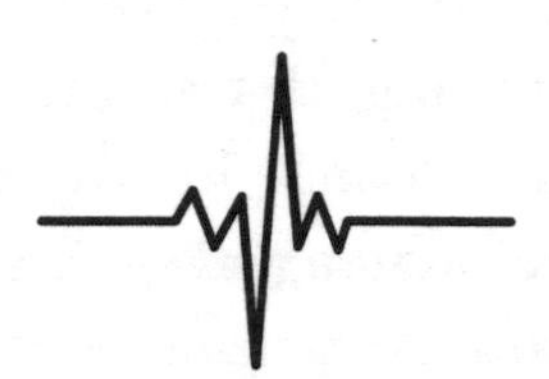

Margot

Tuesday, 9 April 2019, 22:30

I stand before the men, shivering in the dark, my cheek still stinging where Jax struck me to stop my shouting. I went down hard and scraped my cheekbone against the tarmac. My elbow took the brunt of the fall; it will be black and blue by morning.

The men haven't taken their eyes off me.

Two hours must have passed since Anna was taken. At first I presumed they had taken her away to kill her, and imagined all the ways she could have been dying as I stood alone, shivering on the forecourt and wondering how long it would take for them to do the same to me. But as time passed and the panic slowly subsided, it dawned on me that if they were disposing of her, they wouldn't just leave me here. I would be dealt with too. But still we wait.

I need to use the bathroom, and my throat is bone dry. About an hour ago, I asked if I could sit in the car to keep warm, but the men simply continued to stare me down. I have stood here since, shivering and smoking through my pack of cigarettes, leaving a scattering of fag butts at my feet.

An engine revs behind me and I turn around. Headlights are making their way up the uneven track, jolting up and down as they ride the potholes.

It must be her. They've brought her back. Or maybe they've killed her and are coming for me.

The car reaches the end of the lane, veering to the left as if to pass the building, and stops with a sudden jolt. My heart sinks. It isn't the car that Anna was driven away in, but a Porsche Cayman with last year's number plate. It's just another steal.

Damien and Rick get out of the car and step onto the forecourt.

Oh shit.

'What the hell are you doing here?' Damien asks as he strides over to me, with Rick following quickly behind him.

'Oi,' Damien says as he reaches me. 'I asked you a question.'

His eyes are practically bulging with rage. He spots the bruise on my cheek and immediately looks to the men guarding me.

'You do this?'

'Jax,' the man on the left replies. 'She was causing trouble.'

He looks back to me, shaking with fury.

'What kind of trouble?'

'It's hard to explain,' I reply.

He clamps down on my arms.

'I told you not to come back here.'

With his face so close, I can see that his pupils are dilated and there is a white substance framing his nostrils. I glance at Rick behind him; he looks equally as wired.

'Don't look at him,' Damien says, giving me a jolt. 'Look at me. What are you doing here?'

'Hey!' Rick says, and snatches up my hand. 'That's my ring!'

I yank it back and flinch as Damien shouts again, his breath hot against my face.

'Explain yourself. *Now.*'

A bright, white light beams in our eyes. We both squint and turn to see another car pulling onto the forecourt. When the engine turns off, and the lights die out, I recognise it from before.

It's the car Anna was taken in.

The doors open in quick succession, and one masked man after another steps out of the car. I hope to see Anna's head crop up, and each time it doesn't my heart sinks.

Oh God, they really have killed her. She's dead somewhere, been left to rot.

Another figure gets out of the car. It is too dark, and I presume it's just another masked man, until I clock that it isn't a balaclava like the rest, but a hood. I watch as it is yanked off and Anna's blonde hair cuts through the dark.

I pull away from Damien's hold and rush to meet her. She looks strangely calm, but her face is deathly pale. The masked men pass me without a word.

'Are you okay?'

I look her up and down for blood and bruises, but she appears untouched. She nods silently and catches sight of my cheek.

'We need to go,' she says urgently, and turns without another word.

'Well, wait a minute. What happened? I thought—'

I look over my shoulder. Damien and Rick are staring at me, bewildered.

'Margot,' Anna says sharply. She is standing by my car waiting to be let in.

I take one last glance at Damien, and can still see how visibly furious he is with me for coming here. I should try and talk him round, explain it was necessary to get the money, but I can sense Anna growing restless. I can't afford for her to leave without me.

I return to my car, refusing to turn back even when Damien calls my name.

'What happened, then?' I ask, as we get inside the car. 'Did they hurt you?'

I start the engine and swing the car around. She doesn't say a word until we are halfway down the bumpy track.

'I'm fine.'

'What did they want?'

She stares out of the window as if I haven't spoken. I reach the end of the lane and pull out onto the country road, breathing in the smell of fresh sweat coming off her. She jitters her foot nervously against the footwell.

'Anna,' I say sternly. 'What did they want?'

'They will get my son back,' she says, strangely calm. 'But there is something we have to do first.'

'Well, that's great . . .' I reply cautiously, perturbed by her mood. 'What do we have to do?'

She is silent again, staring off into the distance. Almost like she's high or something. Whatever happened to her, she is still reeling from it.

'Ahmed Shabir had a cousin,' she says finally. 'He needs our help.'

Needs our help? Where the hell is she going with this?

'So he needs surgery?' I ask.

'Yes.'

'Well, why is that impossible? You do coronary bypasses every day. You can just book him in and—'

'It has to be off the books,' she interjects, and finally looks me in the eye. 'And it has to be tonight.'

'Wait, wait, wait . . . *what*?' I laugh at how absurd it is and I look back to the road. She doesn't laugh with me. 'How would we do that exactly? We don't have an anaesthetist or perfusionist or . . . *anyone*. We can't perform heart surgery with just the pair of us.'

'We have to find a way,' she replies matter-of-factly.

'Look, I get you want your son back, but you haven't thought this through. How are we going to perform a heart operation without anyone in the hospital knowing?'

'We did it with Ahmed Shabir. We'll follow the same steps we took with him: bring him through the rear of the hospital, close off the ward for deep cleaning, block the theatre off the board so no one attempts to use it. We can do this.'

I'm not sure whether she really believes what she's saying, or whether she is trying to convince herself as well as me. Either way, she sounds mad. In this light she even looks it: pupils dilated by shock, her hands shaking in her lap.

'Oh, really? And what about all the tests you'll need to run? The blood tests, ECG, x-ray, echo, vein-mapping, the list goes on. If you do a single one of them the hospital will be able to trace it back to us, but if you don't, you'll have no way of knowing what we're up against, not completely. Your big plan is to go in blind?'

'If I have to, yes!'

I pull over the car and slam on the brakes. We both lurch forward against our belts.

'Do you hear yourself? This is *insane*.'

'It's the only way I'll get my son back alive,' she replies firmly. 'And the only way you'll get your money.'

I stare at her, enraged and in awe of her stubbornness. This is the most reckless thing we could possibly do. If we were found out, Anna would never be able to perform surgery again, and I would have another crime to add to my charge sheet. Assisting an operation at a hospital I was fired from? I can't even count the amount of reckless endangerment charges that could be brought against me.

But if I don't get the money, I'll be going to prison regardless.

'So what, you think we can pull off a bypass surgery alone?'

'Of course not,' she snaps.

'Then how are we going to do it? Because no one in their right mind would help you do this, not even if you put a bloody gun to their head.'

Anna turns in her seat and stares me straight in the eyes.

'You need to stop acting like we have a choice, Margot. We're both in this now. We only had one threat until your genius idea, and now we have two dangerous groups of people chasing at our heels.

'If we don't do this surgery, and I am discovered for killing Ahmed Shabir, the men who have my son will kill him and then us. But if we do the surgery, the Shabbars will retrieve my son and deal with the men who have him. Two birds, one stone. You get your money, and I get my child. This is our only way out. So we are going to sit in this car and we are not leaving until we have come up with a plan, because I can't see that we have any other choice. Can you?'

Her chest is rising and falling fast, and her eyes are desperate. I turn away and look out at the moonlit road.

'You're forgetting one other outcome,' I say.

'And what's that?'

'If we do this surgery, and the patient dies . . .'

We both fall silent, envisioning the repercussions. I doubt they'd let Anna kill a second member of their family and get away with it.

'Well, we will have to make sure that doesn't happen then, won't we?'

44

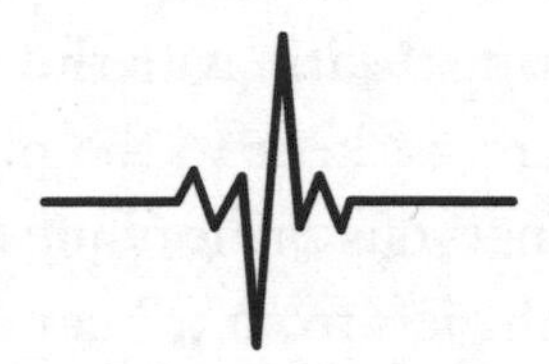

Anna

Wednesday, 10 April 2019, 00:34

I used to think people were being dramatic when describing something as an out-of-body experience, but the last few hours have passed me by in a blur. I have watched myself do things that were risky and reckless and begged myself to stop, only to watch helplessly as I kept going, the desperation to get Zack home forcing one foot in front of the other.

After coming up with our plan and informing the Shabbars, Margot and I reached the hospital at eleven-thirty through the rear entrance of the west wing, and immediately got to work. With PPE masks over our mouths and noses to hide our faces, we set out the very same security measures we had used during Ahmed Shabir's surgery. The hallway leading to the theatre has been cordoned off for deep cleaning, and the theatre's availability has been struck off the board so we don't find ourselves interrupted. Inside, we have prepared every instrument and piece of equipment we might need, and every possible drug that we could conceive of using. Margot really is good at taking things that don't belong to her.

Now all there is to do is wait for the patient to arrive.

I wait in the operating theatre with the two men Mr Shabbar sent over to make sure we kept to the plan, and listen to the tick of the clock, the nervous rattle of my heart. I recognise the voice of the man on the left from the car ride to meet Faheem. They are well built, with the same bronzed skin and dark hair as Faheem, dressed in the surgical scrubs and masks we gave them to disguise themselves the moment they arrived. I hate the way they watch over everything I do, suspecting my motives, but we need them here if we are going to successfully lay the trap for the on-call anaesthetist. I just wish it wasn't Dr Burke.

I go over the plan in my head and obsess over all of the ways it could go wrong. It is only now, as the shock wanes with exhaustion and I have time to think, that I take in how fast we have planned all this. If only we'd had more time to make sure it is absolutely seamless. But tonight is the only night that the abductors expect me to be here at the hospital. And by the looks of my patient, he will be dead within a week without the surgery.

And I can't be away from Zack for a moment longer.

It really is now or never.

The door to the scrub room just beyond the theatre opens with a high-pitched whine. We all snap our heads towards the sound. One of the men must have instinctively reached for his gun, for his hand hovers where it is hidden at his waist.

Margot steps into the room. It isn't until I sigh with relief that I realise I had been holding my breath.

'Dr Burke is out of surgery,' she says.

I look towards the men. The one whose voice I recognise nods back.

It's now or never.

'Page him,' I say.

Margot takes the pager from her hip and sends the page as I get down on my knees and slowly raise my hands. Margot follows suit while the two men walk behind us and aim their guns at the back of our heads.

No one in their right mind would help you do this, not even if you put a bloody gun to their head.

That's what Margot said when I first mentioned the surgery to her, and what struck the idea for how we could elicit help. Because she was wrong, of course someone would help us with the surgery if their life, or the life of someone they love, depended on it. It's exactly how I have found myself in this mess.

My heart is racing, and I can feel the rush of my blood coursing through me, tingling in my knees where I kneel.

This is all for Zack.

Having a gun held to the back of my head squeezes all of the air out of my lungs. I tell myself it is all part of the plan, that he doesn't mean me harm, but the thought of the gun aiming right at me has my lungs shrinking, and my heart beating faster, and faster, and faster, until my breaths grow lighter and my head starts to float and . . .

Dr Burke opens the door.

My heart stops.

I watch as he freezes on the spot, looking down at Margot and me on our knees with his mouth ajar, then back up at the men. His gaze stops on the gun pointed at the back of my head.

'W-what's going on here?' he stutters.

'On your knees,' the man behind Margot orders. He steps forward, his gun aimed at Dr Burke's head. 'I said: *On ... your ... knees.*'

Burke lowers himself towards the floor until he is knelt before me and we are staring each other in the eyes. He is shaking so hard that his shirt is quivering.

'What do you want?' he stutters.

'Dr Jones is going to perform a surgery tonight,' the gunman says. 'And you are going to help her.'

Burke stares at the man, shocked into silence.

'All you have to do is help Dr Jones while she works and never mutter a word of what you saw in this room, and no one gets hurt. Understand?'

Dr Burke stares at the man in a terrified trance. He looks like he is about to scream, or cry, or both.

The gunman behind me slides back the chamber of the gun. I hear the snap of metal and flinch.

'Okay! Okay!' Dr Burke replies desperately. 'Just ... don't hurt us.'

'Dr Burke,' I say, real tears stinging in my eyes, 'I know you're scared. I am too. But if we're going to get out of this we need to stay calm, and we need to trust each other. We can do this.'

Burke looks at me, wired with adrenaline; his eyes are practically jittering in their sockets.

'Do you trust me?'

He tries to speak, but no words come out. His gaze falls back on the gun pointed at my head.

'Burke ...' I say firmly. 'These men, they know where we live. Do you understand what I'm telling you? They know where our *children* live.'

His face drains completely white.

'Your daughter,' the gunman behind me says. 'She sleeps in the bedroom at the front of your house. With the pink curtains, right?'

I feel sick with guilt for telling them that. I only know this because of the Christmas party Adam and I were invited to by the Burkes last year, when I went searching for the bathroom and stumbled into the wrong room. They had been so welcoming to us. Now I am betraying him in the worst possible way. But I would do it again if I had to. Threatening his child is the only way to save mine.

'We must do this surgery, Dr Burke,' I say, at almost a whisper. 'And we must never tell a soul.'

'Never,' he utters. 'I promise.'

A phone rings, and the gunman behind me answers the call in his mother tongue. When he hangs up, the room rings with taut silence, everyone in the room hanging off his next words.

'They are here,' he says.

45

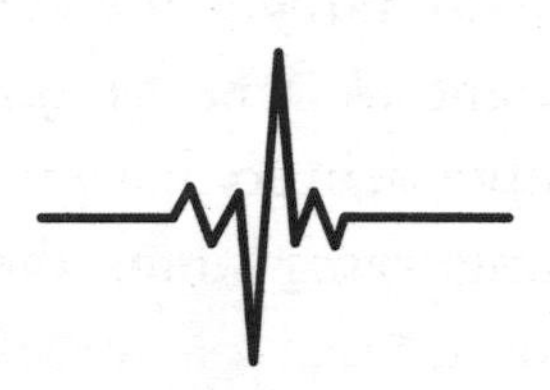

Anna

Wednesday, 10 April 2019, 00:48

I am escorted by one of Shabbar's men. We stand in the lift in silence, but for the amplified breaths behind our masks. I wonder who Ahmed was to this man; I wonder how much he hates me.

The doors open on the ground floor, and we walk along the long, cold corridor towards the rear entrance of the west wing. I have the extra pairs of scrubs and masks piled up in my hands, while the man walks a step behind watching my every move.

The front of the hospital had been newly renovated when I began working here, with the front of the building sporting a whole fresh face; every floor within the public-facing areas had been replaced, every wall painted. But the rear of the hospital hasn't been seen by a decorator in decades, with the west entrance assigned for supply deliveries and secret smoke breaks. The state-of-the-art security system hasn't reached this far either, meaning we can come and go without being caught on camera.

We reach the rear doors, which slide open automatically and let in the cold night air. The patient's transport is waiting, parked in the empty delivery bay: a black, unmarked van with its engine running, ready to tail out of trouble at just a second's notice.

'Go,' the man says.

A rough hand shoves me in my lower back, and I step out onto the tarmac, my heart racing. When I approach the window on the passenger side I jump at the sight of the man on the other side of the glass. He is wearing the same balaclava I had seen earlier in the evening, two dark eyes staring out at me from the holes in the mask. The window lowers, and I pass the scrubs without a word. He takes a pair for himself and passes the rest through a hatch into the back of the truck. When the window rolls back up, I return the way I came.

After only a moment, the man exits the passenger side dressed in the scrubs I gave him, with the surgical mask covering the lower half of his face, and opens the rear doors of the truck. The patient is lowered to the forecourt on a gurney, rasping behind his oxygen mask, and two more men appear from within, dressed in their scrubs disguise. As they wheel the patient towards the doors, I realise one of them is Faheem Shabir himself.

'I didn't think you would be here in person,' I say as he approaches, the truck driving away behind him.

'You thought I'd let you perform surgery on another member

of my family without keeping an eye on you? I thought surgeons were supposed to be smart.'

I lead the way back up the corridor towards the lift, trying not to reveal my nerves. Just a few hours ago this man ordered me dead. I remember the barrel of the gun rising up towards my forehead, watching the stranger's finger tense on the trigger. I am close to death every second I am in Shabbar's presence. All he has to do is say the word.

'Everything is prepared?' he asks.

'Yes,' I reply, trying to keep the stammer from my voice.

'I am still not sure about bringing another person into this.'

'I can't perform the procedure without an anaesthetist, Mr Shabbar.'

'Don't say my name in there,' he warns. 'This Dr Burke, he knows what will happen if he talks?'

Yes. You will kill him. You will kill us all.

'He is aware. I made sure of it.' I lead the way to the lift, the wheels of the gurney squeaking against the lino floor, and look down at the patient as we walk. 'How are you feeling?'

He nods back at me behind the mask, but I can see the fear in his eyes. He still doesn't know if he can trust me. After what I did, I wouldn't trust me either.

We reach the lift and pile inside, cramming around the patient's gurney. The small space soon grows hot from our bodies, and I'm struck by a horrid case of déjà vu: I think back to escorting Ahmed Shabir down to the morgue, with the two abductors riding in the lift with me. The memory is so vivid that I feel the heat of them, smell the blood wafting up as I uncovered Shabir's body. I never thought I would have to do something like this again.

As soon as we enter the theatre, I can sense the panic in the air. Buzzing like a current. Burke is visibly shaking at his station, while Margot stands waiting at the operating table, her eyes wide with angst.

The Shabbars align the patient's gurney next to the operating table, and Dr Burke immediately begins settling up the IV.

'Wait over there, please,' I say to Faheem and his men. 'In the corner and out of the way.'

'If you try anything—' Faheem warns.

'We won't,' I reply firmly.

Margot holds open a pair of gloves and I slip them on, before leaning over to look the patient in the eyes.

'We're going to put you under now, okay? Rest assured that we are here to help you, and nothing more. When you wake up you will be safe at home, feeling much stronger than you do now. Sound good?'

He nods nervously behind his oxygen mask, but I can still see that look of distrust in his eyes. He looks around, searching for someone.

'I think he wants you.'

Mr Shabbar steps forward and leans over the patient, taking his hand. While they whisper to each other under their breaths in prayer, I think over the next steps in my head: as soon as the patient is sedated, Dr Burke will fit the breathing tube and Margot will get to work draping the patient ready to be cut, and I will head to the foot of the bed to dissect the bypass veins myself.

I look to Margot. If she's scared, she is good at concealing it, and I'm glad I have her on side. I need her extra pair of eyes, her strength. For as soon as I make the first cut, there is no going back. The patient must live, or we all die. Zack would never be found. From now until daybreak, all of their lives depend on me.

When Faheem steps away, I nod towards Dr Burke and watch as he injects the anaesthesia into the IV, and step towards the patient.

'Count down from ten for me.'

'Ten . . .' he rasps behind his mask. 'Nine . . .'

Before he can reach eight, his eyes roll and his lids flicker shut.

No going back now.

I move to the end of the table with my pulse thumping in my neck, and lift up the surgical drapes to expose the patient's legs to begin harvesting the veins. My heart drops at what I see.

Large, swollen calves. Fat, purple feet where blood is trapped beneath the skin. I see Margot tense up in the corner of my eye. We both know what this means. I can almost hear her, taunting me from inside her head.

I told you we shouldn't be going in blind.

46

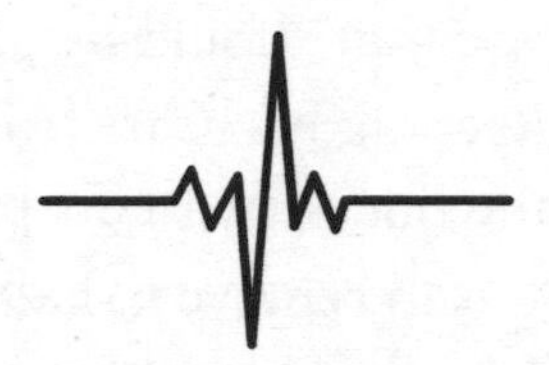

Anna

Wednesday, 10 April 2019, 01:10

'How long have his legs been like this?' I ask.

I try to sound as flippant as I can. The moment I show Faheem weakness, or even the slightest lack of knowledge, his distrust of me will spike. I can't afford to have him trust me any less, especially not this early in the procedure; I haven't even cut into the patient yet. If I'm going to get through this surgery without a hitch, I need him calm.

'About four months,' he says, from the corner of the room.

'And has he experienced a dry cough?'

I watch as Faheem thinks back. 'Yes. Often.'

'And is the shortness of breath worse when he lies down?'

'Yes . . . Why are you asking me these questions?'

'Just continuing my assessment,' I lie. 'Nothing to worry about. Margot, scalpel.'

I take the blade and make the first cut, and begin preparing to dissect veins for the coronary bypasses.

The symptoms Mr Shabbar confirmed suggest that the patient not only has blocked coronary arteries, but constrictive pericarditis: the sac that should be protecting his heart is inflamed. Instead of keeping his heart from harm, the pericardium is choking the life out of it.

The only treatment is to remove it; hell, it's the only way I'll be able do the procedure that we are actually here to perform. But the two procedures need to be tackled in completely different ways. To bypass the coronary arteries, I need to transfer blood circulation to the heart–lung machine, but to remove the pericardium, I need the heart to beat on its own and keep its blood supply going. If the pericardium causes bleeding, I need to know about it before I sew him up; being on the heart–lung machine takes that opportunity away. On another patient, I might perform the coronary artery bypasses off-pump and while the heart is still beating, but it comes with more risks, and this patient's heart is far too weak. If it is put under any more strain there is a high chance it will give up on me.

I should have been more thorough in my assessment when I met the patient. If I had, I might have seen this coming. But I was so eager to get out of there.

I dissect the last of the veins and silently form my plan.

I'll delay using the heart–lung machine and perform the pericardiectomy, then switch to the machine and complete the bypasses. When it's all done, we will restore heart function and wait for as long as we can for any signs of bleeding from the pericardiectomy. That's if we have time to spare at the end of the procedure; if there aren't any other surprises in store.

After I have closed up the incisions on the patient's legs, Margot takes the dissected veins and I move to the top of the operating table towards the chest.

'Dr Burke,' I say calmly, conscious that Faheem is hanging off my every word. 'We'll be delaying bypass initially.'

'Why?' Faheem interjects. 'You said you could do this—'

'I can. But I have to deal with another issue first, which needs to be dealt with while the heart is beating on its own.'

'What do you mean, another issue?' he asks, standing to attention.

'Swollen legs, dry cough, breathing issues exacerbated when lying down . . . these are symptoms of constrictive pericarditis. The sac around his heart that is there to protect it has thickened and hardened, making the heart struggle to do its job. It's not a problem, it just changes our plans slightly.'

I request the scalpel from Margot and turn to Mr Shabbar.

'You may wish to turn away for this bit.'

With the blade poised in my hand, a sense of control comes over me. I slowly run the scalpel along the skin until his flesh and muscle peel away and the white of his breastbone is exposed. I hand the scalpel back to Margot, who passes me the oscillating saw in return.

Faheem flinches as I power the saw. I move the blade up and down through the bone until the pressure gives and the rib cage cracks open, all the while fearing the level of disease I will find beneath. I pass the saw to Margot and take up the retractors to open the chest.

'What are the risks of this other procedure?' Faheem asks.

This is the first time I have had a patient's guardian in the theatre with me, and I can't say I like it. I fit the metal teeth of the retractors between the crack in the bone, and talk as I go.

'Well, there is an increased risk of infection, potential heart displacement—'

'Then you mustn't do it.'

'The alternative is that the patient dies,' I reply flatly. 'Would you like me to save his life?'

Mr Shabbar looks back at me, his cheeks reddening with anger.

'Of course.'

'Then you need to let me do my job. Outside of this room, you can treat me however you like, but in here, during this surgery – you follow my lead. Otherwise the patient will die. Is that clear?'

We stare at each other across the room. A flush of heat prickles across my back from the scrutiny, but I hold his gaze. I can feel Dr Burke squirming from the tension, sense Margot holding her breath. Finally, he nods. I sigh silently behind my mask.

'Thank you.'

I take hold of the retractor and shift the ribcage apart, and slowly reveal the organ beating away inside the chest cavity. Usually Margot and I would jump straight in, tools poised. But instead we stand on either side of the table and stare silently into the chest, before sharing a brief, terrified look.

This is quite possibly the most severe case of constrictive pericarditis I have ever seen.

47

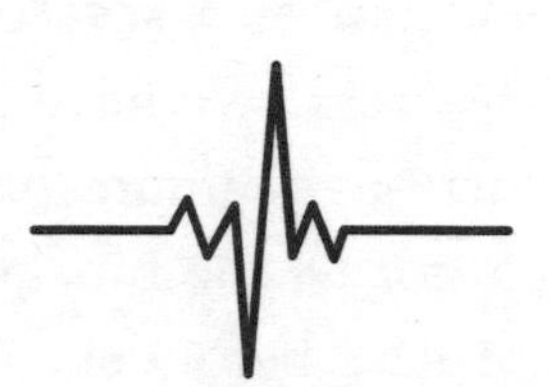

Margot

Wednesday, 10 April 2019, 02:10

'*Slower*,' Dr Jones orders, placing a gloved finger on mine where it is poised along the tweezers. 'Even if you think you're going too lightly – go lighter. These heart walls are extremely friable.'

Friable is putting it lightly. The pericardium hasn't only constricted around the heart, it has calcified, essentially super-gluing itself to the surface of the muscle. It will be impossible to remove it all without tearing the heart to shreds.

'Dr Jones, I'm going as lightly as I can, but—'

'No buts,' she replies harshly. 'Just get it done.'

. . . but it is so difficult to do this while the heart is still beating.

Every time I peel a strip of it away, I have to follow the rhythmic movements of the heart so I don't accidentally stab it with my tool. If I pull away too fast or tug too hard, I could tear the whole thing open. But the patient's heartbeat is irregular due to all of the strain it is under, making its rhythm difficult to predict. The patient may be in his forties, but his heart might as well belong to an eighty-year-old chain smoker.

I check the clock: it's quarter past two in the morning. My head is pounding with stress. We have been performing the pericardiectomy for forty-five minutes, and we are only half done; we haven't even got to the blocked coronary arteries yet. If we aren't out of here before six, we might as well be sitting ducks, waiting for someone to walk inside and catch us in the act.

Shabbar and his men are watching us from the corner of the room. He has his sights set firmly on Dr Jones, looking from her hands to her eyes, and back again. If he does look away, it is to assess me, or Dr Burke sat shaking in the corner.

Dr Burke looks utterly terrified, staring ahead blindly and tapping his foot nervously on the lino floor. I catch his eye and give him a wink over the top of my mask to try and tell him we will be okay, and he smiles briefly before falling back into his shocked, almost catatonic state.

It's a lie, of course – I have no idea if we will get through this. Even if we do save this man's life, we still might each receive a bullet to the back of the head. I imagine the sound of the gunshot, the thud my body would make as it hit the ground.

My breaths get shallower, and shallower.

Don't think of that, I scold. *Stop panicking – just breathe.*

Dr Jones is inevitably tense. While usually she holds herself with relaxed ease, tonight she is working with a stifling rigidity, her muscles frozen into place with fear and angst. Her mask is barely moving due to the pace and depth of her breaths.

'Margot,' she says. Her eyes dart up to meet mine in a flash and I jolt. '*Focus.*'

My cheeks flush and I look back down to the heart.

I have been knowingly avoiding certain pieces of the pericardium, but all of the easier pieces have been removed. I zone in on an area that is reaching around the side of the upper-right atrium, and poise my tweezers.

Slowly, I remind myself, as I assess the rhythm of the patient's heartbeat, and pinch the strip between the tips. Just as I begin to peel it away, the heart beats out of sync and pulls away from my hold, the wall of the right atrium tearing open as it goes. Dark blood immediately gushes out and into the chest cavity. The heart-rate monitor screams.

'*What did you do*?' Dr Jones scolds.

'It wasn't my fault! There was a palpitation and then—'

'Save your excuses and give me suction, *now.*'

I put down the tweezers and take up the suction, aiming the nozzle over the blood filling the chest and blocking the view of the tear, as Dr Jones picks up her needle driver and suture. Just as she is about to hook the needle into the heart wall, we both freeze to the faint yet deafening click of a bullet entering the chamber of a gun.

I look up. Faheem is stood behind Dr Jones, his gun pointed directly at the back of her head. Dr Burke is whimpering. I peer over Dr Jones' shoulder to see another of the men aiming a gun between his eyes.

The third gunman is behind me.

'If he dies, you die, Dr Jones,' Faheem says. 'You all do.'

My stomach drops. Tears instantly fill my eyes. The heart-rate machine gets louder. Screeching into my ears until I can't think straight.

I don't want to die.

I stare into Dr Jones' terrified eyes, stray tears slipping down my cheeks as I watch her process the fear. Faheem prods the barrel of the gun into the back of her head.

'Come on!'

She whimpers as it touches her, and clenches her eyes shut, her lips moving behind her mask as she thinks aloud. Slowly, her breaths calm, and her body stops shaking. When she opens her eyes, I see how focused they have become.

'Burke,' she orders. 'Stats.'

I hear him scramble at his station.

'B-b-b-blood pressure dropping fast.'

'Push nitroprusside and up the blockers. Push his BP down as low as it'll go, and get ready to administer a transfusion or jump on bypass if I need you to. And Margot, for the love of God, *suction*.'

I look down. The patient's chest has filled with blood, sloshing and bubbling where the heart is beating erratically. I thrust the nozzle into the pool and suck it away, as Dr Jones hooks the needle into the heart wall and begins to suture the tear together against the heart's beating.

'Blood volume falling,' Dr Burke calls.

'Start a transfusion,' she orders. 'Give him everything we have.'

The nozzle of the gun grazes the back of my head and the shock of it makes me burst into tears.

I don't want to die. I don't want my baby to die.

'*Margot*,' Dr Jones shouts. 'Look at me.'

I open my eyes, and blink back the tears between whimpers.

'Don't think of the gun,' she says. 'Think of the patient. I can't do this without you. Now *focus*.'

I blink away the tears and look down at the chest cavity, and suction at the blood. I cry and blink, cry and blink, the scene below coming in and out of focus. I hear Dr Jones say something, but it sounds tinny and far away.

'Blood volume is low but staying put,' Burke says in response, as sounds become crisper. 'Pressure slowly stabilising.'

The excess blood has almost gone, and the tear has been sutured shut. The danger is passing. I sigh behind my mask, feeling the tension ease from my shoulders.

Then the heart monitor starts wailing again.

'Heart has fallen into A-fib,' Burke calls.

I stare down at the chest cavity. The heart isn't beating normally: it's trembling minutely, too weak to push the blood from one chamber to the other.

'Margot, paddles.'

I reach around for the defibrillation machine and stare right down the barrel of a gun. I scramble for the buttons with tears in my eyes as the weapon is pressed against my temple.

'Focus, Margot,' Dr Jones calls over the noise. 'Remember – you're thinking of the patient.'

Thinking of the patient, thinking of the patient . . .

I repeat her words as I power up the machine and the gun digs deeper into the side of my head. Something hot is burning into my thighs. I grab the paddles and turn, and almost slip as I pass them across to her.

'Charge to one hundred.'

I turn the dial and wait for the all-clear. The electric current shocks the heart, but there is still no response.

'Charge to two hundred.'

I turn the dial and watch as Dr Jones' whole body jolts with the motion, and looks towards the heart-rate monitor. Everyone's attention is on the screen, watching the lines, longing for a change to the low, ineffective rhythm.

If he dies, you die. You all do.

A tear leaks slowly down my cheek.

The heart jolts back to life.

Every chest in the room deflates with relief, and the guns lower from our heads. The adrenaline seems to seep away the second the gunmen step back, and I feel my body slump with exhaustion.

I look down to where my legs had been burning: my scrubs are soaked through with urine, and I can see it shimmering on the floor. When I slipped while turning to hand over the paddles, I had done so on my own urine that had been silently pooling on the floor. I literally pissed myself in fear.

'Well done, team,' Dr Jones says. She sounds authoritative and in control, but her eyes are wired, and I notice the paddles shaking in her grip as she passes them back to me. 'That's as far as we can go with the pericardiectomy, but it's enough for the heart to beat without restraint.' She blinks furiously and looks up at the clock. 'We have three and a half hours to bypass these arteries. Burke, have the heart–lung machine ready.'

She looks to me across the chest cavity, and puts out her bloodied, gloved hand. 'Margot, scalpel.'

I reach for the tool table and pick up the scalpel, as the last of my energy threatens to wane.

The surgery we came here to do hasn't even begun.

48

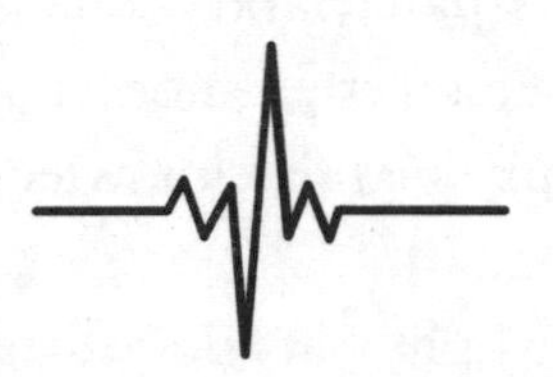

Margot

Wednesday, 10 April 2019, 05:00

Dr Jones is just finishing up with the last vein graft when the clock strikes five.

I have never been so exhausted. My head is pounding, and my teeth and tongue are coated in fur. The scrub trousers have dried now, stuck to my thighs like a second skin.

Dr Jones looks tired too. The whites of her eyes are bloodshot, and the dark circles around them have grown deeper as the night's gone on. But somehow, she has kept us all from breaking. Before I entered this room I hated the woman, but now I feel a level of kinship with her that I can't deny. She must feel it too, for she has been kinder to me tonight than during any of the other surgeries we have worked together. Trauma bonds even the unlikeliest people together, I guess.

Faheem Shabbar is still alert, watching our every move. The men behind him, however, have started to fidget on their feet where the blood will have pooled in them, the pins and needles encroaching up their calves after standing for so many hours.

Dr Burke looks ten years older than he had when he entered the room. His skin is paler, and the bags under his eyes are puffy and swollen. We meet each other's eyes, but we are too exhausted to force smiles, and acknowledge each other silently before looking away again.

It will be growing light outside before long. Soon patients will be arriving for admission, and the nurses will be getting ready to do their handovers. We have just under an hour to get the patient sewn up and off the premises, and for a brief, delusional moment, everything seems as it should: Dr Jones and I are finishing up a surgery, with Dr Burke sat in the corner. But then I catch sight of the Shabbars in the corner of the room with the guns at their waists, and reality slaps the delirium out of me.

'Burke,' Dr Jones calls. 'I think we're ready to come off bypass.'

It's almost over, I tell myself, allowing the pure sense of relief to wash over me.

Dr Jones waits for the all-clear from Dr Burke, and once the blood has returned to the patient's circulatory system, she reaches towards the clamp, keeping the heart isolated from the blood supply. She allows a short burst of blood to enter and wash out the potassium fluid that has kept the heart from beating, and the colour of its flesh slowly brightens. We wait with baited breath, every pair of eyes in the room honing in on the patient's heart.

The heart starts beating.

And then the door to theatre opens from the outside.

49

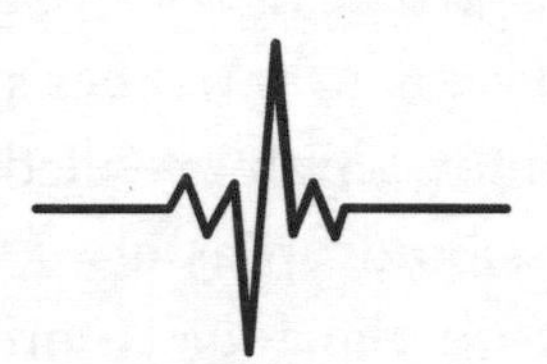

Anna

Wednesday, 10 April 2019, 05:11

David from security is standing in the doorway.

I watch his face change multiple times in just a few seconds. His brow, creased with confusion as he takes in the occupied room; then he recognises me behind my mask – a normal, trustworthy fixture in the theatre – and his face relaxes again. Then he notices the strange men in the corner of the room.

Everyone in the room stands in stunned silence, listening to nothing but the odd beep from the machines, the mechanical inflation of the lungs. The tension is so palpable that the ring in the air pierces like a scream. David doesn't know it, but he has killed us all.

I catch Faheem reaching for his gun in the corner of my eye and my heart lurches.

'David,' I blurt out. 'Can we help you?'

His eyes look up from the open chest cavity and meet mine.

'Sorry, I didn't mean to disturb you. I was checking if the cleaning team were ready to open up the ward. I didn't expect to see—'

'You didn't think, given the last time you and I saw each other, that the cordon might have been put in place to create an element of privacy for a high-profile client?'

I watch his expression drop as his confidence wavers. He looks at the patient on the table, sensing everyone in the room staring back at him. His brow knits together again with another thought.

'Wouldn't one of the security team have been asked to keep the perimeter secure?'

I'm as aggravated by his persistence as I am terrified. I outrank him by a mile, and to interrogate a surgeon like this puts him on very shaky ground; to do so means he has very strong doubts.

Margot is keeping her head down, and I realise why. If David clocks her, he will know something is amiss. There would be absolutely no reason why a fired employee would be brought in to help with a surgery.

Behind her, the Shabbars look like they are growing impatient. Faheem is staring at me. He doesn't say a word, but his message is loud and clear.

Do something, or I will.

'Believe it or not, David,' I say. 'We are perfectly capable of performing heart surgery without you or your team, and frankly, I don't appreciate being interrogated in my own operating theatre. I think you'd benefit from remembering your place.' I give him one of my sharpest glares. 'Or do I have to speak to your superior?'

He looks around the room, his cheeks red from my curt response.

'No, Dr Jones.' He turns to go, when something stops him. I stare at his broad back, my heart racing. He turns to face me again. 'Weren't you suspended?'

I can feel the tension in the room rising. My heart is pounding in my chest, and my face burns from Faheem's glare on the other side of the room. Margot is shaking on her side of the table with her eyes glued on the chest cavity between us. Behind her, Dr Burke is fidgeting, with his eyes set firmly on David in the doorway, his mouth trembling as if he is plucking up the courage to speak.

Oh my God. He's going to say something.

'David,' I snap. 'I don't know what's gotten into you, but I think it would be best if you left. You do not have the authority to walk into an operating theatre – which is growing less and less sterile the longer you're in here – and demand a surgeon to explain themselves. If you value your job, I highly suggest you turn around and go back to manning doors and pacing hallways. You are out of your depth here.'

David stares at me from the doorway. My tone and superiority has visibly shaken him. I glare at him with such rage that his face flushes and eventually, he breaks.

'I'm sorry, Dr Jones. It was my mistake.'

He turns to leave, and the door starts to close behind him.

'David—'

Everyone snaps their eyes to the corner of the room. Dr Burke is staring at the door, his mouth still ajar after calling his name.

You'll kill us all you fucking coward.

David appears in the doorway again. Faheem appears to

finally lose his patience. He reaches for his waist, and I imagine blood spraying from the back of David's head, the thud of his body collapsing on the floor.

'*Dr Burke*,' I snap. 'We really need to press on with this surgery. The patient's life depends on it. His daughter is waiting for her father to come home. Let's not keep her waiting any longer.'

I watch him recoil as I say *daughter*. He meets my eyes and I glare at him with such ferocity that I feel my face burning red and veins pulsing in my neck. Faheem is staring at me from one corner of the room, as David watches me from the other, as if we're all playing some toxic game of Russian roulette, waiting to see which one will fall.

Dr Burke nods and turns to David with a forced smile.

'I was just going to say, David . . . don't worry about all this. We won't take it any further. Lesson learned, hey?'

I turn to look at David in the doorway. He nods, a look of solemnity coming over his face.

'Thank you,' he replies, and turns to me. 'I'm sorry, Dr Jones. It's been a long night, I forgot myself.'

'Okay,' I reply, forcing a smile. 'Let's forget this ever happened. As far as I'm concerned, nothing occurred here tonight.'

'Thank you, Dr Jones.'

David turns and leaves the room, but I'm too scared to let down my guard. Only when I hear the door to the scrub room whine shut, and the ring of silence follow, do I finally exhale. I bite my lip to stop myself from sobbing with relief.

Mr Shabbar lunges across the room with his gun raised and slams Dr Burke into the wall, who whimpers against the tiles and begs for his mother. I should say something, stop him, but I am so angry with Dr Burke that I almost want it done.

He nearly killed us all.

'Dr Jones,' Margot says sharply.

I break away from my thoughts. She is looking at me in disbelief.

'Put down the gun,' I tell Faheem sternly. 'We're not finished here yet.'

Faheem stares at Burke with such rage that I anticipate the sound of a gunshot, and the white tiles on the walls to blast red. But eventually he lowers the gun, and backs away towards the other side of the room. Dr Burke stays flattened against the tiles, whimpering quietly to himself. I should feel for him, understand that he was trying to save us. But he almost killed us all. He almost killed Zack.

It is only when I look to the chest again to begin closing up the patient, that I truly take in what I see: a beating heart, beaming with colour from the healthy blood flow and space to move.

The patient is going to live.

50

Anna

Wednesday, 10 April 2019, 09:19

I wake up in Zack's room.

I know where I am before I even open my eyes. The scent of him is all around me: in the air, on the sheets. I bury my face into his pillow and inhale. It is starting to smell of me more than it is of Zack; I held it to my chest while I slept as if it were him, lying in the crook of me.

They are bringing him back. That's what Faheem said, as the patient was wheeled towards the unmarked van.

It doesn't feel real. The pain of having him ripped from me is now such an integral part of who I am that I can't imagine existing without it, even when he's home, as if it is something I will have to learn to live around. The surgeon in me wishes I could cut it out.

Before meeting with the Shabbars, all of my thoughts had

been on bringing him home. But now that it is a possibility, I can't help but think: once he is, what then? Not only has he experienced intense trauma, but it will have to be kept a secret. All of his painful memories locked up inside him, with me as his only confidant. He will have to lie repeatedly just like I have done, and he will undoubtedly want to know why.

Because Mummy is a killer.

Killer. There is no sugar-coating it, no justifying it. I took a life and watched it bleed out of him, held my breath until the deed was done. Will Zack hate me when he learns of what I did to save him? That I took a life in exchange for his?

Will my son fear me?

The sceptic in me awoke as soon as I got home and laid my head on his pillow, pulling my hope apart like a child picking at an insect's legs, severed limbs still kicking between their fingers. What if the Shabbars fail, and their intervention triggers the abductors to hurt Zack? What if the Shabbars cannot be trusted? *What if? What if? What if?*

I rub my eyes awake, feeling the nakedness of my lids without their lashes. I have only been asleep for an hour or so, but I have woken frustratingly alert. I won't be able to rest properly until Zack is finally home.

All of my phones are laid out beside the bed. I work my way down the line, pressing the home button on each handset to wake the screens, but there are zero notifications.

I stand up from the bed, smooth out the duvet and plump each of the pillows, with the unavoidable sense of the camera watching my every move from the corner of the room. It is strange how I have become so used to them, the extra pair of eyes watching me from all over the house. In a strange way, they help me feel less alone, even if their presence means me harm.

The lack of communication from the abductors disturbs me, but it must mean they believed my lie about spending my night looking into the hospital investigation. If they knew the truth, they wouldn't be holding back and biding their time. That isn't their style. They'd be inside the house right now, guns blazing. Or maybe they do know and they have been following my every move, and they are watching me right now, waiting to see what other lies I will tell them; giving me just enough rope to hang myself with.

The doorbell rings.

I hear Bear run into the hall downstairs, barking as he goes.

What if it's the abductors? I start to pace the room under the camera's watchful glare, my heart rate rising. *Or what if it's the Shabbars? Have they brought Zack home?*

I make my way downstairs, my heart beating so fast that I feel dizzy, and walk shakily towards the door. The only person I can envisage now since thinking of him is Zack.

The banging continues, and Bear barks louder. I raise a shaking hand to shield over the cubbyhole and lean in close.

The detectives are on the other side.

I lean my head against the door, the sight of them hitting me like a physical blow. I had so wanted it to be Zack, almost as if I was willing it into fruition, imagining the feel of his body pressed into mine, the warmth of him as I held him close, breathing in his scent first-hand. I close my eyes and exhale in a shudder. Burying the pain. I take Bear's collar and open the door.

'Yes?'

DS Ryan jumps at the sharpness of my tone. DI Conaty doesn't even blink.

'Dr Jones,' he says. 'We need you to come down to the station.'

'What for now?'

I hate them for not being Zack. My tone is sharp, and my glare searing. I should be softer, appear far more innocent and bewildered. But I can't seem to shake off the rage.

'I've told you everything I know about Paula. I'm sorry you want more, but I can't give it to you.' I look DS Conaty up and down. 'And are you even allowed to be here? Your superior seemed to take my complaint about your conduct seriously.'

'We aren't here about Paula,' she replies, not even trying to hide the joy in her eyes. 'We are here about your son.'

My stomach flips, acid springing up my throat.

'How many times do I have to tell you that he's in Cornwall? Look, Detective, I am sorry about what happened to your child. It is very sad, and it must be extremely hard for you to bear, but that doesn't mean you can harass me by creating this fantasy of trying to save my child, just so you can make up for not protecting your own.'

The smirk falls from her face.

'We have evidence, Dr Jones,' she says sternly. 'Evidence that contradicts your story. We need you to come with us to the station.'

She delivers the last blow. I watch her eyes brighten again at the sight of the panic flooding my face. I inhale a reassuring breath and hold it, an anchor holding me to the spot.

'Am I under arrest?'

'Well,' she says, faltering. 'No . . .'

'Then you can wait. I need to shower and dress.'

I slam the door so fast that the shield over the cubbyhole spins and spins.

51

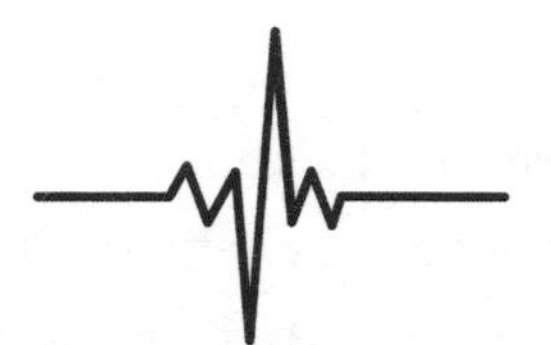

Rachel

Wednesday, 10 April 2019, 11:05

Something is keeping Dr Jones up at night.

Even beneath her make-up, I can see the dark shadows encroaching her eyes, and the sickly white of her neck. It is almost as if she has shrunk since I last saw her, for her frame is smaller, and her features look too big for her face; even her hair looks thinner. When she opened the door this morning, I had barely recognised her.

She hasn't said much since entering the interview room, and the sharpness of her tone that I witnessed at her doorstep has dulled. But by her tight posture and stony expression, it is clear that she is still as guarded as before and ready for our questioning.

I lay the file in front of her on the desk without a word.

'Would you like me to open this?' she asks.

I nod once. 'Please.'

One thing I have noticed about Dr Jones is her fixation on control. When she has it, she seems to excel in anything she puts her mind to. But as she looks down at the card we have played, I can see her resolve starting to unravel. She licks her lips nervously and lifts the cover. When she sees what is inside, her face drains white.

'Could you describe what you see for the tape, Dr Jones?'

A muscle twitches beneath her eye. I can almost see the cogs turning inside her head.

'I see a photo of my brother driving his car, with my niece beside him. It is a photo from a speed camera.'

'And the time and date?' I ask.

'Fourth of April, four thirty-two p.m.'

'Do you see anyone else inside the car?'

Another twitch beneath her eye. I look down at her chest; the open collar of her blouse is pulsing minutely with the racing of her heart.

'Not from the angle of this photo, no. I don't see anyone else.'

'This was taken on the M3 on the day your son was alleged to have travelled to Cornwall. But as you can see by the image here, Zack isn't inside. Why is that?'

The pink tip of her tongue runs across her bottom lip.

'I don't know what to tell you,' she replies. 'My son is in Cornwall. Are you sure this is from the correct day?'

'You can see the time and date on the image for yourself. Your brother lives in London, correct?'

'Yes . . .'

'And he travelled from London to Redwood, collected your son, and then set off for Cornwall, is that right?'

'Yes . . .'

'Then there would be no reason for your brother to be driving along the M3 towards Cornwall without him.'

I can see the panic in her eyes. She is losing her grip on her story; she looks down and closely inspects the image. No loving mother could lie about her missing child like this. For after seeing the footage there is no doubt in my mind: something happened to Zack Jones, and his mother is hell-bent on keeping it hidden.

'This doesn't suggest he isn't in the car,' she says. 'He would be sat in the back; Leila rides up front to prevent travel sickness. From the angle the photo was taken, it isn't possible to see behind her seat.'

'We do also have these,' DS Ryan says.

He slips another file over the desk. Dr Jones looks at the cover for a while, almost like she is trying to conjure an explanation for whatever damning facts might lay inside.

'Open it when you're ready,' DS Ryan says.

She slowly peels back the cover, revealing the CCTV security stills. I watch her take it all in, her eyes dancing across the photos.

'From the time stamp on the speed-camera image, we were able to track your brother's next movements and search for other potential footage that would match the time it would take to reach each landmark on their journey.'

I lean forward and arrange the photos in a line, in conjunction with the timespan.

'These were captured at the service station between junction 4A and junction 5 on the M3,' I say, and point to the first image. 'We see your brother's vehicle enter the car park here . . . We see him park here . . . We see Jeff and Leila exit the vehicle – alone – and head for the services here. We see them head for the toilets here, buying some food here, a takeaway coffee here, before they finally return to the car park. They were gone for twenty-two minutes.'

Dr Jones' mind is working overtime, her eyes busy as thoughts fly around inside her brain.

'I would need to see the footage,' she says, and clears her throat.

I glance to DS Ryan and give him a subtle nod, announcing his departure for the tape. When the door shuts behind him, silence descends on the room. Usually I might see a suspect start to crumble beneath the pressure at this point, wiping their brow, drying their palms on their thighs, glugging water to quench their thirst. But Dr Jones does none of those things. She sits in motionless silence, staring down at the photos on the table, seemingly trying to tie up the loose ends in her story.

Why is she trying so hard to prove us wrong?

If her son isn't missing, she would have been far more compliant during this whole process. She would have called her brother the second she left the interview room the first time to clear up the mistake. Surely, if this is truly a misunderstanding, she would be far more willing to make it go away. But although her motive may not be transparent, her reactions are clear as day. She is hiding something from us. Something she is desperate to conceal.

DS Ryan returns with a laptop and places it before her as I announce his return to the room for the tape, and instruct Dr Jones to play the footage. DS Ryan and I sit in silence watching her eyes, the screen reflecting on their watery surface.

'Here,' she says, pressing pause. 'My brother leans to face the back seat.'

She rewinds the footage and turns the laptop round to face us. I press play.

'He's talking to Zack,' she says. 'And from the angle of the cameras, you still can't see the back seat behind Leila, just like in the speed-camera image. Is this seriously all you have? You've dragged me here once again to try and convince me my son is in danger over *this*? A dodgy camera angle?'

She is right. In the footage, Jeff turns briefly towards the back seats. But there is nothing to suggest he is doing so to speak to someone. He could very well be reaching to retrieve his wallet.

I close the laptop down. DS Ryan removes it from the surface of the desk.

'Even if that were the case,' I say, 'why would your brother leave Zack in the car? They were gone for over twenty minutes.'

She leans back into her seat. Whatever story she is about to spin, she feels confident enough to relax.

'Zack is a very nervous child. His anxiety has worsened since the divorce. He doesn't like crowded places, and his anxiety causes him to have a shy bladder; it is always a struggle to get him to use public toilets.'

'You're telling me your son wouldn't have needed to use the toilet during the five hours it takes to reach Cornwall?'

'Have you searched the CCTV footage of all the service stations on the route?'

I feel DS Ryan tense up at my side.

'No,' he replies.

'Then how do you know he didn't use the bathroom at another service station either before this visit or closer to Cornwall? Although it is very possible that he held it in the whole way. With his shy bladder, he physically cannot go. It's the same when he flies. It's something his father and I are trying to help him with.'

For crying out loud, this woman can conjure an excuse for anything.

'Then why didn't your brother buy food for Zack when they went shopping at the service station?' I pick up the photo of Jeff and Leila at the till. 'You can see the contents of the basket here: two sandwiches, two drinks, two packets of crisps.'

She sighs and crosses her legs, her fingers laced at the knee.

'My son is highly lactose intolerant – even small traces of dairy from cross-contamination during food production can cause a reaction. I made him a packed lunch that morning for Paula to take with her that afternoon when they went to do the exchange.'

'They couldn't even buy him a drink?' DS Ryan asks.

'Well, you can't expect me to answer that question, considering I wasn't there. Quite frankly, I am genuinely disturbed that you have dragged me back here so soon after my complaint about your conduct over something as trivial as this. You're alleging my son has been – what ... kidnapped? Because I made him a packed lunch rather than have his uncle buy him a meal deal?' She pinches the bridge of her nose, shakes her head. 'How many times do I have to tell you? *My son is in Cornwall.*'

Anna Jones is lying. The problem is, she is extremely good at it. Her mind works so quickly that it is almost impossible to catch her out. But I refuse to let her slip out of my reach again.

'On the topic of CCTV footage, we have been able to secure footage from the diner in Redwood you mentioned. You said the plan was for Paula to hand Zack over to your brother Jeff at the diner, but we see no sight of Paula, Zack, your brother, or his car on the footage. Can you explain that?'

'Happily,' she replies. 'I didn't say they were meeting *at* the diner. I said they were meeting *by* the diner.'

I sense DS Ryan glance at me, but I can't take my eyes off her. I try to think back to her exact words.

'It will be on tape,' she says, cocking her head towards the recorder.

'What do you mean, *by* the diner? If they didn't meet at the diner, where did they meet?'

'Just to be absolutely clear,' she says, shaking her head in disbelief. 'You've twisted what I said in our last interview so it fits your version of events, and then used it to justify questioning me all over again? Even after I've already filed a complaint about your conduct, and your disturbing obsession with my child?'

She seems to have premeditated her response for every possible angle we might have come at her from. Her defensiveness is clearly a sign of trying to evade the truth, but the way she does it manages to shut us down at every turn.

'Excuse us a minute,' I say, and announce our departure to the tape before pressing the pause button. I stand from my seat, followed closely by DS Ryan, not saying a word until we step out into the hall and shut the door behind us.

'She has an answer for everything we throw at her.'

DS Ryan says nothing, and after a few seconds of pacing, I look up and meet his eyes. I stop in my tracks when I see doubt flicker on his face.

'Don't turn on me, Mark.'

'I'm not,' he replies softly. 'But maybe her responses sound credible because she's telling the truth.'

'So you *believe* her? After the way she's behaving in there?'

'I don't know,' he replies, running a hand through his hair. 'Maybe she has a point.'

I stare at him for a long time, willing him to believe me, until his cheeks flush pink and he looks down towards his feet.

'I know I'm right, Mark. She will contradict herself at some point. We can't give up now. *Please*.'

He looks up at me and holds my gaze. I see the doubt flash in his eyes, the concern etched on his face.

I'm not crazy. I know I'm right about this.

He sighs quietly and nods toward the door.

'All right.'

I sigh with the relief. 'Thank you. You won't regret this.'

When we enter the room again, Dr Jones is sat up straight and composed, with her shoulders rolled back and her hands resting neatly in her lap. I press play on the tape and announce our return.

'Thank you for your patience,' I say as I take my seat. 'We have some more questions we would like to ask you.'

'What more is there to possibly ask me? I've told you everything I know.'

'Let's start with Ahmed Shabir.'

Her expression falls.

'You were his surgeon, is that right?'

52

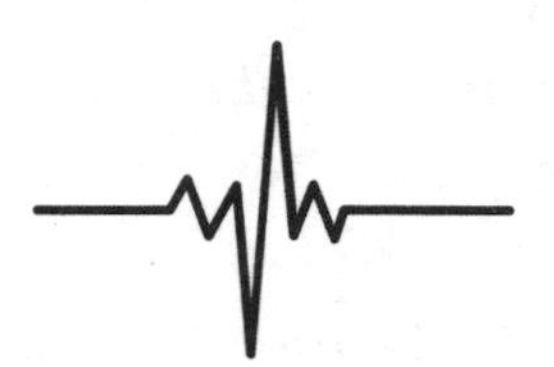

Margot

Wednesday, 10 April 2019, 10:40

The first thing I notice when I wake up is my pulse throbbing in my cheek, and the encroaching pain brings the memories of the night before flooding back: from being struck at the yard and scraping my cheekbone against the asphalt, to Anna being taken away, to performing a surgery with guns to our heads. Just thinking of how the gun grazed the back of my head has me instantly break out in sweat.

I close my eyes and take deep, slow breaths.

It's done now. Soon Anna will have the boy back, and then I will receive my money. And, my God, will I have earned it.

I slip my hand beneath the duvet and run my palm down my abdomen until it reaches the flesh beneath my navel, pulsing with the distant thrum of my heart. It feels like a bump is starting to form. The flesh is bloated and my breasts are tender. At least I'm not feeling sick yet.

You're not ready, Ma says inside my head. *You'll fuck up that kid more than I did with you.*

I should think of a rebuttal to clear my mind, but what if she's right? Am I supposed to feel this terrified? All I can think about are all of the things I might do wrong. It feels so fragile, so helpless, that I am sure it will break inside of me if I turn over too roughly, or lie at the wrong angle. What if I drop it once it's born? Its little neck would shatter like bone china. The thought goes around and around in my head until it is all I can think about. *Thud. Crack. Thud. Crack.*

Someone clears their throat from the other side of the room.

I jump up, snatching at the sheets to cover my body.

Damien is sat in the corner, turning Rick's ring over between his fingers; he must have taken it from the nightstand beside me while I slept.

'What were you doing at the yard, Maggot?'

He isn't looking at me. His eyes are firmly on the ring, watching it glint in the low light where the sun's rays frame the blinds covering the window. It's then, when a brief reflection darts across his face, that I see the dark purple bruising around his eye. He sniffs violently from a night on the gear.

I sit up in bed and try to gauge his mood. His foot is tapping anxiously against the carpet.

He is furious.

'Did someone hit you?' I ask.

'Answer my question. Why were you at the yard?'

'I . . . can't tell you.'

He jumps out of the chair so fast that a small whimper escapes my lips. The second he reaches the bed, he grips onto my arms and forces me down, pressing against me with all of his weight until I can feel the mattress bowing beneath my back.

'Don't you fucking dare,' he shouts, spittle landing on my face. 'I told you not to fuck around, and you did it anyway. You think I care about a black eye and some bruised ribs? I'm lucky this is all they did!'

'Get off!'

He shakes me hard, my neck rattling, and slams me down into the bed again, bringing his face close to mine. His breath smells foul.

'You're supposed to be blackmailing that woman, not giving her a fucking tour of a drug gang's patch. Yeah, that's right. *Drugs.* Jacking cars is just a cover job. You think they want strangers driving up to take a look? If you ask too many questions they won't hesitate to stick a bullet in your head.' He lifts one hand free and prods his finger against the centre of my forehead. 'You understand me? They'll kill you, they'll kill me, and they'll kill Rick. Is that what you want, you fucking idiot?'

I use my free hand to push at his chest, and raise my leg to kick him, but he snatches a hold of my ankle and yanks me off the bed. The shock of the fall shoots up my spine. I desperately snatch at the sheets to cover myself up.

'You don't put Rick and me in danger and get away with it,' he says, grabbing my chin. 'Pack your shit and get out.'

He thrusts me away, as if the mere touch of my skin revolts him, and heads for the door.

'More money for me then,' I reply childishly, with tears brimming my eyes.

He laughs at that. It is a cruel sound, dripping with malice. When he throws his head back I see how white his tongue is, the small halos around each nostril. He crosses the room and crouches down before me. I shuffle back until my spine knocks into the nightstand.

'Don't you think I knew you were going to do a runner with the cash the moment you got your thieving little hands on it?'

The tears are streaming now, following the lines of my nose, wetting my lips.

'Then why did you get me the car? Why did you help me?'

'Because you're my little sister and I loved you, even though I knew you'd use me and fuck off again. It's what you do, Maggot. You use people until they're drained dry, and then run off to find your next victim. Well, you've got what you came for, haven't you? Now fuck off and find some other mug to manipulate.'

He gets up, kicking a pillow out of his path that had slid from the bed in the scuffle, and heads for the door.

'*Manipulate* – that's a big word for you, isn't it?'

He turns to face me, red in the cheeks. I sniff back the tears and dash them away with back of my hand.

'Who do you think I learned it all from?' I stammer. 'I grew up watching you two leeches. Ma hated me because I tried to do something with my life, and you hate me because I didn't take you with me. But why would I? Look at you. Coke around your nostrils before midday and pupils the size of fucking pinwheels. You're a junkie, Damien. You're just like *her*.'

His eyes have become glassy; my words have finally cut deep enough. He swallows hard, his Adam's apple bobbing in his throat.

'You really think you're better than me, don't you?' he asks, his voice hoarse. 'Look at yourself. You're blackmailing a mother trying to save her son, facing prison time for stealing from your friends. And you think you're better than me because I'm working the best way I know how? You're not better ... you're *worse*.' He shakes his head, dashing a tear away with the back of his hand. 'Get dressed, grab your shit, and get out.'

He slams the door with such force that the whole room shakes.

It's only when I'm alone that I finally let the tears flow without fighting them. I sob like I'm a girl again, untangling myself from the sheets and dragging on my clothes.

We always fought rough as kids, but this feels different. Final. I yank the drawstring and raise the blind to let in some light to make sure I have everything, and spot the slice of rainbow on the wall where the sun hits the crack in the pane.

I'll never come back here again.

I snatch up my bag, checking the money and the engagement ring are still inside, and head for the door with the car keys in my grip, determined to take off with the car before Damien thinks to take it back.

The hall smells of bacon and Marlboro Reds, and I can hear the TV whispering up the stairs; but the house is so entwined with the past that I'm not sure what's real anymore and what's in my head.

I've got to get out of here.

I slink along the hall and slide my hand down the banister as I go, every board creaking beneath my feet, and fumble for the latch on the front door when I hear her voice.

I want you to remember that I said this, Maggot: however far you run, however many lies you tell yourself that you're better than the ditch you were born in, it'll always be in your blood. You can't outrun your DNA, Maggot. But I'm sure you'll die trying.

Those were the last words she said, as I was heading out the front door. Stood in this very spot.

I slam the door behind me and a sob bursts out of me. My whole body wracks with it, lips trembling, snot glistening at my nostrils. I rush to the car and shut the door firmly behind me, and rest my head on the wheel.

A sharp pain in my abdomen stops my tears in a second. My mind reels with thoughts as I realise what's happening. My whole world, shifting in a second. I slip my hand to the flesh beneath my belly button.

I have just come on my period.

53

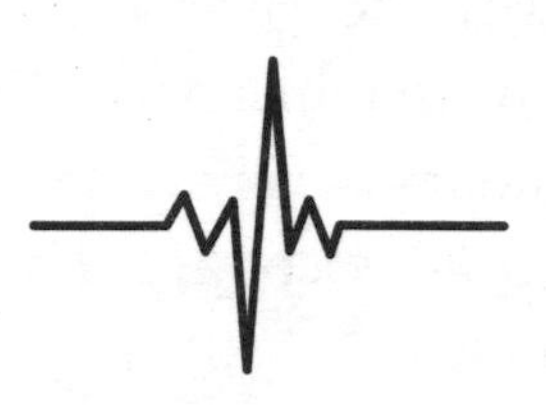

Anna

Wednesday, 10 April 2019, 19:09

I step out of the police station and immediately check the burner phone the abductors gave me. My head is pounding and my stomach is growling with hunger, but all I can think of are all of the missed calls I will find on the screen, a ream of messages asking why I have been in the station so long.

Conaty and her partner kept me in the interview room all day long. They repeated themselves, asked closed questions so I would incriminate myself, twisted everything I said. Every time I threatened to leave, Conaty implied that I must have something to hide, and I sunk down into my seat again. I thought if I stayed and answered all of their questions, it would stop them once and for all. They certainly gave it all they could.

Conaty had veered far too close to the truth. At some points in the interview she practically spelled it out herself, but was so focused on making me trip over my own story that she failed to realise it. She is going to succeed sooner or later. It doesn't matter how many complaints I make about her or how many lies I tell. She isn't going to let this go until she sees Zack with her own two eyes.

But then neither am I.

The sun has almost set. I follow the building round to the car park and take the burner phone from my bag. There are no calls. No texts. They usually know my exact whereabouts and call the moment the coast is clear, or send a threatening text message. I look around me, searching the car park for the black Audi. There is no sign of them.

What does this mean?

My first thought is of Zack. What if they thought the police had finally broken me and I was inside the station confessing everything I know? Did they decide to do away with Zack and run? After all, they got what they wanted – Ahmed is dead.

No. Finding my dead son would only back up my claims – they'd have to kill me off too or I'd talk. But then why haven't they called?

I reach my car and lock the doors the moment I'm inside. The air is hot and stale where the car has sat in the same spot for so many hours. I go through previous messages for the number they use to communicate with me. But they call from a different number every time. They must use each phone once and dispose of it to cover their tracks.

Something is wrong. They definitely should have called by now.

I swallow my nerves and hit call on the latest number.

'The number you have dialled has not been recognised.'

I hang up and call the next number.

'The number you have dialled has—'

I hang up, call another.

And another. And another.

They have all been disconnected.

I hang up the phone and sit in the silence of the car, tears of panic stinging my eyes.

If it's all over, then what have they done with Zack?

A phone rings and I jump, jarring me out of my thoughts. The call is coming from inside my bag.

I throw the burner phone on the passenger seat and rifle through my bag. It's the phone Margot gave me.

What if they found out I told Margot? Have they got her? Has she talked? They could be calling me from her phone to catch me out.

The phone keeps ringing, and ringing. I press the button to receive the call and place the phone to my ear.

'Hello?'

'It's done.'

I freeze on my end of the line. The man's voice is deep, and the accent is thick. I listen to him breathing into the receiver; slow, calm breaths. My mind is so frazzled after so many hours of questioning and so little sleep that it takes me a second to recognise his voice: Faheem Shabbar. I gave him this number because it is the only phone the abductors can't trace.

'What . . . What is?'

A stab of pain twists in my stomach. There are two scenarios that could come from this: either Zack is safe, or he is dead. I can't bear to consider either. To hope he is safe, even for a second, only to find out he is gone, would destroy me.

'Our part of the deal, it's done.'

I don't say a word. I sit, frozen, my jaw hanging open and my eyes brimming with tears.

'We have your son.'

54

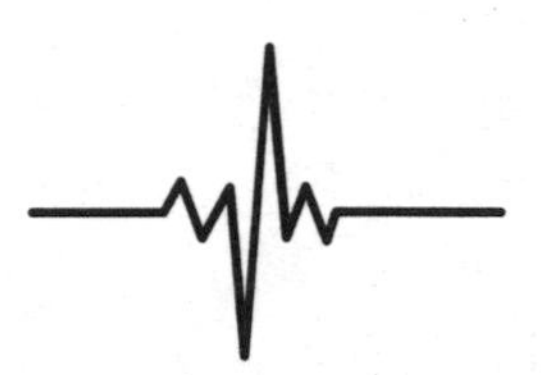

Margot

Wednesday, 10 April 2019, 19:20

I'm not pregnant.

Empty boxes litter the floor of the cubicle, the used tests hidden away in a plastic bag along with the two water bottles I bought and guzzled down to make me go. The smell of the public toilet is revolting; human waste and bleach have formed their own repulsive musk.

I stare into the bag, eyeing the single lines on the test screens where there should be two, and wait for the words to sink in.

Ten pregnancy tests. Ten negative results.

I'm not pregnant. I never was.

I stole a couple of tests from the hospital store cupboard on the day I realised I had missed my period after sleeping with Nick, but I remember now: I only used one. Could it have been a false positive? Did my hormone levels that day trigger an incorrect result or something? Maybe I did something wrong. I should have done more tests, but I didn't want to steal too many and raise suspicions.

Why am I trying to figure out how it happened? I should be happy. I'm free.

Tears form in my eyes until the boxes on the floor blur to nothing against the tiles. I bite down on my bottom lip and clench my eyes shut.

I don't care, I tell myself.

Then I burst into tears.

The sounds bounce off the tiled walls, every whimper and exhale amplified in the tight space of the cubicle, covered in scratch marks and graffiti. Someone has written *Hannah is a slag* in blue Biro. I wonder what they would write about me.

When I first thought I was pregnant, I couldn't bring myself to nurture the life I was supposedly harbouring inside of me. It was a thing, a burden, a clump of my fear made up of flesh and bone. *It*. But the idea of having a baby grew on me, and I slowly learned to love it. Now I know it isn't there, that it never was, there is an aching emptiness within me, a hollowness that brings a breed of loneliness I have never felt before.

I didn't think I ever wanted to be a mother before this. I never showed any maternal instincts; I am selfish and guarded. But maybe I did, and I was too afraid to admit it, even to myself; too afraid to hope that something good might happen only for it to be taken away.

I grit my teeth and blink repeatedly until the tears slowly dissipate, and stare at the grot between the tiles, the chips and cracks that have turned black with dirt from strangers' shoes.

I wanted the baby so I wouldn't be alone anymore. I wanted the baby so I would finally be loved.

I cover my face in my hands and cry silently into my palms, inhaling the foul scent of the room. The severity of my emotions seems irrational for the moment. It wasn't alive. It wasn't real. And yet I am mourning it like I had held the thing in my arms.

I thrust my leg and kick the cubicle door as hard as I can. The whole row clangs with the force.

My involvement in Anna's schemes were for the sake of the baby, and now it is gone, it all seems so pointless. I lost my job, my brother, and for what?

I had been so sure of myself, convinced that I was better than my family, looking down my nose at Damien and Rick. And yet, as I stole and schemed to build myself a better life, I ultimately became the very person who I have been running from my entire life.

I'm just like Ma.

My phone rings.

I reach for my bag hanging from the door handle and wipe my face dry with my sleeve.

I will still have my fresh start, I tell myself. *This doesn't have to change anything. I'll still end up in prison if I don't get the money. After this is over I'll have the fifty grand, only now I'll have nothing to anchor me down. I can change, be better. I don't have to be like them.*

I take a deep breath to compose myself, in through my nose, out through my mouth.

'Hello?'

'Margot!' Anna says. 'They called! It's done!'

She is crying, but her tears sound different to mine. She

is crying from sheer joy. I can hear the relief radiating from her voice.

'What?' I sniff back tears. 'What's done?'

'The Shabbars. They have Zack.'

She releases a sound, caught between a sob and a laugh.

'They are going to hand him over tonight.'

55

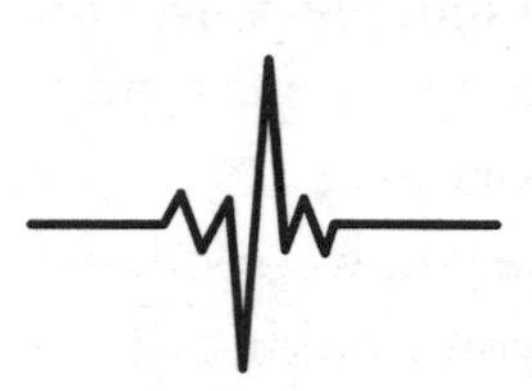

Rachel

Wednesday, 10 April 2019, 19:32

They met by Kathleen's Diner. It's halfway between the school and the M1 junction Jeff uses to reach Redwood.

I pause the tape, rewind, and press play.

They met by Kathleen's Diner. It's halfway—

Pause. Rewind. Play.

. . . by Kathleen's Diner.

I turn off the recorder and sweep my hands through my hair. The way she said it was so subtle that neither DS Ryan nor me picked up on it. Dr Jones seems to set little traps as she talks: sentences laced with minute get-out clauses, phrases she can twist to insinuate one thing but secretly mean another. I have sat at my desk long after home time, listening over our interview tapes and picking up on each little manipulation. I underestimated how smart she is. We all did.

I fast-forward the tape.

As soon as we know Jamie is where you say he is, we can move on.

Zack. The boy's name is Zack.

A knock at the door brings me round. DCI George Whitman is standing in the doorway.

'Sir, I didn't realise you were still here.'

'Whereas I knew you would be,' he replies, approaching the desk. 'I wanted to have a word with you.'

Whatever conversation he plans to have, the fact that he waited until everyone had gone home makes me nervous.

I nod towards the chair and watch as he takes his seat. He seems hesitant to speak, exhibiting tense, closed-off body language. He emits a small sigh before he speaks.

'I have transferred the case to the NCA.'

I stare at him open-mouthed, the rage rising through me like heat. After all of my sleepless nights, my dedication, my sacrifices, he passes the case off to the National Crime Agency. I remain silent, not trusting what I might say should I open my mouth.

'The victim's death shows clear signs of a professional execution. When I ran it by my contact at the NCA, they seemed very confident that the style of killing matches one of their ongoing investigations into a drug-trafficking organisation that uses Redwood as a gateway into the city. They can do far more with this case than we can.'

'*Bullshit*. We'll get them, we just need more time—'

'We don't have more time, Conaty. We have no suspects, no murder scene, no murder weapon. And if I'm being frank, we don't have the resources to hunt down an organised crime ring whose reach will stretch far wider than Redwood. The NCA works with enforcement agencies all over the world to combat organised crime. Do you have those contacts?'

I stare at him, biting my lip. If I don't I will scream, or cry, or worse.

'Do you?'

'No,' I force. 'Look, I may not have a murder suspect yet, but I'm coming at this from an angle that I know the NCA won't think of.'

'Which is what,' he asks, practically rolling his eyes. 'The boy?'

'Yes.'

'For Christ's sake, Conaty! Wake up!'

I jump in my chair from the boom of his voice.

'No one has reported him missing. Not his mother, not his father, not this uncle. You think one of the most renowned surgeons in the country is going to off her kid and expect to get away with it?'

'You're telling me it isn't at all suspicious that the surgeon who performed Ahmed Shabir's fatal heart surgery just so happens to live next to the woman we found dead in a well, with her teeth ripped out and her fingertips sawn off? The same Ahmed Shabir who campaigned for tighter controls on drug-trafficking in the area and pushed legislation for harsher penalties across the country? Which ties *directly* to the organised-crime thread?'

'That's a great theory,' he says, unmoved. 'Do you have any evidence to prove it?'

'Well, not for all of it, no. But look at these.'

I open the file on my desk and place the CCTV photos in front of him.

'These were captured on Jeff Dunn's journey to Cornwall. Where's the boy in these pictures, sir?'

He scans the photos, the frown slowly fading from his face.

'Or how about here,' I say, dropping the speed-camera shot in front of him. 'Do you see him in the car?'

He picks up the photo and inspects it carefully. I see something flash in his eyes. Is it doubt?

'We have a sixty-five-year-old victim exhibiting signs of being executed by an organised crime ring, and the only fathomable reason I can find to connect her to this sort of trouble is her relationship with the boy, who was in her care either right before *or during* her abduction. The same boy who the police down in Cornwall have failed to identify or account for. The same boy whose mother performed the heart surgery that killed Ahmed Shabir.'

A lump lodges in my throat.

'Sir, if you are one hundred per cent certain the boy was on this journey, I will drop it. Should we find out later that this wasn't the case, I'll happily lay the blame at your feet knowing that I tried everything I could to make you listen. This will be on your conscience, not mine. So, are you absolutely certain the boy is where Dr Jones says he is? Are you willing to bet the child's life on it?'

He doesn't say anything for a long time, transfixed by the photograph from the speed camera: Jeff Dunn and the little girl in the front seat, the time and date stamped in the corner. When he looks up at me again, both his frown and his indignation have gone.

'All right, Conaty. I will give the chief down in Cornwall a call and request that officers attend the address and only leave when they receive visual confirmation of the boy. But you'll take the day off tomorrow, no exceptions. I'll call if I hear anything.'

He gets up and heads for the door, his footsteps slow and heavy. He stops in the doorway.

'I really hope you're not wrong about this, Conaty.'

His words linger, even after he has left, and I fear that beneath the sadness of his tone lay a threat.

I'm not wrong, I think, as he leaves. *I have never felt more sure of anything in my life.*

56

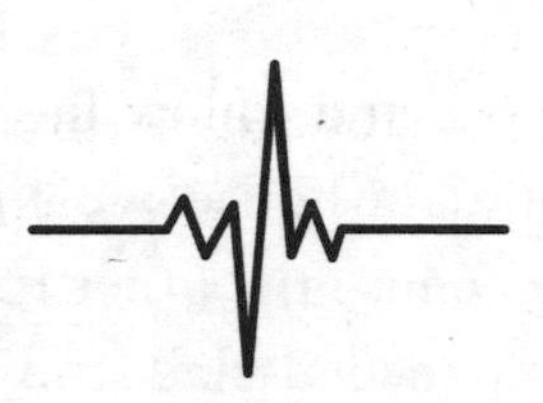

Margot

Wednesday, 10 April 2019, 20:04

'You can come in,' Anna says.

I stand at her front door, staring beyond her and into her home. I see a modern-art sculpture placed on top of the side table against the back wall, and spot the tail-end of a deep green velvet chaise lounge creeping into view. This is just the hallway of the house.

She really had the audacity to tell me she didn't have the money to spare when she's living with lavish shit like this?

'I thought you said there were cameras?' I ask, and crouch down to stroke her dog's curly blond fur, the name *BEAR* dangling from his collar. He is wagging his tail so excitedly that it bangs and thumps into the doorframe.

'Faheem said we didn't have to worry about the abductors anymore. Come in.'

Anna is on edge. I can see from her puffy, pink eyes that she has been crying, and her hands are shaking, whether from anticipation or exhaustion, I'm not sure. We both look as knackered as each other. I stand awkwardly in the hallway as she shuts the door behind me.

'This way.'

I slip out of my shoes and follow her towards the kitchen, breathing in the scent of the house, which is rich in both senses of the word, and glance into the other rooms as I go: a dining table to seat twelve, a panelled-clad study that looks so organised that it seems impossible to think it is used. I can't spot any cameras in any of these rooms either.

She definitely said there were cameras. Was she lying?

I step inside the kitchen and stand at the island unit, secretly admiring the white marble tops as she grabs a bottle of white wine from the fridge. I watch as she pours a glass, then another.

'So what did Faheem say?'

Wine splashes onto the counter when I say his name; she shakily puts the bottle down, and hands the dryer glass to me.

I can drink wine now, I think to myself. *There is no baby to harm.*

My throat tightens, and I swallow down the pain, taking the glass in hand with a forced smile.

'He will call tonight and tell us where to meet him.'

I take a sip. It tastes great, of course. A crate of the stuff would probably cost a small fortune.

'Can't we just meet him now?' I ask.

'We have to wait until it's dark.'

'Why?'

'Oh, for Christ's sake, Margot,' she snaps. 'I don't know.

Why don't you save your questions for him? I know as much as you do.'

There's the Anna I know.

'I guess I'm confused as to why I need to go with you. I've completed my part of the deal. You're getting your son back—'

'You're not off the hook until I hold him in my arms. You're the one who led me to the Shabbars, Margot. Who's got a *brother* working for them. You know these people far better than I do. I'm not going alone.'

It feels like she knows them far better than I do. I might have been the one to suggest going to them, but now they seem to have shut me out. They are the ones having private phone calls and face-to-face meetings. The only time I've met Faheem Shabbar is when he held a gun to the back of Anna's head.

'Nice house,' I say. 'I don't see any cameras?'

She points to the coving above the door. I turn and frown, seeing nothing but white walls and ceilings, but when I look closer, I see that there is a small, white lens peering out from the plaster.

'They're not meant to be easy to spot.'

I had been expecting to see the far more obvious kind that swivel on axles, not minuscule lenses hidden in the walls.

Christ, who are these people?

I turn back and see a flash of something in her eyes at the mention of them: fear, or resentment.

It is times like this that remind me of what our partnership is really about. We aren't friends righting a wrong, or comrades with a shared cause. There is her and her goal, and me and mine. Last night blurred the lines, but it is all clear again now, and being inside her home feels like a bending of the rules. I have a sudden, niggling urge to be free of it.

'So we just hang around here until he calls?'

'Unless you have a better idea,' she replies, and tops up her wine.

'And when will I be getting the rest of the money?'

There is no sudden realisation about our partnership like I had, no change of her demeanour or a shifting of her guard. It was up the whole time. She has always known what this is.

'I will go to the bank first thing in the morning.' She takes a large gulp of wine, and sighs. 'Look, we might as well try and get some sleep until he calls. You look like you've had as much sleep as I have.'

The thought of staying in her home seems unfathomable; I could never close my eyes and allow myself to be vulnerable around her. It would be like curling up to sleep in a snake's nest.

It would mean saving money. No need to pay for a hotel. It's not like I can go back to Damien's.

'All right,' I say finally. 'Sure you don't want to nail anything down while I'm here?'

Her eyes glaze over with worry, as if she is genuinely considering it.

'I was kidding. I won't sleep, though. I'll watch some TV.'

'Suit yourself.'

She picks up her wine glass and heads for the hall.

'I'd like the ring now, if you don't mind.'

She stops in the doorway, and turns to face me slowly, her brow creased with disgust.

'I'm sorry?'

'Your wedding ring . . .' I reply coolly. 'As payment for going with you tonight – putting myself in danger, and all that.'

Her cheeks flush with anger, and she yanks it off her finger and throws it at my feet, as quickly and ferociously as before. She heads up the stairs without another word.

I pick up the ring and slip it on, and admire the two stacked together.

Now I'll have fifty thousand pounds and two rings to flog to keep me going.

I down the glass of wine and pour myself another.

57

Margot

Thursday, 11 April 2019, 02:03

I wake up to a hand clamped over my mouth.

I flinch violently and my eyes clap open, searching frantically for my attacker in the dark. Anna is stood above me.

'Get up. It's time.'

She lifts her palm and I take a deep breath, placing a shaking hand to my chest to dull its racing. My breath reeks of chardonnay after polishing off the bottle.

'You didn't have to bloody smother me,' I hiss, sitting up on the sofa.

'I didn't want you screaming and waking half the neighbourhood.' She heads towards the door for the hall, barely turning her head as she speaks. 'Get your shoes on and meet me by the car. You're driving.'

I sit up and blink frantically to wake myself. I had been in a deep sleep, and I can feel it lingering even now. My head feels dazed and woolly, and my thoughts are fractured, slurring in my head like a drunk's tongue.

The blinds are down and dark with the night. I drag my phone from my pocket and check the time through a squint. It's gone two in the morning.

I lumber up from the sofa and grab my bag, stumbling into the hall half asleep where the front door is open, letting in a wet chill. The driveway is cloaked in darkness. It is only when I have slipped on my shoes and stepped outside to light a cigarette that the nerves set in.

Anna is waiting beside my car, tapping her foot impatiently against the drive. I unlock it on my approach and climb inside.

'Must you?' she asks from the passenger seat, her eyes on the cigarette.

'Yes. Had you given me five minutes before making me—'

'Oh, do what you want, Margot. Let's just go.' She lowers her window to get some fresh air. 'We have to meet him at the old landing strip outside of town. You know where it is?'

'The main gates were welded shut years ago.'

'There's a side entrance. He said to head west of the grounds until we see it.'

'Fine,' I say, and start the car.

We head off without another word.

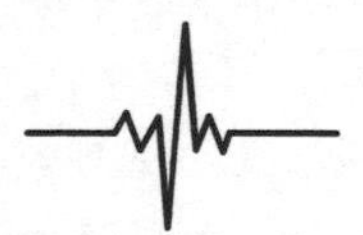

We drive in silence for some time, out of town and up into the countryside, following the winding curves of the lanes. At least twenty minutes pass in silence.

It is at times like this, when we are thrust so close and left alone, that I realise how little we know one another. We stood beside each other every day, giving hundreds of patients a second chance at living, watched as others faded away, and yet we are essentially strangers. I have no idea who she is. But I know what she is capable of.

'Do you feel guilty?' I ask.

I sense her tense up at my questioning. She is so used to controlling her surroundings, but now she can't escape. I wouldn't put it past her to try.

'Do you have kids?' she asks, after a long pause.

The question hits me like a punch, in the very spot I used to caress, where I thought the baby dwelled.

'No,' I force out.

'Then you won't understand protecting your child, whatever the cost. It was Shabir or my son. You want to know the truth?' She is looking at me now. 'If I had to do it again, I would. I would do it a thousand times.'

And yet, that isn't what I asked.

We come up to the main entrance to the landing strip, and I continue on until I see the next turning, and follow the site around the west side. My nerves slowly begin to reveal themselves; my palms grow damp at the wheel.

'What makes you think we can trust them?' I ask.

'That's rich, coming from you. You trusted them when we were headed to the scrapyard.'

'Yeah, and look what happened: you had a hood thrust over your head and were shoved in the back of a car. I mean, we've done what they wanted now; we have nothing to bargain with. What if we're driving into a trap—'

'The gate,' she says, pointing up ahead. 'On the left.'

I ease my foot on the brake and pull up beside it. On the other side is a long, narrow track.

'This has to be it,' she says, and gets out of the car.

I watch her walk before the headlights, her hair darting with the wind, her whole body moving with urgency. She bends her spine to inspect the chain linking the gate to the post and flashes me the padlock, bronze with rust – it has been left unlocked. She opens the gate wide and slips back into the car.

'Keep driving until you see the aeroplane hangars,' she says. 'They told me they would meet us at the end of the landing strip.'

'But Anna, what if—'

'Just *drive,*' she scolds.

She is shaking now. Adrenaline will be pumping through her veins, her heart pounding in her chest. I notice mine picking up too. I lift my foot from the brake and turn down the long, dark track.

We drive in muted silence. The tension forbids conversation. I can almost taste the anticipation in the air, the frustration emanating from her body. When we reach the end of the lane, I pull onto the forecourt where the small aeroplane hangars stand: one is a burnt shell of what it used to be, and the other is covered in graffiti, its roof green from algae as the headlights cast over it. I drive over the forecourt, trying to avoid the many potholes in the tarmac, and head slowly towards the landing strip.

'Can't you go any faster?' she asks.

'If I blow a tyre you'll never get your son home.'

She sighs heavily, and the car falls silent again, rocking as we move along the uneven asphalt.

'Oh, for Christ's sake, stop the car.'

'What? Why?'

'You're going too bloody slow.'

I ease my foot on the brake and watch as she snatches at the door handle, clambers out, and breaks into a sprint towards the landing strip. The passenger door hangs open, letting in the cool breeze. I fix the handbrake and unclip my belt to reach it, cursing her under my breath.

By the time I have slammed it shut and set the car in motion again, she is gone.

58

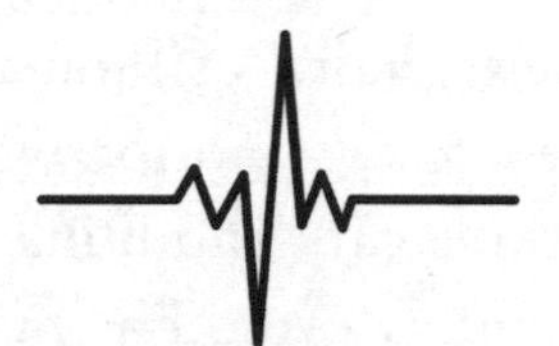

Anna

Thursday, 11 April 2019, 02:39

I run down the dark landing strip with my heart pounding in my throat and sweat breaking out beneath my shirt.

I'm coming, Zack.

The headlights from Margot's car fade until I am almost running blind. But still, I keep running. The air smells of sap and the nervous tang of my breath. I struggle to clear a pothole pitted into the tarmac and I stumble, flailing briefly, before finding my footing again.

I have waited long enough. I have gone a week without hugging him, without kissing him goodnight, without seeing his beaming smile. My need to have him with me is physical, propelling me forward. The thought of seeing his face brings a surge of tears. I push through the pain and the breathlessness, my feet hitting the ground with such force that a burning sensation shoots up my calves.

Headlights turn on at the end of the strip in a sudden bright flash. I stumble to a stop and shield my eyes; two white orbs follow me each way I look. I look ahead through a squint as a door opens and shuts, and listen to the footsteps sounding against the asphalt. A silhouette of a man appears before the lights. He makes a motion with his hand, and the lights dim. I count three cars and blink furiously, desperate to clear the blots from my eyes. The masked man stops ten feet away.

Faheem Shabbar.

'You ran here?' he asks, seemingly amused.

I signal over my shoulder. He spots the headlights of Margot's car glowing in the distance.

'Where is he?' I ask. I don't want to talk. All I want is to hold him and never let go.

Faheem nods to the cars parked behind him.

'How did you—'

'They won't be bothering you anymore,' he says with a dismissive tone. This wasn't only about retrieving my son; the abductors had his nephew killed. I am merely benefiting from an act that they did for their own cause.

If the abductors are dead, it would explain why I didn't hear from them after I stepped out of the police station.

'Where were they keeping him?'

'Hidden away in one of their warehouses. He was sedated when we found him; he is still coming round.'

'I need to see him.'

He nods and turns on his heel, and I follow anxiously behind him, my heart thumping excitedly in my chest.

This is it. After all the worry, and the pain – after everything I have done – I am finally going to have him back.

I feel sick with longing. Every step I take is too slow; each second feels like a lifetime. Faheem stops beside the black Audi and takes hold of the door handle.

'I am paying you this kindness because you saved my nephew,' he says. 'But if I ever see you again, I will kill you. Do you understand?'

I nod furiously, but my eyes remain on the window, desperate to see in through the tinted glass.

Faheem opens the door.

I see his pale hand first: small, slim fingers; pearly-pink fingernails that are half the size of mine. I step forwards, my eyes following up his arm, taking in every inch of him, until I finally see his sweet, beautiful face, his eyes closed with sleep.

The tears stream silently down my cheeks.

I want to admire every bit of him, sit and hold him and never let him go, but my urgency to get him free from these men and this dark world we have both been dragged into dominates my every desire. I lean into the car and reach over him to unclip his belt, cherishing his warmth and sweet scent, and slowly unhook it from under his arm. Just the feel of his skin makes my face crumple with tears.

He is real. I have him back.

'I want my mum.'

His eyes are drowsy, lids flickering. His pupils search for something but never seem to find it. A sob catches in the back of my throat.

'I'm here, baby,' I whisper. 'I found you.'

His brow creases with a frown, and his eyes search more frantically than before. I reach out and stroke his cheek, and watch the frown melt away, a smile flickering on his lips as he recognises my touch. I snatch him up and hold him tight to me, tears streaming silently down my face.

'You're safe now, baby. Mummy's got you.'

59

Margot

Thursday, 11 April 2019, 02:50

I pull up twenty metres from the scene and lift the handbrake, but keep the engine running in fear I might need to turn around in a hurry. The end of the strip is blocked off by three black cars, their headlights beaming at me with men dressed in black suits and balaclavas standing among them. Every one of them is staring towards me.

Anna is standing with the boy in her arms talking to a man who I take for Faheem Shabbar, recognisable behind the balaclava due to his towering height above the other men. Then she heads towards me with the boy's arms wrapped around her neck, and his legs hooked about her middle. I should get out of the car and open the door for her, but I'm frozen in place, too terrified to turn my back on the men staring in at me from afar.

The back door opens, and Anna lowers the boy into the back, sniffing back tears of relief and cooing silently into his ear as she fixes his belt. I look at the child through the rear-view mirror: his limbs are soft and floppy, and his eyes are moving behind closed lids. The poor kid looks high as a kite.

One of the cars flashes its headlights.

'We should go,' I whisper, as though they can hear every word.

'Faheem wants to talk to us,' she says. Her voice is still hoarse with tears.

'No, Anna, just get in the car. We've got your kid. Now let's just—'

'*No*,' she scolds. 'If he wants to talk to us, we'll talk. I won't do anything to jeopardise this. Now get out of the car.'

She gives her son a kiss on the head and then shuts the door behind her.

This is insane. What could they possibly have to say to us now? It's done.

Anna opens the driver's door and stares down at me until I turn off the engine, unclip my belt and place my feet onto the rough, cold road. I go to slip the keys in my pocket when she stops me.

'Leave them,' she says. 'We might need to leave in a hurry.'

What does she think is going to happen?

She stares me down, and a shiver runs down my spine, whether from the cold night air, or the chill in her eyes. I place the keys on the dashboard and close the door behind me.

The wind howls, casting my skin in goosebumps and whipping locks of hair into my eyes. The night is so dark, so quiet. My heart is in my throat.

They're not going to hurt us. They wouldn't have got the boy back if they planned to get rid of us.

The men watch us approach in silence. I spot the handle of a gun pointing from one of their hips and fear zings down my back. I can hear Anna beside me: the clap of her shoes and her quick, nervous breaths. Faheem meets us halfway.

'Good evening,' he says to me, his eyes gleaming with excitement. I swallow hard and keep my head high.

'You wanted to see us?' I ask, the nerves evident in my voice.

'Yes,' he says, and looks to Anna. 'We have one last thing to take care of.'

He raises his hand and clicks his fingers, the edge of his jacket lifting with the motion. My eyes settle on the gun holstered at his hip.

Behind him, a masked gunman ducks into one of the cars and reaches inside, and returns with a man in his grip, yanking a hood off his head. The man is bound and gagged, with dark bruises circling his eyes and dry blood flaking around his cut lips. I watch in silence as he is dragged towards us, listening to his feet trail along the asphalt. Faheem steps aside as the man is thrust to his knees at our feet.

The gunman behind the mask is Damien.

My heart leaps. I stare at him ferociously, longing for him to look at me, but he won't meet my eyes.

How did you get mixed up with these people, Damien? Look at you, at what you've become.

Behind the mask, his pupils look like two black holes, dilated from coke.

Look at me, Damien. Please.

'You seem surprised,' Faheem says through a smirk, staring at Anna's startled face. 'Did you think I killed him for you?'

'I . . . I don't know. When you said they wouldn't be bothering us anymore, I assumed . . .'

This man on his knees must be the abductor. He is smiling up at her from where he kneels on the asphalt, with a bloodied smirk across his face. He has the bluest eyes I have ever seen.

'You thought I'd just take care of your problem for you?' Faheem asks with a laugh.

Anna stares at him helplessly, words dying at the back of her mouth.

'Round here,' he says, 'we clean up our own mess.'

He takes the gun from his hip, and I watch in terror as he turns off the safety, drags back the slide, and holds it out to her.

'Aim between his eyes.'

I stare at the gun, the headlights gleaming in the black metal. My pulse is pounding in my ears. Every bit of moisture has been sapped from my mouth. I try to move, to stop her from doing anything stupid, but I remain deathly still, stuck in fear's grip.

'Take it.'

We both jump at the sudden order, and she snatches up the gun. It looks surprisingly heavy in her grip.

'All you need to do is pull the trigger,' he says.

She stares down at the gun in silence, watching as it shakes in her hand.

'It's not like you haven't killed someone before. This should be easy.'

Faheem yanks the gag from the abductor's mouth. I expect him to beg for his life, or cry, or shout. But he smiles wide, teeth flashing up at Anna as a low, reverberant laugh crawls up his throat.

'You think you can trust him any more than you can trust me?' He laughs until he grows red in the face, and veins swell on his forehead. 'You're dead. You're both dead.'

Anna stares down at him in silence, her finger trembling on the trigger. Almost as if she is considering it.

'Anna,' I whisper. 'Don't.'

Her skin is deathly white, and she is shaking as much as I am. She doesn't look my way.

I stare at Damien, silently begging him to intervene, to make everything okay. But he keeps his eyes ahead. I notice he is shaking too.

'You can kill an innocent man on the operating table,' Faheem says. 'But you can't shoot the man who kidnapped your child?'

Anna tries to reply but she can't. She is frozen with fear, staring at him helplessly. He snatches the gun from her grip.

'Maybe you need some help.'

Faheem stands back and points the gun at the abductor's head.

'I'll pull the trigger. All you have to do is tell me when.'

She stares at him open-mouthed, her eyes sheening over with tears.

'Someone is going to die tonight, Dr Jones. Do you want it to be him, or someone else?'

He glances towards my car, where the boy is.

'*No*,' she warns.

'Then tell me when.'

The abductor is looking up at Anna with those ice-blue eyes, flickering with hate and amusement. Despite kneeling at death's door, he still seems to enjoy watching her squirm, even if she is under another man's thumb rather than his. He smiles so wide that the cut on his lip oozes fresh blood.

She stares down at the man, tears trembling along her jaw. Of course she can't do it. Neither of us could. But the longer she looks at him, the more I see the fear slip away, as hatred fills her eyes. She stares at the man until she has adopted that terrifying coolness she adopts in the operating theatre. Calm. Collected. Unbreakable. When her eyes glaze over, my stomach plummets. The smile slowly dies from the abductor's face. He sees it too.

'Do it,' she says.

Faheem pulls the trigger. Blood bursts from his head and sprays against our legs. His eyes roll in their sockets, and his spine lolls as he turns violently with the blow, before landing flat on his back with his head directly between my feet. He twitches violently, blood spurting from his mouth and bubbling on his lips in pink froth. His eyes never leave mine. It seems like a lifetime passes before he falls still.

I tear my eyes away, tears of shock streaming down my cheeks, the gunshot ringing in my ears, and stumble back. It is only when I see the scene from afar that it sinks in. I see the blood, the chips of skull gleaming under the headlights, brain matter splattered across the tarmac.

I clench my teeth to keep from lurching. The abductor is missing a chunk of his head, the contents soaking into the collar of his shirt. I can't stop staring at the gaping hole between his eyes.

Faheem speaks. All I can see of him are his eyes peering out from the mask. There are blood spots on his shirt.

'You have proved yourself to me,' he says calmly.

'So we can go?' Anna asks, her voice trembling with the rest of her.

'Not just yet. You're not the only person with something to prove.'

He clicks his fingers and Damien steps forward, and raises his mask.

'Damien?' I ask, biting back a sob. I step towards him, and

try to beg for him to get us out of here, but I can't get the words out. All I can do is cry and think of the man's head falling between my feet, his icy-blue eyes staring up at me as he died.

Help me, Damien.

I stare at him pleadingly, longing for him to forgive me and take me home. I can tell him how sorry I am for hurting him; we'll be safe.

Damien is white as a sheet, and trembling as much as I am. When he finally meets my eyes, he stares back at me through tears.

'I told you not to cause trouble,' he says, reaching for his hip. 'You wouldn't listen.'

Damien raises his gun and aims it at my head.

60

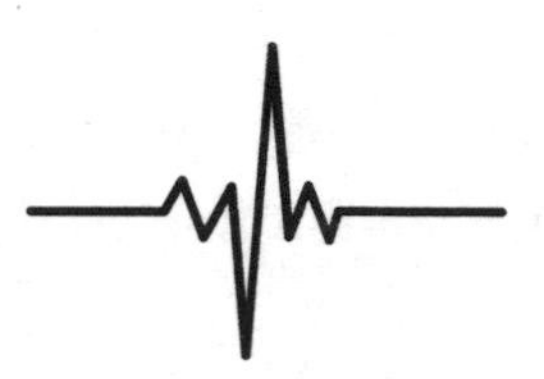

Anna

Thursday, 11 April 2019, 03:03

The second I see the gun, I turn and sprint back towards the car, my heart hammering wildly in my chest.

'Damien—'

'*Shut up.*'

'You wouldn't!' Margot sobs. '*You wouldn't!*'

'*I SAID SHUT UP!*'

Margot screams. The man is crying. I hear the gun's slide snapping back as it loads a bullet.

I sprint as fast as I can and desperately gasp for air, but my lungs have seized with the shock. I can hear Margot's feet pounding against the road.

'*Anna, wait!*'

I scramble into the car and slam the door behind me. The keys are on the dashboard where she left them.

Zack has climbed into the front. He must have come to – oh God, he must have seen everything. He is sobbing in his seat. I lean over to kiss his forehead but he flinches at my touch.

Margot approaches the other side of the glass, breathing heavily from running, and lunges for the door handle.

I lock the door just in time.

'Anna!' she shouts, yanking at the door handle. 'Open the door!'

'Mummy, you locked the—'

'Close your eyes, Zack,' I whisper.

Damien is walking towards her, gun raised. Margot's scream fogs up the window. She looks back to me in the driver's seat and sobs as she pulls at the door handle.

'Anna! Let me in!'

She bangs on the glass, yanks at the handle until I'm sure it will snap off. She could run, she has miles of land to clear, but shock seems to have grounded her. I scramble for the car keys to start the engine and they drop to the footwell.

'Anna, please!'

She pulls at the door behind mine to no avail, and returns to my window, pummelling the glass.

'Open the fucking door!'

'Keep your eyes closed, Zack,' I whisper, as I snatch up the keys.

I glance over to him. He is shaking silently behind his hands. I can smell urine. My hand is trembling so violently that I can't work the key into the ignition.

'No,' Margot says. '*No!*'

I look towards the glass and our eyes meet. I see the fear

coursing through her, the tears shimmering on her cheeks, her eyes desperate and enraged. She finally understands what I have done.

'You bitch! Let me in this fucking car!'

She looks to Damien and screams as he nears her, tears gleaming on both of their faces. She starts to wail and beg, banging on the glass, pleading to the man by name. I'm sure I hear the pane crack.

I clamp my eyes shut and wait.

'You bitch! You traitorous, evil bi—'

The gun blasts. I hear the fleshy thud of her body hit the ground, a high-pitched ringing in my ears. Zack is sobbing, heaving for breath to fill his little lungs.

I open my eyes and look to where she stood: there are blood splatters on the window. The man is stood above where her body lies, staring down at what he has done in pale-faced shock. Faheem comes up behind him and pats the man on the shoulder, sending him back to the blockade, and reaches down for something. When he approaches the car, I turn the key in the ignition and lower the window.

'I believe these are yours.' He places my rings in my palm. 'Now go. I will call you with next steps.'

Next steps . . . next steps . . . It never seems to end.

I nod frantically and raise the window, slipping the rings on my finger. When I place my hands on the wheel, I notice the rings are flecked with her blood.

'Mu-mu-mummy . . .' Zack sobs.

'It's okay, baby,' I say, strangely calm. I don't sound like myself. 'Keep those eyes closed until I say.'

The car smells of her: cigarettes and cheap perfume. I breathe through my mouth and turn the ignition key. The engine turns over with a low growl.

I pull the car in reverse, make a swift turn in the road, and slam my foot on the accelerator until the back wheels spit dust and we are barrelling down the strip. We jolt across the potholes until we pass the gate and I pull out onto the road.

Zack won't stop crying, heaving for air between sobs. I glance down at him. His pyjama bottoms are soaked through.

I stare out ahead at the road, the tears drying on my cheeks, adrenaline-fuelled breaths heaving in and out of me.

'You can open your eyes, baby. You're safe now.'

'There's one more thing.'

Faheem nods, waiting for me to speak.

'It is something we must discuss alone.'

He turns to the woman and speaks in his native tongue. She glares at me and leaves the room without another word.

Only then, when the door is shut and we are left alone with the sleeping patient, do I speak.

'Margot,' I say. 'The woman who led me to the scrapyard. She cannot be trusted.'

He stares at me awhile, a mix of caution and admiration. He must think me as cutthroat as he is. Maybe I am.

'And what do you suppose we do about it?'

He knows exactly what I'm insinuating. I look down at my hands. How much more blood can I shed with them? How far am I willing to go?

I think of Zack, so beautiful, so innocent. His terrified voice, groggy from the drugs, calling for me at the other end of the phone. Even if I get him back, there is no knowing what Margot will do next. What she will demand. Who she will tell. If her extortion will ever end. Zack and I will forever be looking over our shoulders.

I stare Faheem directly in the eyes.

'We kill her.'

61

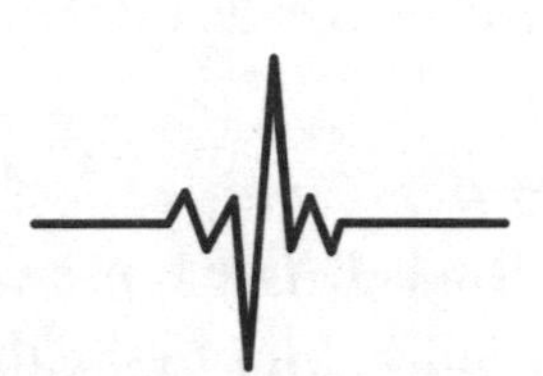

Rachel

Thursday, 11 April 2019, 13:16

I wake up to the sound of my phone ringing.

I am on the sofa, face pressed into the cushion, with my head pounding and a patch of cold drool hardening beneath my lips. The TV is on, the volume at a whisper. Jamie stares down at me from the walls.

I paw the coffee table for my phone, knocking the empty wine glass on its side, and squint at the screen. When I see the name flashing on the phone I scramble to a sitting position and clear my throat.

'Morning, sir.'

'It's the afternoon, Conaty,' DCI Whitman replies.

Christ, I haven't slept this late in years. The wine must have knocked me clean out.

'You have news?'

'I do,' he says, almost reluctantly. 'Why don't you come into the office? We can talk about it then.'

He has that tone to his voice again; his words laced with pity.

'I'd prefer you tell me now, sir.'

Oh God. They've found the boy harmed.

He sighs heavily.

God, man. Just say it.

'You were wrong, Rachel. The boy's fine.'

I sit on the sofa in silence. I try to speak but the words fail to form, clicking and clucking at the back of my mouth.

'Conaty. You there?'

'I don't understand . . .'

'Officers down in Cornwall made contact with Jeff Dunn this morning. He explained that after you interviewed Dr Jones yesterday, she set off for Cornwall straight away to bring her son home and clear everything up.'

I picture her bombing it up the M3 from the coast with her hair flicking wildly at the open window, and the boy smiling by her side.

'No, that doesn't make sense at all.'

'Conaty . . .' he warns.

'Have you seen him for yourself?'

'The boy?' He unfurls another heavy sigh. 'Not with my own eyes, no.'

'And did the officers down in Cornwall see him?'

'Conaty, I don't know how to say this to you. It's over. I gave you a case and you fucked it, it's as simple as that. Anything you do now will only make your situation worse—'

I end the call and jump up from the sofa, thrusting my phone deep into my pocket, the same work trousers I wore the day before. There is a red-wine stain on my shirt, creased from tossing and turning. I move about the room, conscious of Jamie framed above the mantle; I wonder if he would be embarrassed of me looking like this.

I go to turn the TV off when I see Ahmed Shabir on the screen. I frantically turn up the volume.

'Our source reveals that the hospital's internal investigation has reached its verdict on the cause of death: Shabir's death has been attributed to a secret chronic health condition causing complications during surgery. It is believed he kept his condition out of the public eye to prevent it from negatively impacting his chances of becoming leader of the Labour Party and running successfully in the next general election.'

No, I think, reading the breaking-news banner as it laps the bottom of the page. *No, no, no, no, no.*

Everything I believed before closing my eyes has fallen apart.

I rush into the hall and snag my jacket from the hook, catching sight of my reflection in the mirror on the wall. My hair is wild from sleep, plastered to my scalp on one side, knotted and frayed on the other. I rub the crust from the corner of my eyes, snatch my keys from the sideboard and slam the door behind me.

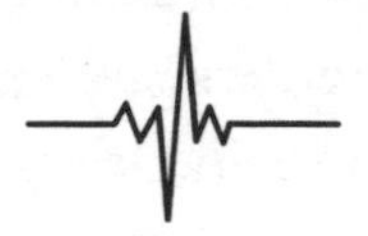

I'd been managing fine before this case. Before the boy.

I had found a balance between holding myself together and falling apart. A seesaw of grief and closure, dipping to one side, but always returning to the other. A process I could trust. But seeing that little boy on tape did something to me. It split me open, and all of my grief came gushing out. Now I'm all but drowning in it.

I speed down the road towards Dr Jones' address, overtaking car after car with the accelerator pushed to the floor.

I can't show up at the house like this. But the anger is free now; I've held it down for so many years, ignored its kicking, its thrashing, ripping me up from the inside as it tried to claw its way out. I wish I had something to blame for it – just one sole reason for my rage. But it is an amalgamation of so many things, singed and clotted into one dark mass. It was Dr Jones who woke the beast.

I know she is lying. It isn't mere intuition toiling in my gut, or a detective's hunch eating away at me. I know it as a mother. I know what it means to lose a child, to bury the despair to prove to the world that you're coping. I saw the very same fight in her eyes: the defensiveness, the panic. The stiff posture we hold so as not to fall apart at the seams.

I turn down The Avenue. There are people in their front gardens, kids playing with a ball in the middle of the road, snatching it up and running to the side so I can pass. Their neighbour was murdered a week ago, but no one would think it. People did the same with Jamie. For a week, there was an outpouring of rage, the whole country seemingly sickened by the idea that a stranger could snatch a child in broad daylight. But the very next week, when no leads came, their anger turned on me. I was the mother who failed to protect him, the mother who didn't cry enough at the press briefing, the mother who dared to brush her hair. It never fails to shock me, how quickly people turn.

I pull up at the end of her driveway and step out, not caring that my hair is littered with knots or that my breath smells of sleep. It takes all of my willpower to smother my anger and keep it beneath the surface.

I raise my fist and knock on the door three times.

The dog barks behind the door. I hear the shuffling of feet, a muffled voice. I picture her face when she sees me: her complexion paling, jaw slackening at the hinges.

The door opens.

Dr Jones stares back at me, but her face doesn't change like I expected. Her lips stay in a firm line, and her eyes remain unmoved. She looks better than she has in days. Her hair is washed, and her face emits a glow that it didn't have before.

Standing beside her is the boy.

This is the first time I have seen Zack in the flesh. He has icy-blue eyes like his mother's, the same button nose. He is holding onto his mother's hand, blushing as I stare at him. He doesn't look like how I imagined he would. But of course he wouldn't.

I was picturing Jamie this whole time.

'Yes?' Dr Jones asks.

I break away from the boy and look towards her, tears itching at my eyes.

'I, er . . . I just wanted to . . .' I clear my throat. 'I just wanted to meet Zack.'

'Say hello, Zack,' she says.

'Hello.'

His voice is so sweet, yet it cuts at me like a razor. I force a smile while barely able to see him through the tears.

'I've heard a lot about you, Zack,' I say, my voice hoarse. 'What a handsome boy you are.'

He looks to his feet, shuffling awkwardly.

'Why don't you go and give Bear a treat?' she says, caressing his hair. 'But only one.'

He looks up at his mother, love and trust pooled in his eyes. Just like the way Jamie used to look up at me.

This is agonising.

I watch as he slips out of view, giving a cautious look over his shoulder at the crazy woman standing at his doorstep.

Don't cry, I tell myself. *Don't you dare cry.*

'Are you satisfied?' she asks.

'Dr Jones . . . I don't know what to say.'

'I think this answers any more questions you might have?'

'It does,' I say. 'I'm sorry.'

My chest is burning: my lungs, my ribs, my heart. Everything feels fit to burst.

'I hear the hospital investigation has come to a close,' I force myself to say. 'Congratulations.'

'It's a relief, yes. I'm so glad we can move on. All of us.'

She stares at me over the threshold, that motherly glare I remember so well. If we were animals, it would be a low-bodied growl, warning me away from her young.

'I trust I won't be seeing you any time soon?'

I need to get out of here.

I wasn't prepared to see the boy; I was so convinced she was lying, and that by coming here I could expose her. The tears are coming now, shame and grief swelling up inside me. Innate sadness that has long been disguised as rage.

'No,' I say. 'That will be all.'

She nods once, her stare relentless and unwavering, and shuts the door. I head back to the car as fast as I can, sobs working their way up my throat. I jump behind the wheel, swing out of the driveway, and speed down the track, the wheels spitting gravel and his name screaming in my brain.

Jamie. Jamie. Jamie.

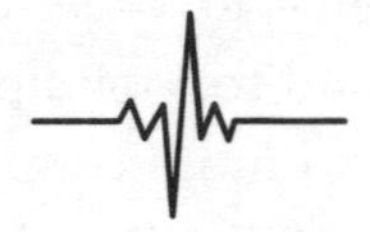

I have sat behind the wheel for an hour, parked up at the turn in the road where The Avenue meets the track, when my phone rings inside my pocket.

I feel completely numb. The eruption of tears has drained the life out of me, and my head is throbbing with pain. I catch sight of myself in the rear-view mirror as I reach for my phone. My eyes are tinged red with burst vessels.

'What?' I snap.

'I'm sorry, Conaty,' DCI Whitman says.

He must have known I would go to her, to see the boy for myself. Watching the clock, waiting to see if I'd call.

'No, you're not,' I reply with a violent sniff. 'You love to be right.'

'Not about this,' he says. His tone is solemn and quiet. 'Are you all right?'

When tears come to my eyes, I almost want to laugh. How can there be more tears inside of me?

'Not really.'

He sighs on the other end of the line.

'You need to cut yourself some slack. This grief, it's eating you alive. You've let it destroy you for fifteen years – how long are you going to keep punishing yourself?'

'My son was taken, George. That isn't something you forget.'

'Of course it isn't. I'm not saying that. But you're stuck, Conaty. You've wrapped yourself up in grief and held on for dear life. You live it, breathe it. You're killing yourself.'

I bite down on my lip, shake my head.

'You wouldn't understand.'

'Then help me try.'

No one has said that to me, not once in fifteen years. Not even my ex-husband, who failed to relate to a mother's grief so much that he bolted and left me among the ruins.

'If I stop grieving him . . . I will lose him.'

'What do you mean?'

I lean back into the seat with my eyes closed, inhaling a deep breath. I hold it there until the tears melt away.

'If I allow myself to move on, I'll be leaving him behind. If I don't hold onto the small things, I'll lose them. I know I will.'

I think of all the parts of Jamie I have lost over the years: the sound of his voice, his laugh, the feel of his hair, the patter of his feet on the stairs. The tears rise up again, biting at my eyes.

'I don't even remember the sound of my son's voice, George.'

'You will never forget him completely. You will always have your memories of him. But tell me . . . is this fight you have in yourself every day, this battle to hold onto every part of the past – is it worth it? Would Jamie want this for you?'

The tears fall in heavy, silent streams. I think of the shame I felt at home, blushing under his photographs, wondering if he would be embarrassed of me. If he would pity me like everyone else.

I shake my head.

'I can't do it anymore, George. It's . . . agonising.'

'It's time to try a different way now, Conaty,' he says softly in my ear. 'A way that's easier to bear. You're not to blame for what happened to him.'

'Stop it,' I beg.

'You're not to blame, Rachel.'

'Sir, please—'

'You're not to blame.'

I break down in sobs, my whole body racking with them. But this time the tears are from a different part of me. I'm not crying from the pain. I am crying with relief. I have wanted to hear someone say it for fifteen years.

I'm not to blame.

62

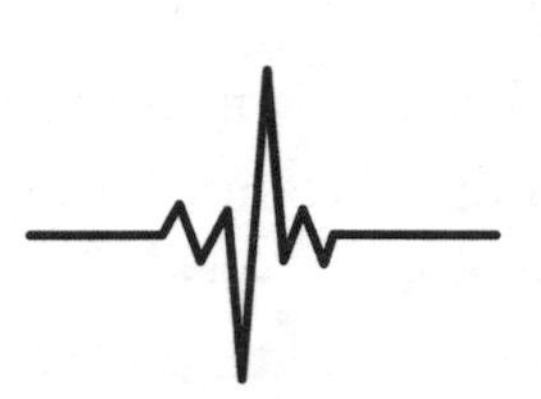

Anna

Thursday, 11 April 2019, 16:30

I would give anything to know what Zack is thinking.

The house is silent but for the jut of the flathead screwdriver hitting the plaster and the creaking stepladder beneath my feet. I dig the tool beneath the camera lens and pop it out. The abductors did a rush job; the wires snaking from the back of the cameras aren't fused to the main electrical circuit, but merely coiled around it using naked copper cables. No wonder they were able to fit them so quickly.

Zack is sat cross-legged on the floor, playing silently with the toy he used to love. It appears like he no longer recognises it. There is no resonance of the joy it used to bring, no excitement in his eyes. He runs the doll's blonde locks through his hand, fixated on her frozen face. He chose it because he said it looked like me. Maybe that's why he doesn't like it anymore.

'Can I watch TV?' he asks.

I look at him with a wide smile, the corners of my mouth cutting into my cheeks.

You're trying too hard.

'Not yet, darling.' I step down from the ladder and carry it to the opposite corner of the room. 'I had to turn the electricity off, remember? Or I could get hurt.'

I reach the top of the stepladder and stare down the barrel of the lens. Faheem said the abductors had been dealt with, and the blue-eyed man's death happened right in front of me, and yet, even with the power turned off, I can't shake the thought of someone lurking behind the camera, staring back at me. I dig the flathead beneath the lens to crank it out and slowly uncoil the copper wire from the circuit. I find the work strangely comforting. Working with wires and electrical currents isn't too different from fixing a heart.

'Why did that man shoot the lady?'

I freeze on the stepladder, gripping the camera wires in my fist.

There is a small comfort in knowing that he will never know her name, that when he thinks back to that night she will just be the strange woman who was too dangerous to let inside the car. The woman who fell to the ground and didn't get back up again.

'It's complicated,' I say finally. 'But it's over. Everything can go back to normal now, can't it?'

He says nothing, plucking at the hairs on the doll. I watch the white-blonde fibres drift silently to the carpet. Has he watched me do that? Is he doing to the doll what he has seen me do to myself?

I haven't given into the urge since he has been home. I need to take control now: control of myself, of Zack, of any potential dangers we might face. I manage the need, swallowing it down and distracting myself to quieten the teasing whispers. Zack is home now. He is all I need to feel whole.

I watch him from the ladder. He stares at the doll, deep in thought. I wish I could see inside his head, lift the scalp and part his skull, press my ear to his brain and listen to the whispered secrets inside.

Tell me what you're thinking, Zack. Please.

I wonder how he will be affected by all this. Not only the trauma, but the lies too. I think of all the things he must have seen, the masked strangers who will haunt him in his dreams, the sound of the gunshot ricocheting through his memories. The mother who made him lie to cover her own crimes, who won't let him utter a word about any of it to another living soul. No therapists, no friends. I wonder if he will love me for it, or whether he will come to hate me. It is always the parents' fault.

'You're seeing Daddy tomorrow. Remember what we talked about?'

I watch him think back.

'This is our little secret,' he says. I can almost hear myself in his words; I had knelt by his bed this morning and made him repeat after me, begging for his silence in a hushed tone. *I did something bad to save you. Now you must keep it a secret to protect me.*

'Good boy. And when Daddy asks you where you've been, what do you tell him?'

'Cornwall with Uncle Jeff.'

'And Leila,' I add.

'And Leila.'

'Good boy. What did you do there?'

'We went to the beach . . .' He looks up, the tip of his tongue poking out between his lips as he thinks back to the activities I told him to say. 'We caught crabs. We went on a boat.'

'That's good. We can go over the rest later.'

I give him a smile, willing his lips to curve in return, to see a glimpse of his tiny milk teeth. He looks down at the doll again without another word.

The smile slowly fades from my face.

Give him time.

I slip the two cameras in the back pocket of my jeans and step down from the ladder, the flathead under my arm.

'Do you feel bad?'

I freeze on the ladder, my grip tightening around the metal frame until my knuckles turn white.

Do I?

It was only when I laid my head on the pillow after Zack and I returned home that my mind drifted to what I had done. I waited for the guilt to hit me, that crushing sensation on my chest, the nausea in my gut. But I felt nothing. Not even a twinge.

I'd felt bad about taking a life before the surgery, hadn't I? I tried to think of any other way; dreaded meeting Shabir and his wife before stepping into the operating theatre. But was it guilt? Or was it being out of control that I couldn't stand?

I have had to deprive myself of human emotions to survive my job. Switch off the morality, shield myself from dwelling on lives lost on the operating table. If I didn't, I'd go mad. It was my defence mechanism that facilitated my ability to take a life on the operating table, urged the bullet from Faheem's gun to kill the abductor without remorse, made me wait with bated breath until Margot was blown away right next to me. Now I almost will myself to feel something. Flip the switch; be human again. But I had meant what I said to Margot. I really would do it all a thousand more times if I had to.

Zack is staring, waiting for me to respond. I can almost see him searching for the guilt in my eyes, longing for there to be a good person beneath the surface. I wish I knew what he sees in me, the woman lurking behind the smile.

I must have a heart, for I love him more than anything.

'Yes,' I lie. 'But there is nothing I wouldn't do for you, Zack. Nothing.'

He nods slowly and looks back down to the doll. He almost looks disappointed. Did I say the wrong thing? I wish I knew what he wanted me to say, for I would say it again and again until he believed every word.

'I'm going to move into the kitchen now. Want to come with me?'

He shakes his head.

Stop trying so hard. Let him come to you.

I set up the ladder in the kitchen and climb the steps. Zack might struggle to trust me for a while, but I will wait for as long as he needs. Everything has worked in my favour up to now, and this will too. I will jump through whatever hoops he throws at me.

I reach for the flathead poking out from my back pocket and glance at the letter on the breakfast table, 'Redwood Hospital' printed at the top of the page. When I woke up from my brief sleep this morning, I found the envelope waiting for me on the doormat, hidden among half a dozen bills. The second autopsy declared that the cause of death was a ruptured aorta, caused by a suspected thoracic aortic aneurysm brought on by his health condition that weakened the artery walls, and the incision made to fit the bypass tube into place would have greatly increased the risk of rupture. No suspicion of foul play; no police investigation. The hospital's verdict was announced on the news before midday, and will be featured on every front page tomorrow morning. But by next week, Ahmed Shabir will be old news.

As for Margot, she will be seen to have skipped bail and gone on the run. She will just be another face on the list of the wanted, her name listed at airports in case she tries to flee the country. There is no one to miss her, no one who will wonder where she went. I certainly won't. She knew my son was taken from me and still chose to exploit me for money and, worse still, she would never have stopped – she would've continued to blackmail us for the rest of our lives. Thankfully she had left her bag in the footwell of the car, and the cash I had given her was hidden inside. I got back my rings, my money and, most importantly, my son.

I wonder what they did with her body, whether they buried her, burned her, crushed her inside the stolen car that the Shabbars collected from my driveway in the night, and added her to the rusting metal walls around the scrapyard, trapped for eternity in a coffin of scrap metal.

At least David the security guard will get a more respectful burial. It was a hit-and-run, according to the local news sites. Struck down as he left work yesterday morning and left to die. I wonder which one of Faheem's men did it to keep him from talking.

Dr Burke, however, was allowed to live. I received a text from nurse Val just this morning, asking if I wanted to chip in towards his leaving present, what with him and his family returning to his wife's native Germany at the end of the week. 'Emergency family situation', she put in brackets. No doubt Faheem will be watching Burke and his family closely until then. I'm sure they will be keeping a close eye on Zack and me for years to come, making sure we keep our mouths shut. Perhaps for the rest of our lives.

I think of the two snakes, good and evil, described as lurking within all of us. Does it change things if one outweighs the other? If there is more evil in a person than good?

To save Zack, I had to do wicked, unforgivable things. Things that should haunt me for the rest of my life. But it was for the greater good, I must keep reminding myself of that. It wouldn't be the first time.

I have had to make so many tough decisions in my career: who to save, who to kill; who is the most eligible for a heart transplant, and who must continue to wait on the list, knowing they will die without it. I have been playing God for years. If I can't apply the same logic to my own life, then why play God at all? Maybe that's why I don't feel unfathomable guilt the way any normal person would. Perhaps I have been playing God for too long.

I reach in to uncoil the copper and scream. A hot, white spark shoots out from the main circuit in the wall and zaps the tips of my fingers. I stumble down the ladder with my fingers in my mouth, and rush into the hall to inspect the fuse box.

The power has been turned back on.

I walk up to it, massaging my hot fingers with my tongue, trying to see how it could have happened. Could the switch have turned on by itself? Some fault in the trip?

I look inside the cupboard. The shoe rack I keep hidden inside so as not to clutter up the hall has been dragged closer to the fuse box. Zack often uses it to climb up and reach the coat hooks.

He watched me flick the switch to turn it off. Did he copy me?

I hear something coming from the living room. I dare to hope that he might be talking to himself, or playing a game with the doll, rather than what I suspect. I walk in and find him sat on the sofa, his heels kicking against the base.

He is watching TV.

'Zack.' I snatch up the remote and turn off the TV. 'What are you doing?'

He looks up at me briefly and shrugs his shoulders, his heels kicking harder against the base of the sofa. *Thump–thump. Thump-thump.*

'You could have killed me. I told you I'd get hurt.'

He doesn't apologise. He doesn't do anything. His eyes stay on his lap, and his heels continue to kick, and kick.

Did he do it on purpose?

A vile thought comes to mind, and I bat it away.

Like mother, like son.

'Don't do that again. You hear me?'

I sigh and make my way back into the kitchen, flicking off the power as I go, and inspect the tips of my finger and thumb. The skin has turned a livid red, the flesh still hot.

He wouldn't have understood why it was dangerous. I didn't explain it well enough.

I pick up the flathead from the floor where I dropped it with the shock and climb the ladder, enjoying the feel of the cold metal against my hot fingertips. The camera is still there, coiled to the main circuit. I reach in, tapping it cautiously with the tip of the tool before reaching in with my fingers.

But that doesn't stop me from glancing into the hall towards the fuse box, waiting for Zack to flick the switch again.

A lock of hair slips from my bun, drifting silently towards my cheek. I raise my hand and tuck it behind my ear, but as I return to my task, I see one lone hair, dangling in my line of sight.

I don't need to give into it anymore, I tell myself. *I'm in control.*

But the urge is still there, wriggling inside my mind, twitching in my hands.

I pinch the hair between my fingers.

And pluck.

Acknowledgements

No book is complete without the help and guidance from so many amazing people, to whom I owe the following thanks.

Firstly, to my agent, Madeleine Milburn, whose passion and enthusiasm is truly unrivalled (I call her 'The Dream Maker'), as well as her team, Liv Maidment and Rachel Yeoh, and Georgia McVeigh for her thoughts on the very first draft. I would also like to thank the rights department at the Madeleine Milburn Literary, TV and Film Agency, for getting my books translated into other languages, and being so lovely to work with: Liane-Louise Smith, Georgina Simmonds and Valentina Paulmichl.

At my publishers, Simon & Schuster, my first thanks goes to my editor, Bethan Jones, whose passion for this story won me over instantly. Her guidance, trust and enthusiasm are what I have always dreamed of in an editor. I also owe huge and special thanks to Clare Hey, Katherine Armstrong, Richard Vlietstra, Sarah Jeffcoate and Harriett Collins for all of their amazing support in-house, and Craig Fraser for the beautiful cover. Dream team!

Many thanks to my copyeditor Ian Allen, and my proof-reader Clare Wallis, for helping me make *Do No Harm* the best it could possibly be.

I would also like to thank the following people for their initial guidance and enthusiasm for *Do No Harm*: Phoebe Morgan, Cal Kenny, Gaia Banks and Sophie Lambert. I also owe a heartfelt thanks to John Marrs and Holly Seddon for their kindness when my journey in publishing was rather rocky.

As always, I would like to thank the phenomenal team at Waterstones Colchester – if it weren't for their love and support, this book might not have been possible. I would like to make a special mention of Jon 'Bitch with the Pitch' Clark, who has sold a staggering amount of my books by hand, and whose kindness and dedication goes unrivalled (and who was one of the very first people to read *Do No Harm*). To the team, past and present: Helen Wood, Jon Clark, Clive Parsons, Liv Quinn, Karl and Chloe Hollinshead, Mark Vickery, Joe Oliver Eason, thank you. Also, special thanks to Gaby Lee and Bea Carvalho for their amazing support and kindness.

I owe huge thanks to my main support system, my family and friends, who have supported me through thick and thin and never let me give up, even when it seemed the more logical option. I couldn't have reached this point in my career without the following: Sandra and Carl Jarrad, Pamela and Tony Jordan, Jess Savoury, Abbi Houghton, Martin Chester, and special thanks to my Brighton babe, Anna Burtt, and to the best boy, Bowie.

And lastly, a huge thank you to every author who gave quotes, and bloggers and reviewers who shared their thoughts on the early copies of *Do No Harm*, thank you so much for all of your support (with a special shoutout to the phenomenal Stu Cummins!). And then you, the reader: thank *you* for picking up this book, and for making my dreams come true – I hope you enjoyed it, and that you also enjoy the books yet to come.